For certainly we be determined rather to
adventure and commit us to the peril of our lives,
and jeopardy of death, than to live in such
thraldom and bondage as we have done long
time heretofore, oppressed and injured by
Extortions and new Impositions against the
Law of God, and Man, and the liberties, and old
policy, and Laws of this Land, wherein every
Englishman is inherited. Our Lord God King of
all Kings, by whose infinite goodness, and
eternal providence, all things been principally
governed in this world, lighten your Soul, and
grant you grace to do as well in this matter as in
all others, that which may be according to his
will and pleasure, and to the common and public
weal of this land. So that after great clouds,
troubles, storms, and tempests, the Sun of Justice
and of Grace may shine upon us, to the joy and
comfort of all true-hearted Englishmen.
PETITION OF THE THREE ESTATES
TO DUKE RICHARD OF GLOUCESTER

And al the wikkednesse in this world
that man mighte worche or thinke
Ne is no more to the mercy of God
than in the see a glede.
Wm. Langland : *Visio de Petro Plowman*

Under the Hog

An Historical Novel

PATRICK CARLETON

SPHERE BOOKS LIMITED
30/32 Gray's Inn Road, London WC1X 8JL

First published in Great Britain 1937
First Sphere Books edition 1973

for Cyril Edward Spencer Noakes
with love

Set in Intertype Baskerville

Printed in Great Britain by
Hazell Watson & Viney Ltd
Aylesbury, Bucks

ISBN 0 7221 2203 9

PREFACE

HARDLY any of the characters in this novel are fictitious. All the important political and diplomatic events described in it really took place.

Where, under given circumstances, I have not been able to discover how this or that historical personage actually behaved, I have been at pains to light upon some way in which he was at least capable of behaving.

To my friends Dr. Patrick Du Val and Mr. Philip Bramwell, and to my Father, I am much in debt: to the former for his expert advice on certain points of Heraldry and Genealogy, to the latter for their really valuable and understanding criticisms.

PATRICK CARLETON.

Contents

CHAPTER ONE

KING-MAKING

(*France:* 1470–1471)

Berry est mort,
Bretaigne dort,
Bourgongne hongne—
Le Roy besogne.
                    French popular song, fifteenth century.

AMBOISE, June evening with red sunshine : Duke, Kingmaker and the Christian King were at it in the Castle, in a
private room, watched by Christ above the prie-dieu on the
northern wall and by Sir William Monypeny, the Sieur de
Concressault, who sat apart from them on a hard bench, not
saying anything.

The Duke sat by the table, on which were flagons and
bright cups, with his legs out in front of him. He was tall,
twenty-one; wore peach-coloured clothes and a short gown
of crimson cloth-of-gold lined with white. His yellow hair
was in big curls round his forehead. He might have been
beautiful, but his features seemed too small for his face, and
his eyes were narrow. Kingmaker was his cousin, and now
his father-in-law; sat upright at the table's other end with
his right elbow on it. Five rings on his closed hand spat at
the sunlight, and the gold chain round his neck shone. He
was dressed in purple and dull red, so that, as he sat stiff
and attentive in his low-backed chair, he matched the thick,
rusty colours of the evening. Sir William Monypeny, who
had known him a long time, still found his face interesting.
It was long from eyes to chin, and its nose long and
arrogant. The small, tight mouth turned upward at the
corners. The brown hair had gone a little from the top of
the head : helmet-baldness. It was a quiet evening, and
sheep could be heard bleating a long way off. There were

9

thick shadows in the cone of the roof and below the windows.

The Duke was talking, in a young, high voice.

". . . so my late father, it follows, Richard Duke of York, was true heir to the throne of England."

No one said anything, and he went on :

"How much love, anyway, can your Grace feel for the house of Lancaster? Family of brigands : good God, they were never at ease unless they were spilling war, pillage, and all the devils in hell over your unhappy kingdom! Harry of Monmouth, who called himself King Henry V, was the plague of France. It's on record. Sore subject : I've no wish to dwell on it, but your Grace will scarcely have forgotten Azincourt."

A deep settle by the arched empty fireplace had its back to the windows. A mastiff, tan-coloured, with crimson leather collar, lay beside it on the rushes. All to be seen of the King was his hand limply dropped over its arm to play with the dog's ears.

"Well, however badly the King my brother's behaved— we're not here to take his part, God knows—your Grace must see it is to your advantage to maintain our house in England. The name of my father-in-law is a guarantee of my own goodwill to you, Sire. The Lancastrian usurpers gained one kingdom by murder and bled it white trying to snatch another by arms. But we are the heirs of that anointed King filthily murdered by Henry Bolingbroke : Richard II, Richard of Bordeaux, the constant friend of France . . ."

"Son of the Black Prince."

The King's voice came huskily out of the dark of the settle like a talking magpie's. The Duke flicked his long, white-lined sleeve across his knees and looked sideways. He was a good deal of a bore, Sir William Monypeny thought. English politics were hopelessly complicated, as he, who had been King Louis' ambassador to Edward IV, knew well enough. It was seventy years since Henry Bolingbroke had alleged thirty-three separate articles of misgovernment against Richard II; elbowed him out of the throne and out of life. That was forgotten. It was with Bolingbroke's mad grandson, the most pious prince since Edward the Confessor, that the trouble began : marching and fighting of nobles

10

and their armies all up and down the kingdom, red roses and white roses, betrayals, coalitions dissolving and re-forming, attainders, executions. His style until the final fall had been Henry VI, by the grace of God King of England and France, Lord of Ireland; but most Englishmen called him Holy Harry of Windsor and tapped their foreheads. It was his wife they hated: Marguerite of Anjou, who was neither mad nor pious. The old Duke of York was backed by Kingmaker, the Earl of Warwick, when he demanded the crown, and by Parliament; might at this moment have been King if Marguerite had not raised men in the North, struck quickly at him whilst he was keeping Christmas in Yorkshire and sent him to prosecute his claim before a higher court. She defeated the Earl next and took her husband from him, before her luck changed. Her army was of thieves, flayers, banished men, Scots, and she could not hold them. They plundered south of Trent; made her hated. To save the sack of London, Holy Harry went back to the North with them, and the thanks he got was:

He that London did forsake
We will no more to us take:

rhyme yelped from mouth to mouth. They wanted, in London, a King that they could see. The Duke of York's eldest son was six feet four inches high, as lovely as a girl; was called the Rose. He was nineteen. The Earl got him crowned somehow, after battles, as King Edward IV. That was nine years ago. Marguerite and her son lived on the charity of King Louis, a thin diet, now, and Holy Harry was in the Tower of London, fumbling his beads and mumbling his prayers and wondering how he had stopped being the King of England. Sir William knew all about it. What he wanted now to know was how exactly Kingmaker had come to quarrel with the King he made, so that he and the King's brother had run over to France with the name 'traitor' shouted after them. He guessed a little, but wondered more. King Edward's disgraceful marriage would be at the back of it for certain. If Duke George would stop chattering and let his father-in-law have a word, they might hear something. He looked at the Earl. He was still sitting upright and staring at the wall a little to the left of the King's settle, with an expression as though he were engaged in some important business not being transacted in this place. It seemed unlikely that he was listening to his son-in-law.

"No one feels more than we do how serious an affront my brother's ill-contrived marriage was to your Grace : and the whole nobility of England feels it. One thing has been clear to me from the beginning. There was sorcery in it. My brother was bewitched."

There was a stir in the shadows. Sir William guessed the King was crossing himself. Edward of England had done two startling things in his life. He had won the battle of Towton in a howling snowstorm against a Lancastrian army that outnumbered him by two to one and had the advantage of the ground; and he had secretly married an obscure gentlewoman of no family, at the very time when King-maker was working to betroth him to King Louis' sister-in-law.

"What other possible explanation is there? A widow seven years older than he is, with two sons and a whole hamper-ful of poor relations : widow of a Lancastrian at that. Something addled his wits. She's not even a Duke's or an Earl's daughter. He's had ladies of better blood than hers for concubines. Her mother, the Duchess of Bedford, married a simple knight. Her own first husband, Sir John Grey, was nothing better, and he was killed fighting for Marguerite at St. Albans. She may be the child of a Duchess and the Count of St. Pol's niece, but she's no wife for a King. Why the devil couldn't he have bedded her and no more words about it? The Duchess of Bedford knows a thing. She could tell you how to brew a love-philtre as well as any witch that ever straddled a broomstick; and God's truth, she has her reward. The Queen's kin are everywhere. Greys and Wyd-vylles, Wydvylles and Greys; you couldn't toss a tennis-ball in England without hitting one : and they marry. Queen Elizabeth's sisters have pouched three Earls' sons and a Duke between them already; and what does your Grace say to her brother John, nineteen years old, married to a Duchess of eighty?"

"Doubtless she also used magic," said the King, "to beglamour the poor young man. They seem very given to sorcery, your English ladies."

The Duke laughed, making a noise in the quiet place.

"A Wydvylle would marry the devil's grandmother for a hundred marks a year and a patent of nobility. The Dowager Duchess of Norfolk is the richest woman in England. She's a widow again now. We could not do much, but we settled accounts with Sir John Wydvylle before our misfortunes came."

Sir William looked at Kingmaker again. In the sinking light it was not easy to see whether he was smiling; but it must have been a good moment for him when Sir John's head left his shoulders. Sir William knew what Kingmaker must think of the Wydvylles and their clever marriages. His own family, the Nevilles, had had a genius for the game. He himself quartered the arms of Beauchamp, Clare, Montacute, Newburgh and Monthermer, and his eldest daughter was a King's sister-in-law now. He would not be happy, watching a new house scrambling to splendour up the same ladder.

"That was an extreme proceeding, my Lord Duke."

The King's voice suggested nothing at all, and he was still playing with his hound's ears. The Duke drew in his legs and leaned forward.

"And a more extreme one would have been a greater charity to the commonwealth. The Queen's family have been the cause of every misfortune that's overtaken England these five years past. 'Apes in scarlet' is an old saying, your Grace. Their insolence is beyond words. They care for nothing but the enriching of themselves and their blood. My brother has as good livelihood and possessions as ever a King of England had; but his wife's kin are drinking him dry. He's debased the coinage already. That's by their guiding. He crushes the commons flat with taxes with one hand and then twists forced loans out of them with the other, until they curse him out of the side of their mouths as he rides past; and he was loved once. A prince of your piety would hardly credit it, Sire, but those horse-leeches he's married himself into have even seduced him into spending the goods of the Holy Father, which were given to him for defence of the Christian faith, and bringing the whole land in jeopardy of interdiction : and the money goes up the sleeve of my Lord Scales, the Queen's brother, may the devil haul him through hell, and the Duchess of Bedford, who would be burned in a tar-barrel if all had their own, and their good

13

friend Sir John Fogg. Those are our masters. They rule the King and they rule England. It's not to be endured, Sire, and it will not be endured much longer."

The Duke was talking very loudly now. Sir William was not surprised to hear that he was angry. Queen Elizabeth, as he remembered from his own last visit to the English Court, liked herself very well. Coloured cloth-of-gold and double velvet were her wear. She had a throne overlaid with gold like the King's, and even her own mother had to kneel to her. He remembered the small, proud face under a heap of yellow curls from which, in private, she was probably plucking an occasional grey hair already, and the fixed, curiously shallow-looking eyes, more green than blue. Her voice was shrill and rather irritating, but she carried herself well. As for her relatives, both her father's and her first husband's, they were certainly everywhere, and hated everywhere. Whilst he had been in England a mob had torn up the palings of one of her father's deer-parks and massacred the deer. The widow of a little country knight : it was odd she should have caused so much trouble.

The bells had started to ring vespers : cold sprinkles of sound over Amboise. Sir William looked to see whether the King would say a prayer; but he did not. As though the bells had awakened him from some kind of drowse, the Earl of Warwick stood up suddenly. He was long-legged, and his shape, at forty-three, was young still. He stood with his feet apart and his thumbs in his girdle, looking into the shadow that the King sat in. Hard lines of his profile showed against the fading windows, the nose jutting and the under-jaw pushed out. He said in a low voice, speaking better French than the Duke :

"My son-in-law is quite right, Sire. It will not be endured."

The King's voice was lower still; sounded like a priest's mutter.

"Have you no remedy in your own hands, then?"

The Earl made a stiff gesture like movement of a man in armour. The whole carriage of his body in its rich clothes still suggested harness.

"We have tried and failed. Your Grace knows. There was trouble in Yorkshire last year. The King went North to deal with it. We took charge of him. Old Rivers and Sir

14

John Wydvylle and the two Herberts we headed, to put an end to their mischief. Edward promised seas and mountains to us. He would be advised by us in all things. There should be no more bleeding of the commons. The Queen's kin should be punished for their ill-guidance. Oh yes, he promised everything!"

The Earl sat down again; passed his hand slowly two or three times over his chin, let it fall with a tiny slap onto the table.

"We had the wolf by the ears. We dared not loose him and could not hold him. He's a strange creature, Edward: clay and iron in him. Mould the clay as you please. You will scrape the iron bare in the end and cut your fingers. He is besotted by these Wydvylles, and we had killed two of them. He slipped away from us in October and was back in London, mustering men as fast as God would let him, the Queen at his elbow yelling vengeance for her father and brother. He said everywhere that we were his best friends; but his household-men had other language. I can see flies in milk, Sire. We had gone too far or not far enough."

"So," said Duke George, "seeing that my brother had shown himself unworthy to rule, and that I, after him, am the next heir to the house of York . . ."

Kingmaker went on as though he had not been interrupted.

"Our only retreat was to advance. We raised Lincolnshire against him, and told our people that when the matter came near the point of battle, they should call upon my Lord of Clarence, here, to be King."

It was out now. Sir William realised that he had never quite believed it. He could not picture Duke George as King of England. The Earl's low voice began again :

"Edward had a great power of artillery. Robert Welles, who was the leader of our people, retreated from him. Edward had Welles' father and Thomas Dymmoke for hostages. He headed them both."

"Contrary to faith and promise given," put in the Duke, "and to the worst example that might be."

The Earl nodded.

"Yes, he was angry. Welles stood before him then, without waiting for us. The artillery was too much for him. He was taken and headed."

15

"Requiescat in pace anima eius, et animae omnium fidelium," the King muttered disconcertingly.

The Earl crossed himself, saying Amen, and then went on:

"We were in a bad case. I asked help of Thomas Stanley, but he flatly refused to bear arms against Edward. Then Edward's summons came. Robert Welles confessed before he died, it seems. We were to surrender ourselves to the King's grace or be proclaimed traitors: and the King's grace would have meant the Queen's grace. We thought best, Sire, to leave England for a time."

It was a quiet way, thought Sir William, in which to describe what looked like ultimate disaster. Kingmaker and his son-in-law had taken ship from Exmouth, he had heard, and had meant to put in again at Dartmouth: but the Queen's brother, Anthony Lord Scales—Lord Rivers, too, since his father's execution—had driven them off. They headed for Calais. Kingmaker had been Governor there for fifteen years. His own lieutenant, Lord Wenlock, fired on them and would not let them land, even though King-maker's daughter, the Duchess of Clarence, was being brought to bed of a son on board the ship. They had got ashore between Harfleur and Honfleur at the upshot. Now Kingmaker was asking favours of King Louis, who, in past times, had treated him almost as a reigning prince. The silence in the room was prolonging itself. Even the Duke seemed to have nothing left to say. The tan-coloured mastiff yawned, King Louis' fingers still busy with its scruff and ears. The Earl looked thoughtfully at the rings on his hand. Then he repeated:

"It will not be endured, Sire."

The King's voice was huskier than ever.

"And who is left in England to resent it? Your Captain Welles is dead. Lord Stanley and Lord Wenlock have parted company with you; and I have heard your noble brother, the Marquis Montacute, was on King Edward's side in this late affair."

The Earl, looking at his rings still, smiled.

"I do not despair of my brother, Sire. Edward made a mistake when he took the Earldom of Northumberland away from him and gave him a magpie's nest to maintain his state with. Marquis Montacute: it's a fine title, but I

16

think my brother would rather have kept the lands that Edward gave back to the Percys : and for the rest, there are the common people."

"Are they all the hope Edward has left you?"

"Remember, Sire, they are different from the commons of France. They are not serfs. They wear wool and eat flesh and fish, and if they ever drink water, it is by way of penance. They are rich men beside yours. Also, they are very good archers. The commons of England are powerful people, Sire; and they regret my exile. I have been a kind lord all my life. Men trust me : and they are getting very tired of Edward. He is jolly and hearty; but they know which is worth more : a kind word and a clap on the back or an abatement of taxes. When we crowned him they believed he would amend everything the house of Lancaster had done amiss. All he has given them is more battles, loss of their goods, ruin of their trade, continual calls to leave their homes at their own charges and fight his rebels. His marriage stinks in their nostrils as much as mine, too. They would be glad to see the world change again."

"I wonder how you will change it."

"As I set out to do, your Grace : Edward has shown himself unworthy to rule. At least, I can persuade England that he has. I crowned him. I shall uncrown him. My son-in-law has set forth the reasons why we ought still to maintain the right of York against the right of Lancaster, and as he himself says, he is the next heir after his brother. I need only ships and money. If your Grace will help me with those, I can make Duke George King of England."

"There is another brother, is there not?"

The Earl looked sideways. The question seemed to have surprised him.

"A child," he said.

"Sickly," added the Duke.

"In such a quarrel as you are making, however, he would be for one of his brothers and against the other. That is, you may say, inevitable. Whom would he favour?"

"Edward," said the Duke; "he is his shadow."

The Earl shrugged his shoulders.

"I assure your Grace it is of no importance. He is only seventeen, very undersized for his years, bookish. He has ailed from birth; will never make old bones I fancy; has no name in the country."

"Then it seems that we need not regard him. But tell me, my Lord of Warwick. You will have some plan, I make no doubt, for dealing with Edward when he is deposed. An uncrowned King is a very dangerous and difficult person."

"I hope his death may not be necessary. I'm fond of the lad. We were friends once. I had thought of imprisonment : in the Tower probably."

"Mercy is a precious thing, my Lord. We ought all to be merciful and long-suffering, because bloodshed offends God."

Sir William moved his shoulders a little on the hard wall against which he sat. He always experienced a slightly chilly feeling when the King talked of mercy and the eschewing of bloodshed.

"You would doubtless require men as well as ships, my dear Lord?"

The Earl and the Duke leaned forward. The Duke drew his chair up a little nearer to the King's settle. The Earl said :

"Not many, Sire : once landed in England I could raise twenty thousand; and it would damage the Duke's cause if he arrived with a large foreign troop. Artillery would help more. We shall need that; and money."

"Money."

The King was almost whispering now.

"Against good and sufficient pledges, of course."

"Then with ships and artillery and a loan against good pledges, you can uncrown King Edward?"

"As surely as God made me, your Grace."

There was a long quiet in the room. Suddenly, the King lifted his hand. The big dog looked to see why the scratching of its ears had stopped.

"I regret it with all my heart, my dear Lord, but I will not lend you either a fishing-smack or a Paris sol to make Duke George King of England."

It appeared to Sir William, that of the two, the Earl was more surprised. He sat up quickly, like a man who has been stabbed under the ribs, and put his hand to his gold chain. The Duke lifted his voice :

"But, Sire, you cannot . . ."

Kingmaker threw out his right hand, the palm toward him, stopping his words. Then he stood up; began to walk about the room. His feet hissed on the rushes. The King was stroking the dog again. Presently, the Earl stopped. It was growing very dark now.

"My Lord King, I have known your Grace too long to think that you do anything without counsel. Our enterprise must seem perilous to your Grace: too perilous, perhaps. But there is one consideration I have not spoken of tonight. It has been handled between us before now. It touches your Grace's own crown very nearly. Edward of England is allied with the Duke of Burgundy."

"I know it."

The magpie-voice was so faint now that it seemed to speak inside the listeners' heads, like a voice in memory.

"Your Grace knows also that Charles of Burgundy will turn his duchy into a kingdom if God gives him scope. He would be at open war with you now if he could find support. Your Grace, Edward is no longer popular in England: but there is one way by which any King of England can gain popularity, if he were as wicked as John or as mad as Henry. It is by a successful war with France."

In the increasing shadows, the Earl seemed very tall. He stretched out one arm stiffly toward the settle.

"Make your market for it, my Lord King. You have trusted me before. Trust me in this. If you refuse us your help to dethrone Edward, then within two years the allied forces of Burgundy and England will invade France. I will borrow the words of my Lord Duke, 'Your Grace will scarcely have forgotten Azincourt.'"

There was a sudden scuffling in the rushes as the mastiff jerked itself. The King must have pulled its ears too hard. Sir William heard its ribs sound under his hand as he patted it. His voice suddenly had become round and cheerful.

"My very dear Lord, and you my dear Lord Duke, it seems my foolish tongue has done me some injury. Forgive me. I have not explained myself. I beg your forgiveness. I said I could do nothing to make you, my Lord Duke, King of England. I did not say I wished your brother to continue in that dignity. I never said it."

His face came round the edge of the settle like the face of a village idiot playing at peek-a-boo with the farmer's children. A look of peculiar absurdity was given him by his black velvet cap with the nap rubbed off it, which was very greasy and stuck full of holy medals, and under which the hair was scraped into a fringe on his low forehead. He was as yellow as cheese, with a long nose and a loose mouth. His whole appearance suggested a country curate much given to good works and not quite right in his wits. Harmless, one would have said.

"It does not seem to be according to God's will that King Edward should continue in contempt of his fellow-princes and of his own people. You tell me that he oppresses his poor commons and lavishes extorted money upon unworthy and profligate companions. Under God, I have always tried to aid what was right and just. His behaviour appears to me to be scandalous. It would not be right for us to let him rule any longer."

The Earl had sat down again; propped his chin on his fist and was staring. The Duke of Clarence grabbed the back of his chair with both hands, twisting his body into a school-boy's attitude; called out:

"Then you will help us, Sire?"

"No," said the King, "you will help me."

He stood up and began to shamble about the room, stooping, in a black gown to his ankles, wiping his mouth with his hand.

"My Lord of Clarence, I feel great affection and respect for you. You seem to me a most worthy young prince. But I am not so ignorant of English affairs as you suppose. When Sir Robert Welles told his men to shout: 'Clarence for King,' no one heard them outside Lincolnshire. You have been driven out of England, and I do not think that anyone has made much protest. In effect, it would seem that the English do not want you for their King, and that though your noble father-in-law might put you on the throne, he could not keep you there. Your brother, I am informed, has still some following in his kingdom, so that people have not observed your greater merits. I fear, my dear Lord, that the English would never see the sense of pulling down one Yorkist King merely to put up another."

"But I am the next heir after Edward."

The Duke sounded like a child who has been promised a

treat and will not forget it. The King wiped his mouth again.

"People are very foolish," he said vaguely; "we have a Yorkist King who must be pulled down at whatever cost. So it seems to me, speaking under correction, that it is time for us to think about the house of Lancaster."

Sir William heard the Duke gasp as though he were winded, and the Earl's fist dropped with a faint smashing noise onto his knee. The King halted with his back to the empty fireplace, his head down and his hands closed behind him, and went on:

"The course of action which I shall suggest to you is that we should approach the Lady Marguerite, the wife of your King Henry, and discuss with her the means of restoring her husband to his crown and dignities."

The Duke exploded onto his feet and began shouting:

"God's truth, am I mad or is the rest of the world? Is it possible that you're asking me, me, to make an alliance with the she-devil who killed my father? D'you know that after Wakefield her people hacked off my father's head and put a paper crown on it, mocking him as the Jews mocked Christ, and stuck it on a spike over Micklegate Bar, like the head of a murderer; and that they served my brother, the Earl of Rutland, in the same way? That was Marguerite. Now you want me to shake hands with her and give up the crown I ought to have to her old madman of a husband. Do you, by Christ's blood? I'll see the whole kingdom of France sunk in the sea first."

"George, George," the Earl had found words now, "hold your tongue, for the love of God. Sire, you will not be offended. My son-in-law's a little upset. Your Grace's suggestion took him by surprise. It was unlooked for; startles us. Sire, can you have considered what this means? Say York and Lancaster, you say cat and dog. My son-in-law believes strongly in the justice of his father's claim. You ask him to waive it on behalf of a prince whom we both look on as a usurper: mad, too. And think of me, Sire. The Lady Marguerite regards me as her worst enemy in the world. I have been against her. It was I who published it that she is an adultress and that the late Duke of Suffolk was the father of her son. I hounded her out of England. I fought a dozen battles against her. When Harry of Windsor was captured it

21

was I who cut off his spurs and led him through London as a traitor. How in God's name am I to make an alliance with her now? You might ask a lamb to ally itself with a wolf. She'd give her immortal soul to put my head where she put the Duke of York's."

The King said to no one in particular:

"One might make some means,"

and the Duke snapped at him:

"But we don't want means."

A thick, shaking sigh came from the Earl of Warwick.

"No, Sire, it's not possible. It's not even to be thought of: an alliance of Trojans and Greeks, something outside imagination. Even if I and the Duke of Clarence were willing to go down on our knees to her and say that all we've done and thought these last ten years has been rebellion and bloody treason, that when I took arms against her I was not defending the right but destroying it, she could not listen. If she were on the throne again I should be shorter by a head before she'd sat there long enough to warm it. Set up the house of Lancaster again, Sire, and you sentence me to exile for life."

"You are an exile now, my dear Lord. As you yourself said, with much eloquence, your only retreat is to advance. King Edward assuredly will have nothing more to say to you. I have told you, with such poor plainness as I can command, that I, for my part, will have nothing to say to King George. So there is King Henry. You tell me—and I do not doubt it—that with ships and artillery and a loan against good pledges you can uncrown King Edward. Do so, I say, and put King Henry, whose sorrows I pity and whose piety I unfeignedly admire, in his place. Patience: allow me to continue. You were about to tell me again that he is mad and that his wife would never have you as a friend. My Lord, his wife is desperate. That she does not think you an angel I, who have often heard her speak of you, am thoroughly aware; but she has the best reasons in the world for knowing your name is powerful in England; and she has a son: a most noble young prince, eighteen years of age, wonderfully handsome. Your younger daughter is fourteen, if I remember: marriageable. Bear with me a little longer. Were King Henry on the throne again, some sort of regency would be necessary. That sacred man, a true

22

child of God if ever there was one : well, in effect, his pre-
occupation with heavenly things has perhaps a little unfitted
him for the cares of this world. Yes, a regency certainly
seems indicated. The Queen, of course, and the Prince :
they would both have their share in it, and then the Prince's
father-in-law, the father of whatever young lady he might
marry. A fourth person would be desirable. The son-in-law
of the Prince's father-in-law would have no great claim by
blood. The relationship is a remote one. But if the son-in-
law of the Prince's father-in-law had powerfully helped the
Prince to gain his rights, even making war on his own
brother in that quarrel, then I think he ought to be
rewarded.

"These June evenings are oppressive, I find. They make
one sleepy. You, my Lord of Warwick, will have a great
deal to talk over with your son-in-law, your future plans to
discuss. It is a heavy responsibility to undertake the regency
of a kingdom : but you will rise to it. My Lord of Concressault, will you tell the people in the ante-room to
conduct the Earl of Warwick and the Duke of Clarence to
their apartments? A most illuminating chat we've had; and
there was a remark you made, my dear Lord of Warwick,
that I thought was very apt and memorable about advancing and retreating. I must remember that. How pleasant it
is when people can sit down and discuss all their agreements
and disagreements frankly and quietly like this. No, no, not
another word, I beg of you. I won't keep you now."

The King's speech was becoming disarticulated. As Sir
William opened the door and shouted to the valets for
torches, he could still hear him scattering sentences all ways
like small coins of largesse.

"An adjustment here, a small concession there, and one
finds things arrange themselves neatly enough in the end.
Oh yes, things arrange themselves not at all badly. It is a
question of viewpoint. Eighteen is a ripe age, too, and he is
really a most amiable young man. A desperate woman, my
Lords, and of a consuming ambition : she will come to
terms. It is only a matter of adjustment and the virtue of
charity. We must not bear grudges. If all you tell me is
true, these Wydvylles must be shocking people, and of
course my sister-in-law was very much disappointed. Piety
outwears adversity. Beati sunt humiles. I could manage the

23

artillery, I think. This June weather exhausts one, don't you find? And I wonder whether anything could be done about Lord Wenlock? But let us say no more about it now : not another word this evening. Are you fond of dogs, my Lord of Clarence? To me they seem the most admirable of creatures : faithful, unambitious. We shall have to think about the Burgundian navy, too. You must have a talk with the Bastard of Bourbon. He understands such things. Here are the torches at last. A thousand goodnights to you both, dear friends : think over what I've said; and my Lord of Warwick, offer my most distinguished compliments to your younger daughter : a thousand goodnights."

Torches spilled into the room a pink-gold glow and smell of resin. Sir William bowed to the two Englishmen going out. Kingmaker's mouth was stiff and a vertical cleft was marked between his eyebrows; but his expression did not tell much. The Duke of Clarence breathed through his nose; was red. Their feet sounded loudly in the ante-chamber and went away. A valet lighted candles on the table.

"You may sit."

Sir William took the chair the Duke had left. The King was in his settle again. By candle-light his complexion was almost deadly. He sat with his mouth open and his eyes nowhere. Sir William noticed how his shoddy gown was marked by the droppings and dribblings of his meals.

"You are tired, Sire. Shall I call your people?"

"Burgundy." The King whispered the name and let it dangle, adding nothing to it.

"Or let me give you a drink of wine?"

"Be quiet. Burgundy, England : which have we most to fear from, de Concressault?"

"Burgundy, Sire."

"No : Charles the Hardy by himself I can deal with. I don't fear him without England. But England alone was too much for us in Henry of Monmouth's time. We must fear England most."

The King's eyes were brightening a little, fixed straight in front of him.

"Is it really possible that your Grace can contrive an alliance between Marguerite and the Earl of Warwick now? Is it not too late in the day?"

"They call him 'Kingmaker' don't they—a maker of Kings? He'll never swallow exile; pocket his pride first. So will she, that odious woman. Adversity is a strong argument."

"But to marry her son to his daughter . . ."

"A detestable youth : I am sorry for the Earl's daughter with all my heart. We shall contrive it, though; and that's the end of Edward : Warwick as the ruler of England; and Warwick is my friend."

"I do believe he is, your Grace."

"I have more reason to speak well of him than of many others, my own relations not excepted. He was always a friend to my crown; and he hates Burgundy."

The King's chin had sunk down onto his chest. He twisted his long fingers together for a little. Then he threw his head up and his laughter, like something being torn apart, screeched round the room.

"Charles the Hardy, Charles the foolhardy, Charles the ass's head! De Concressault, listen now ! It's a comedy. In God's name it is. Charles means to hammer his coronet into a crown, does he, and with my France for his anvil? Yes, and Charles perfectly loves the house of Lancaster : but when Edward of York climbed up to be the King of England, Charles saw an ally and put his love of Lancaster in his pocket. Didn't he marry Edward's sister? Didn't he invest Edward with the Golden Fleece and let Edward invest him with the Garter? Qui fodit foveam incidet in eam. That's Holy Writ, de Concressault. The man who digs a ditch falls into it. At the moment when he says : 'Now I have England at my elbow,' I put my hand out, I give a push, and down goes the house of York he hates and flatters, and up goes the house of Lancaster he loved and betrayed. And now who's Lancaster's ally but I who put them on their throne again? And when Charles and I reckon up our accounts at last, whose elbow does England stand at? not Burgundy's."

He was leaning forward in his settle now and his hands were wagging. A glint of saliva appeared at the corner of his mouth.

"It'll be my England, de Concressault, an England that I call the tune in : not a strong kingdom any more. They need not help me. What must be certain is that they cannot help

Charles; and with a madman, a child, a Frenchwoman and my loyal friend ruling in it, Lord God, I shall see England weak again."

He thrust to his feet. There was a slither and slur in the rushes and then he was kneeling at the prie-dieu, his eyes fixed on Christ and a babble of prayers starting from his lips.

Isobel, Duchess of Clarence, was embroidering with threads of several colours her father's arms, Kingmaker's. She had finished already the fesse and crosslets of Beauchamp and the Clare chevrons; was at work now on the three lozenges gules of Montacute. Anne, her young sister, was using only blue and gold threads for the leopards and lilies of England that would be quartered with the Neville blazons when she married the Prince, Queen Marguerite's son. The tapestry was to be part of her trousseau. They sat in their room at Angers, side by side, with the heavy cloth across their knees, and stitched. A French maid watched them from a window-seat; bored, fiddled with the ribbons on her lute. It was July and hot, bees fooling about the room noisily and butting against the flowers on the high oak table. The Duchess felt heavy and wretched again that morning, four months after she had had the birth-pangs in a little stinking ship rolling first one rail under and then the other outside Calais harbour. Everything had begun with messengers from her father coming to her husband's castles before sunrise, having travelled by night, and her husband writing with his secretary, Mr. Stacy, the Oxford bachelor, and drinking more than ever, clashing the lid of his pot down and asking her how she would like to be Queen of England. Treason was what that was, and she knew it. George was her father's choice of a husband, and not hers, but she was fond of him. He and his young brother Richard and she and Anne had been children together. It gave her a little cold, like a knife's slippery cold, inside herself when she thought of what was done to traitors. They were not hanged till they were dead, but cut down alive, unmanned, gutted; and what had been inside them was burnt on the scaffold. A hangman who knew his job could get the tripes into the fire before his man had died. She did not want that to happen to George; only a silly boy. It was so stupid, anyway, that he should

26

want to go rampaging about, trying to be a King and making war on his big brother, the Rose of Rouen, Edward. Edward was a giant and had fought seven pitched battles without losing one of them; and even her father said George might be able to handle a sword, but he was no soldier; and neither did his hopes last long. She could remember, in March, him and her father in the castle at Leicester, looking up every time they heard hooves, and the wind blowing to deafen them, and a man coming at last, riding with his left foot out of the stirrup, hose of his left leg black, blood-stiffened, holding on by his horse's mane in the courtyard, shouting between grunts up to the window they stood in: ". . . all over . . . the big guns . . . not a hope . . . Sir Robert, he's taken . . .," and her father looking at George with a stretched smile lifting his lips at their ends. "Unless Stanley helps us now it must be Calais. I am at least sure of Wenlock." They had gone South and West and there had been torment at sea, and Lord Wenlock not letting her land, sending out to their ship only wine and a midwife and word to her father that he was holding Calais for King Edward against rebels and traitors. People said the Duke of Burgundy had bribed him to do that. At Amboise she suckled her boy whilst George and her father talked to the King of France, and one night George had come back in a rage and got drunk, making a noise as he stumbled about the room. He spilled wine and said: "But I'll never give up my right. I'll renounce God first," cursing King Louis and Queen Marguerite. It had astonished her, too: her father talking about Holy Harry as though he were the true King after all: but she understood that it was the only thing left for him. Edward in England was putting people to the brake, hanging them up by the hands and forcing their teeth out, to discover all her father's secrets. They would never be friends again: and now Anne would be Queen of England one day. When they had come to Angers and met Queen Marguerite there, her father had gone down on his knees to her, kneeling for a quarter of an hour, with King Louis' courtiers and the Lancastrian nobles he had chased away from England looking on. The Queen had forgiven him and he had done formal homage to her; sworn to be a good faithful subject until death to her, whom he had fought against, and to Holy Harry, whom he had arrested as a

27

traitor, and to the Prince, whom he had called a bastard. It seemed like magic to Isobel. The magician was the shuffling little French King in scrubby clothes with the holy medals in his hat. He had worked it.

She looked at Anne sewing a royal golden leopard on its azure field : small face rather pale except over the cheekbones, lips very red. Not really beautiful, she thought. She had their father's forward chin, though her nose was short. Her hair was fair-brown, hidden now under a square coiffe, white gauze edged with silver. She sat and frowned a little with her plucked eyebrows over the stitching. Her hand quickly went up and down.

How will she like being married, Isobel wondered—and to Marguerite's boy? It seems only the other day that she and little Richard and George and I were all playing ball together at Warwick. She was always so fond of poor little Richard. Now I've married George and she's going to marry the Prince of Wales (it does seem odd to have to call him that again), and our husbands are going to make war on Edward and Richard and probably kill them. It is all tangled, like threads a cat has played with. The cat is King Louis. We are both fond of Edward and Richard ourselves. When Holy Harry dies—and I mustn't call him that any more either—she will be Queen. It is agreed, too, that if she and the Prince die before us without any children, George is their heir : so I may be Queen, too, in the end. I don't think that I want to be.

"Isobel."

"Yes, Anne dear."

"Do you think we shall have to see the Queen again to-day?"

"I don't know. I expect not. She'll be in council all day with father and the others, most likely."

"Thank God."

Anne went on with her sewing. She had not looked up to speak. Isobel chose a green thread with which to begin the eagle displayed of Monthermer, and thought of Queen Marguerite. She was thin; had black eyes and grey hair; looked at one as though she meant to bite. Her voice was harsh, as though she had been screaming and shouting all her life. When anything was wrong she stamped her foot hard. She had her pages whipped very often and looked on whilst it was done. They said she had been beautiful when King Henry married her. Her son was good-looking after a fashion certainly, but very sulky, and with her temper. It would have done no harm if she had whipped him sometimes and let the pages be. He had never fought an action in his life, but talked about nothing but war and chopping heads off, as though everything were in his hands and he were the god of battles, or safely on his throne, at least.

Anne asked:

"Did George tell you anything last night of when they mean to sail to England?"

"No; only something about going over with father first, and you and mother staying behind with the Queen."

Anne left her needle in the tapestry and looked up.

"Staying behind?"

"Only until the fighting's over: that's what he said. I don't know if he knows anything about it really."

"He must know that much."

"Father tells him very little now. He complains of it."

"Well, it was different when we thought he was going to be King. You can't think father would want to tell him things, and now there's no cause why he should. I must ask father. There's no other way then."

"I shouldn't, dear."

"Mother Mary, it's only in nature that I should want to know what will become of me, left alone with that Queen."

"You'll have our mother: and you'll be married by that time. Father will never invade England till that's done."

"Yes, he means to be a King's father-in-law, fall back, fall edge. Oh, God, if Edward had married one of us we should never have been in this case. He might have done, for the matter of that."

"We were never good enough for him, I suppose, my dear. He was fierce with anger when I married George."

"As though that were monstrous: I can't see."

"We did always say when we were playing that George was my bridegroom, and . . ."

"And Richard was mine: well away, he won't be, it seems. The world's changed again."

Anne got up; looked tall for fourteen in her blue narrow mantle with silver edgings. She put her end of the tapestry onto her chair and walked to a window; propped her right fist on the edge of the embrasure, level with her head.

"I'm tired of sewing. I wish we had a fool here or a juggler. Do you remember how Edward always loved our fool at home? That was something about Edward. He was always merry."

"And he did look a King in the beautiful clothes he wore : not like . . ."

Isobel remembered the French maid, whom she suspected of knowing more English than she owned to; did not go on. Anne twisted her short, bright lips down oddly at the corners.

"He'd have made you a better husband than George, Isobel; and if he'd married you, our father would still be in favour."

"My dear Anne, he never thought of me : but why he need have married that harlot . . ."

"Go on. There's one blessing in having turned Lancastrian. We can say what we like about Elizabeth Wydvylle."

"Yes, she's the root of our ills."

"I tell you again, Isobel: you should have married Edward."

"Oh, I've no quarrel with George."

"There are folk in plenty who'd call George a traitor."

"And our father."

"That's another tale. George is Edward's brother."

"God have mercy on all sinners."

"Amen."

Isobel stopped sewing too, and thought of George and Edward and Cain and Abel. But if it came to that, she thought, her Uncle Montacute was against her father. Everyone was against everyone in England. Edward himself was known for breaking his word. He had headed Dymmoke and old Welles after swearing their safety; and his father, the old Duke, had broken his oath to King Henry. There was nothing sure in England; and after all the battles and turning of colours everyone had a grudge against everyone else now. There were revenges. Edmund, Earl of Rutland, George's and Edward's brother, had begged for his life, they said, at the battle of Wakefield. He was only seventeen. But Black Clifford, who had him down, said : "By God's blood, your father killed mine and so will I you." They were all bitter now, and perjured too, most of them. No one cared more for his side than himself in England. God have mercy on all sinners, then.

Anne touched the French girl on the shoulder. She said:
"Chante donc, Yvonne. Nous nous ennuyons tant."

Yvonne came to life: flash of her teeth in her white, quickly-smiling face; took her lute up. She fretted with the strings a little, nodding and working her eyebrows. Then her face stilled and she began to sing in a good treble:

"De triste cœur chanter joyeusement
    Et rire en deuil c'est chose fort à faire,
    De son penser montrer tout le contraire,
    N'issir doux ris de doulent sentiment.

"Ainsi me faut faire communement,
    Et me convient, pour celer mon affaire,
    De triste cœur chanter joyeusement."

Anne interrupted her.
"Qu'est-ce que c'est cette chanson?"

Yvonne turned her head sharply; looked put-out.
"C'est un vieux rondeau de la noble dame Christine, dite de Pisan, Mademoiselle. J'espère bien qu'il vous plaît."

"I never heard of her before," said Anne.
"She was a learned lady, very skilful in rhetoric and such-like," Isobel told her.
"And very unhappy as well, I think."

Mist, Calais, October, thin drizzle dropping down into stinking, narrow streets and the wind cold: a fair-haired young man in good clothes was peering at the door of his inn, remembering words shouted as he and his people came into the town: "Burgundian whorsons." The inn-door looked odd; was scribbled over with crosses and words in two languages. The young man spoke French, as well as Flemish, from birth and

Chaqu'un Bourguignon est marry
    De la bonne alliance
Accordée au bon roy Harry
    De par le roy de Fraunce.

31

helped him to guess at :

> Therle of Warrewyke in a happy tyde
> wth the ffrensshe kynge is wel allyed.

The crosses, he supposed, were for the Neville blazon of
gules a saltire argent. Slantingly, in a corner, to leave no
doubt, someone had scrawled :

> godde bles Kynge herry,

God curse King Harry,
was what the young man thought; and shrugged his fur
cloak more warmly about his shoulders. His names were
Philippes de Commynes and Philippus van den Clyte. At
twenty-four he was Charles of Burgundy's most trusted
ambassador already; wished at the moment heavily that
he were not : looking up trouble on his Duke's behalf for
King Louis was one pair of shoes; but coming to Calais in
the foam of an English revolution when Burgundy had
backed the wrong side was another, and pinched. He had
come on official business often before, and this was the first
time he had found it necessary to ask for a passport. He had
it with him, and Duke Charles' ring too, that he was to show
if the English put him in prison. The Duke had almost
begged him, using filthier language even than usual, but
keeping his temper, to undertake this mission, saying he had
need to be served in the matter : which was all very fine
and large; but where, de Commynes wondered, would he be,
ring and passport or no ring and passport, if a couple of
drunken English soldiers met him in a dark alley and
decided that there was no need of Burgundians about the
place, seeing the house of Lancaster was up again and
Charles the Hardy was allied with the house of York? He
would be in a hole and, the next thing, a hole would be in
him. Four years ago he had taken part in the battle against
King Louis at Montlhéry; could still remember the look of
pikes, their steel heads showing up on the wooden dark
shafts, levelled at one; how a man kicked when an axe had
gone into his brain; and the noise a sword-stroke made :
short, heavy hiss in the air like a cat spitting. That was a
startling sound. Remembering it, he overcomingly felt the
sensation of a dagger lifted up, now, for a blow, behind his

32

shoulder-blades; looked round with a twitch. There were only his own people at his back. They stood in the drizzle and pulled their furs high under their noses. The house opposite was blind, dull, with heavily overleaning gables, a pair of gilt shears swinging from them for a sign. A lean pig grouted in the rubbish of the kennel. Farther up the street a hawker was shouting flatly : "Que voulez-vous, que voulez-vous. Whaddyou lack, say, whaddyou lack?" His voice was dreamlike and profoundly desolate. De Commynes told one of his men to knock on the door.

The landlord, who was anglicised French, scrubby and talkative, showed them their rooms. Good ones : but they had the chalk scratchings round the doors again. The sight of the sprawled white X and the easy rhyme, repeated in both languages, of France and alliance began to irritate him furiously. Belly of God, he thought, there's no need to remind me that they're in alliance : I am in no danger of forgetting it. He pointed to the devices and asked the landlord sharply who wrote them there. The fellow showed him an arch silly smile, moving his shoulders, eyelids and eyebrows all at the same time.

"C'est les gens de la ville, mon Seigneur."

"Mais pourquoi, en nom Dieu?"

"Ah, très puissant, illustre Seigneur, ne sais rien, moi; mais c'est que les piétons du très illustre Comte de Varrouic sont venus ici, les pieds blancs, et maintenant on dit partout : Vive King 'Arry."

"Merci, va-t-en."

Thinking, he walked about the room. His valets knelt on the floor to unpack his boxes. Yes, they would all have to say for the moment : Vive King 'Arry. Bitterly he reviewed his dealings of the last five months with John, Lord Wenlock, Governor of Calais, Knight of the Garter, and the shiftiest time-server, he had always suspected and was now certain, between London and Byzantium. When the news came to Duke Charles that Kingmaker, running from the hornet's nest he had stirred up in England, had been refused at Calais, he was very well pleased. Kingmaker, he had always maintained, had only two ideas in his head. One was to marry his daughters royally; and that did not matter to anybody. The other was an alliance between England and France. That mattered more than a rush to the Duke. He

packed de Commynes off to Calais to kiss Wenlock cere-
moniously on both cheeks, offer him a pension of a thousand
crowns from the Ducal treasury and desire him to continue
that affection which he had already showed to King
Edward. De Commynes tapped his lip with his finger as he
remembered the scene in the Hall of the Staple on a fine
June day when, kneeling before him as the Duke's proxy,
Wenlock put his hands between his own and swore that he
would serve Edward IV, by God's grace King of England
and France, against all opposers whatsoever and be a true
friend of Edward's noble and illustrious brother-in-law,
Charles, Duke of Burgundy, Brabant and Luxemburg,
Count of Flanders, Holland and Zeeland. There had been
the whiff of a rat in it, even then : a score or so of Warwick's retainers still in the town and drawing their pay
from Wenlock, and Wenlock looking sideways, and hinting
that if the Earl sailed back to England again, well, let him :
no need for the fleet Charles was fitting out at Boulogne to
engage him in the Channel. Edward could crush him as
soon as he landed : oh, easily. Then the news came, and
made the Duke throw the plate he was eating from out of
the window, that Louis had managed, by the help of the
devil presumably, to patch something up between Warwick
and Marguerite. Duke Charles ranted and cursed till it
seemed all the pimples on his face would jet fire like vol-
canoes. If the Earl of Warwick, he said, had turned Lancastrian, then he fully expected to meet the devil in heaven;
and he wrote to his brother-in-law that the age of miracles
had begun again and that Warwick with a French fleet
would invade England as sure as the Mass, before autumn.
It did not seem that Edward of York had taken much
notice; but the Duke was right this time, which was more
than he always was. De Commynes himself had been in
Calais when the world heard how Kingmaker and his son-
in-law had crossed the Channel whilst the Burgundian navy
that should have stopped them was stormbound; had landed
at Dartmouth along with Jaspar Tydder, Earl of Pembroke,
and John Vere, Earl of Oxford, the two best soldiers among
the Lancastrians; had raised all the West country; had
camped within three leagues of the King. There were worse
rumours than that, but wild ones. He flogged his horses

34

from Calais to Boulogne, and a frightened man in an ante-room caught at his sleeve.

"Go to the Duke."

He went. Charles the Hardy had thrown off his gown on to the floor and was standing in doublet and hose. His upper lip was sawing from side to side in a way that made his moustache writhe like a snake and showed the ugly gap in his teeth.

"Where the devil have you come from, hey?"

"From Calais, my Lord."

"Then go back there."

"My Lord?"

Charles looked round the room for something to smash. His large, long-nailed hand closed on a chair-back. His shoulders heaved and his arm stiffened. The chair clattered against the wall and fell over with one leg snapped.

"I said go back there. Jesus Christ, Holy Virgin, have you gone deaf? Go back and set fire to the place. Go back and kiss Lord Wenlock again. Go and sell your body to an Albanian for a steeple-crowned hat, for all I care. Everything in the world's gone to twenty million black devils. My calf's-headed fool of a brother-in-law landed in Holland yesterday."

He had to listen to the Duke numbering all the instruments of the passion and sorrows of Mary, and the bodies of God the Father and God the Son member by member, before he could learn the details. They were serious. Edward of York had marched on Kingmaker with a large army, but it was not trustworthy. Its chief commander was Kingmaker's own brother, the Marquis Montacute. There had been no battle. Whilst Edward was at dinner in some little farm with a moat round it, the Marquis mounted a horse and told his levies to shout for King Henry; and there were six thousand of them. That was confusion, and awakening for Edward out of a dream of being safe. He ran for it with his brother-in-law, Lord Rivers, his young brother, the Duke of Gloucester, Lord Hastings and some more. De Commynes imagined them with white faces leaving the plates and bowls of food still hot, and piling anyhow, all in a bunch together, out of the shadowy farm-hall, and their men quarrelling in whispers about letting the drawbridge down. Some of them would run up the road with weapons

35

in their hands to watch for the Marquis, and the man who held the King's horse would look away whilst he was mounting. They got somehow to the port of King's Lynn and took ship in their armour, the gap widening between the side of the boat and the shore, and between the white rose of York and the Kingdom of England.

"I had word from Gruthuys to-day," the Duke said, and tapped his foot on the floor. "When they landed at Alkmaar they hadn't a penny to bless themselves with. He's sent them on to the Haag. Edward had to give the ship's captain his cloak to pay for their passage. That's the fellow whose sister I married, the Rose of Rouen : and I thought he was going to be some use against Louis. I wish to God he'd been killed in battle. It's his running over here to us that's going to be the ruin of everything. If he were dead we could have patched something up with the Lancastrians. Now they'll invade us, as if we hadn't enough on our plate as it is. God's teeth, but I wish I'd never dirtied my hands with the house of York." He went with two steps to the sideboard; began slopping the tisane he always drank into a bowl. He was at war with Louis of France and having no pleasure from it; was in a fair way to lose St. Quentin and Amiens. "There's no hope of making an understanding with England whilst he's here. We'll have Warwick's men down on top of us before we can cry haro. Oh, Holy Virgin, why didn't I kill Louis when I had the chance at Péronne? This is all his doing. Now we shall be destroyed." It shocked de Commynes to realise what his own thoughts were. It was not the pikes and guns, the moving of men toward them in ships and down roads to smash everything small that they had built up from the War of Public Good till now, Louis' hands crooking themselves round the rich cities, what they had wrung out at Conflans and strengthened at Péronne melting like ice away, that he saw, but as though he were looking at something beautiful a long way off, the adroitness of the Most Christian King. He is inspired by something, he thought, the Holy Ghost or the devil. What he has done is as beautiful as music : in five months to reconcile two old venomous enemies, chased exiles, and put them into alliance and make them powerful, making a famous fighting King run like a coward, and all without even mounting his horse, and all to destroy us. It is what God would do, or a great saint. He is wonderful.

They had seen how wonderful next day, when they heard that the Earl of Warwick, barely Master of England, had remembered who were his friends and sent men already to invade the Boulonnais on behalf of France. Letters of defiance in Henry VI's name would come next, and Charles the Hardy would be at war with two kingdoms at once, chained bull with a dog at each ear. He gave de Commynes his ring then and told him to risk his blood and go back to Calais; persuade somehow Lord Wenlock and the English that the alliance between Burgundy and the house of York must stand between Burgundy and the house of Lancaster.

De Commynes walked over to his bed and sat down on it. It was a tall, painted bed with hangings of green-and-white arras a good deal frayed. The paintings were of flowers and castles and men riding horses and blowing horns. He began to lay out hopes and questions in his mind as coins are laid out on a table to count them: what he must fear and what he need not, how much truth to tell and how many lies. It would be silly to pretend now that he was not in danger. He remembered King Louis at Péronne, under Charles' hand, smiling with terror, looking from one side to the other and talking very fast, whispering bribes and promises to everyone that would listen to him, and Charles shaking all over with hate, so nearly, so very nearly making up his mind to murder him. Well, it was Louis' turn. The danger had been to him then and was to them now: Louis down and Charles up, Warwick in exile and Edward at ease, Charles down and Louis up, Edward in exile and Warwick at ease. It was a boat that rocked up and down on a swell. Anchored, it sailed nowhere.

There was a noise under his window: feet and English voices, then a sound that made him stand up quickly with the odd, unpleasant feeling between his shoulders again: clank and thump, weapons. He looked out. There were half a dozen men-at-arms in the street, standing in a bunch by the door, well-dressed and smart-looking. They wore scarlet tunics badged on back and breast with the Neville saltire; had steel sallets on their heads and swords in their belts, and carried pikes. One of them held a saddled horse. De Commynes put his right hand to the left side of his girdle where his dagger was. For a moment he stood stiff, with his muscles drawn, looking down on them. Then his hand moved; went from the dagger-hilt to his scrip and opened it. He took out the English passport with the obscurely scribbled signature at the bottom. *Joh. Wenloke de Wenloke,* and the Duke's ring. It was a gold ring with an intaglio of a lamb, emblem of the Golden Fleece. Little things, he thought bitterly, turning them over : a few scribbles on a bit of paper and a trifle of jewellery. It was to be hoped they would be more help to him than his dagger.

Steps quickly and obscurely thudded up the stairs and his door was knocked. The landlord bowed a pink-faced young Englishman in fine clothes— a squire, de Commynes guessed —into the room. The lad bent himself courteously until his long sleeves touched the ground; announced in bad French that Lord Wenlock had sent to ask the pleasure of his company at dinner. De Commynes bowed too. His heart was going a little faster than was pleasant. He pointed to the window and said coolly and sternly :

"My Lord Wenlock has always showed me the most distinguished courtesy; but this is the first time he has accorded me the honour of an armed guard."

The squire smiled as pleasantly as a schoolboy; but, de Commynes reflected, an Englishman will smile when he is in act to cut your throat.

"It is for the safety of your person, sir. The people of the town are a little excited. The recent happy events in England have aroused their enthusiasm. My Lord Wenlock would never forgive himself if a misfortune were to overtake you in his jurisdiction."

"I am very gratified to hear it. You'll drink something with me before we start?"

"You are very kind."

De Commynes shouted through the door for wine, and it was brought them. He observed in the squire's neat velvet bonnet a gold ragged staff, another badge of the Kingmaker. I wonder, he thought, that the good Earl doesn't take the throne for himself and have done with it. He has turned the entire nation of English into his household-retainers already.

"God bless King Henry," said the squire, drinking.

"Amen," said de Commynes, "and your very good

health." This may, he added to himself, be the last wine I shall drink in this world. They may mean to murder me.

"Where do we dine?" he asked. "In the Hall of the Staple?"

"In the Castle."

"The Castle? Just so: a strong place: would you mind giving me some idea of when I shall be returning here? For the convenience of my servants, you understand."

The squire looked puzzled, and de Commynes, not waiting for an answer, went to the door and called his secretary.

"Dirk," he said in Flemish, "I am going out now. Take this ring. If I've not returned by sunset, ride to the Duke. Give it him and tell him the English have seized me."

A quick look of understanding went like light on water over the secretary's flat face. He dropped the ring into his scrip.

"Now get my horse," de Commynes told him, and turned to the squire again. "Dismal weather we're having. My people are just saddling my horse. Then I'm at your disposal. In the meanwhile, do tell me all the latest news from England."

The young man, standing with his back to the window, finished the wine; began to speak enthusiastically:

"Why, sir, you can guess how overjoyed we all are at the restoration of the true blood at last. Our troubles are over now. The woman Elizabeth, late calling herself Queen of England, has fled into sanctuary at Westminster. You've heard of Westminster, sir, our great Abbey? That's where she's gone: and the usurper Edward's fled, as you know. The great Earl's come to London with Lord Stanley, and our good King is free again, lodging in the Bishop's Palace, I believe. The latest news is that the Butcher—the Earl of Worcester, sir; Butcher's what we all call him—has been taken and is going to be tried for high treason. He was the one who helped Edward in all his tyrannies: a monster of cruelty. I wish I might be there when they rip his collar off for the axe."

"You speak very feelingly. Has your family suffered much in the quarrel of the house of Lancaster?"

The squire's face became a little red and he fidgeted with the collar of his own doublet. "My house is retained by his

39

good Grace, the Earl of Warwick," he said gruffly. "We have followed him in all quarrels."

"Just so," de Commynes said : "my horse will be ready. Shall we start now?"

Outside, the rain had thickened and the wind was blowing uncomfortably from the sea. They jogged along together over the slimy cobbles, three men with shouldered weapons slouching in front of them, three men with shouldered weapons slouching behind. From indoors singing came and a close reek of cooking. A man in rough clothes passed them, whistling a slow, dignified air that de Commynes thought he recognised as the old war-song of the house of Lancaster. He paused to see their procession pass; stared after them and spat. The whole town of Calais seemed almost decomposing, like broken fungus under the rain. Even the news from England and the tavern singing gave it no festal air. Yet it was a place bought with blood by England and held with swords : a valued thing. The Mayor had once told him that he would gladly pay the King fifteen thousand écus a year for the farm of the customs there. It was the narrow gate by which the bales of English wool went all through Christendom. That is what Kings are greedy for, de Commynes thought : the towns of trade, rich markets. Louis will have Ghent and Bruges from us unless God forbids, and perhaps this place from the English, too. Narrow-streeted towns slimy with rain in winter, filthy with dust in summer, each with a castle and a guildhall and a stone wall all round : those are the things he loves. One day he will be master of every town in France, he or a successor of his. Berri, Provence, Brittany, Burgundy : he'll tipple the Dukes out of their thrones and be cock of the dunghill. One France, one prince : and our Duke wants six Frances and six princes; and between him and Louis and Warwick and Edward I'm caught and go ambling along in the rain to dinner or death, whichever Lord Wenlock is pleased to give me. The rulers bang about, each with his own game to play, and we poor devils of ambassadors must field the balls for them and risk knocks. But Louis is a cleverer player than Duke Charles, it seems.

At the gates of the Castle more men in the Earl's scarlet saluted, thumping the butts of their pikes down onto the cobbles. The young squire bowed to him again :

"Will you follow me, sir?"

The great hall was full of people : indistinct mutter and sibilation of English everywhere. A fire burned gaily and much silver winked on the long tables. Men with napkins round their waists darted about, carrying hot dishes and jacks of wine. A group of people in fine clothes, furred long-sleeved gowns and velvet bonnets with bright scarves round them, broke up and showed Lord Wenlock. He came forward hastily, both hands held out : a tall, well-shaped man, very striking in his rich green dress laced with gold, his pointed yellow beard and frizzed hair barely touched with grey yet. His face was shrewd, friendly, marked permanently with wrinkles of smiling : only his greenish eyes, set close together, had something of suspicion and indecision about them, as though, were one to make a sudden movement before him, he might start back instinctively and grab at his dagger.

"Ah, my dear de Commynes, this is really a pleasure. But what cursed weather you've brought with you to Calais. Wet, are you? Here, one of you good-for-nothings, take Monsieur de Commynes' cloak. How are you, my dear sir, how are you?"

"Very well, thank you, my Lord : and you?"

You dirty old strawpresser, he added to himself, what would I give to pull that goat's beard of yours.

"Come and take your seat, my friend. You'll be hungry, eh? I'm in the best of health : no medicine like good news, eh? Come along. Come along."

They went up the hall to the high table. People on either side of them bowed courteously and gravely. Display of the good manners for which the English were well known, it meant nothing. De Commynes found himself on Lord Wenlock's left. The pages, in leaf-yellow suits so neat that they showed every muscle of their calves and thighs, brought water and fringed napkins. He washed his hands. With a scurrying and whispering of pantlers behind their chairs, broth and the best white bread were served. Lord Wenlock smiled and nodded to the pages, dismissing them to their own table. Over his broth, de Commynes observed the people who sat near him : a respectable company. Wenlock and several more had golden ragged staves in their bonnets; and those who could not wear the emblem in gold had it in cloth. A little way down the board to his left he recognised two of Warwick's household-men whom he had wished Wenlock to turn out of Calais six months ago. It is a good thing that they do not know that, he thought. Those sitting near them were treating them with great attention.

Lord Wenlock's hearty voice boomed in his ear:

"You're noticing changes here, I expect, Monsieur de Commynes."

"I am."

"Well, well, you mustn't let it disconcert you, you know. The true blood's come into its own again. It was bound to happen sooner or later. It was a bad day for Edward of York when he broke with the Earl. There's not a man here, I can tell you, won't follow the ragged staff through fire and sea. Why, within a quarter of an hour of the news coming that he was landed in England again everyone in the town was wearing this."

He touched the gold badge in his bonnet. Sewers began serving, one after another, different kinds of meat. De Commynes heaped his plate in silence and cut himself a slice of bread. It was the first time that he had realised how unstable were the affairs of this world.

Lord Wenlock smilingly chattered on. It was extremely hard to believe that only six months had gone since he was firing cannon at his beloved Earl and refusing shelter to his daughter in her difficult hour.

"Now we can hope there'll be some honesty in England again. Really, you wouldn't believe the state the country was in under the usurper. You wouldn't believe it. If he'd only married a lady of royal birth, there might've been some hope for him; but that woman Elizabeth: well, I won't offend your ears, eh? She and her brother, Lord Rivers, and Butcher Tiptoft and Sir John Fogg, they ruined him between them, treating the old nobility like dirt and pilling and polling the poor commons to get money for their luxuries and pageants: not good enough, by the Mass, not half good enough. I mean to say, there's measure in everything, eh? You can't do that sort of thing in England."

His close-set eyes flicked round the table, as though he wanted someone to agree with him. Several people had stopped eating to listen. Now, one after another, like hounds answering each other on a hot scent, they began to talk. Their faces reddened and their chins stuck out. From all

42

parts of the table, injuries began to heap themselves upon King Edward and his wife's relations. One fat little man in a fox-furred gown, whom de Commynes recognised as a London wool merchant, accused them of having ruined the Calais trade, and talked of a certain sum of 32,821 pounds which he seemed to think the King should have paid out of his own pocket. Several people mentioned the beheading of Welles and Dymmoke, and the man on his left had much to tell of the cruelties of Butcher Tiptoft as Earl-Marshal of England. It seemed that his habit of impaling upon pointed stakes the bodies of those whom he had hanged was disapproved of. The charges became wilder. Queen Elizabeth and her mother, the Dowager Duchess of Bedford, were called whores and witches. Why, said one man, rudely leaning forward with his knife upright in his hand, it had been proved by witnesses that the Duchess used little puppets of lead to beglamour the King into marrying her ditch-begotten daughter; and the Queen herself had a dubious sort of priest, one Friar Bungay, always with her, a necromancer and poisoner if ever there was one. Farther down the table someone laughed and said:

"What of it? Edward could tell you more of necromancy himself than most wizards. Alchemy was all the rage when I was at Court last: everybody chattering about Azoth and red lions and lapis philosophorum. Pity he didn't turn dross into coin instead of coin into dross when he issued the new money."

The first speaker grinned; showed ugly teeth. "Turning honest women into whores is more his mystery. Remember Elizabeth Lucy."

"Aye, you've hit it there, Ralph: except when he turned a whore into an honest woman. Remember Elizabeth Grey."

A great bark of laughter went up from the table. De Commynes looked down the line of talking faces, flushed, sweaty, vehement, and blinked his eyes. He was not easily startled by hypocrisy, which was his trade, but this loud sudden snarling at the heels of York went past his understanding. It was the ones who he had thought were most for Edward who now most abused him. Some of those there, no doubt, were genuine Lancastrians. More, and perhaps Wenlock at heart was among these, would shout for any King made by the Kingmaker. But the rest, surely, could only be trimming their sails to the day's wind. Set Edward up again, Kingmaker or no Kingmaker, and they would shout for him. It seemed, too, that the chief hate of all of them was against the Queen. No words were hard enough for her and her family : and yet, he thought, if it comes to that, no one ever has pretended that Queen Marguerite is a saint of God. One has heard tales about that lady. As for King Henry, everybody knows he is a very foolish man and nearly insane. Yet to listen to these English now, one would suppose it was Christ and the Virgin Mary that they had got to rule over them again. I never saw such changes in the world before.

He asked Lord Wenlock :

"No doubt all the nobility of England have joined my Lord of Warwick by now and declared for King Henry?"

Wenlock wiped his mouth with a piece of bread.

"All that matter, anyway : Thomas Stanley, one of the chief lords of the North, has joined him, and the Percys are quiet in Northumberland. Shrewsbury's with him, too; and then there're the nobles who've always been on the Lancastrian party : Pembroke, Oxford, the Courtneys; and his brother Montacute, of course."

"That will be very pleasant hearing for my Lords of Somerset and Exeter, who are the guests of my master the Duke just now. They're true Lancastrians. The Duke sheltered them gladly in their time of adversity. Now I suppose they'll be leaving us to take up their estates again. Well, it's a pleasure to think we were able to do something for them."

Lord Wenlock looked queerly at him.

"God's bones, is that how his Grace the Duke looks at the matter?"

De Commynes shrugged and helped himself to salted almonds.

"But naturally : whomever you repute to be your King, we shall; and remember, the Duke himself is related to your noble King Henry, being, in effect, the great-grandson of John of Ghent, the founder of the house of Lancaster. I assure you he is very much pleased at the turn things have taken. Admittedly, he is married to the late King Edward's sister : but, then, we must all serve the turn of the times, must we not? At the date of that marriage there seemed no

44

hope of a Lancastrian revolution. But now it has pleased God to bring this about, we are very content with it."

"But here, just a moment, my dear sir; aren't you forgetting that his Grace of Warwick has concluded an alliance with France? I mean to say . . ."

"Not at all : it's unfortunate that we are at war with King Louis ourselves just at present : but if it comes to treaties of alliance, isn't there one between us and yourselves?"

"But that was made in Edward's time."

"What of it? I won't rehearse the text to you. That would indeed be talking Latin to monks. But you'll remember that, in consideration of past changes, we introduced the words *with the King and the Kingdom.* The treaty stands, my lord, York or Lancaster."

He took a long drink of the Moselle wine that was in front of him. I may snatch the chestnuts out of the fire yet, he thought. If only Edward were not with us it would be almost simple.

"That's very ingenious, Monsieur de Commynes. You have God by the toe and the devil by the nose, eh? But what about Edward? We all know he's in Burgundian territory; sailed for the Low Countries as soon as Montacute declared for King Harry. You can't expect us to be very interested in this talk about treaties whilst your Duke's aiding and comforting our great enemy. We're not fools, you know."

De Commynes set down his tankard, chose a piece of green ginger from a silver dish and chewed it slowly. He felt suddenly calm and at his ease, seeing as though by the white instant blink of lightning how all this jar and grind of opposites, Charles and Louis, York and Lancaster, the tangle of turncoat nobles and arrogant Queens, matchmaking, treaty-breaking, intrigue, annexation and war, could be for the moment be stilled and ordered by one lie from him. He looked coldly into Lord Wenlock's unsure eyes and said :

"Edward of York, my lord, will not be aided by my master or by any prince of christendom. Edward of York is dead."

On an afternoon in January of the year 1471, the month in which the great comet appeared, low and menacing like a blazing whip on the horizon, the Duchess of Burgundy sat

45

down to write a confidential letter to her brother, the Duke of Clarence. The letter was discreet, saying only that her two other brothers, Edward King of England and Richard Duke of Gloucester, were in health and wished, despite the differences that had arisen between them, to be remembered fraternally to Duke George. For other news she besought him to give credence to the bearer, a trustworthy man, and she remained, ever praying that God would have him in keeping, his sister and hearty lover.

She remained, in fact, with strung nerves, her temper worn : sister of one of the two most headstrong princes in Christendom and married to the other one. It was a marriage, of course, of policy : no love in it. Charles the Hardy disliked the house of York; had asked for her hand only to prevent Edward, in the days when he was planted safely on his throne, from making alliance with King Louis. He would not have got her, for the matter of that, if any of the counter-suitors whom Louis, on his part, suggested had been worth Edward's while. They were not, so two and a half years ago she had gone to Charles and Burgundy, instead of to Milan and Galeazzo Sforza or Piedmont and Prince Philbert or Savoy and Duke Amadis, as the Christian King had hoped she might. She had no objections; grew even fond of her ferocious, ugly husband as she might have been of some rather dangerous and imposing wild beast that one kept about the house to impress visitors. She taught him English, to which he took very kindly because of the new fields of blasphemy and obscenity that it opened to him; made him eat a conserve of roses with his breakfast every morning to keep his blood cool; listened to his one repeated doctrine that the great lords of the French provinces ought to be kings, not simply vassals of the crown of France; spent much of the money which he, as generous as he was brutal, poured into her lap, on books, tapestries and musicians. She knew him placidly for what he was : a man whose virtues had swollen to the proportion of vices, with whom courage was a disease, pride a madness and activity demented, a monstrous man-animal like a centaur. She was not in the least in love with him. The only persons she loved in the world were her three brothers. Neither, certainly, did she hate him. She hated only her namesake, the French princess who had been the scourge of England, Marguerite of Anjou. George and

Richard had been children on the day of Wakefield. But she, like Edward, had been old enough to understand the story the survivors told : the brave soldier, her father, smashed down to death by the very weight of the armoured men who crowded round him, her delicate brother Edmund disarmed and on his knees before Black Clifford, having his throat cut like a calf, and their two heads, her father's with a paper garland round it, rotting and stinking in rain and sun above a gate in York, lips shrivelling back to show the teeth, eye-sockets hollowed by crows' greedy beaks, the skin turning from green to black. Her care was to see the house that were to thank for that stamped in the mud and her three brothers riding over them. She had seen it : and now, because Edward had married like a fool for love and made an enemy of the man who crowned him, it was all to do again. The following of the white rose had narrowed to a few dozen knights and noblemen hiding for their lives in English sanctuaries and the remnant of a court, without money, without dignity, living somehow on credit and faint hope, vivant de cœur, she said to herself in the language that was as usual now to her as her own, in the town of St. Pol in Artois : a court of exiles. Her brother was there, the Rose himself, Edward, with that huge and perfect body that moved with the sureness of a royal stag, the large, dark-blue eyes and the good, smiling mouth. He still smiled, although what he had lost was a kingdom; pretended that the greatest of his troubles was the coarse food he had to eat now after the meats cooked with twenty spices, the pike stewed in wine, the demaine bread and the foreign novelties, caviare and roast porcupine farced with truffles, that had been served every day of the week in his Palace at Westminster. He loved food and drink, hunting, fighting, clothes, books, music, and women above all things. There was little hunting and no fighting in Artois, and his clothes wore out. The idea of him, of all men, as a shabby dependant on a foreign government nagged his sister like an aching tooth. If ever a man had been designed by God to be a King it was the Rose of Rouen, the tallest and handsomest lad in his own kingdom, with charm in his voice and smile that delighted his worst enemies. He had killed the most deer, won the most fields and spoiled the most virginities of any man in a court of hunters, soldiers and wenchers; and now he was a

47

conquered King. She thought of the people who were with him, loyal still : Lord Say, melancholy and preoccupied, Lord Hastings, gloomily distracting himself with the Artois peasant-girls. William Hastings was half French, one of Edward's best friends, a dark-eyed, slim man with an affectionate manner, shrewder than one would think. If ever the world changed again, he would have more share in changing it than Lord Say; had still a following in England.

Lord Rivers, Anthony Wydvylle, Queen Elizabeth's brother, was the next of them. The Duchess frowned a little when she thought of him : his good clothes, neat little golden beard, manners that were almost too elegant, too easy. He was more than a fop, she thought : was one of the most learned nobles in christendom. A philosopher, student of the classics, he accepted misfortune gently, with a smooth face. When Edward regretted the almond pastries and roast herons of Westminster, he answered that his own chief sorrow was for the beheading of the Earl of Worcester, who had been the best-read peer in England. The saints knew what had been done with his library. It seemed neither of them spoke of what must really smart in their minds : that Queen Elizabeth, alone in sanctuary whilst her enemies tramped the streets and manned the Tower, had given birth at long last to a son who might never see his father and never be called Prince of Wales or King of England. The Abbot and Prior of Westminster had stood godfathers, as they were accustomed in charity to do for poor and nameless children born in that place. Well, be it so, the Duchess thought. Neither the Queen nor any other Wydvylle had much room to grumble at a revolution their own too much pride had brought about. Let Queen Elizabeth, suckling her boy in the stinks and shadows of Broad Sanctuary, and Anthony Rivers reading his book in a tilt-roofed attic in St. Pol, be grateful for the fat past years they had enjoyed. Much more than enough that a Plantagenet had ever mated with them : the badge of the old Duke of York had been a falcon, a bird that does not foul its own nest.

Of the other English at St. Pol, two likely-looking East-Anglian knights, Sir Robert Chamberlaine and Sir Gilbert Debenham, attended chiefly on the Duchess' youngest brother, Duke Richard of Gloucester. Richard had changed more than Edward, she thought, in the last three years. He had ridden beside her to Margate, a pale-faced, chétif little boy of fifteen, thin as a lizard and not five feet high, to see her aboard the *New Ellen* when she sailed for Burgundy. He was still pale and had grown hardly at all; looked a shade ridiculous beside Edward; but he had seen his first field last year against the Lincolnshire rebels, and blooded himself. Edward had made him Warden of the West Marches against Scotland afterward. That post was no one's plaything. He had pleasant manners, more reserved than Edward's; was quiet; sat patiently and attentively in the background whilst the others talked, keeping his grey eyes on their faces. He had retained though, the Duchess noted, a boy's nervous habit of sliding his dagger up and down in its sheath, or twiddling a ring on his finger : shy, probably. He told nothing of what his thoughts were in this new world : but she was sure he had thoughts. At least he was a better brother than George; devoted, she guessed to Edward; might come in useful one day.

Absently, she scribbled at the top of her letter to Duke George the one word *Jesus,* half as a symbol of good faith, half as a talisman. The time had come for them to risk something. Even her husband was beginning to see that. He had only had one interview with Edward at St. Pol. Their servants quarrelled : scufflings in passages, groups standing apart in antechambers, muttering and looking at each other under their eyebrows. Edward used all his charm : his laugh that could make any girl forget what her mother told her; boyish, slightly uncertain gestures of hands which he kept so clean that it was impossible to believe he had killed dozens of men with them; lively humorous talk; caressing looks. Duke Charles, with pimples all over his face and half his front teeth missing, looked scarcely human in his company; told her afterwards that he was a fool.

"They've kicked him out. Why the devil should I sweat my skin to put him back again, that playboy, that long-legged fop? He should have held on tight to his crown while he had it. I tell you frankly, if I can come to an understanding with the Lancastrians, I'll see him to twenty thousand basketsful of black devils before I'll help him. Virtue of God, I'm a Lancastrian myself if it comes to that. It's only that damned fellow Warwick I don't trust."

It looked at first as though the understanding with the

Lancastrians might come about, too : days when the Duchess felt numb and out of hope; knelt in her oratory, praying in anger and not devotion, whilst the Duke held conference with his Lancastrian guests, the Dukes of Exeter and Somerset, who were getting ready to leave for England. They, it seemed, trusted Kingmaker about as well as Duke Charles did. Edmund Beaufort of Somerset had lost his father in the first battle at St. Albans, and his elder brother had been beheaded by the brother of Kingmaker, the Marquis Montacute. "These things," he said drily to Duke Charles, "stick in a man's memory"; and he had not forgotten, either, who it was that had led King Henry bound through Cheapside, shouting down from his saddle to the peering people in the shop-doors : "Here's the traitor." Henry Holland of Exeter said that, for his part, he had no desire for a French alliance. He and his cousin of Somerset, when they were home again, would use their influence against Kingmaker. The devil, having got into heaven, was being cold-shouldered by the saints.

Unfortunately, they were a little late in starting. Kingmaker, doubtless mindful of the parable which promises to those who have worked but one hour in the vineyard the same reward as to them who have borne the heat and burden of the day, waited neither for them nor for Queen Marguerite before calling a Parliament. His brother, the Archbishop of York, opened the deliberations with an eloquent sermon on a text of Jeremiah : Revertimini ad me filii revertentes, ego enim vir vester. Edward of York was declared, obviously enough, a rebel and traitor to his sovereign lord, King Henry VI, now restored by God's especial providence to his rights and dignities. His acts were annulled and damned and his Dukedom of York presented to his brother Duke George. A ten years' treaty was ratified with King Louis. King Henry himself did not take any very active part in these proceedings, though some of the sounds which escaped his small, protruding lips were understood to express his gratitude to God and the Earl of Warwick. The Earl talked to the French ambassadors about sending over two or three thousand men to Calais as an advance-guard. He, himself, would follow with ten thousand good archers and as many levies as could be raised, and France and England would take order with the Duke of Burgundy. His share of the proceeds, it was understood, was to be the counties of Zeeland and Holland.

Amiens was still occupied by royal French troops. Duke Charles, cursing vilely, began to listen to his wife.

The Duchess shook a little bell of ivory and silver that stood on her painted escritoire. The man who had been waiting in the passage came in : a short man, dark and attentive-looking, wearing the clothes of a pilgrim. She sealed her letter and held it out to him at arm's length, saying in English :

"This is only a letter of credence. I'll tell you what you've to say in a minute. Have you decided which shrine you'll be visiting?"

"I'd thought of Canterbury, your Ladyship. It's the most central, you see."

"Yes, a good idea : if by any chance you should really go there, you might offer a candle for our success. I mean that. Now listen. You're to begin by telling the Duke of Clarence that their Lordships of Exeter and Somerset will be sailing for England very shortly, and they've been using very hostile language about him, and he may expect trouble from them when they land. They've been heard to say that once Queen Marguerite and her son cross over from France and are established in England again there'll be no further need of him, and as Queen Marguerite hates all the house of York, it will be easy to find some means of getting rid of him."

"I quite understand, your Ladyship."

"That should make him reflect. Then if he goes on to speak of my brother the King, say that he and Duke Richard have had many messages from our friends in England. Say that if they were to return and enjoy their former state, neither of them would bear grudges, as their one desire is for trust and amity between all the children of our great father, sweet Jesus have mercy on his soul, and that is my desire also. You follow me?"

"Perfectly, your Ladyship."

"Good : now go carefully here. If—only if—he shows you encouragement, you may say that his Grace King Edward has entered into a secret understanding with Duke François of Brittany, who will aid him in a brotherly manner to recover his kingdom."

"I'm very glad to hear it, my Lady."

"So should I be if it were true. He is going to write to Duke François, but the saints know if there'll anything come of it. We must put our hopes on England. Tell Duke George to believe no tales that my brother and my husband are not in amity. They are only put about to deceive King Louis. Be firm in that; but don't run before your horse to market. Sound him cleverly; and if you think he has begun to lean our way, then you may ask him—say that I ask him—what he has gained by destroying our father's house, and whether his state is better now than when the Rose of Rouen was King."

"I will ask him that. He should know the answer, I think."

"So do I think. All he's gained is the name of Duke of York and the Lieutenantship of Ireland that he had before. But there's no telling where you have him : a weathercock. You must go to work carefully : nothing sudden. Get a word, if you can, with my lady mother or the Cardinal of Canterbury. You may be plain with them. Tell them I'm at my husband day and night to help us. The news of the Parliament has shaken him. Say my brother is writing to Brittany. My mother should sound Lord Stanley. He might take our part again. That family are always turning their coats. The Mowbrays have hated Lancaster ever since Richard of Bordeaux's days. We shall need to hire German ships, I think. My brother and Lord Rivers are going to Bruges soon on that business. Tell my mother if she can send a thousand pounds it would be blessed. Be on your way now. If you're taken and tortured, hold fast to your faith and confess nothing. All saints be good to you."

The man bowed with a jerk; had gone. The Duchess of Burgundy placed for a second the palms of her hands upon her eyes. It was a gambler's game that she was playing, matching against Kingmaker and the soft, fluid devilry of the Christian King nothing stronger than her husband's grudged help and the chance that George, with his too-small eyes and his loud voice, since he had been a traitor once, might be a traitor twice. She felt hope suddenly leak out of her and leave her empty. The odds were ruinous. Queen Marguerite and her son were still in France, but at the first word that Edward was in England again surely they would be across the Channel in King Louis' ships, with King Louis' mercenaries, to join the Earl. Forty thousand, fifty thousand men might take the field for the red rose, swords, axes, pikes, crossbows and longbows, big iron and brass guns on their carriages, horses trampling the fields to mud, ranks spreading out of sight on either side, vanward, middleward and rearward, drawn up before some quiet market-town to roll over and stamp flat a slender company of Yorkists. Edward would die like his father in a ringfence of enemies. She stood up and crossed herself, meaning to pray. There were two faces in her mind. One was long from eyes to chin, its small mouth tilting ironically upward at the corners : face of Kingmaker, the unmaker of Kings. Edward's was the other, smooth as a boy's, with the straight Plantagenet nose and arched, fine eyebrows, the wide eyes matching the sapphires in the ring he wore. He was smiling; had smiled himself and smiled all England and Burgundy into this coil of troubles; smiled at a woman, laughed at a jealous friend, and paid with a kingdom. My husband is a cruel man, thought the Duchess, with devils of arrogance and anger all at rage in him. But Edward is, by far, more terrible; is ruinous because people love him. His charm will bring more sorrows into God's world than Charles' anger or Louis' policy or Queen Marguerite's hate. Bright Mary, star of the sea, help me to help him out of his troubles for now.

CHAPTER TWO

FOG

(*England*: 1471)

Entre vous, Franchois,
Jectez pleures et larmes.
Vervic, votre choix,
Est vaincu par armes.
Burgundian popular song, fifteenth century.

MARCHING and going on marching down the uneven roads
and sleeping where he could, sweating under his leather jack
and catching his feet in ruts, was all he had seen up to now
of soldiering.

His name was Young Ralph at Mill, but now they were
all calling him Ralph Miller. He was tired of carrying heavy
cornsacks. When they said in his village that Sir William
Parr was getting men together to fight for a King—they
could not tell which—he went up to the Manor and they
gave him his jack and a pike and an old steel sallet. His
cousin, Red Tom, was a man-at-arms of Sir William's and
knew him again. They were nicer to him than people had
been in the village; and Sir William mustered them all in
the park and said he was going to pay them threepence a
day. So they marched to Nottingham, and found the city as
full as at Goose Fair, and everyone armed, and heard tales.
He could understand part of them. The York King, Edward,
the one Kingmaker chased out last year, had come back;
was at Doncaster. Some people said he had taken an oath
not to fight the mad King, King Harry; only wanted his
friends to come with him to London, in arms, to ask King
Harry to give him his dukedom again. Red Tom grinned
and asked Ralph : "Isn't it likely?" When they marched out
for Leicester they were more men than Ralph ever saw in
his life : fellows in sallets and jacks like his own, and men-
at-arms in real steel armour like Tom's, and archers by

hundreds. Knights rode among them, steel from sole to crown, metal men. But Red Tom pulled a face and said :

"I don't like this. If these're all the friends Edward Longlegs has got, he'd 've been better to stay out of England."

"Nay, but Tom, there's crowds of us."

"Crowds, you holy innocent : d'you know how many we had at Towton when we beat the old Queen? Forty thousand. There's not four thousand here."

"What was Towton like, Tom?"

"Like hell : snowing fit to cool the devil, and the Lancastrian thieves on top of the goddam' hill and us at the bottom of it, and the Duke of Norfolk was late bringing his men up. Seven hours of it and twenty-seven thousand dead at the upshot : Christ keep me out of another field like Towton."

"Will we likely have to fight a field this journey?"

"Oh, holy St. Anthony, what d'you think you've got that toothpick in your hand for : to scratch your arse with?"

The men began to talk about what their captains were planning and who their enemies were. They were heading for Newark to fight the Earl of Oxford, they said. He was a famous captain and his soldiers came from East Anglia; would be as stout as trees. Then it was said he had retreated, and they turned back to Leicester again. Then a new name began to be spoken from file to file, under the breath mostly : "Kingmaker." He was at Leicester, the great Earl, with an army. Ralph didn't pretend he knew much, but he knew what that meant. Tom told him how Kingmaker fought at Towton when he was friends with King Edward. There had been dead men round him, heaped up like faggots. He hefted his long pike in his hands; wondered what it was like to see one of those knights coming down at you, swinging his sword about.

"Jab at his horse," Tom said, "in the neck if you can. It's worth it. There's pickings on a dead lord if you've time to strip him. I got one at Towton : ten angels and a gold ring with stones in it."

Eh, thought Ralph, you could buy land with that.

No battle was drawn up in front of Leicester. They marched into the town, and people watched them out of windows. But Kingmaker had been there; had marched out the day before, with seven thousand men wearing the ragged staff and the silver saltire, the townsmen said, and taken the Coventry road. Was he running away? Waiting for re-inforcements more like, the old soldiers said. It was his fashion. His brother, Marquis Montacute, had one army and Lord Oxford another. They would all three join, and then the dance would start. The only comfort was that men were coming into Leicester in troops of two and three hundred at a time, very well arrayed, saying they were for Lord Hastings and the white rose. Ralph had seen Lord Hastings once or twice, a handsome, dark-faced gentleman in splendid armour. It would seem he had friends in these parts. Their own Lord, Sir William, had given them a quarter-royal each as advance on wages. That was a lot of money. He went with Tom and two lads in his village to an inn in a fine street and they had strong beer and broth and beef and a capon and white bread; drank Lord Hastings' health and Edward of York's.

"And he can take his crown again as well as his dukedom for all of me," Tom said. "He's a soldier, and he's got what you might call the looks for a King. I banned him when he brought that new-fangled money in, it's so cursedly hard to reckon it, but I'd as soon him as Holy Harry."

They had another gallon between them, and one of Sir James Harrington's men came in, swaying and bedazed, drunk as a gleeman's bitch. He pointed to them and stammered : "Have you heard it?"

"Heard what, man?"

"The talk of the town: goddam' Duke of Clarence coming this road with seven thousand men to join Kingmaker. I've some of my pay left, and I'm going to have a Mass said for me when I'm dead."

It was true, too. They were all roused out of the town and on the road by dawn. It seemed very unkind to Ralph that the Duke of Clarence should be for fighting his own brother; but, then, he didn't understand Lords' policies : they were too high for him. Red Tom was glum and would not talk much, except to say there were a bare six thousand of them and Clarence and Kingmaker would have twelve thousand between them at the smallest.

"We'll be shent," he said.

They marched a sullen day over the flat Leicestershire plain, touched by spring, from Narborough to Hinckley, from Hinckley to Nuneaton, places and names that he had never heard of. He felt hideously far from home. The men who knew the countryside began to whisper to each other.

"Making for Coventry," he heard one say, and Red Tom answered:

"Aye, it's our only chance."

"But isn't Kingmaker there?" he asked.

"Why yes, addlewit: Edward's best play's to try the issue with him before the Duke comes. You'll see a field, my lad, before you're two days older."

He saw, in the doubtful owl-light when his thighs ached with marching, a city with a wall and trees about it. Some-one pointed to a spire, standing up black against the sunset, and said: "Christ's Church."

He leaned on his pike and looked and looked. The men all round were silent. He knew why. Under the spire, inside the walls that had the red West like a threatening flag behind them, the great Earl was. They had come South for this: to stand and wait and look, whilst shadows closed in on them, until Kingmaker sounded his trumpets and rushed out destructively. The men's faces were lined, pensive under the curved brims, shiny with sunset, of their sallets. They turned their tired eyes on the city. Ralph looked from one to another of them. They had been good to march with and they might all be dead to-morrow. He did not understand the garboyles of the two Kings and two roses; but he knew the tales of Kingmaker that were told in his village. King-maker had won bloody victories; had defeated everyone. He was rich past words. The money that a plain man saw in the whole of his life would not amount to the price of his horse or his bed-hangings; and his castles were everywhere. When he was in a town, any fellow could come in his kitchen; take as much cooked meat away as would go on a dagger. He never missed it. Kingmaker was more of a matter than forty Kings. It seemed unnatural for the armoured captains to be riding through their ranks now, giving orders to forage and bivouac. Could they mean them to go to sleep so close to the Kingmaker?

There was a queer thing next morning. They were wakened by trumpets, having slept with their jacks on and

57

their pikes beside them. Their own lord, Sir William, was in the saddle already, harnessed except for his helmet, and shouting out in his loud angry voice: "Come on there. Stumble up there. Follow on after me."

All over the fields in which they lay, knights and captains were getting their files together, leading them down to the crossroads. There was a vast crowd there and banners were showing. Ralph had learned some of the blazons. The white boar with the golden bristles belonged to Edward of York's young brother, the Duke of Gloucester, an easy one to remember; and Edward's own device he could see too: a white rose inside a gold sun with rays all round it. There were men of all sorts streaming down to join the crowd. He saw some queer ones with good armour and beards, that he had not noticed before. A man near him said:

"There go the Flemings."

Sir William pushed his horse through the mob, and they followed behind him. There was a clear space in the midst of the crowd, a ring kept by knights and lords, wearing sur-coats of all sorts of colours over their armour, sitting their horses and looking proud and solemn. It was still misty, and the breaths of the crowd made smoke, but the sun streamed pure fire over the armour, blue, white and black, so that men's heads and shoulders burned. It was all gorgeous for Ralph to see. The Lords were like saints and angels shining each in his place. Their horses were big and beautiful, stand-ing stock-still, with gay saddle-cloths and their tackle all polished. He could see into the middle-space, peering between Sir William's horse and another's. There were people on horseback: Lord Hastings for one, and a tiny little man on a white horse who must be the Duke of Gloucester. There were heralds on foot, holding trumpets. But there in the middle, high on a black horse, wearing armour of black and gold, was someone he knew in a flash. No one but Edward of York could so tower like a ship's mast over the rest of the crowd. His helmet was off, and his hair, the colour of copper, took the light like his harness. Ralph gazed. He had been King of England once. Suddenly a great blare of trumpets ripped open the silence, and a man's voice sounded, sing-songing words, such fine language that Ralph understood only half of it:

"We, Edward, by the Grace of God and by lawful inheritance King of England and France and Lord of Ireland . . ."

He gulped, excitement thrilling him; caught more words :

". . . resume and take upon us again the said right, title, dignity and estate of the crowns of the realms of England and France and of the lordship and land of Ireland, of right, law and custom appertaining to us, as well by inheritance as by lawful election . . ."

He puzzled what could lawful election mean; missed something and then listened again.

". . . pardon and oblivion for all such offences by them committed, except only such as are capital enemies to our said crown and dignity, without punishment of whom good peace and prosperity of this realm cannot be had, and except all such as at this time make any resistance against us . . ."

Nay, he thought, but the tales I'll have to tell when I get home : me hearing all this like as if I was a fine Parliament gentleman.

". . . all well-disposed persons of this realm to take and repute the said Henry of Lancaster, calling himself King of England, to be our rebel and traitor, and neither to comfort nor assist him as they would eschew our heavy indignation. *Long live King Edward!*"

Then it seemed as though the pale March sky would split. The tearing noise of trumpets and loud burst of voices went up together, making the eardrums shake. "King Edward! King Edward!"

They waited all day for Kingmaker to come out of Coventry, and had no ease in their waiting, watching the roads and walls and listening for music. The old men said, who had seen wars before, that Edward had chosen today for calling himself King again so as to draw Kingmaker like a badger and fight him before Montacute came from the North or Clarence from the West. Archers that day saw to the feathers of their arrows and tried their bows out. Such armourers as were with them lighted fires, and one heard everywhere the quick, sweet language of their little hammers : ting-tingtang. But no men with the silver X on their tunics and banners of ragged staves moved out across the green-and-brown March fields. Christ's Church tower and the castle looked at each other. Smoke flickered up from chimneys, and the city was shut like a box, and mute.

They ate and sang at night round the big wood fires, their faces reddened by them; but the city and its silence and nearness were in their minds, as near as the dark was near, and they were uneasy. They slept and woke again. Then the lords were among them again, flaming in armour, telling them to break camp and march. Ralph's feet were blistered. Red Tom had told him to tear a little off his shirt and wrap his toes up separately; but he limped still. Here in Warwickshire, in Kingmaker's county, no one cheered when they passed. An old man by the roadside shouted :

"White-rose bastards, long live King Harry!"

A mounted man-at-arms smashed him across the face with the butt of his demi-lance; knocked him heels-upward into the ditch. They dropped into the Vale of Evesham and crossed the Fosse Way before they camped; slouched on through the dull next day, a crowd of men on foot and in saddles, chafed by harness and carrying weapons, and the baggage-carts, four-wheeled and ponderous, requisitioned hay-waggons mostly, creaked and croaked behind them with a guard of mounted archers. Ralph had begun to think, moved to it by new things he had seen and felt and by the largeness of England. The marching and the sight of great men and expectations of battle and the words that had been read by the herald forced his mind open. What he thought was : All this is still England, and there is more of it yet, and it is all the King's. We are going about, just so many of us, to change the King as though these towns and roads belonged to us. Four armies already are on the march to stop that. How could we ever do it?

When they had trudged, thirsty and sulking, uphill out of the Vale again and could see Wroxton Abbey far off, they were halted. They stood dumb like sheep, and fresh orders were given. Ralph stroked the rough down on his chin, missing his weekly shave. A fellow near him spat and said softly under his breath :

"Oh Jesus."

The Duke of Gloucester, looking no bigger than a monkey on his big white horse, came down the road toward them from the head of the column, riding at a hand-canter. He reined in hardly twenty feet away, so that Ralph could see his beautiful armour, blued steel with the boar in hammered silver and gold on it, and hear his clear voice which was young and low, very pleasant. He said :

"Sir William Parr?"

Sir William kicked his slow roan mare into a trot and came up saluting, making the men jump out of his way.

"Here, your Grace."

The Duke saluted him. He had his vizor down and lifted one gauntlet to it sharply and formally. Eh, but he's a little one, Ralph thought, not like his brother. It gave him an obscure kind of pleasure to see the little, shiny, erect shape on the tall horse and hear the impersonal voice, coldly friendly, coming from behind the ribs of the vizor, quiet and unpassionate.

"Sir James Harrington?"

"Your Grace?"

Sir James rode up, wiping his mouth with his bare hand. He had been taking a draught from the flask of watered wine that his squire carried.

"You two and Debenham and Chamberlaine are posted to the vanward under me. March your men up the road and join the others. We deploy on the right of the middleward, of course. The King's Grace will take the middleward, Lord Hastings the rearward. Our outriders have just reported the Duke of Clarence at Banbury with his people. If they make a stand, we shall be pitching battle in about an hour. Ride on and take your places."

The men ahead stood from the road to let them march past. It seemed to Ralph that the soldiers like Tom who had fought before had turned cheerful now they had heard there would be a battle. He felt coldish and sickish. Red Tom was whistling. It's Lent, but I've been eating meat, Ralph thought. If I die I shall go to hell. There were men waiting for them at the head of the column. Some of them were the bearded strangers he had seen before. They had swords, and strange things like deep brass cups on the end of poles. Tom jerked his thumb at them.

"Hand-gunners from Burgundy," he said. "Germans and Dutch mostly : I reckon a rush to them." Then he called out queer words Ralph could not understand : "Hey, Heinrich, Duke kommt. Fechten. Schlag tot."

A hand-gunner with a yellow beard down to his shoulders, a fat man, grinned. "Recht so : wohl schlagen wir tot." He pushed the brass part of his strange weapon forward. "Boom!"

"Silly whorsons," Tom said, "I've seen a many of them."

From behind their backs came suddenly the young, cold voice that Ralph knew already: "Outriders on": and a hundred or more on horseback, well armed, began to trot. They followed; marched past the Abbey and down the Salt Way. There was a difference now in their marching. They did not slouch, but kept step together; kept close. The archers had uncased their bows and most of them carried one arrow ready in their hand. The knights had their vizors down. I've not been to confession, Ralph thought, for ever so long. I'll be put into hell, and our priest never taught us prayers properly. How does it go? Pater noster qui es in ... something, I can't remember, ne nos inducas in tentationem sed libera nos, and some more, amen: and the saints, now: the blessed Virgin and St. Joseph the joiner and St. Anne and St. Antony, St. George, St. Dunstan, St. Cuthbert, St. Thomas the holy martyr: I do hope they'll remember me. I won't eat meat in Lent any more.

In front, people shouted. A horseman came rattling down on them, went forward, galloping so that they barely had time to make place for him. Then they were halted. Voices called. An archer in the company just ahead twanged his string twice and held up his wetted finger to try the wind. There were orders given abruptly and loudly, and they were leaving the road, all the column of them, and stumbling through fields. The knights and captains rode close beside their commands, jostling and herding them.

"Slope pikes."

"Keep rank there, God damn you."

"Right of those trees."

He was on the inside of the column; could see nothing; but he felt his flesh shrinking together, trying to make itself small, at the expectation of danger coming suddenly down on them; pressed himself close to the man on his right.

"Halt. Turn about. Form battle."

The column faced round and became a line, five deep, of men, pikes thrust out from it, wavering at first and then steadying. He could see better now: could see level fields and the road and their own line with plumps of archers and pikemen or men-at-arms placed alternately; peered over

62

shoulders, pushing his pike, as he had been taught, between the bodies of men in front of him. Music was playing some-where : chatter of drums and vaunting of fifes and trumpets. Away to his right he could see horsemen, the end of their line. He realised clearly and suddenly what they were : an army straddling a road. The King himself, Edward Long-legs, was there on the road with the middleward, and far on their left was the rearward under Lord Hastings. We are the vanguard, he thought, and our captain is the Duke of Gloucester, whose badge is a boar. We are going to fight. Then he saw the enemy.

They had not spread out into the fields; were coming in a column like their own down the road, moving slowly, with banners. He looked and looked, thinking : Perhaps some-where there, in a man's hand or his quiver, is something to kill me. But the queer thing was that those men coming up the road were the Duke of Clarence's men, and he was King Edward's brother. Two brothers on this side, he thought, and one on the other, and us here to fight for the two against the one. Eh, it's all daft. The column came on; was near enough for him to tell separate movements of legs and arms. Its top was a single sheen like a river, because all the men were helmed; but below, it was broken in colours of clothes and glimmer of harness. Horsemen rode with a banner in its front, and he could not see the end yet. He felt himself almost hiccoughing with afraid expectation. Then, with a jerk, the column halted, light ceasing to ripple on its steel top and beginning to shine steadily. A loud call sounded from trumpets not theirs, and by theirs was answered. A strange twitch and shiver passed along the rank that he was in. Some gripped their pikes more firmly; but others straightened their backs and let the points droop. A dull rough voice behind him said :

"Praise God and St. Bernard."

From the head of the column two or three horsemen had moved and were riding alone—bright, small shapes—up the road. All the rest of the compact, long troop stood still. He heard hooves drumming, and the Duke of Gloucester and two knights went past, riding to the road. Ralph saw him go up to the moving horsemen, not lifting any weapon, and they all halted together; were shiny, still points on the road's white, to which, from the middleward and rearward, more riders came. He wondered was this how a battle always began. For a long time everything was still and he could hear rooks caw-cawing a long way away. Then, in a knot, all those horsemen who had sat in their saddles between the armies moved in one direction; moved toward him slowly; and behind him the music blew up again. From the middle-ward came cheering. He cried out, not bearing to be puzzled any longer:

"But what are they at?"

The cheering spread sideways from the vanward; was loudening up the line toward where he stood: an unshaped clamour. The voice that had thanked God and St. Bernard loudly said:

"Haven't you eyes? Cheer, you fool. Duke of Clarence has turned his coat. He's come over to us. We'll crown Edward King in London again before Easter day now. Go on, you addlewit. Cheer for the Duke of Clarence."

That was it, and now they were going to London, a great conquering army, conquering without a blow. When they left Banbury he stepped out in pride on his sore feet, with his head full of music. He had seen wonderful things; would have something to talk about all his life; and he was going to see London and help crown a King there.

They were fifteen thousand now, and people cheered here and there as they went by. Seven thousand had come up out of the South-west shires behind the Duke of Clarence's banner, which was a black bull, and were queer fellows to Ralph, speaking an English he could barely comprehend: said Ich for I and turned their esses into zeds. They said the Duke had never meant to fight his brother; had brought white-rose favours in his baggage ready to distribute to them when the right time was. Some of them did not seem pleased to change. People in their parts, they said, held with the house of Lancaster. They had news, too, that the old Queen, Holy Harry's wife, and her son were coming from France with a good army; were expected on the West coast any day now. They would join their troops to those of Kingmaker and there would be bloodletting.

"And when it comes," Tom told Ralph, "if our King's wise he'll keep his kind brother and these West-country sheep-stealers under his eye. The half of 'em are red-rose men at stomach; and as for the Duke of Clarence, a man who's turned his coat once'll turn it twenty times; and that's what."

He said this whilst they were lounging, a hundred or so of them, before a church in Daventry. Their King was in the church at his prayers, and his fifteen thousand took a little rest about the town, drinking and playing shove-groat on the steps of the market cross. They were for Northampton, the word was, and then St. Albans; and from St. Albans for London.

"You've seen London, Tom," he said. His mind was always on the city now. No one had ever been there from his village.

"Aye, three or four times. That's a city, I'll tell you. There're strong whores in Cock's Lane and the best eel-pies ever I've eaten : and I'll tell you a thing. If you've any manner of goods that you want to chaffer and no words said—something you've found, say—take it to the Lombards. They'll buy it off you and no questions. What the devil's to do?"

A man had come out of the church, a squire with a staring face, and was shouting :

"A miracle, a miracle, loved be God, a wonderful sign!"

Then Sir William came out, pushing the squire aside, and cried in his high voice, furiously : "On your knees, you bastards : get on your knees and a pox on it. Fifty million devils, d'you think the goddam' saints work a miracle every day of your lousy lives. Kneel down and be damned. Here, one of you run for a priest and let's have some christian prayers in the devil's name."

They slumped by ones and threes down on the cobbles, wondering, uncovering their heads. A fat priest was hustled onto the church steps and blessed them. Sir William nudged him and whispered. He nodded; began to talk gabblingly and uncertainly.

"My sons, I announce to you great joy. Populus, as it stands in the Book, qui ambulabat in tenebris vidit lucem magnam. It has pleased almighty God to approve by a most marvellous working the justice of the Lord Edward's quarrel. Whilst the King in excellent piety, as he is a most pious and godly prince, was kneeling in discharge of a vow —Oh my sons, it is good to pay vows—before the image of the blessed St. Anne, that great saint, the mother of the mother of God, a kindly lady whose ears are always open to prayer, that great saint, I say . . ."

He paused, having lost, it seemed, his discourse; began again :

"The holy image was covered, as is the custom of the Church during this season of Lent, with a screen of boards. Behold a miracle. As the Lord Edward knelt before it, the boards opened of themselves, visibly parting by the work of no man's hand. They closed again. Is it not good to pay vows? They opened yet again, and widely, so that the image of the blessed saint, the dear mother of our Lady, was plainly seen by all. There is a miracle, my sons. There is a sign that the cause in which you bear arms is pleasing to God, and for the amendment of your naughty lives. Amen, dico vobis. Do not harden your wicked hearts. Here is a marvellous opportunity of grace. The holy image is here, here in this church of God. See that you all, by some pious work, show the kind saint that this token of her love has not been wasted on you. Bring forth fruits meet for repentance. Abstain from riotousness and ill-guidance whilst you are in this town where the power of God has been so gloriously manifested. See that your prayers, your vows, your alms show God and the dear kindly saint your gratitude. Amen."

"Amen," said Ralph, and men said Amen all round him. He could not get into the church to see the holy image because of the crowd of knights and nobles there; but he found a little Christ at a street-corner and said his prayers to him : "Sweet Christ, our priest never taught us prayers properly, but you know what I mean. Sweet Christ, thank you for the holy miracle, and I will live cleanly. Don't damn me at doomsday because of Lent. I won't sin so again, and I'll be shriven at Easter, and I've got a farthing I'll give the next begging friar we meet. Don't let me be killed in a battle, for the sake of our Lady and blessed St. Anne, and God bless King Edward and the Duke of Gloucester. Amen."

On the Thursday before Easter they were in London.

Ralph could not rightly believe that he was there. He realised now, had not known before, why in the first place he had taken livery and gone along with Sir William. He had gone along to see London. They had a two days' wait at St. Albans whilst King Edward, people said, was writing letters to Queen Elizabeth in sanctuary and to the Bishop of London and the Archbishop of Canterbury. Then they went in, and there were people shouting and waving hands, and cloths hung out of the windows and aldermen riding in scarlet and rich citizens in violet, and they marched through more streets than Ralph ever saw and were heroes; had come into London and brought King Edward the Rose with them again. No one had stopped them, and Ralph did not understand how poor fellows like him could matter so much to grand Londoners; why women smiled and blew kisses and men called : "God bless you." It seemed he and Red Tom and Sir William and the hand-gunners from Burgundy and all the rest of them had done something marvellous. The miracle of St. Anne might be part of that; but then, after a little, he understood that it was because everyone in London loved beautiful King Edward. They wanted him back again, and had a welcome for poor, simple folk from the North and the Midlands who had guarded him across England.

London was amazement to him : the many streets and the many churches; the tangle without end of houses whose lower storeys were brick or stone; the shops where all things in the world were to buy or sell; cookhouses where you could have any dish that you asked for, like a Lord's kitchen but open for common folk; Londoners talking their odd, clear talk; Lombards and Germans and Genoese; armourers' shops making harness for knights; a vast bridge with real houses upon it; hot baths open to all; many hundreds of houses each having its own sign, so that a rank of them hung out at different levels, like a row of pikes, over the street : the bear, the crown, the mitre, the fess, the rose, the crescent, the bull, the foot. People looked cheerfully at him everywhere. God bless King Edward and À York were passwords. The grand people, in violet and mulberry, who walked down Cheapside as though it were theirs had white roses stuck in their bonnets. The first day a pretty girl, very well dressed, ran out of a shop as he passed, with a mazer of wine.

"Mother says, if you're one of King Edward's men, drink and God love you."

He had only drunk wine four or five times in his life; smiled and fumbled with the wooden bowl, frightened to look at the girl; gulped pink claret and lifted his hand to his sallet.

"God bless you and long live King Edward; à York."

He heard wonderful gossip. The Londoners talked all the time. There was no sitting still in a tavern or on a market-bench, wondering who a stranger might be. Anybody was somebody to a Londoner. They all talked to him. An apprentice as nicely dressed as a squire and able, as he said, to speak French told him how, two days before they came in, the Archbishop of York, Kingmaker's brother, had raised six hundred men and ridden about the City with King Harry, calling on everyone to stand by the true blood of Lancaster.

"But you never saw such a miserable sight," the apprentice said, "Holy Harry sitting his horse like a sack and mumbling. He's no make of a King, and everyone knew you were all of you lying at St. Albans. We've no use for King Harry. They had the guards out guarding the City, but Recorder Urswick—he's clever—he told 'em all to go home to dinner when he heard you were coming, and so King Edward was let in. I'll tell you what. I'd like to fight for the white rose myself. I'm tired of trade. You're a lucky one. I'll tell you. Why shouldn't you sup with me, if my master'll let me off, to-morrow night; and bring some of your company? I'll give you a London supper. My master's a white-rose man, belly and bones. He might give me a groat towards it."

Ralph hardly knew how to answer. This was London, and they were all being kind to him. He thought how his father used to beat him and how the girls in the village called him silly: and here I am, he said to himself, walking about London and making grand friends like a knight or an alderman. I know what I'll do, by St. Anne : I'll get someone to write a letter to our priest to read to mother, telling all about the Duke of Clarence and the miracle and the fine life I'm living. I'll find someone to take it, so it'll get there before I'm home. A letter from London : mother'll be in her pomp about it and all the village'll talk for weeks. They'll see then what a fellow I am.

They had their supper on Saturday at a tavern in St. Botolph's parish. Ralph asked Tom and an archer he knew called Hick Tanner, a silent, small Yorkshireman. The apprentice's name was Ned Taylor, and he was bound to a silversmith in Cheapside. He was a decent, godly lad who blessed himself before he ate, and kept Lent, so they had no meat : but it surprised Ralph the wonderful fish that there were. They had broth of barley and fennel-seed and a pike stewed in wine and dressed with a sauce of eggs, sugar, milk of almonds and cream. Then there was a huge square eel-pie. When Red Tom saw it he shouted to Ned : "God bless you, lad. I love you," and plunged in his hand to the wrist. Last of all they had stewed lampreys, greasy and hot, in an open dish. Ned ordered a quart of sweet wine and paid sixpence for it.

"Master gave me a silver sixpence," he said. "He's a good master and all for the Rose of Rouen. You see, there's several gentlemen of the party of York who owe him money. Now we've got the Rose again they may pay him, so he's glad."

He told them how, when the news came that Edward was at St. Albans and had passed the danger of the great Earl, all the Yorkists in sanctuary at Westminster and St. Martin's-le-Grand broke out and ran about the streets cheering for York. The Duke of Somerset left the City with his brother and the Earl of Devonshire. Some said they had gone North to join Kingmaker and some said they had gone West to meet Queen Marguerite. Red Tom took a long drink of wine.

"Aye," he said. "We're not out of the wood yet. There'll be a battle."

"But York'll win it," said Ned.

"Please the pigs, aye. I hear the Bourchiers have come in with seven thousand tall fellows. That makes us above the twenty thousand. We can show Lancaster a thing now."

Ned wanted to hear all about battles and fighting. Ralph was picqued a little that he took so much notice of Tom; but Tom could tell wonderful tales for certain : about God's great providence at Towton when, at the moment of the Yorkists' advance, the wind changed, hurling snow in the faces of the Lancastrians and making their arrows wheel back in flight like peewhits.

"And there was more red than white on the snow that day. The dead hindered the living from coming to quarters, they lay so thick. That was a field, by God's soul. Let go the

cup, lads. Aye, that was a field : and I'll give you a piece of
good teaching, young Ralph, since you're new to the wars.
I learnt it at Mortimer's Cross when a dam' Welchman
nearly had me shent myself with it. Edward Longlegs' first
victory that was : a while ago. Here 'tis. If the field breaks
and you find you're alone and no man on each side of you,
and you make a pass at a fellow with your pike and miss
him, swing the butt round like a scythe and knock his legs
from under him. Don't try to recover and lunge again.
Swing the butt round. That's wisdom. I've handled a pike
myself."

"I was at Mortimer's Cross and all," said Hick Tanner.

"Were you, by the holy blood? I never knew that before.
Short and sharp field, wasn't it?"

"Aye."

"D'you remember Owain Tydder, Earl of Pembroke's
father, being headed after; and the mad wench lighting the
candles around his dead body and washing the blood off it?
That was a queer game."

"It was that. I was on guard at his heading. I could tell
you the last thing he said."

"Could you so, Hick; and what was it?"

Hick narrowed his small, very grey eyes and said slowly :
"He had a fine red velvet doublet on, and when they ripped
the collar off it he said : That head shall lie on the block
that was wont to lie on Queen Katherine's lap. Those were
his last words. I can see him now. They made quick dispatch
with him. His head was off with the first cut. Clever headsman they had there."

Ralph was puzzled. He asked :

"What's that about Queen Katherine? I never heard tell
of her."

Red Tom shouted to the drawer for more wine.

"I'll be gaffer this turn, lads. I'll tell you, Ralph. That
Queen Katherine, she was Holy Harry's mother, wife to
Harry of Monmouth. After Harry of Monmouth died—him
that fought Azincourt—it seems she took up with the Welch
fellow, Tydder; had two sons by him, I believe."

"Earl of Pembroke, and the Earl of Richmond that was,"
Ned told them, nodding.

"That's it. Anyroad, our Edward had the head off this

70

Tydder after Mortimer's Cross, same as Hick and I've been telling you. That's, oh, ten years back. Let go the cup."

The inn was packed tight with soldiers, men of Lord Hastings and the Duke of Clarence and the Bourchiers, drunk mostly and wearing white roses. They passed the wooden mazers from hand to hand, supping loudly like cows; belched and broke wind in sweaty, unharnessed ease. One of them was boasting that he had had three Flemish whores—strong, fat ones—in Cock's Lane last night. He praised the second one, "Plump as a sow, like a featherbed"; gloated; moved his hands in the air, cupping curves. There was shouting singing of loud songs with nonsense choruses: "How, trolly-lolly!" The air smelt of woodsmoke, wine, fish, sweat and garlick. Two drunk citizens in a corner were playing a game of barter, one setting his doublet against the other's dagger. Two or three dogs snarled over bones under the trestle-tables. A quack-salver in queer, parti-coloured clothes was trying to sell two of the Duke of Clarence's men an infallible cure against swordcuts. The fat wife of the innkeeper talked to a sober fellow in a black gown about Queen Elizabeth, sentimentally nodding.

"I'll wager the King's happy, bless his lovely face, seeing her again and the dear little Prince as was born in sanctuary. Wasn't that a sad, wicked thing, him to be driven out so just when she was expecting: his firstborn son, too, the poor lady. Well, well, his misfortune's all turned into bliss now. After sorrow, joy; that's the course of the world. He'll be comforting the Queen now, I make no doubt."

"And other ladies too," said the man in black drily.

"Oh, you naughty fellow: to say such a thing."

"Well, perhaps I'm in the wrong. Perhaps he's only saying the paternoster backwards and turning the seive and shears with his bosom-counsellors Friar Bungay and Mr. Dominic."

A man with the Duke of Norfolk's badge of the white lion jumped up, staring and handling his dagger.

"I'll renounce God if we haven't a lousy Lancastrian horse-thief here, accusing our Lord King of necromancy. You'll take that back, master goodman, or I'll shove it down your stinking throat, so God help me."

The man in black looked unhappy. All round the room mazers and tankards stopped on their way to men's mouths, and eyes turned on him.

"No, no, friend, you do me wrong. I'll take it on my conscience to say there's not a better Yorkist in this house than I am. I meant no harm. I was there in St. John's field in Clerkenwell that day, ten years ago, when the Lord Edward was first called King. I shouted for him along with the rest. Aye, and I've been in service in his Grace's household. I'm a proper white rose man."

The Norfolk man did not sit down. He said : "You don't talk like one."

"Oh Lord, that was only silly gossip and a joke. Good King Edward does use astrology and geometrical arts, and what harm. It's not sinful. Here, take a drink from my cup and be christian. If I've offended anyone here I'm sorry; but if I thought I'd offended the King, by the Mass I'd go hang myself."

He handed his tankard to the man with the white lion, who took it; looked at him unsurely for a minute; said : "Well, if you say that all's well. I'm a quiet one. I'm not quarrelsome; but by the Road of Bromholme I'll not hear a word against York," and drank.

"That's right," said the innkeeper's wife. "We're all honest here, I'm sure. For my part, I never could abide that King Harry after the Good Duke Humphrey was murdered when I was a girl; and I'm sure the Rose of Rouen's got the prettiest face in the world. So I'm for York."

A drunk man in a corner shouted : "What's that, mother : the prettiest face or the . . ." but a noise stopped his mouth.

Someone had brought in a blind gleeman, an old bearded man with a head like a snowed bush, and was calling for silence. The old man was given a drink of pudding-ale and drawn into the middle of the room with his lute and his dog. A man called out :

"Hush up, lads. Here's an old one knows the Rose of Rouen song. Let's have it, grandfather."

"Yes, let's have it."

"Come on, old Joseph with the long beard. Blessed be the time."

The old man nodded his blind head and grinned, tuning his strings and tapping with his foot. Then, in a shaky voice, he sang, and Ralph heard for the first time the ballad of the Rose of Rouen, telling how the terrible Northern army of Queen Marguerite broke the Yorkists at St. Albans and was broken by them at Towton, in the year that Edward was crowned King. The song went to a quick, swinging tune, the gleeman wagging his beard in time to it. Everybody watched him, and some shaped the words with their mouths, smiling proudly.

"Betwixt Christmas and Candlemas, a little before
  the Lent,
All the lords of the North, they wrought by one
  assent.
For to 'stroy the South-country they did all their
  intent.
Had not the Rose of Rouen been, all England had
  been shent.
Blessed be the time that ever God spread that
  flower.

"Upon a Shrove Tuesday, on a green lede
Betwixt Sandridge and St. Albans, many men 'gan
  bleed.
On an Ash Wednesday we lived in mickle dread.
Then came the Rose of Rouen down to help us at
  our need.
Blessed be the time that ever God spread that
  flower."

Ralph felt the quick proud tune get into him and liven his blood. I'm a soldier, he thought, and I've come, too, to help London at their need. I'm ready to fight. I'd like to fight. The soldiers were swaying their bodies and rapping the table with mazers and dagger-hilts. Their eyes were all fixed on the old man in a kind of haughty excitement.

"The Northern men, they made their boast when
  they had done that deed :
'We will dwell in the South-country and take all
  that we need :
These wives and their daughters, our purpose shall
  they speed,'
Then said the Rose of Rouen : Nay, that work
  shall I forbid !"
"Blessed be the time that ever God spread that
  flower!"

All round the room, people shouted the catchline and then leaned forward for the next verse. Fixed grins were on their hot faces and their eyes shone. Ned Taylor looked ready to cry. Tom was smiling into his red, short beard. They were all drunk with the tune and the boasting words. Even the man in the black gown was beating time with a hand that had a silver ring on it.

"For to save all England,"

sang the old man,

"the Rose did his intent,
With Calais and with London, with Essex and
  with Kent
And all the South of England unto the water of
  Trent,
And when he saw the time best, the Rose from
  London went."

Ralph shouted with the rest of them. Excitement was like a live animal in his chest.

*"Blessed be the time that ever God spread that
  flower!"*

"The way into the North-country, the Rose full fast
  he sought.
With him went the Ragged Staff . . ."

"Hey there!"
"What's that, a devil with it?"
"Shut your mouth, you old addlewit."
Six or seven of them shouted and swore at once to remind the gleeman that the Earl of Warwick and his ragged staff were not on the Rose of Rouen's side now. The old man turned his blind, yellow face, his lips wobbling, looking feeble and frightened suddenly. His dog dropped her tail and crouched down, knowing the noise of anger. Red Tom called:
"No harm, old lad, only leave that bit out. Let go the cup, fellows. He's all right. Sing up."

> "The Northern party made them strong with spear
> and with shield.
> On Palm Sunday after the noon they met us in the
> field.
> Within an hour they were right fain . . ."

"Bills and bows! Bills and bows! On, up there!"
It was a great new voice crying from the doorway.
"Bills and bows! Up, out of it!"
He looked to the door. A man was there with his sallet on
his head and the King's own badge of the rose in the rayed
sun painted on his steel jack. He stood with the April dusk
behind him, a tall man, scowling; had not come to the inn
for wine. The room suddenly was as quiet as a winter field.
One or two men got up. He shouted again:
"Come on out of it, you fatherless beggars. Come up, I
tell you. God's soul, don't you know there's a war on?"
Hick Tanner stood up in his place and quietly, as he did
everything, pulled his long dagger out. He said: "What's
amiss, then?"
The man with the King's badge looked at him.
"What's amiss? Kingmaker's amiss, lying at Barnet Heath
with thirty thousand. They're all there: Oxford, Somerset,
Montacute, the whole fry of them, thirty thousand; be on
top of us to-morrow if we aren't on top of them. The King's
commands: we muster in half an hour at Moorgate."
On the blank Moor a fog was shaping itself, clots and
strings of vapour dropping down out of the white, low sky
and beginning to crawl along the ground. Ralph watched
the outriders disappear into it, trotting with a clash and
creak of armour. The air was desolate and tinged with wet.
A horse coughed and blew through noisy nostrils. On the
road in front, a company of bowmen, Hick Tanner with it,
was being drawn up in a strange formation of parallel short
ranks facing all one way, making a square mass wider than
the road. There were more outriders on the flanks, men-at-
arms with demi-lances. Captains rode up and down,
anxious-looking, giving their orders in sharp, nervous voices
or reining-in to whisper to each other at the side of the road.
The men did not talk. Sir William was there; began to form
his people into a square like the archers: twelve columns of
twenty men each, men-at-arms on the outside, pikes in the

centre. Behind was more tramping and clattering, more clink of arms, then a loud order : "Forward-on !" and they were marching.

Ralph did not think much or very clearly; was heavy with what he had had to eat and drink. He watched the man immediately in front of him : square shoulders in a stiff black leather jack, longish brown hair, tangled, escaping under the back of the polished sallet, pike sloped, a brass-studded belt with a dagger in it : just a man. He did not know his name. The mist and the dark were drifting steadily down on them. They were walking into the mist like walking out of the world. The thing he had begun privately to believe would never come was coming now; was in the mist ahead of them. They were going to fight Kingmaker.

In blackness, after three hours, when they could see no stars, they came to Barnet.

The village was dead asleep. Houses showed in the fog only when they were very close to them. Ralph could see three men : the man before him and the two at his two sides. Beyond that, fog was, and he was alone with these three in the world. They halted and they moved on, and he heard the noise of thousands who moved on in front of him and behind him; saw nothing. They were going uphill now : turf under their feet, slimy. He thought : This is the Heath. We shall fight here : now, or when?

The dark grew a seed of light that blossomed—red, unsure patch made by torches held close together—and advanced upon him. They were halted again. There was nothing but the yellowed blur, higher than a man's height, coming nearer and growing, and the awareness of the men near him and a squelching of hooves. He was sickly tired. Then, in the middle of the torch-glow, he saw a gleam and a face : gleam of a steel basnet with the vizor raised, and inside it, deeply shadowed round the mouth and eyes, a firm-chinned, short face, looking as white as white cloth, looking through a bright hole in the fog : the Duke of Gloucester. The torches were upheld on either side of his horse; spilled a little light down as far as the gorget and pauldrons on his neck and shoulders; showed his horse's pricked ears. He was still, in the dark that framed him like a portrait : a boy's face with a string of steel and a halo of fire round it. His mouth was so shaded that Ralph did not see the lips move when he called gently for Sir William. From the fog there was the answer : "Here, your Grace."

"This is the place, Sir William. You can harbour here. Unsaddle the horses; but your men must sleep harnessed. I've posted a troop of horse under Sir Gilbert Debenham on your right. The rest of our wing will form on your left. Is all well?"

"Aye, your Grace; but I don't like this fog."

"We must content ourselves with it. I'm going on down the line now. Choose good sentinels. Goodnight to you."

"Goodnight, your Grace."

The torch-glow wobbled and went faintly away. Ralph watched the shine of the Duke's basnet out of sight, and was walled up in fog again. After the Duke's low voice Sir William's sounded brutal.

"Now then, lads, break your ranks, but don't go wandering like sheep. Keep touch. Best get some sleep while you can : we'll be busy to-morrow. Horses to the rear : unsaddle and hobble 'em, and hold fast by your arms. If I catch a man lying unarmed, by God's mother I'll brain him. Stop that garboyling noise there. D'you want the enemy to hear you? God alone knows how near they are. You bowmen, see you keep your strings dry. It's a whorson damp night. Now keep quiet."

He walked his horse on, talking still. Ralph stared into fog that seemed to press upon his actual eyelids. His body was one pain of tiredness. Unbodied voices round him softly complained : "Here's a lovely harbourage. Let's say our prayers and sleep." "It'll be a wicked morning. Curse the fog." He could hear men lying down on the dewed turf : grunts and leather creakings. Another voice said : "All the devils in hell fly away with the Earl of Warwick. I'll have a tertian fever to-morrow." "Cold steel's a grand medicine for that," somebody answered. "Then may you have a dose of it, whoever you are." He lay down, his pike beside him. A man whispered : "Hell fire singe your rump. Look where you're coming with that thing." They lay as close as paupers' burials in that field, so that they heard each other's breaths in the blind dark. A horse whinnied sadly, far away. The turf was not as wet as Ralph had thought. He rolled over onto his stomach; laid his face on his crossed arms with a small sigh.

Thud:

it was a thick deep noise in the dark before him, seeming to make the ground jerk, and after it came a strange swishing whistle.

Thud,

as though God had struck the earth with his fist in anger: he raised himself on his elbows, afraid.

Thud whheeww, thud whheeww:

twice in succession and nearer: two whistling birds flew overhead and, as if they had fallen heavily down like hawks, he heard distantly behind him two short, brutal sounds, like blows of a cleaver upon meat. Someone cried sharply:

"Guns!"

He felt his body slowly becoming jelly, liquefying so as to sink in escape into the ground. He pressed his face down on his leather arms, terrors swarming like lice upon his skin. Far away, far to his left, he heard the thuds again. "Oh, St. Anne!" he prayed, scratching with his fingers in the turf, "Oh, St. Anne, St. Anne, St. Anne!"

Thud whheeww thump:

the shot had passed very near him. He knew it; believed he had felt the wind of it passing and that it had plumped down not a yard behind his heels. His bowels were loosening with fear. A man on his right began loud Latin prayers: "Ave Maria, plena gratia, Dominus tecum, benedicta tu in mulieribus . . ." Then there was the low-pitched voice of a squire or captain, urgent and carrying.

"Quiet, you fool, quiet: they're over-shooting us. No noise, any of you, else they'll know where we are and level on us."

The man next him on the left whispered: "Christ, but they must be near."

"Don't talk, you fools. I'll stab the next man that talks."

Thud, thud:

at each crash of gunfire the earth's skin seemed delicately and instantly to twitch, like a horse's hide. The explosions were regular and moved, as the cheering had moved on the day the Duke of Clarence turned his coat, up the line from left to right, loudening successively as they came. First, on the far left, was a single smothered bang, and then another. A cruel silence of waiting was then, and after it two louder detonations followed on each other's heels, so near that he could hear the swishing of the balls. There were two more obscure shots on the left, and he waited for the next with his teeth clenched on grass. The sound of it was hardly at his left at all : seemed almost in front of him, and the ground shook again when the shot fell. No one cried out. He expected men to scream in furious torment when the falling stone balls smashed their bones into the earth, but there was only quiet, and presently he knew that the captain was telling the truth and that the shots all fell beyond them.

So for that night the Rose of Rouen's twenty thousand men lay close together upon turf, their arms at their sides and their harness on their backs, not seeing, not speaking. In front of them, behind a fence of fog and night, Kingmaker's guns bellowed for Lancaster, and behind them the innocent earth was pitted with his shots that went too far.

At perhaps three in the morning the bombardment ceased. Stiff, clammy, twitching, he listened for the next gun, but no next gun fired. He dared to move, unbrace muscles he had braced five hours ago. His body was without feeling, and sleep closed on him with the speed of a blow. He was kicked awake, and saw the fog was yellow now and not black, but close still, so that he could not see a hundred yards. It was Red Tom who kicked him :

"Up and pray, my lad."

He rolled onto an elbow. Aches gnawed his loins and back. For a second, he could not remember where he was. Then he was afraid again. He asked : "Is it now?"

Red Tom was looking pleased and thoughtful. There was dew in his beard. "It's now, boy, a field at last. God damn this fog, though. We'll be playing hoodman-blind with them."

Ralph stood up; leaned on his pike. "I'm hungry."

"Didn't you think to bring food with you?"

"No."

"You innocent : well, take this and a murrain." Tom opened the pouch at his belt and gave him a piece of black bread. "Stay your belly with that. We've not much time. The Duke's been to the King and come back again. I saw him."

He tore the sour bread with his teeth. His belly was queer. He thought : It's come at last. It's really happened.

"Now then, lads."

Sir William was among them, on foot, all armoured. The dew had taken the brightness from the street. He had his long-handled sword in his right hand and a short mace slung at his girdle. He lifted his voice : "Listen to me, all of you. I'm no speaker : that God knows. I shan't make an oration. You know we're here for the right cause, so every one of you fight your hardest and stand your strongest, and trust God and our dear Lady and the blessed St. Anne to defend our quarrel. I'll be with you and do my share. Attend to this now. The enemy don't know how near we are to 'em. Haven't they burned powder all night shooting over our heads? But the King suffered no guns to be shot on his side. We'll surprise them. Go bravely when the signal's given, and we'll catch thtem unready, please God. Form your ranks now, and St. George for the white rose."

He was the second rank; did not know why or how; was jostled there as the line formed. They were a line now, five deep, the men-at-arms with swords or langues-de-bœuf in front and the pikemen behind them. He had his pike against Red Tom's hip and another pike stuck out past his own shoulder. His heart was knocking, but he felt happier in a crowd with men close by him. Suddenly, from the left, a noise to split the ground began : thump after thump of guns.

"Our ordnance at last," Tom said over his shoulder. "Don't joggle your pike so. I'm ticklish. We shan't miss 'em either. Lord, listen."

The guns were blaring one after another like repeated thunder-claps when a storm rolls round and round a valley.

"They're all massed in our centre, by the sound of 'em. That's the way, boys. Puff it at 'em. Singe their hides. Wonder who we've got in front of us. Kingmaker himself, I wouldn't wonder. He mostly commands the left. Well, our little Duke'll show him a thing. Got the makings of a captain, that lad has."

"Make way, there."

"Macht Platz."

"What the devil's to do here?"

Their ranks were being parted toward the right to make room for a file of hand-gunners. There were thirty or forty of them, each with his strange, long-stocked gun over his shoulder and a lighted match dangling at his wrist. An armoured English squire in the Duke of Gloucester's livery was with them. He said : "Duke's orders : these men'll advance in front of you, fire and then fall back behind your line."

"I believe you," said Tom under his breath.

One of the gunners grinned at him : the man to whom he had spoken outside Banbury : "Grüss Gott, Kamerad."

"Greet God yourself. They're no use to anyone with their new-fangled nonsense," he went on to Ralph. "Give me a crossbow any day; and they can't see in this whorish mist."

A trumpet sounded very far away. Something tightened like a string in Ralph's belly. There were more trumpets, nearer, and quick drum-taps. Sir William shouted at the top of his voice. "On, up! St. George for the white rose. Avant Banner!"

They were advancing.

It was difficult to keep rank, to keep his pike thrust out beyond Red Tom's harnessed moving body as they went, crowded together, at a slow walk into the fog. The grey-and-yellow coils still wreathed themselves like sluggish snakes floating in air; and there was nothing, still, to see. But he knew the fog was a curtain and Kingmaker might part it suddenly, charging at them with his thousands. He counted their steps. At twenty paces nothing had happened, and at fifty nothing. Only the drums pattered behind them and the strung-out line of gunners marched in front. At a hundred paces the trumpets shouted to the fog and they stopped. The English squire said something to the hand-gunners.

Tom grunted. "It's a waste of dear time, so it is," he said. "They'll do no good in this."

The gunners, scattered in a line, were talking to each other in their strange, crooning language and pouring powder from horns into the short, wide barrels of their guns. Bullets were put in next, after the powder had been rammed down : lead balls as big as a man's eye. The gunners looked at each other and rested the long stocks of their weapons, like spear-butts, on the ground, holding them with the right hand and the burning matches with the left.

"Foreign nonsense," said Tom, "more like a May-game than a battle."

The English squire, who had an axe in his hand, called : "Fertig?"

"Fertig" : the word went hissing along from one man to another.

"Los !"

With a queerly flourishing conceited gesture, the Germans put their yellow smouldering matches to the touch-holes. Ralph watched them brace their bodies, and clamped his teeth. He was full of a hatred of gunpowder. There was, suddenly, a series of loud, thick explosions, and clots of smoke began to float backward. The guns did not all go off together, so that the noise was like that of many stones slithering over a cliff. Towards the end there was a louder bang and a flare of yellow fire, just before Ralph. The man who had talked to Tom dropped his gun, tossing his arms up, and went backward, his head obscured by a great cloud of smoke. He lay spread and still where he had fallen. His mouth and lower jaw had quite disappeared. In their place was an irregular, wide black hole with a red edge. His nose, too, was snubbed back oddly, so that the look of his face was that of a pig, snouty and chinless. There was a quantity of blood on the ground round him. His gun had burst in his face. Ralph felt sick. A low, small chuckle grew up among the Englishmen, and a deep voice somewhere said :

"Silly foreigners."

The Germans, having fired, shouldered their weapons and marched off. One of them looked at the dead man and shook his head. "Kaputt," he said, "armes Leut." Then the trumpets blew again and they were marching again. Ralph thought : Someone will walk right over that dead man. He had not seen death until then. In front, they had the fog still, and more death behind it, waiting for them. There was, he realised, an enormous noise going on. It seemed to come from their left; was shapeless and hungry, like the noise of a river running when it was swollen. Then, leaping out of the fog with the leap of an evil goblin, a stunted small hedge was in front of them and Sir William called : "Halt !"

They halted. Nothing came from behind the hedge : no charge of men or volley of arrows. Only, on his left, the confused baaing and murmuring loudened and loudened, and he could hear under it a quick, tinkling noise like the noise of a forge.

Red Tom said : "Where in the devil's name have we got to ?"

They waited; saw only the dull twigs of the hedge making a black lower-border for the mist, and after a long time heard hooves and a shout.

"Sir William Parr, the Duke's commands : bring your men up, through that hedge. We're overlapping them. Past their left wing we are. The Duke's engaged them. Bring your men up and outflank them : quick, quick."

And Sir William : "Forward, lads, St. George : knock that damned hedge down and bear to your left. St. George for the white rose, à York !"

Twigs scratched him. Men shouted. Noise was on his left side still. The hedge gave. They were through it and swinging, he felt them swing, sideways and blindly. "À York, à York !" They were running without sight; running into fog blindly. Then, like a terrible miracle, they were in daylight : a break in the mist. The early sun cleanly and gaily shone on grass and on men near them, turning to look at them : two hundred or five hundred men like themselves, standing with pikes in their hands and the fog behind them. Ralph felt their line check. The men with their backs to the fog were turning, lowering pikes and drawing swords, ranking themselves. Tom called out happily :

"Steady lads, here comes all Warwickshire in a hurry."

Then men were running. In the emancipated sun the level row of shiny pikeheads looked like some strange fluted ornament of metal. Ralph's fingers on his own pike ached with gripping. He could see their clothes, brown, green and grey, and their watching faces. A man on a red-roan horse, in blue armour, was riding at the end of their line and waving an axe. Sir William's voice came, louder than ever :

"Archers loose !"

He had not known that they had archers with them. But out of fog he heard the twang-twang like breaking fiddle-strings and a buzzing like bees; and a man of the enemy suddenly and queerly jumped, in the middle of a stride, clean off the ground; dropped his pike and fell down on it. Then there was something horrible for him to see. All one end of the hurrying line began to melt, break up, the men falling full-length by threes and fours or else dropping down on their knees and rolling over, so quickly that they struck one another before they reached the ground. He heard the archers shouting "Ha !" "Ha !" each time they drew their strings. The line came on, spreading out as it ran, spreading into the zone of arrow-fire and being shortened by it again, so that its movement was like that of a piece of string writhing on hot coals.

"Forward-on!"

He was running with the rest; was one of a crowd of men running to meet another running crowd. He could not see much. There were two shouts: "À York!" and "À Holland!" very loud. Then there was a shock that crashed Red Tom's steel back into his chest; jarred all his body; and faces looked and grimaced over the shoulders of the front rank at him and they were all straining and shoving like men with a bogged waggon. Something pushed at his pike and he pushed back. Someone near him shrieked, "Aiee!" a shrill, mounting noise, and all round him they were shouting: 'St. George, à York!" Past Red Tom's head a steel blade jabbed at him. He wried his face away and with his pike desperately pushed forward and up. There was a heavy weight on it. They had gone forward a pace and were more loudly yelling. He was jammed between the men in front and the men behind; was deaf with noise; and there was more noise yet; was noise of horse-hooves and fresh shouting. In the air, behind the enemy, he saw them: faces and arms of riders swinging swords and axes, pushing with lances. A horse suddenly and terribly reared with beating forefeet and blown nostrils and went backwards. There was no pressure. Faces were not staring. The enemy mass had turned into knots of men walking backward, thrusting with pikes and turning and running away. He saw a man with a short axe lean down from his saddle, lift the axe up and strike a running man on the head. The man dropped. They were standing and gasping. Ralph felt something pull at his arm. One of their own men was tugging at it, sinking as though his knees failed. He turned up a foolish, open-mouthed face and said softly, surprised: "In my belly." Then his eyes rolled back under his eyelids and he fell down. Another voice said, as if speaking of cattle:

"Those were Henry Holland's men, Duke of Exeter."

"Forward-on, lads."

It was not easy to keep rank. There were men lying on the ground. He tripped. Their line was opening, some hurrying past others, and the fog was on them again. It was a

84

fog with noise in it : clamour of voices and metal clashings. Then horsemen, vague in mist like rocking and swaying towers, were in front of them and they began to run; ran into fog and for a long time saw nothing. Suddenly a great wave of voices shot up. "À Warwick, à Warwick!" He was caught in a backrush. People ran past him, and almost in his ear there was the shout again "À Warwick!"

There was a man in front of him : dark face, smooth-shaved, open mouth. He saw the device on his jack of a ragged staff and saw him swing his hand up, a short mace in it. He did not know what he was doing until it was done. The man's face seemed to crumble and put off humanity as his pike caught him in the throat; and he fell backward. Then men from behind were all round him and he was running and yelling with them.

Fear and tiredness went out of him and his mind became shrunken; narrowed away from the edges of consciousness down to the single business of hurrying and fighting. They fought in mist; were a line sometimes that pushed another line, and sometimes were small backward-and-forward moving groups weaving like particles of dust in a shaft of light. When they went back, others ran up and passed them, and now and again a mounted man was seen, hurling himself from greyness into greyness. Twice out of the din and dark an ordered company came striding, shouting for Warwick, and split through the straggling row in front of it; left men struggling or quiet on the ground where it had been. Then there was tumult from behind and the fight turned again, Warwick's men moving backwards, a step at a time, hacked and poked on both sides and in front by men-at-arms and archers who had slung their bows and used their lead hammers. Men died. Even in the mist he saw wounds given and fighters thrown to the ground and trodden into it. Some crawled on their hands and knees away, or lay grunting and moaning. The second wave knocked him from his balance, a soldier with the device of a burning cresset on his chest swiping with his axe at him, the blade missing him and the shaft catching his thigh. He got up and saw the advance turned, a crowd of men, close-packed and roaring, facing two ways and moving one, with those who had been squeezed from the line ranging about, like sheep-dogs round a flock, for a fresh opening. He forced his pike between others' bodies to reach the ringed-in enemies; put his weight to it, grunting and sighing.

Light was coming. The mist had broken into milk-coloured banks and thinned. With the others, shouting with the others, he jostled after the retreating company of Lancastrians that split and spread so that presently there was no thick mass of men together, but only a scattering, over the whole range of sight, of separate retreats and separate contests. A man on the ground struck with a knife at his legs. He swung his pike up as though it were a flail and hit him with it. Then another was coming with a halberd at him, but there was a rush from behind, half-a-dozen archers shouting : "À York," and swinging axes. The halberdier was swallowed by them, and when they had gone on he lay on his back and had no top to his head. Ralph jumped his body, running and yelling. The main battle had passed him now. Between two banks of mist, in a space where sun was, he saw the rider on the roan horse pulled down, three archers and a pikeman at him. The pikeman stuck him under the vizor, gaffing him like a fish and pitchforking him out of the saddle, as one of the archers cut the horse's throat. Both fell in a tangle. He did not stop; went past them and past where, in a line like a pack of cards flicked from the hand, hundreds were dead together; had died standing. Here wounded were moving. One man, his face bright crimson, knelt and groped at the corpses near him as though he were looking for something in the dark. Another was screaming. He went forward. Behind him, chiefly, it seemed, and much to his left, the shapeless and untiring din went on; but round him there was no battle and he was lost; walked only through dead men and over ground the fight had used and given up. The mist had closed again. Something gave under his foot : an arm hacked through at the shoulder. The green wool sleeve, soaked red, looked odd on it. Tiredness caught him suddenly again. He would rest a little; stood and leaned on his pike. He would have liked to sit down, but did not dare. Have we won, he thought, or been beaten? The battle-noise was going farther away. He had somewhere in his mind the thought of finding the Duke of Exeter's man that he had killed, and stripping him. Then there were figures coming to him out of the mist, two of them, walking slowly and dragging between them an unmoving third, and he levelled his pike again, breathing sharply.

"Whose man are you?"

"Sir William Parr's."

"God be loved. Come here with you. Here's Lord Say—hurt."

They were two squires who strained, bending forward, to draw a trailing and steel-plated limp body over the ground. Ralph helped them to lay it down and unfasten the basnet. One of them was saying over and over and over again: "What a field, what a devil's field."

He asked the other: "What's doing? I was lost in the fog, but I killed two of them."

The squire looked at him across their work. "I think I've killed ten. By God, we're winning. Where in hell's name've you been? The Duke of Gloucester's smashed their van back into their middleward. By God, I never saw anyone do like him. We've swung 'em clean round like a wheel. They're facing the way they came."

Ralph saw that the front of his body was all streaked and splashed with blood and that there were many bright scratches on his armour. Lord Say's basnet came away under their hands. Lord Say had a thin, tired face with a hole in it, rather above the right eyebrow, and a red stain down the cheek.

The other squire began to cry. "Dead," he said, "our kind lord, dead, right through his vizor."

Ralph looked across the heath. Not far away, two more corpses were. One was an archer. He lay crucified and a wound had split his chest. From where he was, Ralph could see the splinters of bone looking out through the red cleft, white and clean. The other man lay on his face. Beyond, he began to see more corpses, single or piled together, foolish-looking, then more. The mist was walking away from him very slowly, like an edge of cloth being trailed languidly over the ground. His mind was timeless, drowned in the noise he could still hear.

One of the squires said: "We'd best wait a little till the fog breaks again." Then, as soon as he had said it, he stood up and drew the dagger of mercy hanging at his right side. The battle had begun to come toward them again.

On the edge of the mist they could see people running.

87

They were not charging, but flinging along with their heads thrown back and their hands weaponless. One came a little toward them, holding his side, and then pitched to the ground. The men as they ran shouted a new word, and voices from the fog answered and shouted it back to them:

"Treason! treason!"

"Come on!" called the squire with the dagger. He ran holding the long, thin blade level with his chest, and Ralph followed. Out of the milky, moving curtain an archer came. Ralph saw the ragged staff on his clothes and saw the squire strike him as he passed. The man staggered and threw his hands forward. Ralph drove at him; felt his weight on the pike and saw him step backward slowly, fall down and lie. Then he was in a clear place again, a wide patch of light, and men with the cresset or ragged staff were all round him, but were not fighting. They streamed past in thick groups. He heard the sob of their breath and, again and again, the word gasped or cried out: "Treason!" A great surge of happiness and excitement filled him. Men with the white rose were coming, tearing down on the runners, hacking those they could reach or with pike-thrusts skewring them through. A mounted knight with a mace rode among them; called out: "No quarter, men! Lancaster thieves!" We are winning, he thought. We have broken them, King-maker's men. There was something else to see: an armoured lord running away. He came into the patch of clearness running top-heavily with short, tripping steps. He had a sword in his hand, and his armour was damascened; shone in two colours. Half a dozen Yorkists with the Duke's own badge of the silver boar were after him. But Ralph saw, a hundred yards separating him from the place, a knot of running Lancastrians, badged with the silver X, come between. There was fighting, but the man in armour ran hobbling on. He looked helpless and laughable, stiffly moving like a man with clogged legs in a nightmare. Then in his mind Ralph heard Red Tom say: "There's pickings on a dead lord if you've time to strip him."

As he ran, there were all sorts of pictures in his mind of spending money in his village and telling tales. He could hear other people behind him now and a voice shout: "After him, after him: don't let him slip." But I'm leading the field, he thought. I shall get him and kill him. I have helped to make Edward of York King of England again, and I'll kill a lord and I'll be rich on it. The tottering, shining figure was just ahead and the pursuers were just behind. It was a helpless thing, mail-clogged and slow, he was hunting, he thought, and shortened his pike. With a queer little stumble and swerve the mailed man suddenly ran round in a little circle, as a rolling coin circles before it falls, and was facing him, holding the sword in both hands, the point downward. With great clearness, Ralph saw the quarterings on his breastplate of an eagle displayed and three lozenges, and a tiny gold bear on his helmet with a ragged staff in its paws. He was a tall man. If that on his helmet is gold, I could buy a farm, Ralph thought. I must strike now. He lunged, but the steel man before him swayed sideways from the point, lifting, as a woodman his axe, the long, wide blade of his sword upward from his shoulder. Ralph thought : I am glad Tom taught me the trick I must use. I will swing the butt round and trip him, and then he is mine. He swung his pike quickly as the steel man brought his sword downward and forward. The blade caught him in the left side. He felt a moment's shock and deathly sickness, and tried to breathe. His life faded and finished in his body like the fading red of a small coal.

CHAPTER THREE

BLOOD-LETTING

(*England:* 1471)

"*Sum Rex, sum Princeps,*"	*neutrum fortasse deinceps.*
O qui iura regis	*Christi specialia Regis,*
Hoc quod agas melius,	*iustus es, esto pius.*
Nudum ius a te	*vestiri vult pietate:*
Qualia vis metere	*talia grana sere!*
Si ius nudatur,	*nudo de iure metatur:*
Si seritur pietas,	*de pietate metas.*

Wm. Langland, *Visio De Petro Plowman.*

RAIN and black night were over Dorsetshire as though God had stripped a wet cloak from his shoulders and thrown it down there. The rain clucked and chattered in the gutters of Cerne Abbas, heavying the clothes of the men who went out on watch. Alone in the guest-hall of the Abbey, the Lady Anne, Princess of Wales in the right of Lancaster, could hear what they were singing as they clumped out into the wet.

> Deo gratias, Anglia, redde pro victoria!"
> Our King went forth to Normandy
> With grace and might of chivalry,
> There God for him wrought marvellously,
> Wherefore England may call and cry:
> Deo gratias,
> Deo gratias, Anglia, redde pro victoria!"

It was the old triumphal song of the victory of Harry of Monmouth at Azincourt, slow and noble; but in the rainy night it sounded like a Dies Irae.

90

There was a good fire in the guest hall. Our King went forth to Normandy, thought the Lady Anne. I wish this Queen might never have come forth from there. I wish to God I were well out of this.

A great deal had happened to her in the last year : being told by her father that Edward of York, the big, laughing King that he had made and quarrelled with, was no King for them now; that the old, terrible Queen, Marguerite of Anjou, and her mad husband in the Tower were true Queen and true King, after all; that the old Queen's son, whom he had called a bastard begotten in adultery, was a fine young Prince. That had been the beginning, last year in France, after they had run hurriedly across the Channel and she had crouched in the after-cabin listening to the screams of her sister Isobel in child-bed and the slamming of the guns Lord Wenlock fired at them from Calais : and later her father had said more. He had said the old Queen's son was a well-conditioned youth, and very handsome. They married her to him in Amboise with all the bells ringing for the strange alliance of the exiled House of Neville with the exiled House of Lancaster. The French King had been there, smiling close to people's faces and talking very rapidly. He stooped to pat a dog as they came out of the Cathedral. Whilst she was walking solemnly and glimpsing the dog's waving tail—all dogs loved Louis of France—out of the corner of her eye, she realised suddenly, like seeing the mottled sky between two roofs, that she was actually the wife now of the pretty-faced boy whose mother had had the head from her grandfather's shoulders and who, though he had never fought a battle, talked of little else but chopping heads off.

The wife and not the wife : that was a discovery she made later. These were very confused times that she was living in. When she was married there was talk that Edward, whom her father had chased out of England and who had landed in the possessions of the Duke of Burgundy, was dead. Then he was alive again, but Holy Harry—and she had to remember very carefully that he was now her father-in-law—was on the throne. The old Queen talked daily of setting sail for England, but somehow the year turned and February stretched to March whilst they were idle at Dieppe, hearing stories of how the great Earl and the old King contented the people after the long tyranny and usurpation of the House of York. Anne dined under a cloth of state at the Queen's left hand and her husband sat at the Queen's right. He bowed to her when they took their places, and she curtsied; but the staircase that went up to his bedroom did not go to hers.

It took her a long time to understand it. At first she thought that there must be some question of the Pope's dispensation, and that her husband had scruples of religion. She was in no hurry, for her part, to have things different. Something of the shrinking and chilling she felt in the presence of the Queen came on her in the presence of the Queen's handsome son. They were not canny, these two. When they were silent she felt that their four black eyes were always watching the same picture : blood squirting from wounds or running down the blades of swords. Her father had fought many battles and signed many death-warrants; but his eyes never looked like the eyes of a cat watching a bird. He had turned King Edward out of England without striking a blow, but this did not seem to please Queen Marguerite or her son. "Your father was too cautious," the Prince told her in his sharp voice. "If I had commanded, I would have forced that traitor to a battle and made a finish of him." The old Queen nodded at that, and tapped her hand on the table as though impatient for something. It was strange, Anne thought, that in all the nursery years when her governess had shaken a finger and said : "If you're not good the Queen will come for you," she had not been afraid; had never understood why her father's nostrils stiffened when he said : "Lancaster" or "the Queen's party" : and now she did. Now that her father was the Queen's friend, she understood most perfectly why he had been her enemy.

It was only after they had kept Christmas and gone down to Dieppe, with the cold wind blowing and the sea shrugging grey shoulders between them and England, that she realised that she need not fear the consummation of her marriage. It came to her in a cold shock of understanding and anger, freezing something inside her that would never wholly thaw again. They did not trust her father yet, this black-eyed

92

pair, the old she-wolf and the young whelp. Marriages had been dissolved before to-day, and the more easily when the married pair had no carnal dealing with one another. If her father failed his promise, then give the Queen half an hour's talk with a Papal Legate and Anne Neville might go packing to the nearest nunnery, neither maid, wife nor widow. The woman who had been hard enough to make that match for her one son would be hard enough, and to spare, to break it. Anne knew how a good cloak or a ring must feel when it was put in pawn in Lombard Street.

She held her hands to the fire. The mantle was carved with a device of the last supper. Christ sat among the twelve with wine and bread, and Judas, leaning forward, upset the salt. The noise of the men singing had dropped away and she could hear only rain : English rain that was perhaps falling on her father too, wetting the flanks of his great horse as he rode South to meet them and join his army with theirs for the new campaign. She would see him soon, and perhaps the world, that had felt like twitching bog under her feet these months, might harden into security again. They had sailed for England hurriedly enough when it came to it, blown on the breath of a fantastic rumour which had proved to be fantastic truth. Edward, the over-grown schoolboy, the laughable fellow who had once been King and had bolted like a chased hare out of his kingdom, was back in England with his young brother Richard. He had landed at Ravenspur, the ill-omened port from which Henry Bolingbroke once marched to steal the crown from Richard of Bordeaux, and was coming South, 'accompanied,' her father wrote to them, 'with Flemings, Easterlings and Danes, not exceeding the number of two thousand persons, nor the country as he cometh not falling to him.' The old Queen gritted her teeth and called up the French mercenaries that King Louis had promised her; and her young son looked hopeful. He would fight a field, after all, and have blood-letting. They rode seventeen days at anchor on a merciless sea. It was strange to Anne, shut in a cabin with the Queen and feeling the boat endlessly and sickeningly dancing under her, that all this unreal interlude of France and intrigue and separation should end, as it began, in dirty weather in the Channel. She was going back to her father again, who governed England again, even if he did it in King Henry's name now, and not King Edward's.

This was her second night in England. The Queen was asleep and the Prince had gone with the Earl of Devon on inspection. She was quite alone. The Lancastrian nobles did not pay much court to their Princess. Sir John Fortescu, the wise, kind old man who had once been Chancellor, spoke to her as often as he could, asking little questions about how she had slept and whether the wine they had was to her taste. She would have liked to reply cordially and make him sit down beside her and talk of the books he had read and the great men—the Good Duke Humphrey and the Cardinal of Winchester—he had known in the old days : but she did not seem able to talk now. Words lost their meaning on the way between her mind and tongue. Lord Wenlock, with his yellow beard and his eyes rather close together, was still more attentive. He explained that he had always been a loyal man to her father, and that when he fired his guns at them from Calais it had been only policy. He was of a piece, she thought, with all the rest of her life as Princess of Wales in the right of Lancaster. He spoke and moved, and one would take him for a man; but there was something hollow.

Nothing is real, she thought. Big Edward and little Richard once seemed real to me; but that Queen and her son, my husband, never. Lancaster is not real; is a name they frightened me with when I was little. My father has a green eagle in his quarterings. On a shield or a tapestry it looks right enough; but not flying in the sky or stooping at a lamb, behaving as birds do behave. These Lancastrians are the same. I believe in them when I remember stories my father told me about St. Albans and Towton and how Queen Marguerite and the Earl of Wiltshire laid a plot to kill him : but I do not believe that I am eating and drinking with them, and shall be always. Only my father is real, now riding toward us from London through the wet, my father who has chosen to pretend these ghosts are men, for his own purposes.

There had been voices, and horses clicking and stamping in the Abbey courtyard whilst she thought of these things. Now suddenly a door flew open and there was a man in the room. She could not see him, for the firelight did not reach the door, but she heard his voice : voice of a gentleman, but loud, strained, impatient and enormously tired.

"The Queen, I must see the Queen. Has that squire not announced me? Is no one doing anything?"

She did not answer at once; was startled. The man came forward a foot or two and said :

"In God's great name, Madam, I am the Duke of Somerset with news of the first urgency for the Queen. Oh, Christ's passion, êtes-vous Française? Alors, écoutez-moi. Je suis le Duc de Sombrasset . . ."

"I am English, my Lord Duke."

Somerset : the man in the shadow between the hearth and the door was Edmund Beaufort, a great Lancastrian. The hate between her family and his was old and personal; transcended politics, so that St. Albans and Wakefield, Sandridge and Towton and Hexham had been as much battles of Neville and Beaufort as of York and Lancaster. Her father, almost as often in the secure old days as he had talked of Queen Marguerite and her bastard, had talked of the Bloody Beauforts.

He came right into the firelight now : a big, heavy-boned man in sopping clothes and with his wet bonnet still on his head and wet black curls coming from under it.

"Your pardon : to whom have I the honour to talk? Perhaps you will carry a message from me to the Queen's Grace. I am sorry I spoke so rudely, but I am over-tired."

His face was a little reddened with weather, broad across the cheekbones, with a thin, short nose and a pointed chin. His black eyebrows were very heavy and sullen, but there was nothing horrible about him. Steam began to rise from his soaked clothes in the warmth of the fire.

"The Queen's Grace is over-tired, too. We were seventeen days stormbound at Dieppe, and the road here from Weymouth was cruel. Must we break her rest now? Look how you're wet. You'll have an ague. Sit down by the fire and I shall send for some wine."

The Duke of Somerset shoved both palms against his forehead; then drew them slowly down across his face. He said in a slow, wondering voice, as though the discovery surprised him :

"If I drink anything now I shall be drunk."

"Sit down and rest, then, at least. Have you ridden far?"

He twitched his bonnet off; dropped his cloak round his feet; groped backward for the chair opposite hers. He moved like a man who has been tortured, put to the brake.

"From London."

"Tell me your news before we trouble the Queen. There's not been a battle?"

He nodded.

"Yesterday at Barnet Heath, in the morning."

She found that her hands jerked up suddenly and came together at the level of her breasts.

"Who had it, sir? Who had it?"

"Edward of York."

He went on in a shout, leaning forward and shouting up to her face:

"Gone, all gone, everything that we had our hopes in: there was sorcery. Edward's neocromancers darkened the sun against us; made our guns shoot wide. The fool Oxford broke his ranks and rode off on a wild-goose chase. Then someone cried treason, and that opened the pit of hell. I heard old soldiers calling out to Christ to have mercy on them in the fog. Christ has no mercy for Lancaster, Madam, or the Earl of Warwick would be alive now."

It was as though one of the great guns had boomed suddenly in her ears: a ringing shock of noise, explosion, blowing out the light in the brain.

She became unaware of her own body, or aware of it only as a downward tube through which her blood and senses were emptying into the ground. There was no realisation and no pain. She put her hand against the wall in order to feel that it was there. Presently, through the echoes in her mind, she heard him talking.

"Does that give you a start now? He was killed yesterday, the great Kingmaker who ruined all our fortunes and was going to restore them all again. I tell you Christ has no mercy for Lancaster, or why did he preserve that master-traitor of the world in a dozen rebellions against us and drop him dead the first time he drew his sword for the true blood? He killed my father at St. Albans and prospered after it. His brother sent my brother to the scaffold and God did nothing: but when our Queen was so reduced at last that she would even make alliance, alliance of blood, with him—the subject who dared call himself a maker of Kings

—if he would undo what he had done, then down with him to join my father and my brother and every other honest Lord he ever butchered. All the good he did us in the last winter's died with him. Edward of York's back in London. Our holy King Henry's in the Tower again : and all we've gained is the marriage of our Prince to a dead rebel's daughter."

She said, not speaking to him, speaking to assure herself that she had still the use of her mouth :

"Holy Mary have pity on me."

"Holy Mary have pity on all of us. Who are you if you want pity more than the Queen? I've this news to tell to her yet : our greatest hope smashed, and she's gained nothing, nothing at all on earth, by stooping to make that shameful marriage for her son. Or look at my case. Seven years I've been an exile in Burgundy waiting for the red rose to flower : and now by God it's flowered. I shook hands with my father's murderer for nothing. Don't I need pity?"

"My lord, if we have both lost our fathers we can pity one another."

The Duke looked oddly at her and heaved himself with a grunt out of his chair.

"You have not told me who you are, Madam."

"The Princess Anne."

"God forgive me," said Edmund Beaufort, and went down slowly on his knees.

Shameful marriage, she thought, marriage of our Prince to a dead rebel's daughter : he thinks the words have hurt me.

"Stand up, sir; I do not know why you kneel."

"I am kneeling for pardon, your Grace. As God sees me, I did not know who you were."

"Who are we, any of us? It does not matter. But stand up, and for charity's sake tell me how my father died."

The Duke had to help himself to his feet by the chair-arm. She thought : He must be dead weary with riding. But he blessed himself formally and slowly. The titles of his hereditary enemy rolled in his mouth as though he were a herald at a tournament.

"Madam, your great father, the high and noble Earl of Warwick, Aumarle and Newburgh, Grand Chamberlain and premier Earl of England, fought like a second Hector yesterday; never budged a foot while there was hope; and when he did retreat, it was with his sword in his hand after his people had thrown down their weapons and run past him. I saw him almost at the end, Madam. A common pikeman, one of the North-country scum Edward had with him, tried to trip him with his pike. He turned and cut him in two. I lost him then, but I have heard he got to his horse and rode into a little wood. Its name is Wrotham Wood. There is no way out of it. They surrounded him there, and he gave up his soul to Christ, by whom I pray that he has been accepted."

"Thank you, sir. That is generous. For some of what he did he will need your prayers."

"Let me call your women, Madam. It is terrible for you. I wish I might have had my tongue cut out . . ."

"No, please, my Lord : we'll sit together a little."

His mouth and tired eyes opened a little. He said softly :

"By God, now I see you are your father's daughter."

"Do not quarrel with me for that. He was my father, though it was little enough I knew of him."

"He was a man of endless deeds. I can understand he would not spend much time in his homes."

"And yet he was always at the back of our lives. The crown went from Lancaster to York or York to Lancaster, but there was still my father. It is strange I have never wondered until this moment whether he was a very wicked man or a very wise one."

"We hated each other. But I will say this freely. If he did wrong and drew blood unjustly, we can hope that his death has been an atonement for all his transgressions. Your father was at the back of many lives as well as yours, Lady. I do not think we can judge him like a common man."

"That is generous too. Don't blame yourself for what you said before, sir. But oh, God, who would ever have prophesied that Edmund Beaufort would comfort Anne Neville? Tell me what has happened; if any of my friends are left, my uncle Montacute . . ."

He looked away from her, and made the sign of the cross again. Then there is nothing real now anywhere, she thought, except Edward and Richard who are now our enemies. She asked :

"Was it such a slaughter?"

"Your father and your uncle dead, God rest them, Henry Holland of Exeter dead or wounded, John Vere of Oxford fugitive : only I and my young brother have come to join the Queen here."

"You say there was a cry of treason."

"Do you wish to hear the battle, Lady?"

"I think so. It is best to know."

"There was a mist. We bombarded what we thought was Edward's line all night. He was nearer than we ever dreamed, though. Sorcery, I say : his friend Friar Bungay. When it was morning your father spoke to the troops. He reminded them they were fighting against a tyrant who had wickedly invaded the royal seat. Edward set upon us with shot first, and then with hand-strokes. Our battles were not front-to-front. Oxford on our right over-reached the York-ists and must needs go in chase after them as far as Barnet. God pardon John Vere of Oxford, for I never will. He lost that field for us. On our left it was worse. Your father and Exeter commanded there. Who d'you suppose was opposite to them? Edward of York's dwarf brother, little Dickon of Gloucester, a boy of eighteen, and no bigger than a wet cat, against the greatest soldier in Christendom. You need not tell me the devil cares for his own. All of us on the field had proof he does. Madam, that little boy fought like a fiend from hell. The Yorkist battle over-reached us at that end. He led them, on a white horse twice as tall as himself : and in the centre there was Edward Longlegs, like Colbrand the Giant. I saw him over the heads of the men even though he was on foot, and tried to come at him. I could not. He beat and bore down before him all that stood in his way. I had the marshalling of our middleward with the archers. All the arrows in the world couldn't hold Edward's rush. It was like the sea : and your father was being driven back toward us where Gloucester had turned our flank. No one knew who had the better. It was all jolting and running in the mist. But we were being ringed in closer all the while, with Edward in front of us and Gloucester thrusting at our side and Oxford God knows where. They told me Henry Holland was down. Someone cut his horse's throat under him, they said. It lasted three hours, till Oxford came back and then—oh, my God."

He stopped and rubbed his eyes.

99

"The whole field had turned a circle like a wheel. We were facing back the way we'd come; and Oxford charged our rear. That was the end. He smashed into us and thought he'd saved the day. The saints know how many he killed before he found out his mistake. Our men took the silver mullet of Vere for Edward's blazon of the rose and sun and loosed arrows at him. When he found we weren't Yorkists, he thought we must be traitors. Or perhaps our people raised the shout first. All one : treason was shouted and we broke; and when a battle breaks after three hours' fighting it does not form again. I did my best. I brained a standard-bearer who threw my banner down. But the next thing I knew, there were Yorkists all round me and I'd my blood to save. You have heard the rest."

"You say Duke Richard had the battle opposite my father."

He looked a little dully, as though he had not expected that question.

"Yes, Lady, an under-sized child who was riding his hobby when your father was commanding armies. I saw him toward the finish, not three spears' length away. The devil can make the strangest instruments terrible. That little thing like an ape, perched up there on his great horse and all bloody from his hand to his shoulder : Jesus, there was something horrible in it, unnatural."

"Sir, was he there when . . . ?"

"I do not think so, my Lady. I heard it was common men who followed your father into Wrotham Wood."

"I am glad of that. Duke Richard and I were children together. My father was a foster-father to him in the old days. The world changes and changes, and it seems not even hate or love mean anything for long. What sort of a world is it, in God's name, when a man's fosterling commands the army that kills him and his old enemy comforts his daughter for his death? I am only a foolish little girl, though you call me a Princess now. I am in the dark. I cannot understand these things."

"I think it is the will of God that in this world we breed up our own destruction. For ten years your great father carried the House of York on his shoulders. Now it has broken his back. My Lady, you knew all three of the brothers very well : Edward the giant and Dickon the dwarf

100

and George—God blind his eyes—the turncoat. Do you not think they have a devil?"

"No, my Lord, I only thought they were three familiar laughing boys, very human and kind. Dickon—Richard of Gloucester—was quieter than his brother, and George of Clarence was always feather-headed. But I saw no devil."

"Am I to believe that God was on their side, then? Something not earthly was. Consider. Six weeks ago Edward of York was a conquered King, living on charity at Charles the Hardy's Court, and no man in Christendom believed that he would ever see his throne again. A month ago he lands in England with a bare thousand men. The commons of Yorkshire, to the number of seven thousand, rise against him; but he takes no harm. Your uncle Montacute and Percy and Vere and Holland are all in the North with power enough to crush him ten times over. He slips past them and never draws a sword. Your father himself is ready for him at Coventry. But your father hears that George the traitor is on his way North with a huge army, and holds his hand, which was to his destruction, as it happened afterward. George the traitor shows himself to be George the traitor: and that at least we might have foreseen. I and my brother in London hear that your people have landed, and ride West to meet you. Edward slips like a fox into a goosepen into London almost before our backs are turned. But you, with the army that should have joined our forces and your father's, are delayed by storm. We ride back again. We aren't out of hope yet. Is not Warwick on our side? But that's not enough, says the devil who sent the storm: so he sends the fog as well. He turns a boy of eighteen into a great captain. He makes Oxford blunder into his own allies as though he were pixie-led. Is all that chance? Or has Edward or George or Richard or all three of them a familiar spirit? It was the elements themselves were York's best allies: and we know who it is that is called Prince of the Powers of Air."

A crust had formed over her mind. Memories could take shape and move under it, and it kept out the essential news she had not got by heart yet : that her father, on a cold morning of mist, had ridden his horse into Wrotham Wood and had not ridden out again.

She sat and thought calmly, save for the ticking and

101

twitching of muscles in her thighs and belly, folding her small hands and thinking back to the old days before King-maker had quarrelled with King Edward. She remembered Middleham Castle in the rare sunlight of a Yorkshire Spring, and four children in fine clothes taking the air in the base-court. George of Clarence was there, grown-up, really, and the three others listened to him. He was telling them, in his voice of seventeen years, first gruff, then squeaky, about the fine times at his brother Edward's Court, hunting and dancing, viols, bitter honey that came in odd-shaped jars from Candia, lions and leopards and Holy Harry of Wind-sor, all on show in their prisons at the Tower. "And when I asked him," he told them : " 'How did you take it upon you to be King of England, seeing that that was my great father's right and my brother Edward's after him?' he shook his head at me like a sick cow. You would've laughed. 'My help cometh of God,' he says, 'who preserveth them that are true of heart.' Mad as Bedlam : 'My help cometh of God,' he says. I couldn't keep my face straight." She remembered how her sister Isobel laughed at that, throwing her head back and showing her white teeth. Little Richard—he was fourteen then, and already Duke of Gloucester—had looked inquisitively at his brother and said in his attractively low voice : "But, George, was that courtesy, to ask our defeated enemy that kind of question?" George laughed irritably. "Why, what in God's name's courtesy to do with it? I've told you, this was Harry of Windsor I was talking to." "I only wanted to know," said Richard meekly. George went on talking, and presently Richard and Anne wandered away from him and Isobel and began to play ball. Richard was always very kind to Anne, in spite of being three years older, and she was not afraid of him, as she might have been of other older boys, because he was so small. George teased him for it, but he did not seem to mind. "I know I'm little," he told her once secretly, "but I can lift my Lord of Warwick's sword if I use both hands. He let me try yesterday, and I did." Anne had been very much impressed by that. Her father's long-hilted two-handed sword was taller than she was, and could whip a man's head off at one swing.

She sat with fixed eyes and remembered that : her father's sword with the killing double edge, and the well-spoken

102

little boy who could lift it if he used both hands. Presently she said:

"My Lord of Somerset, I believe you are my kind friend and will not impeach my loyalty to the Queen if I answer what you ask me. George's treachery has sold my father to Edward's and Richard's swords: but for all that, the Duke of York's three sons do not seem devils to me."

Edmund of Somerset nodded.

"I am the better pleased to hear it," he said seriously, "for we shall have to do with them. This game's not ended yet. The Bastard of Fauconberg is lying at Calais with ships. He will be loyal, and if we could draw Edward down into the West he could make a snatch at London."

"So you'll still fight?"

"Yes, by God's passion, we'll still fight. We've the troops King Louis sent along with you, and the Courtneys' men; and Jaspar of Pembroke will raise all Wales for the red rose. We'll fight. Give us time and we could face Edward in an open field: but before that, if God's any way good to us, the Bastard will be in London, and we'll have Edward and Richard and our double-dealing George between two hot fires."

"As easily as that, my Lord?"

"I do venture to hope so, my Lady: and the North's not quiet yet. Percy might declare for us and lead his men on London. Oh, there's still hope. London and the Eastern shires are Yorkist; but here in the West, and even northward in Edward's own duchy, we have all the friends. We'll lure him down to us and keep him running until the Calais fleet is in the Thames."

"And if we fail?"

The Duke looked at her frankly and opened his hand like a man dropping something.

"Destruction: they will not show a tittle of mercy. If we fail now, we fail for good. Louis of France will do nothing more for us now your father's gone. Burgundy's handfast to York after all his shuffling. His clever envoy, de Commynes, saved Edward's skin when he told Wenlock that lie that he was dead. Brittany will go where the cat jumps. The Scots are useless. One more defeat, and the red rose is bled white forever. I shall die in harness or on the scaffold; and I don't mind that. It's the way my father and my brother went to God, and I've been an exile long enough to like an English grave better than a Flemish bed. All I care for is to persuade our Queen that we've still hope. But you, Lady—it is different for you, harder : but I think if the worst came about—which God defend—you could find some means of grace with Edward, could you not? The world's mad, as you say, and all changes are possible. Duke George is your brother-in-law. He and his wife would stand between you and the extreme of malice."

She shook her head.

"The world's mad, my Lord, and there's an end of it. York or Lancaster, I feel there is nothing left now to call real."

He did not answer, except to shake his head. They sat on in dark and firelight of the guest-hall, as though under the shadow of dark wings.

On Tuesday April the sixteenth of the year 1471, the Lancastrian army marched out of Cerne Abbas toward Exeter. Its leader was the Prince of Wales, Queen Marguerite's son, but since he was without experience of warfare, the guidance of the campaign fell upon Edmund Beaufort, Duke of Somerset, John Courtney, Earl of Devon, their brothers Lord John Beaufort and Sir Hugh Courtney, Lord Wenlock, and Sir John Langstrother, Prior of the Knights of St. John, who were all soldiers. With them went Queen Marguerite and the young Princess of Wales, daughter of the Earl of Warwick now deceased. It had been a hard business to persuade Queen Marguerite to this step. She and Lord Wenlock, of whom the news of his great master's death had made a frightened man, were for retreat to France : but Somerset and Devon had had their bellyful of exile. They argued till midnight round the large fire, swearing and pounding the chair-arms with their fists, until the thin-faced Queen agreed to draw Edward of York into the West so that the Calais fleet might make its raid on London. "I pray God speed us well," she said in the end, with a dead look.

From Exeter they moved to Taunton first and gathered strength. Then their road swung North-east, and their troubles began. The mercenaries who had fought under Queen Marguerite ten years ago, the Scots and Bretons and

Normans, got out of hand. At Wells they sacked the Bishop's Palace and sang the old plunder-song of the Lancastrian army before Towton:

"Hop! Hop! Willikin, hop!
England is mine and thine":

words that had caused the name of Lancaster to stink from Trent to Severn; and at Bath they had news that Edward was at Cirencester, camping three miles South of the town on the Bath road. Somerset blessed God then and would have made a stand, and the Prince spoke hopefully of meeting Edward himself in the battle, or at least his perjured brother-in-law George of Clarence: but the others were for retreat until Jaspar Tydder of Pembroke should have brought up his Welch to their support. They made for Bristol, and the news met them almost at the city gate that Edward had come down to Malmesbury; was shouldering them inch by inch over the Cotswolds and into the water of Severn. That was on Wednesday. On Thursday their outriders met and skirmished in the streets of Sodbury. "We must make for Gloucester," Lord Wenlock urged, "and hold it till Pembroke can come up." So they marched all that night. But in the morning the town gates were shut and the walls manned, and when they demanded entrance in the name of Queen Marguerite and her son, they were told that Gloucester was firm and fast to Duke Richard.

This was the ugliest setback they had had. Edward and his two brothers were very near them now, and it seemed their best hope to slip over Severn by the ford at Tewkesbury, some five hours away. They were very roadworn, and the foul weather, which had darkened the sky as though the devil did not mean that God should watch the fall of Kingmaker, had given place now to an unnatural early heat. Nevertheless, they reached the abbey town that afternoon and, sending the Queen and Princess to take shelter in a house of religion on the Worcester road, pitched camp and got some rest.

King Edward and his brothers had halted at the village of Cheltenham. They arrived before Tewkesbury on Saturday the fourth of May and deployed their forces in the order they had kept at Barnet; the Lancastrians were entrenched very securely upon the edge of a rise, having a broad trough of lower ground before them, and behind them the small River Tirle. Devon commanded their right, which lay nearest the ford and town of Tewkesbury, and the left was in the charge of Somerset. Lord Wenlock had the middleward. With him were the Prior of St. John's and the young Prince of Wales.

King Edward had brought his great artillery: the guns *Meg, Messenger, Dijon, Fowler of the Tower* and *Fowler of Chester,* the bombardels, *Edward* and *Richard* and the iron guns *Newcastle* and *London.* He emplaced these opposite Somerset's division, under the command of his young brother, Richard of Gloucester; and presently the Duke, annoyed by the sharp shower of balls and arrows that Duke Richard gave him, sent word to Lord Wenlock to advance in his support and charged the middleward of the enemy.

Lord Wenlock, sitting his horse upon the ridge with the pleasant scent of apple-orchards in his nostrils, could see the attack, in an oblique hurrying line of gleams and colours, streaming past below him. He could see also the ambush of spears which had been set by Edward in a little copse, emerge and take Somerset in his right flank and the Duke of Gloucester swing his line through a half-circle on his left to crush him. He remarked to the Prior of St. John's that the time had come for disobeying orders: and after a while, Edmund of Somerset, having lost above two-thirds of his man, and his own brother among them, seemed to realise that he was at hopeless work, for he turned and hacked his way out of the press and rode, with tears streaming down his face, for his own centre. Finding Lord Wenlock there, with his reins still slack upon his horse's neck, the smell of apples blowing coolly round him from the cider-orchards by the river, he swung his axe for the last time that day and struck the brains out of his skull.

King Edward and Duke Richard now advanced to fold up the Lancastrian force from right to left. The ford of Tewkesbury being a little one, only a few of those who ran got over it. Many were drowned by the mill, but most were herded along the bank, first of the Tirle and then of the Avon, until they came to a sunken meadow with a line of willows down its middle, which was called after that Saturday, the Bloody Meadow, and there killed miserably. King Edward, when he came to regain England, had told his

106

followers to give no quarter, so the carnage in this place was absolute, and the Prince of Wales, who was the last of his house and fourth in descent from John of Ghent, was cut down with the rest, although he cried for succour to his brother-in-law, the Duke of Clarence.

Of those who got their bodies and lives over the Tewkesbury ford, most ran at once through the town and toward Wales. But the Duke of Somerset, the Prior of the Order of St. John and Sir John Fortescu, with twenty-three other knights and squires and some common people, threw themselves into the Benedictine Abbey which lay to the right of their road and dropped like hares in a forme among the Clare and Despencer tombs there. A priest, disturbed at his Mass, turned round with the ciborium in his hands to find that the house of God was full of bleeding men. He was an old, short-sighted priest, not much in touch with politics, and this invasion so startled him that he almost forgot what he was at. He came from his altar and stood in the pillared nave, wholly bemused, whilst his acolyte, who was only a boy and inquisitive, ranged about like a dog in a barn, peering at the grand gentlemen. Then a sudden and abominable tumult began outside. Men shouted brutally, there was a screech as though a spirit had been sent to its account from the Abbey's very threshold, and the door was hurled open by an enormous figure, all blazing and splendid, that swung a yard and a half of steel in its hand and shouted : "Lancaster thieves; no quarter, men, kill the lot!" Its voice fetched echoes from the painted roof where angels played their drums and cornets to the honour of God. The men sprawling on the pavement, with blood oozing through their broken armour so that they looked like lizards that a cat had mauled, appeared to dwindle at the sound of it. The priest, who was learned, remembered a very terrible story in the Gesta Regum : how a woman of wicked life was buried in a certain church, in a stone coffin with chains round it, and fifty clerks sang Dirige and fifty priests said Masses for three nights for her; but on the third night a tall demon smashed the doors of the church to fragments with impetuous violence and, going arrogantly up to the coffin, plucked the poor woman out of it and carried her whither she would not. This thing, he thought, was happening again to-day. He knew that he was only a foolish old man, but, remembering

107

what he had in the ciborium, he did not feel afraid. He walked up to the shining monster in the doorway and said boldly :

"My son, you will kill no one in this place."

The immense figure—to the gold crest on its basnet, it was more than seven feet high—lifted a steel fist to knock its vizor up. The old priest saw that its azure surcoat was quartered in gold with leopards passant and fleurs-de-lys. Then he found himself looking up into a flushed face, straight-nosed, as smooth as a boy's, in which the eyes blazed like the blued steel studs on the head of a mace. The loud voice said :

"Stand aside, father. You see who commands you now."

"You see who commands you, my son," answered the priest, feeling no fear. He lifted the ciborium and held it before King Edward's eyes. "Are you not ashamed to be waving that sword in the presence of your Redeemer?"

The King stepped backward, and the panting and blood-splashed men in steel who had been crowding up behind him stopped their rush.

"Go out," said the priest firmly, "and think how narrowly you have been spared from a terrible sin."

King Edward crossed himself and mumbled. He looked sheepish.

"You have menaced Christ himself with that sword of yours. Now you shall kill no one who is here. I forbid it."

"Aye," muttered King Edward, like a man who does not understand clearly what is happening, "aye, anything." He swung round and shouted angrily at the men behind him :

"Go on, the lot of you. Get out of here."

The priest watched them go to the road again, shapes of flaring steel in sunlight, badges of the rose and sun, the silver boar, the black bull, the manche, the talbot. Monks peered from doorways and narrow windows at their retreat before issuing into the green-turfed garth to help one or two who had not retreated, but lay moving or quiet, where they had been overtaken. From the road, the din of pursuit and slaughter still went on, and there were sounds as though the doors of houses were being battered in.

The priest went back into the cool of the Abbey. He replaced upon the altar the body of God in its gold lodging.

Then he told the men who crouched, more of them than stood, among the tombs and pillars that King Edward had promised their lives to Christ, and they had nothing to fear.

The monks brought them food and drink, urging them timidly to lay off their hacked armour and let the infirmarian ransack their wounds. Two lay-brothers began to swab up the puddles of blood that had formed on the flagstones. The excited acolyte was cuffed over the ears and sent about his business. The broken men began to breathe as though life were flowing back into them after drowning. They ate and spoke to each other. But when they peered out of the door of the Abbey, they saw pikemen and archers posted on guard, wearing the Yorkist livery.

The hall where the Court sat was low and stuffy and hung with a rather bad threadbare arras of the Seven Worthies of Christendom. Sun came through the windows and painted stripes of dust along the air, and when a cart passed outside the noise was painful. Bored men-at-arms in scarlet, badged with the silver boar of Gloucester, were lined down the two walls. The chairs placed for the Earl Marshal and the Lord High Constable of England were behind a long table of pale oak at whose end a busy little fellow in a clerk's gown was scribbling, taking no notice of anything, apparently.

Edmund Beaufort of Somerset, standing bareheaded among his fellow-prisoners, found his mind drifting. He knew remotely, a little incredulously, that he was probably within a few hours of his death. It did not move him; had been coming anyway, for so many years. The Beaufort destiny was to hold by Queen Marguerite and the red rose, and die. His brother had discharged the duty two days earlier, toppling sideways off his horse with a Yorkist spearpoint under his arm. Now, he and his sisters and his cousin, the Lady Margaret, were the last Beauforts left alive. Distantly, the thought satisfied him : that his name would go out on the same breeze as blew out for good the cause and quarrel of the House of Lancaster.

Tired with standing, he shifted his feet. Pictures were forming in his mind : Wenlock's face of sudden terror as he swung his axe at him, the ripple of light on lance-heads when the Yorkist ambush broke out of the wood to turn his flank, the smashed body of the Prince of Wales carried up into the Abbey from the Bloody Meadow after his first and last battle. He remembered a firelit room and a girl in a white coiffe, sitting very still in a big chair and whispering without tears; "Holy Mary, have pity on me." That poor, brave, lovely child, he thought, what will become of her now, orphaned, widowed and outlawed at fifteen? I hope she need not be broken in our fall, the daughter of my old enemy, who forgave me so simply for the rough things I said to her. I hope her sister and her brother-in-law of Clarence will take care of her.

The men-at-arms grounded their demi-lances with a series of thuds and stood to attention, and the little scribbling clerk rose from his stool. The judges had entered, and now took their places. John Mowbray, Duke of Norfolk, was Earl Marshal: a middle-aged man with a smooth shaven, square face that looked somehow as though it were made of iron and growing rusty. His expression was that of someone attending the funeral of a distant relative. Next to him, seeming tiny in the wide chair with carved arms, sat Richard Plantagenet, Duke of Gloucester, Earl of Carlisle, Lord High Admiral of England, Warden of the West Marches against Scotland, Chief Justice and Chamberlain of North and South Wales, Lord High Constable of England. He was very quietly dressed in black velvet slashed and reversed with violet silk and a black velvet beret with a jewel in it: but about his shoulders, like a bright noose, there flamed the Yorkist livery-collar of gemmed and enamelled gold. Edmund Beaufort's eyes, once on him, did not move again. He was thinking: I can see the face of our destruction now. This is the little boy in his 'teens who persuaded Clarence to betray us, who broke Kingmaker's ranks at Barnet and mine here on Saturday, to please his big brother. He has been Edward's angel all these months past. It is fitting he should be the one to pronounce our death-sentence and put a keystone to his work.

The Earl Marshal began to read from a list of names the clerk had pushed across to him. He read badly, in a rough, loud voice that stumbled sometimes:

"Humphrey Audley, Edmund Beaufort calling himself Duke of Somerset, William Carey . . ."

Edmund Beaufort did not listen. Between his black head-dress and the violet turnup of his doublet, the face of Duke

110

Richard was astonishingly pale : not sick or haggard, but bloodlessly clear and white like limestone. His straight hair, combed until it gleamed, was a brown frame round it. He sat back in his chair with his chin dropped and his hands, as white too as a girl's, lifted in front of him. The finger and thumb of the left hand drew ceaselessly up and down a large ring on the little finger of the right one. His eyelids were lowered over this play, and all that was visible of his face was a pair of delicate eyebrows, slanting a little upward toward the forehead, and with a scholar's frown between them, and a tight, lipless mouth, muscled at the corners like a grown man's. He is not nineteen years old yet, thought Edmund Beaufort, our destroyer. Boys of his age are being birched to teach them Latin in the colleges and the novices' schools. Yet he has known exile and intrigue and won battles, and he is sitting here to order my death.

"You and each one of you," rasped the Earl Marshal, "are indicted and accused of the crime of high treason against our Sovereign Lord, Edward, by the Grace of God King of England and France and Lord of Ireland; forasmuch as you have wickedly, seditiously and maliciously levied war against our said Sovereign Lord in his dominions, entering the same in arms and with banners displayed; moving and seducing his lawful subjects to great riots, tumults and insurrections in divers places, to the jeopardy of their lives and against the peace of our said Sovereign Lord, whereby the prosperity of this realm was like to have been utterly destroyed; and treasonably, sinisterly and maliciously resisting in arms the loyal part-takers of our said Sovereign Lord, to the effusion of Christian blood and the great annoyance of the commonwealth; imagining and intending by this the destruction of our said Sovereign Lord's most royal person and the subversion of this his realm. All of which you have done in the name and by the stirring of Henry of Lancaster, late calling himself King of England, and of Marguerite his wife, and with the aid and by the stirring of the ancient adversary of this realm, the King of France; contrary to the faith and allegiance which you and each one of you owe and should bear to our said most Sovereign Lord, King Edward.

"What have you to answer touching these charges?"

No one spoke. The trampling and gossiping of common

111

people in the street came through the windows with the sunshine. Edmund Beaufort still watched Duke Richard. He had not moved whilst the indictment was being read; had continued, with a grave air and bowed head, to draw the shining ring up to the top joint of his little finger and shoot it down again. Once or twice, when the Earl Marshal stumbled in his reading, he wrinkled his forehead and sighed gently. A curious thought crossed Edmund of Somerset's mind, drowsy with the foreknowledge of death : If we were not all certainly condemned already, if there were a loophole for us, I should be glad we had this boy for our judge. The Earl Marshal laid down his paper and coughed.

"Does any of you deny bearing arms against our Lord King in the field here on Saturday : No? Then we need not call witnesses. Does any of you make exception to the tenor of this indictment?"

Edmund Beaufort recognised the voice of young James Gower, the Prince of Wales' swordbearer.

"I plead the King's pardon."

The Duke of Gloucester, without moving his chin from his chest, lifted his eyes. In doing so, he immediately altered the whole character of the scene; made it alive. His eyes, narrow and set far apart, were a pale, blazing grey, and seemed to take the light like the diamond in his cap. A deep, straight wrinkle, underlining each of them, aged his face as much as the stiff muscles round his mouth.

"What's that?" said the Earl Marshal. "Pardon? This is the first I've heard of it. Mr. Catesby, have you any writing of pardon from the King's Grace to these accused?"

The little clerk shuffled his papers with quick hands; looked up.

"I have letters of pardon under Privy Seal for Sir John Fortescu and others whom we dealt with earlier, my lord."

"Yes, yes, we know all about that : but these prisoners, man."

"I have no writing concerning them but the indictment and your Graces' commission to put them on their assize."

"Just what I thought : we've seen all the pardons there are. You, fellow, can you produce exemplification under seal of this pardon?"

James Gower's voice quickened. He began to stammer.

"The pardon and assurance of safety he swore to the priest

112

that turned out at his Mass, and the sacrament in his hands, when King Edward came with his sword into the church; required him by the virtue of the sacrament to kill none of us that were there : we stayed still in the church on trust of that pardon when we might have gone and saved our lives."

The Earl Marshal pulled his lip. Then he turned and bowed very respectfully to the Duke of Gloucester.

"I don't see how we can take this into account, your Grace."

The Duke stopped playing with his ring, and without moving his curious eyes from the prisoners, began to speak. His voice was as unexpected as his look. It was low-pitched, gentle, extraordinarily winning, and at the same time distant, like a clerk's voice reading the Gospel. If there was an emotion in it, it was a kind of frigid tenderness.

"I fear you have cheated yourselves into a cruel hope. My royal brother's oath, which he respects, was no more than to refrain from bloodshed in the church precincts. His Grace is not a tyrant who takes pleasure in homicide, and all those who by possibility could be admitted to mercy and been so admitted. But there was no talk of general pardon. How could there be?"

Suddenly and disconcertingly, James Gower began to yell :

"Devils, devils and pledge-breakers, you're going to murder us, and your lying King's lying word's worth nothing. He swore it on the sacrament, I tell you. He swore it on the body of Jesus Christ. He'll be damned for this. You'll all be damned. Why isn't he here now? He's afraid to face us : liar and coward and murderer. You, Richard of Gloucester, he's sent you to judge us to death because he's afraid to look at us himself. Are you going to take your brother's sins on you? Take care of your precious soul, Dickon of Gloucester, or you'll serve your brother over the edge of hell."

The Duke did not open his mouth or move his eyes; but the Earl Marshal, as though he had forgotten his office and remembered that he was a Mowbray speaking to a Lancastrian, shouted :

"Shut your goddamned mouth, you traitor."

The Duke lifted his hand at that, frowning a little. Then he said more gently than ever :

113

"Sir, will you not be brave? Bravery is better for you than hope now. You spoke of murder; but in neither God's law nor man's is the execution of a rebel against the King's crown called murder. My brother is King of England; and consider what in the last twenty years has been the portion of England : wars and commotions and feigned rumours, division of county against county and hundred against hundred, continual effusion of blood. That is what comes when the crown of a kingdom is in dispute. That is what my brother's Grace is utterly determined to end : and it shall end. If you talk of murder, think of the poor commons who lived easily and were agreed until you called them from the sheepwalk and the plough-tail and sent them to their deaths in your quarrel with us. They were murdered; and you know in your souls that if we spared you now you would only wait your day to begin this madness of civil war again. Your Prince is dead. The house of Lancaster is broken down, and whoever raises it again must do so on a great heap of poor men's bodies. You shall not do it. We must have peace; and that there can never be in England in your lifetimes."

He stood up abruptly and uncovered his head. The Earl Marshal rose beside him, over-topping him. The loud breathing of the prisoners could be heard.

"You and each one of you are guilty of rebellion and high treason against our Sovereign Lord, King Edward, and the sentence of the court is :

"that after time given for the shrift of your souls, upon this present day, you be had severally to a scaffold in the market-place of this town and your heads there smitten from your bodies, and all your lands, titles and estates be escheat and forfeit into the hands of the King's Grace : but though it is in the authority of this court to see your bodies dismembered and your quarters hung upon the highway to the admonition of ill-disposed persons, nevertheless, the King's Grace, of his mere mercy, is pleased to grant that after execution you shall be buried according to the usage of Holy Church, without any quartering or division of your limbs."

And so, thought Edmund Beaufort, we come to the end.

"What I can't for the life of me see is why that little fox

114

John Morton, that little Rector of St. Dunstan's or what he calls himself, has to be left alive. Make a clean sweep, I would. Everybody knows he was the whole wits of the Lancastrians, he and Fortescu."

"Wits without hands aren't dangerous. I'd never head Fortescu, anyway : such a distinguished old fellow, great scholar. As to Morton, if he can see flies in milk he'll forget the red rose and make himself useful now. He's a learned man, too."

"Scholars and priests : I never did like scholars."

"We know that, Thomas. We know that."

"Well, I was never one for learning : waste of dear time. What's a man want with books when he can get a lance in his hand?"

"You mustn't talk like that, Thomas, or you'll offend Anthony. Our Anthony's a great man in a tournament as well as a scholar, remember. Will, wake up and give me a drink. No, not the claret, man : can't you see I'm drinking hippocras? You know, you fellows, what I really want is a woman. God's blessed Lady, it's good to see London girls again after those ugly bitches in Artois : faces like mules, and stinking of sweat and garlic to knock you down. I swear I'd 've taken a vow of chastity if we'd stopped there much longer."

"Talking of women . . ."

"Yes, let's talk of women. I summon Will here to tell us about his first woman. Search your mind, Will. Cast your memory back and count on your fingers. Well, no, not your fingers, perhaps : try the hairs of your head. How old were you?"

"These are the secrets of the confessional."

"Don't talk about confessionals. It upsets Thomas. How old were you, Will?"

"I was fourteen, and she said she'd tell her mother."

"And did she?"

"No, I found out afterwards she was an orphan. That taught me never to take women at their word."

"Oh, Solomon!"

"Have you ever done penance for adultery, William?"

"Yes, whenever my wife got to hear of it."

"Talking of adultery, I wonder if that story's really true. I'd like to know that."

"What story? If it's one of Will's, it isn't."

"About Marguerite's son being a bastard."

"Why, holy God, surely there's no doubt about it."

"I never heard it questioned before now."

"Not a doubt, man."

"Well, since you ask, Anthony, I tell you plainly that for my part I'm not sure. Warwick began the tale, and he swore to me that he had proof of it. But didn't Warwick marry his own daughter to that same bastard when he thought it paid him? He was a deep one, Warwick. If he ever had those proofs he told me of, we can be sure that he destroyed them then. Marguerite had carnal doings with Suffolk, and Wiltshire too. I'm sure of that : a French whore. They say when Harry of Windsor heard she was with child he counted on his fingers and said it must be by the Holy Ghost : but Harry of Windsor's mad. We'll never know the truth; and the brat's dead and gone now."

"Aye, killed flying : and that's not like a grandson of Harry of Monmouth."

"It saved the headsman a job, at least. There's the end of Lancaster."

"Amen."

"Not quite the end, your Grace : Have you not heard who the rebels say is heir to the crown now?"

"Good God, I'm no chronicler. The Staffords trace their descent from Edward III, I believe."

"It is not Henry Stafford, though."

"Well, who, then?"

"Jaspar of Pembroke's nephew, Henry Tydder, son of the old Earl of Richmond and Lady Margaret Beaufort."

There was a bellow of laughter. Edward IV of England leaned his huge body back in his chair and beat his hands against his silk-sheathed knees. He jerked his head, and the sun from the window sent snakes of light twisting among his copper-coloured hair and made the jewels on his chest and neck flash. His laughter was delightful, as true as a child's, compelling to anyone who heard it. The richly-dressed noblemen of the Cabinet Council—the unconstitutional small body that, much more than the official Privy Council, ruled England—clapped their hands and held their sides. Even the young Duke of Gloucester, that precociously straight-faced boy, chuckled with the rest. Lord William

Hastings, the Court Chamberlain, who had told the news, made a brief effort not to applaud his own joke and then succumbed.

"A Welchman," gasped Edward presently, "a Welchman to rule England : by God's blessed Lady that's rich. Oh, that's wonderful. I suppose the eldest sons of his royal house'll be styled Prince of England. Where's the capital of the realm to be : Conway or Caernarvon? Oh Jesus, Will, you mustn't say these things. I shall hurt myself. A Welchman : and what after him : a Scot perhaps?"

Duke Richard of Gloucester, with a suggestion of colour in his usually bloodless face, asked :

"You're not serious, surely, Hastings?"

"As the Gospel of the Mass, your Grace."

"But for God's love, Will," said the King, "they can't think they've any law or reason behind this moonshine concoction."

"I understand, your Grace," said Hastings in the hushed voice of a man about to giggle, "that the main point is that this Henry Tydder—who is a child about ten years old, by the way—is descended on his father's side from Harry of Monmouth's widow, Queen Katherine, and that his mother's a Beaufort, and so descended from John of Ghent."

"But all that amounts to," said the King with a kind of strained reasonableness, "is that he's descended from two several sets of bastards. His grandfather, that old fellow I had the head off after Mortimer's Cross, was never married to Queen Katherine. Their children were got in open adultery : and as for the Beauforts, the whole world knows they're bastards. Good God, the thing's unheard of. The claim of Lancaster to the crown is false enough, but if it were as strong as mine and my father's it would do this Welch brat no good. He's no more Harry of Windsor's heir than I'm the Duke of Muscovy's."

"I only tell the tale I heard."

"Well, I'll renounce Mahomet," said the King euphemistically. "Can the Tydders themselves believe such a cockand-pie story, d'you suppose? It passes my simple understanding altogether."

Hastings shrugged.

"Don't ask me, your Grace. They're Welchmen : and of course they're descended from ten thousand generations of most royal and puissant no-one-Ap-nobodies who were all Kings before Noah."

"Did you ever meet a jenkin who wasn't? All the same, I wish we might have laid hands on Jaspar of Pembroke. His head would look well on a pike over the Bridge. That fellow Vaughan we sent after him into Wales is a damned bungler. I ought to 've sent you, Dickon, when you asked me."

Duke Richard of Gloucester, sitting a trifle apart from the others, had been abstractedly sliding his extremely beautiful Italian dagger up and down in its gold sheath. He looked up with his quick, serious smile when his brother spoke to him.

"I should have been very glad to serve your Grace in the matter," he said formally; then added, with the manner of making fun of his own gravity :

"A little work comes as a change after last winter."

Edward smiled over his shoulder at him.

"Oh yes," he said, "it's time we gave you something to do. You've been idle these last months, haven't you? Only led a wing in two battles, headed fifteen rebels, and then nearly cried with rage because the Bastard of Fauconberg wasn't here to meet us. Can you never be still?"

"I'm young," said Duke Richard with perfect seriousness.

There was an odd intimacy in this exchange between the two brothers, as though they were alone together in the room. Even Duke George, sprawling his legs in a window-seat, appeared shut out by it.

"You're young," said the King, "but you'll have your bellyful of work before you're older. I'm like the man in the tale who raised the devil and had to keep him busy. You shall make ropes of sand."

Anthony Wydvylle, Earl Rivers, the King's brother-in-law, looked and listened. A man of no family, a made Lord, despised by the old nobility and detested by the common people, it was his principal business in life to keep his fingers on the pulse of Edward's mind. His sister Elizabeth—a woman, as he did not conceal from himself, of small imagination—had thought their troubles over when she netted the twentytwo-year-old King into a quiet little marriage at Grafton Regis on an April morning seven years ago. He had known better; though he could hardly have foreseen that Kingmaker's angry jealousy was to mean a revolution, two deaths in the Wydvylle family and four pitched battles. His care was for his own advancement and his kinfolk's; and since it was hard for beggars on horseback to make friends, he watched the King.

Edward, at the moment, was a sight to see. He was dressed with the magnificence that was characteristic of him and that led him frequently into astonishing expenditure. Jewels glistened on his fingers and rippled in bands across his plum-coloured Genoese velvet doublet: pearls and sapphires to match his teeth and eyes and heighten the colour of his hair. His gown was damson-coloured cloth of gold and his hose damson silk, and though the occasion was not a ceremonious one, he wore his Garter. Eight weeks' campaigning had sweated the fat of exile from his vast bones and fined down the lines of neck and face. He was twenty-nine and looked nineteen. Duke Richard, with his small, prim mouth and the queer horizontal wrinkles below his eyes, might have been his elder rather than his younger brother. Certainly, no one who saw him now, sprawling in one padded chair with his feet on another, would imagine that three months ago his position had been hopeless enough to inspire a Milanese diplomat to an epigram about the difficulty of climbing in through the window when one has been kicked out of the door. Still less would anyone who heard his delightful laugh suppose that he had only that morning come to London, victor of the decisive battle of his life, or that after that battle he had stood in a window looking onto Tewkesbury market-place, listening to the dull repeated crash of the axe and watching the thin spurts of blood jet onto the sawdust, as fifteen rebels and gentlemen, all of whom believed he had sworn their pardon on the sacrament, were made shorter by a head. In many ways, thought Lord Anthony, a studious reader of chronicles, he must be the oddest King that ever ruled in England. Some people complained, with careful euphemism, that his abundant humanity caused him to use himself more familiarly among private persons than the honour of his majesty required. Elder statesmen who remembered the godly dowdiness of Harry of Windsor's Court and the frozen etiquette of Harry of Monmouth's felt like travellers to a new country when they waited on the Rose of Rouen in his state apartments, that were always hung with the finest French and Flemish

119

arras and full of pretty women and tame monkeys. It distressed them to be given drink in a trick goblet that spurted wine into their sleeves, or to hear the King seriously commend some squeaky-voiced brat on being able to spit farther than any other page in the Palace. Royal mistresses, too, had been out of fashion in the previous generations. Under the Rose of Rouen they had come in again with a vengeance. To those who ventured—very circumspectly—to deplore his taste for exotic fashions, nursery amusements and the wives and daughters of his loyal subjects, Edward might fairly have pointed out that he had never lost a battle in his life and could outface any man in his kingdom either in the hunting-field, in the tiltyard or at the butts. Instead, he generally contented himself with saying that he did not mean taking Holy Orders just at present. People who pressed the matter farther had been known to leave his presence with white faces. The Plantagenet temper, which his family got, along with their drooping eyelid, from Black Fulk of Anjou who sold his soul to the devil, was not dead in him, but simply sleeping. Lord Anthony, of all people, was careful never to disturb its slumbers. If he and his family once dropped from royal favour, it would be into everlasting destruction. His friends and colleagues of the Cabinet Council would see to that.

"The Tydders'll have slipped across to France now," continued Edward to his brother. "But you shall go and chase the Bastard if it'll keep you happy. Thank God and St. Anne I've not your energy; and now we'd better hear just how much damage that same Bastard's done in our loyal city of London and just how much our loyal citizens blame me for not being there when he arrived. Tell us all about it, Will. We must do some business this morning, I suppose."

William Hastings, very elegant in apple-green silk reversed with cloth-of-silver, looked sideways at Lord Anthony. Lord Anthony returned the glance. He had never regarded the affable and decorative Court Chamberlain in any other light than that of a rival. Charm, intelligence and the peculiar mixture of brutality and refinement which King Edward demanded of his playfellows—all the qualities Lord Anthony knew himself to possess—Lord Hastings possessed too. Had William Hastings had a pretty sister who knew how to take and hold King Edward's fancy, then William Hastings would have been where Anthony Rivers was. The two were invincibly cordial to one another and distrusted one another from the bottom of their souls.

"I think Lord Rivers can answer that best," said Hastings, "considering his service to your Grace in the matter."

"Then speak up, Anthony, and let's hear the worst of it."

"The Bastard and his men arrived here on the fifth, Sire, shouting for King Harry; and I don't mind telling you that some of those loyal citizens of yours would 've let them in, malgré myself, the Lord Mayor and all his brethren. There's a devlish ugly Lancastrian spirit abroad still. But these Kentish whorsons flung their own chance over the dyke; started plundering the beer-shops on the way and lifting cattle. That gave our dear Cockneys a notion of what they'd have to content themselves with if they opened the gates. Then Fauconberg got cannon from his ships and bombarded the Bridge. The Southwark gate and thirteen houses are destroyed; and he did the same at Bishopsgate. After that I think there was no one in London wouldn't 've eaten his liver without salt if they got the chance. My Lord of Essex here and myself asked for men and got all we needed. I took six thousand of the loyallest and drove him off Aldgate, and I will say my Cockneys followed me most lovingly. We killed over two hundred before the chase was done. My Lord of Essex and the aldermen made a sortie from Bishopsgate and killed about the same number; didn't you, my Lord?"

"About seven hundred, I made it," said Henry Bourchier of Essex shortly. He was an old-fashioned nobleman and disliked the Wydvylle family beyond measure. Lord Anthony shrugged; smiled; went on:

"Ah, my Lord, we young men cannot compete with you veterans of the French Wars: more than seven hundred, then. But there were plenty left. It was three days before they retreated as far as Blackheath: and, believe me, if the Bastard had not been so free with his gunpowder in the first place, you might have found us besieged in the Tower when you came home. It was something a great deal more than a mere riot and commotion. Their strength was very little under twenty thousand: not simply the Bastard's pirates, but the commons of Kent in droves. He'd roused the whole county. Remember it, your Grace. The Lancastrians may be dead and buried at Tewkesbury, but the Lancastrian spirit's alive and flaring in Kent, and in London too. Holy Harry's name still stirs people. Why our dear English should want a saint to rule over them, God only knows, but it would seem they do; and saint, Sire, is one of the few names not even your enemies have ventured to apply to you."

Edward drew down his arched, delicate eyebrows in a perplexed grimace; looked almost wistful.

"But God's blessed Lady, aren't I a better King for them than that old lunatic? I never said I was a saint; don't pretend to be. But I do rule, and as far as God lets me I rule justly: more than he ever did. He never thought of anything but his own precious soul. So long as he could spend his time with the angels, all the devils in hell might have charge of the commonwealth for what he cared. People howled loud enough when he was on the throne and they'd the Beauforts and Ormonde and Suffolk to squeeze them. There was some sense in it when Warwick was alive and helping him : but who in God's name's mad enough to want him back now?"

"Enough men to make things very uncomfortable here a week ago. He's Harry of Monmouth's son. Never forget that, Sire, for the commons of England never do. He may be a witless idiot, but his father fought Azincourt."

"Yes, when he found he couldn't buy himself off. Jesus God, if that's all they've got against me I'll show them a thing. I've a monstrous crow to pick with Louis, and the saints know I promised Charles of Burgundy often enough to invade France. Azincourt'll be a hen's turd to a dunghill to what I'll do. I'll have Normandy and Guienne, and everything in between 'em for good measure. So God help and save me, I will. But I've got to have the country quiet first, haven't I? Well, go on. Tell me how much damage was done last week."

"Jack Cade never did worse. It's pitiable. There's the Bridge for one thing. You could see the smoke for miles off. Then they burnt some fine houses at Aldgate and did shameful damage along the river-front; and to judge by the complaints I've had since, there's not a farmer between here and Canterbury hasn't had his cattle lifted. As long as Holy Harry's alive you may expect this sort of thing whenever your back's turned."

Lord Anthony stooped; took a pull from the goblet of claret at his elbow and looked round him. He wished his words to go below the surface of his hearers' minds; had said them with a purpose. Duke Richard and Lord Hastings were watching him attentively. They were both intelligent men, he thought; would let no mere distrust of his ambitions or dislike of his family blind them to the good sense of what he might advise. Hastings was gentle, a warm-hearted man who might deplore extremes. As for Duke Richard, it did not appear from his activities in these last two months that he had any special horror of them. He moved his eyes to other faces. Henry Bourchier of Essex, bald and bearded, wearing mourning for his son Humphrey Cromwell, who had gone down before Oxford's furious charge at Barnet, and John Mowbray of Norfolk, had both been forced to ally their blood with the aspiring blood of Wydvylle, and resented it. Fortunately, though they were notable Yorkists, the King did not find these two especially amusing. Essex was Treasurer and Norfolk hereditary Earl Marshal; and Edward generally found it easier to think of them as officials than as people. The powerful Northern Baron, Lord Thomas Stanley, a gross, ugly man with small eyes sunk like a pig's in the fat of his face, was more of an enigma. He came of a not particularly distinguished family which had a reputation for going where the cat jumped, and was remarkable for two things : the immense strength of his hands and his illiteracy, which, in a polite age, was such that he could hardly write his name. The King liked him. George Duke of Clarence, in his seat at the window, was pouring out another cup of hippocras. Lord Anthony watched him speculatively. At the rate he was going, he would be drunk by supper time; had not his elder brother's head for liquor. He was only twenty-two, but his quite handsome face was permanently flushed and getting heavy. An opportunist and a philosopher, Lord Anthony could not help being impressed by the adroitness with which this decorative young man had turned traitor for just long enough to marry the co-heiress to the Warwick estates and then remembered his loyalty in time to come in out of the rain. But he did not hide from himself the plain truth that Duke George, for all his cunning, was an ass. A cunning ass,

123

a cunning ambitious ass: there was no telling where you were with such a combination.

The remaining member of the Cabinet Council was Sir John Fogg, and there were moments when even Lord Anthony felt that he had no business to be there. He had jockeyed him into the King's favour, attached him by every lawful and unlawful bond to his own interests; but he could not like him, and doubted very much whether anyone else could. He was a thin, dark, hungry person with a wet mouth and cheekbones that stood out like the handles of a pot. Everything that he did advertised him as a man who would rather make a dishonest farthing than an honest penny. Even the gesture with which, as his patron watched him, he took a sweet wafer from a dish was that of a sneak-thief. We are well told, thought Lord Anthony, to put no trust in Princes. Those of us who do are forced, in the upshot, into trusting such far meaner creatures.

The Duke of Clarence, having filled his cup and drunk from it, said:

"Hang about half Kent, I would; show the whorsons who's master."

Edward's dark blue eyes appeared suddenly to grow lighter. "Yes," he said deliberately, "I think there will be hangings. King I am and King I'll be, and if it costs a few fathoms of strong rope, well, I can afford it. The Kentishmen are dirt and always have been. I'm going to Canterbury to-morrow."

Hastings put up his eyebrows.

"So soon?"

"Sooner the better: by God's body, I'll show the Bastard and all the other bastards what it amounts to, shooting guns at my London. But I've had another thought, too. We've friends in the City as well as enemies. Good, then we'll reward 'em. Anthony, I want you to round up the Mayor and Urswick—the Recorder, you know, clever fellow who got the guards out of our way in April—and about half a dozen of the Aldermen you like best. I'll knight the lot this afternoon."

The Duke of Norfolk coughed and looked sideways at the Earl of Essex.

"Is that really necessary, your Grace?" he asked. "For my

part, I feel that these mercers fishmongers are quite puffed-up enough already."

"Very true," said Duke George, "very true."

"Nonsense," said the King easily, "I like the citizens, and most of 'em like me; and one knighthood of that soil'll get us more following than twenty hangings. What d'you say, Anthony?"

"I wholly agree with your Grace."

"And I," said Hastings.

"When it comes to raising people's estate, Lord Rivers should know best," said Duke George. His smile was at once childish and malicious; gave his face an odd look of spoilt youth, as though something were destroyed in him. It is remarkable, thought Lord Anthony, the genius that young man has for being offensive. It must be the knowledge of what England thinks of his own shifts that makes him so ready to talk of cockerels to St. Peter. Clarence the turncoat: he knows they call him that. He bowed slightly.

"Considering the unnatural treacheries which have lately been exemplified in the realm, I think we should lose no effort to confirm a loyalty which, after all, is only of very recent growth."

Edward grinned faintly; but before Duke George had seen the insult, Duke Richard, who had been fiddling with his dagger again, said:

"Are there other matters to be gone into?"

Lord Stanley leaned forward. He had a fat voice:

"As I said before, your Grace, I wish you'd have the head off that John Morton. He's as clever as a fou'mart, and there isn't an honest bone in his skin."

The King shook his head.

"Can't do it. Think what the Pope would say."

"Damn the Pope," said Lord Stanley. "The Pope's curse wouldn't kill a fly. There's another churchman whose gown wants shortening by the hood, and that's George Neville."

"The Archbishop of York: God's blessed Lady, Stanley, have you had too much to drink? I can't kill an Archbishop."

"Harry of Bolingbroke killed Archbishop Scrope."

"Yes, and Harry II killed St. Thomas of Canterbury. I tell you I've had enough trouble with Rome, without heading any bishops."

"He's Kingmaker's brother, your Grace."

"I've not forgotten whose brother he is. I've a little bill to settle with the reverend father in God, George Neville. But it can wait; and I shan't go so far as to shorten his days for him. Now what's next?"

Lord Anthony opened his mouth, but Hastings had stood up. He stroked his chin with two fingers and had a shadow of trouble on his forehead; said hesitantly:

"There are the women captured at Tewkesbury, your Grace."

Edward swung his feet from the chair they had been resting on and locked hands round his knees. He looked less like a boy now. Duke Richard turned his face a little toward him. Duke George looked at the carpet and his underlip projected queerly. The King said:

"I don't know what to do with 'em. So God save me, I don't. Women have no business meddling in affairs of Princes."

He pushed jewelled fingers into the sheen of his hair, frowning.

"There's Marguerite herself," went on Hastings, "Lady Courtney, Lady Vaux, and Warwick's daughter Anne—your sister-in-law, my Lord of Clarence."

"As to Marguerite," said the King, "there's only one fate for her: perpetual imprisonment. Let her thank her saints she was born a woman. If she'd been a man I'd have sent here where I sent Edmund Beaufort."

There was a grunt of agreement from Essex "She'd get no more than her due if she were burned for a witch," he said.

Norfolk shrugged his shoulders. "They say she is almost out of her mind since her son's death."

"Then there's Warwick's Anne," said Hastings thoughtfully.

"Oh God, yes," said Edward. "Well, what the devil are we to do with the chit? She's in your charge at present, George, isn't she? Though quite how you managed to get hold of her, I don't know."

Essex rubbed his bald skull. "If I may make a suggestion, your Grace, I think she should be treated mercifully."

Sir John Fogg raised his reddish vulpine face with pink-rimmed eyes; peered round him; broke silence to say in a rather nasal voice:

"A rebel's daughter, sirs, attained in blood."

"That's just where you're wrong," said Hastings. "Warwick hasn't been attainted, and can't be till Parliament sits. That cock won't fight."

Essex said emphatically :

"I hope it never may fight, poor little lass. Sire, do you intend to attaint the late Earl in Parliament?"

"God knows. Attainders aren't popular. I think of reversing some of the old ones of the year 'sixty-one. Something must be done about the Warwick lands, though : and there's his wife to be remembered too. You haven't by any chance got hold of her as well, George?"

"I have not."

Hastings smiled.

"A mother-in-law's never much sought after, is she, your Grace? As a matter of fact, the Countess is in sanctuary with the Cistercians at Beaulieu Abbey, a liberty which I am told is ample and as large as the Franchise of Westminister."

"She can stop there for me," said the King, "but I'll send some people down to see she doesn't slip over to France with half Warwick's fortune tied up in her skirts. She's another pair of shoes from little Anne : clever woman in her way."

"Speaking of sanctuary," said Norfolk, "the Lady Anne might enter a good house of religion. That would be a solution."

"What of?" asked Duke George. "What the devil are we all talking about?"

"Yes, what indeed, George?" agreed Edward. "I'm not going to harry the girl. You've got her. Well, let you and your wife make formal intercession to me on her behalf at the next Council, and I'll admit her to mercy : no fault of hers if her father married her off to Marguerite's brat."

Duke George filled his cup again. He put his hand to his mouth to smother a belch.

"Oh God, you can attaint her for all I care, and good luck to you. Let her go to all the devils in hell."

Essex and Norfolk looked shocked. Hastings' expressive eyebrows rose as though they wished to escape altogether from his forehead; and Lord Anthony reflected that a converted Jew usually eats pork three times a day : but Duke George was overdoing his loyalty. What he had just said was indecent.

"That's very unkind of you, George," the King said smoothly.

Duke George looked at his feet. He mumbled:

"Fuss about nothing: the girl's either a rebel or she isn't. What she does or where she goes doesn't matter a rush. It's where she stands with the law."

Duke Richard of Gloucester had stopped playing with his Italian dagger and was regarding his brother with narrowed, serious eyes.

"We have just been told," he said gently, "that the law's no danger to her."

Duke George's underlip was projecting more than ever. He sat with his elbows on his knees, his body forward; said emphatically:

"And I say she's just as much in danger of the law as the men you headed at Tewkesbury."

Duke Richard sighed.

"I can't prevent your making foolish remarks, George; and I do not need to show the others that they are foolish. The men that Norfolk and I condemned were dangerous traitors. Anne Neville, whom we've known since childhood, is a perfectly harmless girl you should be sheltering with all your interest. She's your wife's sister. What in the name of charity is your spite against her? Has she offended you in some way?"

"I've nothing against her," said Duke George instantly. "It's a question of law."

"Then leave it to the lawyers." Duke Richard turned to the King. "My Lord brother, since you are disposed to be merciful in this case, may I suggest that if our brother of Clarence does not care to be responsible for the Lady Anne, then some other reputable person may be found to take charge of her?"

Duke George slammed his cup down so violently that Lord Anthony thought the hippocras would slop out of it, but it was too far emptied. His face was as red as beef.

"Forty thousand devils," he shouted, "body and bones of God! So that's it, is it? Somebody else take charge of her: you, I suppose."

"Hardly that," said Duke Richard in his remotest voice. "I am unmarried."

Duke George uttered one of his high feminine laughs.

"How true, my dear brother, you are unmarried. Christ's blood and passion, you must think my wits are as paltry as your body if . . ."

"George!" King Edward had stopped lounging. He sat in his chair as though it were the King's Bench. "George, if you can't keep your temper when you're in my Palace, then I wish to God you'd stay out of it. I've a fine mind to make you apologise to Dickon. What the devil you're both quarrelling about I don't know, but I'll have no more of it. Now be quiet, the pair of you."

Lord Anthony thought : When all's said, it is amazing how we hang from him like fruit, how he is our centre. We play with him as you would play with a lion-cub, but only until he shows his teeth. What is it in him? He is a self-indulgent, pretty overgrown boy, no more; but we obey him. That trick of mastership is the one thing he has that I have not. They say there is a curse on the whole family of Plantagenet. Very like : where there is so great a gift there must be, in reason, a great payment. If I can turn his temper to my advantage now, I shall get my purpose. They have angered him out of his conceit of mercy for a while. He stood up.

"Your Grace," he said carefully, "the question of the Lady Anne's future, the question of the punishment of the Archbishop of York and of the rebels in Kent, will be decided by your good pleasure : but only provided that you remain King for long enough to attend to them."

He looked round to see the ripples spreading from his flung stone. Stanley, Essex, Hastings and Norfolk looked at him as though they were concerned for his wits. Sir John Fogg passed thin fingers across his mouth and squinted out of the corner of his eye at the King. Duke Richard's busy hands fell still again. Even Duke George's look of a whipped child was replaced slowly by a puzzled dull one. Edward was still sitting upright. He looked at Lord Anthony and said coldly :

"I take it, Anthony, that you mean something by that very curious speech?"

"I do indeed mean something," Lord Anthony said with a planned gesture. "The Beauforts and the Courtneys and Kingmaker and Montacute are dead, and Marguerite's boy. Henry Holland's licking his wounds in Broad Sanctuary.

129

Marguerite is your prisoner. Yes, but have you taken and headed the Bastard yet, or Oxford or the Tydders? Have you hanged the seven thousand who tried to stop our way to York? You have not. Has Calais sent in its submission? Has a single foreign ambassador come to congratulate you on regaining your crown and dignities? Have the people of Wales manifested any desire to salute that hopeful boy your son, my nephew, as their Prince? Why, half the counties North of Trent have not acknowledged us even yet. On the very day you were winning worship at Tewkesbury, Percy was risking his blood to put down a great Lancastrian rising in the North, and my Lord of Essex and I were victualling the Tower against the Bastard. You are not King of England. You are master of London, with your enemies for the moment in confusion. So was your great father before Wakefield. The mob cheered him in the streets as they cheered you this morning : and at that very moment the sword was sharpening somewhere in the North that was to take his head off."

"Come to your point," said the King shortly.

"It's as plain as the point of a spear. You've broken the back of Lancaster, but an adder can still bite with its back broken. There are tens of thousands still living in this realm who hold by Harry of Windsor. For the time, they are harmless because they want a leader. One day or another, a leader will be found—Oxford, Jaspar Tydder or his nephew, no matter—and our work will be to do again. The tinder and spark are there. It only wants a hand to bring them together, and the roof is fired over our heads."

The small sounds of men at ease, enjoying drinks and sweetmeats, had died out of the room. The King was frowning unhappily. He never liked to hear uncomfortable things. Duke Richard, with his eyes almost shut, was rubbing his underlip along his teeth. Hastings looked impressed. The spell was working.

"You can be as just as Solomon, Sire," went on Lord Anthony, "and as bold as David. Many will love you : but there will always be others who remember that poor, witless creature in the Tower whose father fought Azincourt."

Edward's fist, which could snap a sword-blade, came down with a thud onto his knee.

"Mother of God, am I to have no peace all my days because a little monkish fellow with a long nose won a victory before I was born? William, Thomas, you've heard what Anthony says. Are the English really so besotted by the memory of two ploughed fields in France that they'd rather have a lunatic to their King than a sane man?"

"The English, no," said Hastings judicially. "I think there are as many in this realm for us as for Lancaster, especially now Warwick's gone. But, as Lord Rivers says, there are tens of thousands who do love Harry of Windsor for the sake of Harry of Monmouth."

"Harry of Windsor," said Edward with extraordinary bitterness, "who lost England every rood of ground in France that Harry of Monmouth won for her."

"They blame Marguerite for that."

"She's not unloved herself," said Stanley, "in the North." Edward seized on the word.

"I shall take order with the North. There shall be no more trouble there. In Warwick's day it was more his kingdom than mine : but I'll find someone to fill his room, and someone I can trust utterly. That's certain."

"Yes," said Hastings, "we want no more Kingmakers."

"Kingmaker or no Kingmaker," interrupted Lord Anthony, "North or no North, troubles we've had and troubles we shall have, for just so long as any high-stomached nobleman or common rogue who chooses to be displeased with the King's pleasure can raise a shout of the true blood and start pulling down the King that is and putting up the King that was. My Lords, has even last year not shown you Fortune is a whore? The English have been taught a fatal lesson : that a King may be put on and off like a doublet. At the first discontent now—and there must always be discontents whilst there are Princes and subjects —they'll be for changing the colour of the rose again. Your Grace, it's not only for yourself I say this. You know I love you. There's your son. Is he to be Prince of Wales, and King of England in God's good time, or is he to die on a battlefield in his 'teens like your brother Rutland or be murdered privately in a dungeon like Richard of Bordeaux?"

Edward disordered his hair again. The droop of his mouth was like a child's.

131

"Anthony," he said, "you've given me a sour drink to swallow."

"So do physicians."

"To a sick man."

"Your Grace is sick : all this broad kingdom—sick. It's a plague that's destroyed very many : your father, your brother Rutland, my father, my brother John, the two Herberts, Tiptoft, old Salisbury, the good Lord Say, Lord Cromwell, Warwick and Montacute who were your friends before they were your enemies. We want physic in England."

Duke Richard suddenly drew his chair closer into the circle. He thrust his young, bloodless face forward over his joined hands; said with the beginnings of animation :

"And by the grace of God we shall have physic now. Justice without vengeance and without corruption; proper care for the poor; repression of law-breakers and law-twisters, not here and there as the fancy takes us, but everywhere, absolutely : that's our physic for a sick commonwealth : that and a settling of accounts with France."

"That is just such a noble sentiment as I should have expected from your Grace," said Lord Anthony quickly. "But consider that the country enjoyed the blessings of which you speak for ten years, and still revolted at the end of them."

Duke Richard looked full at him, and Lord Anthony experienced a small shock. Those very grey eyes were too hard, too seeing, and especially too unreadable to those who looked at them, to be in a boy's face.

"The country did not enjoy them. Many of the King my brother's acts were unpopular."

Lord Anthony fingered his beard; looked away. He knew King Edward's unforgiven act was his marriage and the advancement to honour after honour of his wife's kin. He had not forgotten the blunt phrases of Kingmaker's proclamation of two years ago that condemned the 'deceivable covetous rule and guiding' of the Queen, himself and their relations. This boy is going to be more difficult than his brother, he thought. I must get young Thomas into the Cabinet Council, and brother Ned. We want more voices. Bowing with a grave air of concurrence to the Duke, he said :

"At least it enjoyed them in greater measure than in the days of Harry of Windsor and his wife; and there was a Lancastrian revolt for all that. I repeat, your Grace, that we have no security whilst Harry of Windsor is alive."

King Edward moved his head from side to side like an irked beast. He said:

"Well, even if that's true, the old idiot can't live for ever."

Lord Anthony drew a slow breath. Then, staring directly at him, he spaced his words:

"You have said it, your Grace. Harry of Windsor cannot live for ever."

He looked round him narrowly. No one else would have had the bowels to say that, he thought, for no one else would dare to think it. Now I have voiced it, now I have dared to look farther than they into the dark, half of them will be with me, the men of the old nobility who sneer at me for a made Lord and man of yesterday; let them hate me for climbing by my wits to where they stand by birth, and once there, for elbowing them from the good marriages and profitable appointments. Let them hate me, so they follow me. They do not know the proper meaning of what they were born to, these Howards and Bourchiers and Stanleys, as I do who have crept to it by difficult ways. Rulership is a stag in their coverts, driven up to them by the keepers and shot from the butts. But I am the poacher who tracks it down alone, worming up to it on my belly, reading the tale of its slot and fumes.

Hastings had got the meaning of what he said. His mouth opened a little and his eyes narrowed. A curious and disconcerting look of intelligence came and went, like the glint of a swung lantern over water at night, across the gross face of Thomas Stanley. Sir John Fogg twiddled with the sleeves of his unconvincingly smart gown. Edward of England stared at Lord Anthony as though he had grown suddenly and miraculously out of the ground.

"But what . . ."

"The spark is there and the tinder is there, I have told you. There's only the hand wanted to bring them together, and our thatch is fired. Damp the tinder? There's too much of it. Cut off the hand? We don't know whose. But put the spark out. That would be very easy."

"Be plain. Anthony, I order you to speak plainly."

133

Lord Anthony could feel his knees twitching a very little. He jerked his thumb toward a window that looked eastward.

"Holy Harry of Windsor is in the Tower there at your disposal. Send him to God."

The Cabinet Council were like the painted figures put up over great men's coffins. The midday sunlight, entering the room, made much of the jewels on their chests and fingers and of the gold threads in their clothes; and they sat stiff and inadequate. Their eyes were off each other; searched the carpet. Have I said enough? wondered Lord Anthony. Shall I say more? He counted ten to himself and spoke. No one else in the room had uttered a sound.

"Neither you nor your son is safe, Sire, whilst he is outside Heaven."

The King's voice was thick and pleading.

"Think. Oh God, think what you're asking, man."

"I have thought. I am asking for your safety and your son's. I will ask for that until you silence me. Your son was born under a Lancastrian King, in sanctuary like a beggar's bastard. Either he will die under a Lancastrian King, too, or the Lancastrian King dies in the Tower now, to-day, under the Yorkist one. Why did we come from Burgundy and fight Kingmaker and Marguerite and win against odds no one would believe? To stretch our legs and wear cloth-of-gold for a little before the Lancastrians chase us out again, or to make the throne of the house of York so sure that your son and your son's grandson shall sit on it? You have your choice. But choose now. This world moves."

He stopped, aware of being intently looked at by someone who was not the King. Duke Richard had twisted his meagre body round in his chair and was staring at him with the blazing intensity of a leopard or a hawk. His mouth was as tight as a crack between two paving-stones; then opened as he took a loud breath, drawing his chin into his chest. Lord Anthony was sure that he would speak; but he did not; only wrinkled up his wide, flaring eyes until they were two slits in his face, and stared. It was Lord Anthony now who felt like a beast at a stake. In spite of the suspense of the moment, he was aware of an extraordinary discomfort, as though he were a child caught in some dirtiness by an elder. He pointed a finger at the Duke and burst out:

"His wife's moss-troopers crowned your great father's head with paper and put it on a common spike."

It was King Edward who answered. His voice came almost as a shout :

"Mother of God, do I need any of you to remind me of that?" He closed his right hand and pushed it repeatedly against the arm of his chair. "But my father himself would not want that poor, silly creature's life."

"Your father has two more sons in this room, Sire. What do they say?"

"George, do you want his life?"

Heavy and red, Duke George took his cup in both hands and stared into it like a diviner.

"We should be safer with him gone. It could be done privately."

"Dickon?"

"They killed our father. We killed his son : even and quit."

Lord Anthony said :

"Why cut the branch and leave the root in the ground?"

He felt easier now. Duke Richard was not looking at him. He had moved his eyes to the distressed face of the King and was saying in a voice that was wonderfully persuasive :

"Lord Rivers is your Grace's brother-in-law, not your brother. If we do not wish to make a pagan sacrifice on our father's grave, then why should he? Is it any wish of yours to be called Bloody King Edward?"

"It is not," said the King vigorously.

"Then leave this wretched old man to end in peace."

I must cut in here, thought Lord Anthony, or lose my pains. I must cut in now, before it's too late. He spoke in a louder voice than he had used before.

"Your son, Sire, remember him."

"Oh God !" shouted Edward, and got on his feet sending his chair skidding. His mouth was twisted and his eyes narrowed, not like his brother's, but with distress. Impersonally, Lord Anthony was sorry for him; said to himself : Poor boy. He looked round the Council; spread out his hand.

"My Lords, is it not time you did your duty? We are the King's Cabinet Council to give advice in his affairs, and you are leaving him to make this very hard decision alone."

135

He looked at Lord Stanley. No weakness of pity in those hanging chops and little eyes, he thought, and no scruples either. The big man moved in his chair and cleared his throat.

"Speak to the King, sir," Lord Anthony insisted.

"Your Grace," said Stanley.

Edward drew his hand down the side of his face and looked at him like a hurt child.

"Yes, Thomas?"

"Your Grace is merciful. Your Grace is too merciful, by God. Lord Rivers is in the right of it. That's my opinion."

Lord Anthony heaved a deep sigh; did not care who heard it. Stanley, Clarence, that's two, he thought. We shall win him over. The made Lord will kill a King.

"I swore not to hurt him," said Edward in a repressed voice.

"You swore to spare Beaufort at Tewkesbury, Sire," answered Stanley flatly.

Duke Richard spoke urgently, as though his unnatural calm were breaking and showing something underneath.

"That is a lie," he said. "His Grace swore only to respect the church. You make me a murderer if you say that."

"Oh, Christ, I don't know what I swore now. Beaufort could not have been spared, anyway : but Henry . . ."

"You at least know that you swore his safety. You know that for sure. William, are you going to sit still while these men plot murder? My Lord of Essex, since when have the Bourchiers listened to talk of assassination? Is this how you and my father conducted your wars in France? Holy St. Paul, are we Irishmen or Turks, or are we the nobility of England? I'm the youngest of you, I should keep silence. But you old men, you must have taken your vows of knighthood so long ago that you've forgotten them, I think."

Duke Richard was leaning far forward and talking with a peculiar checked vehemence that suggested two hard words for every moderate one he used. Everyone turned to him, staring, a little blockish. Hastings' face was wrinkled with distress. Duke George's mouth hung open. Henry Bourchier's old, rough voice suddenly barked out like a wheezy cannon :

"Well said, sir ! Your father would never have listened to such talk, God rest his soul."

"If he had," suggested Lord Anthony gently, "he might be alive now."

The old man rounded on him in a bristling fury.

"Yes, sir, and if he'd run like a coward from the battle of Wakefield he might be alive too. But he wasn't a coward and he wasn't a murderer, and so he's dead, and a sort of people that he wouldn't have permitted to hold his squire's horse are alive, and you can go to the devil."

"Gently, gently, my Lords," exclaimed Hastings; "let's have decency at least. My Lord Rivers, tell me plainly, do you really think it necessary for his Grace's safety to be so extreme? A foolish, infirm old man whom the citizens hardly raised a finger to help last month . . ."

"As I hope for salvation, I do think it necessary."

"Salvation of the devil's grandmother," shouted Essex furiously.

He rose and stamped to the far end of the room, where he stood staring out of a window, muttering and pulling his beard. Lord Anthony turned to the Duke of Norfolk. He was a man of honour, but the hatred of the Mowbrays for the house of Lancaster was part of English history.

"Your Grace of Norfolk, you were in England during the exile of our King. You had a taste of the Lancastrian hand then. They say you had to make suit to John Vere of Oxford as humbly as your own tenants ever did to you. Now answer me, my Lord, is the life of one impotent madman too high a price to pay to assure that those black days shall not come back again? Is it? I know you love our Lord King as much as I do, and I know you cherish your honour as much as my Lord of Essex; but answer that question."

Norfolk looked away from him, rapping his knuckles on his teeth. Edward had dropped into his chair again. He called out like a man at the end of his strength :

"Damn you, Mowbray, answer him. All of you speak, all of you. I won't be left alone to this."

Norfolk fixed his eyes on the tapestried wall opposite to him and said to it :

"His death would be our security. My Lord Rivers is right. We cannot afford to leave him alive."

Duke Richard's voice was as cold as a school-teacher's.

"You surprise me, my Lord of Norfolk."

Norfolk fell to tapping his teeth again and gave no answer.

"You, Fogg?" said the King thickly.

"Kill him, Sire."

"Do not say kill," said Duke Richard. "Say murder."

"William?"

William Hastings put both hands in front of his face. With an inarticulate noise the King was out of his chair; seized his wrists and dragged them down with such force that the Chamberlain, turning a white look on him, was almost over-balanced.

"Will you speak?" said Edward through his teeth. "You've heard the others. Now speak."

"Christ," said Hastings weakly. Then he twisted in the King's hands and faced Lord Anthony, his dark eyes staring. "The devil put this in your mind. You're right; and I think you've damned yourself and the rest of us. Sire, Henry is better dead, but I wish to all the saints this thing had never been spoken of. We shall be dishonoured as long as men have memories."

The King dropped his hands.

"Perjury and murder," was all he said.

With the speed of some dangerous small animal, a weasel, Duke Richard flashed out of his chair and across the room to him. Even now, his face did not explain what was the chief impulse in his mind. His expression was not indignant, anxious, distressed; was merely intent. He caught his brother's arm and looked up at him.

"Let me alone, Dickon. For Jesus Christ's sake let me alone."

"Edward, you know whose the disgrace will be. Your brother-in-law and all the rest of them can hide behind you. Lord Rivers is thinking of his skin, not yours. He's making you his butcher. Do you allow that?"

The King jerked himself away and turned his face to the wall.

"Let the Lancastrians revolt," went on Duke Richard. "Is a harmless fool in prison as good as a weapon to them as a cry of murder? God has worked two miracles as a sign of his favour to us, because our cause is the just one. When we desert justice, he will desert us."

The King threw up both hands as though to snatch something and tear it. His breathing was plainly audible. Stanley and Duke George watched him. Hastings sat miserably with his hands between his knees and his eyes on the floor. Norfolk was plucking at the collar of his doublet as though it irked him, and cursing under his breath. Sir John Fogg looked at Lord Anthony, who gave him a tiny nod and got to his feet. One last throw, he thought, and I have my game.

"Your Grace, we must all fear the judgment of God, but the actions of Kings when they defend their thrones and assure peace are not judged by God like those of subjects. England and your son are in question. God will forgive you this because it is for the prosperity of England; and your son will bless you for it."

Edward, over Duke Richard's shoulder, turned eyes of profound distress on him.

"You win, Anthony," he said in a smothered voice. "But you shall be my butcher. I order you to do it yourself, to-night."

Forty thousand devils, twenty thousand thunders, hell, death and corruption, scourging and crown of thorns: George Duke of Clarence was riding home to his mansion in the Strand after the Cabinet Council and, being rather drunk and furiously angry, was keeping time to his horse's steps with an interior rhythm of curses. His anger was large, wide-embracing, and sprang from several causes. He had not forgotten that he had had a chance of being King himself last year. His late father-in-law had been perfectly serious about it. But that ill-dressed little dog-fancier of a French King, whose soul God rot and wither in endless fire, had put a stop to that. I will not lend you either a fishing-smack or a Paris sol to make Duke George King of England. Duke George, a mediocre horseman, tugged his hackney's mouth as he remembered the words. The abused beast jibbed, and he damned it at the top of his voice for the next hundred yards. His head was hot, and he felt as though a sow had farrowed in his mouth. After the disappointment in France he had at least expected the Lancastrians to treat him well, considering that he had actually deserted his brother to be of use to them : but the pestilent, unthankful villains had hardly been polite. The cold-shouldering he had received last winter at King Henry's patched-up Court had been more than flesh and blood could bear. Really no christian soul could blame him for having deserted them for Edward again, especially since blood was thicker than water. Indeed, if his sister Margaret of Burgundy could be believed, they had even been plotting to do away with him. Bloody murderers, the pack of them : served them right that their old idiot of a King was going to be put under ground to-night.

In deserting to Edward he had at least been sure of one thing : that with his father-in-law dead or in exile (better dead, the affair at Barnet had been most satisfactory in that respect) he would inherit in his wife's right the vast Warwick estates, the castles of Middleham and Sheriffhutton, the manors and parks and chases and warrens sewn broadcast over all the counties of England. That was worth something; would make him the greatest royal Prince since John of Ghent. Now, hell, devils and martyrdom, it seemed to have gone over the dyke too. Little Anne, although she had actually married Marguerite's detestable son, was not going to be outlawed, after all. She was going to be admitted to mercy; and the next thing would be young Richard would marry her and poach half the inheritance. Duke George had no delusions upon that score. Richard and Anne had been in love with each other since they could talk, almost, and though Richard—hypocritical little prig—had a couple of bastards to his credit now, they were probably still as mawkish about each other as ever. In any case, love or no love, Richard would have to be a greater fool than he took him for to peep between his fingers at such a dowry. Dowry : the word sent a fresh wave of blood throbbing painfully to Duke George's head. As a sailor sees a pitch-black squall pop up over the horizon and come hurrying down the sky toward him, he saw exactly the course events would follow. Holy Harry of Windsor would be with the angels to-night, helped to the place for which all his earthly life had been a preparation by the sword of that jumped-up coxcomb Anthony Wydvylle. To-morrow Edward, with a smarting conscience, would have one of his fits of clemency. Pardons and amnesties would fly like hail, thick and three-fold. That sentimental poseur, Hastings, and that bloated bullfrog Stanley, were both related by marriage to the

Nevilles. One or other of them would make formal intercession on Anne's behalf. She would be commended almost with tears to their affection and care. Then Richard would arrive like a knight-errant in a ballad, there would be a Papal dispensation—since they were cousins—a wedding-feast and a settlement; and that settlement would be half the fortune and half the lands that Duke George had fully expected to enjoy in undivided happiness. God damn and blast Anne Neville, Richard Plantagenet, Harry of Windsor and Louis of France in one heap to eternal blazing hell and all devils, amen.

It was unfair, Duke George repeated to himself with increasing conviction. It was unfair. No one would stir a finger to get him his rights, see that he was rewarded in full for his return to the Yorkist fold. Richard was liked by Edward, admired by Hastings and the old nobility. Edward was loved by all of them. He, George, only was friendless, looked at sideways by Yorkists almost as much as by Lancastrians: Clarence the turncoat, the man who had sold his brother to his father-in-law and his father-in-law to his brother. They would all laugh if at the end of it he lost his wages. No one trusts me, he told himself, and felt his eyes prickling with the intensity of his conviction of wrong. I'd be a different man if people trusted me, if people understood me. I'd be a different man.

He had arrived at his own gate. Porters swung the iron-studded oak leaves apart, and in the cobbled courtyard a page held his stirrup. He dropped to the ground, jarring his headache to life again, and went up the steps to the main door. The obsequious major-domo bowed to him. Would his Grace be pleased to dine?

"Go to the devil," said his Grace, "and send me a pottle of sweet wine into the presence-chamber."

"At once, your Grace, and may it please your Grace . . ."

"It doesn't," snarled the Duke, and banged the door of the presence-chamber behind him.

The room was large, rather cheerless, and hung with painted cloth, once the property of Kingmaker, which displayed the exploits of Guy of Warwick. At one of the oaken tables a dark-dressed, dark-haired man with a close mouth was writing. He stood up respectfully. This was Mr. Stacy

141

of Oxford, the Duke's secretary, a man born to be some-one's jackal, and with the look of it on him.

"Good-day, your Grace."

The Duke unclasped his cloak and held his arms out. Mr. Stacy disembarrassed him of it and fetched up the best chair. Duke George dropped into it and clasped his head, eyes shut, until a cough at his elbow announced the wine.

"Fill the cup, leave the pottle and get out," he told the page.

The boy obeyed; coughed again from the door and said nervously:

"Please your Grace, the Lady Anne desires . . ."

Something twanged like a lute string in Duke George's head and he sat up.

"Stacy," he yelled, "see that little bastard gets a whip-ping to-night. Didn't I tell him to get out?"

The page got out, whimpering, and Duke George put down two cups of sugary Greek wine, tasting of resin, before he said:

"The Lady Anne, the Lady Anne indeed: Stacy, there's the devil to pay."

"My Lord?"

The Greek wine was making Duke George feel worse instead of better. He belched, but without experiencing relief.

"They're all against me, Stacy, sneering, plotting, all against me."

"No, no, your Grace."

"All against me: and they're murderers. Holy Harry's going to be murdered."

Mr. Stacy pursed his lips and raised his eyebrows.

"In the Tower to-night; that Rivers is going to do it: bloody murder."

"Things will be safer, no doubt, when he is gone."

"Safer for Edward: Holy Harry gone and that little beast of a Prince gone—shouted to me for succour: I'd give him succour—and then where are we? You remember the agreement with Marguerite we drew up. You remember it?"

"Well, your Grace."

"Good, you remember it. When Holy Harry was dead

and his son was dead, I was to be King. That's devilish funny."

Mr. Stacy glanced round him.

"The world has changed since then, your Grace."

"It's changed. By the sacrament of the altar yes, it's changed. Nothing for poor Clarence now : he can go to the devil. Nobody minds him. Now d'you know what they're going to do to me, after all I've done for them?"

"What, my Lord?"

The Duke told him. It took a long time, because he was beginning to feel that he might be showing his drink a little and had, in order to counteract this, to use the longest and gravest words at his command, some of which he repeated more than once, for greater clarity. Mr. Stacy helped by occasionally finishing a phrase for him and by clicking his tongue and looking outraged.

"If only we could hide her," concluded Duke George. "You know. Hide her. Put her away, so Richard wouldn't find her. All the trouble I took to get hold of her after Tewkesbury : and now I wish to God I'd let her alone. If we could hide her somewhere . . ."

Mr. Stacy fingered his lip and looked cunning.

"That would be difficult," he said, "if the King's seeking her. We could hardly force her against her will."

"Damned obstinate little bitch," shouted the Duke, feeling that some observation was required of him.

Mr. Stacy tucked his hands into his sleeves and appeared to go into a doze. Duke George helped himself to more wine, spilling a good deal of it. There was a dull interval. Finally the secretary said :

"The only way I see, my Lord, is to make the lady willing to hide herself."

"You're a silly fool," said Duke George. "You're a damned silly fool. How the devil are we to make her want to hide herself; hide herself from little peeky priggish Richard? She wouldn't want to hide herself from Richard. You don't understand, you silly fool; must be thinking of somebody else. I just told you she's in love with Richard. God damn you, what are you such a silly fool for when I'm talking to you?"

"I try to be of help, your Grace."

143

"That's right, Stacy; good Stacy! You be of help. That's right."

"After all, your Grace, there's no need to tell her that the Duke of Gloucester is in search of her, or that the King's inclined to mercy."

"That's right."

"She is a captured rebel. Suppose—only suppose, your Grace—that she were in terror of King Edward's severity. Suppose she expected nothing but harsh treatment, humiliation. You have befriended her; might bear her a timely warning that King Edward's bent on extremes. You heard it in the Cabinet Council this morning; can protect her no longer. Her only chance—escape, flight, hiding; even disguise or a change of name."

"Sanctuary : she'd only go into sanctuary, and then little whorson Dickon'd go and get her out again. Come out, little Anne, and I'll marry you and have half the Warwick lands, and poor goddam' George can hang himself. That's what : poor George."

"Not sanctuary, your Grace : but that could be avoided. The King has got himself a certain name as touches sanctuaries. There was that very questionable piece of dealing after Tewkesbury. It would be easy to tell the Lady Anne that the Church could not protect her any more than it did Edmund Beaufort."

"Tewkesbury Abbey had no right of sanctuary, though. Abbot told me so himself; told Edward so : quite different."

Mr. Stacy sighed loudly and clicked his fingers.

"The Lady Anne doesn't know that. We're not debating what's the truth, but what we can make her think's the truth. Listen to me, my Lord."

"I am listening," said Duke George indignantly.

"If we can persuade the Lady Anne that neither your protection nor even the liberties of the Church can shelter her from the extreme vengeance of the King; and if, that done, we leave the door open and look the other way, what will she do? She'll run : a brave, high-spirited young lady, not afraid of a small risk to save a greater one. She'll disappear."

"Clever," said the Duke heavily, "clever : but what I want to know is, how do we persuade her in the first place?"

Mr. Stacy pondered that, his hands in his sleeves again.

Duke George's sensations of discomfort were lodged in his stomach now, leaving his brain a little clearer. He stared at his long-toed shoes for some time and compared them unfavourably with the jewelled pair he had seen on Edward's feet that morning : a dressy fellow, Edward, with his silks and enamels, a vain dressy peacock of a fellow, always thinking of the ladies—a wencher.

"Holy St. Catherine !" yelled the Duke suddenly.

Mr. Stacy jumped violently. Duke George pointed an uncertain finger at him and shut one eye.

"Edward's a wencher," he said solemnly. The information did not appear to convey anything, so he repeated it. "Edward's a wencher, lecher, an evil liver. No decent woman's safe from him. Elizabeth Lucy, Lady Elenor Butler : he played a very naughty game with them. No woman's honour . . ."

A slow, beatified smile, like the smile of a cat, dawned and widened on the tight-mouthed face of Mr. Stacy.

"Subtle," he said in a small, satisfied voice, "subtle—oh, very cunning !"

"My sister-in-law's honour," said Duke George, twisting a thick tongue round the words, his eyes closing, "my sister-in-law's honour : I must warn her. Fly, hide, save herself, not to be dishonoured."

Anthony Wydvylle, Lord Rivers, hesitated on the stairs leading from the banqueting-hall. The night was cool and clear, with few clouds, and a great gout of moonlight slithered, bland as milk-of-almonds, down the square, despotic mass of the White Tower, making the blind fortress that Bishop Gundulph built for the Conqueror four centuries ago ride like a ship before the eyes. The rest of the party who had supped that evening in the Tower of London were ahead, following the small figure of the Duke of Gloucester. The Duke had abruptly suggested a turn in the fresh air after they had discussed the armament he was taking to Sandwich in the morning against the Bastard of Fauconberg. Lord Anthony watched them. They had turned left toward Tower Green, and might be proposing either a circuit of the Inner Bailey, bringing them back to the point from which they started, or an emergence upon the river-front to watch the few barges of night-roysterers sliding home to London and hear the water-men singing. They were at the foot of the Garden Tower now. Perhaps they only meant to stroll round the little enclosed pleasance and pick some fruit of which Duke Richard was notoriously fond. But no : the Duke had stopped for a second to speak over his shoulder to someone, and now they were all trooping like sheep into the Outer Bailey. Lord Anthony, conscious of a certain tickling in his midriff, turned and beckoned into the shadows behind him to Sir John Fogg. The disappearance of that little figure, clearly etched by moonlight at the head of its troop of larger followers, had made the whole situation realler, more immediate for him. He and Sir John Fogg walked quickly onto the Green and, without ceremony, pushed open the door of the Lieutenant's lodging. Richard Hawte, the Chief Warder, had been waiting for them; was just inside the door. His tanned face was stiff except for the mouth, which moved a little.

"They've gone into the Outer Bailey," said Lord Anthony.

"I know. That's very near where . . . very near us. If they heard anything?"

"We must do it quietly, then."

Sir John Fogg pushed softly past Lord Anthony's shoulder. The light from inside the lodging showed up his face with the disproportionate cheekbones and the glistening lips. He said in a wet whisper :

"Have you a sword?"

"Here," said Richard Hawte, who was himself girt with one. He stepped back into the narrow lobby and brought out an unsheathed two-handed sword; passed it over. "I sharpened it."

"Good," said Sir John Fogg. He tucked the blade under his arm as a schoolmaster would his ferrula; tapped Lord Anthony gently. "Time we were moving, sir : not long to waste."

"The sooner the better," said Lord Anthony, swallowing. Why the devil isn't there a sheath to that sword, he thought : carrying a naked blade like that, advertising our purpose to everyone. I argued for it this morning against them all, and now don't like it : the craziness of what we wish and what we get, contradiction; Fortune always wrying the opposite way from us at the last minute.

A warder challenged them at the foot of the Wakefield Tower. Richard Hawte stood in front of him and said calmly :

"Bring your fellows down here to me, everyone out of the tower, quickly; and make no noise."

The man's eyes showed in the moonlight. He went up the tiny staircase, and there was a wait. Lord Anthony's silk-sheathed legs began to quiver. Then broad shoulders of men bobbed out of the narrow doorway, one behind another.

"Now your keys," said Hawte softly.

Something jingled and was given him by someone. Lord Anthony had turned to look at the White Tower again, not meaning any of them to recognise his face. Footsteps went away quietly, the men not talking. Hawte's voice said :

"They are gone now, my Lord."

This is the way, thought Lord Anthony, up this dark stairway, with the King's permission, so that no one may question us, so that all England must keep its mouth shut. This is our safety, mine, Elizabeth's, all our house who are secure only in the King's security. He found he was at the top of the stairs and before a door.

"Remember," he told Sir John Fogg, "not till I say."

Hawte's face, in the light of the spitting and stinking flambeau at the stairhead, worked obscurely. He licked his lips.

"You'll be rewarded for this," said Lord Anthony.

"I'm in your hands, sir," said the Chief Warder, and unlocked the door.

The room was very simply furnished, and only a rush-light, doubled up so that both ends burned, showed the plain table, the buffet with a pottle of wine and pitcher of water beside a wooden cup, and the low truckle-bed. Some books stood on a small clothes-chest in the window alcove, and opposite was the arch, contrived in the thickness of the wall, of a little oratory. This was well furnished. Gospels and Missal, their illuminated pages showing in the poor light as puddles of colour, were open on the cushioned prie-dieu, and above them, in painted alabaster, Christ bled between the two Marys, who held up folded, resigned hands, whilst on the one side God, the bearded Father, received the corpse into his lap, and on the other the Holy Ghost, a golden dove, swooped down upon the twelve

147

Apostles. Candles were on a pricket below, not lighted yet. The smell of the room was close and old.

In a chair by the table, his hand propping his head over a book, sat the man Lord Anthony had seen more than once before and did not mean to see again, Holy Harry of Windsor, Duke of Lancaster, recipient from the Pope, for piety, of the Golden Rose, once King of England and France and Lord of Ireland. He wore a plain frieze gown to his ankles and there was a knotted cord round his waist. He did not move at once, but presently, with a slowness that gave the movement some false air of cunning, he turned his face. Yellow-grey tangles of hair sprouted uncertainly round his small mouth. His face was long, chinless, the forehead low and the eyes wandering, unable to focus themselves certainly on anything.

"You are welcome, gentlemen."

His voice was unnaturally high, toneless, and as inexpressive as a bird's cheep. His whole personality affected Lord Anthony, as it had always done, with a sense of distance from reality, from the live world. Lazarus, he thought, might have looked with such unmeaning eyes, and spoken so. Lazarus had lived and died and lived again; and Holy Harry, in the real world of men and policies, had also risen from the grave for a little, and must be put into a surer grave now.

It was Sir John Fogg, surprisingly, who answered the greeting as though he had not a drawn sword under his arm.

"We wish you good evening, my Lord of Lancaster."

He spoke with the suavity of a tooth-drawer at a country fair. It shan't hurt, I promise you. Open your gob a trifle wider and trust me. Holy Harry of Windsor appeared to consider his words a moment; then said:

"There have been lights, music, one of those ceremonies they made me attend. I would rather be without them. This is the Tower, I think. Who is in the Tower to-night?"

"The Duke of Gloucester."

All the muscles in Holy Harry's face moved, as though trying to produce some human and comprehensible expression. He dropped back in his chair; crossed himself.

"No," he said urgently, "no, Gloucester is dead. My Lords and commons—and you, my Lords Spiritual—I call

148

all of you to witness I am innocent. They say he was murdered, but it is a lie. He died of palsy. Truly, truly, I would never have consented to put him to death."

With a chill of complete horror, Lord Anthony realised that Henry was talking of his uncle, the Good Duke Humphrey, who had died mysteriously in prison twenty-four years ago. He said, scarcely aware of his own words:

"No one accuses you. Gloucester of York, Duke Richard, Edward of Rouen's brother, supped here to-night. The title has been conferred again."

"He was a loud-voiced man," said Harry of Windsor, looking nowhere: "hurt my ears, shouting: but I never meant his death. It is written, 'Blessed are the merciful.' They blame me for so many things: and Gloucester was always an accursed Dukedom; does not prosper. But, sirs, I have hated bloodshed all my life. The brave Suffolk: they struck his head off over a ship's side like a common pirate, and my cousin Somerset; and Bishop Aiscough; they stoned him. Oh, sirs, what wickedness that was, to kill a priest of God."

"The commonwealth is at peace now," said Sir John Fogg.

"I know. The angels told me. I heard guns last week, the mortal noise of them, killing men, displeasing our Lord God. Then two angels came. They were all in very pure white and under their feet was like fire, and they told me there would be no more killing. Donum Spiritus sancti est pax. They told me, and they stayed with me more than an hour, to comfort me."

Behind Lord Anthony, Hawte was praying softly under his breath. The hair on Lord Anthony's neck prickled and his fingers shook. Harry of Windsor, in his meaningless voice, went on:

"They are not angry with me because I am King of England. The angels are not angry with me. My father and my grandfather were Kings, anointed; and if there has been blood shed in my time, my Lords, truly I am not to blame. Sitis homines benevolentiae, I told them, et caritatis, sicut filii patris uni, qui est Deus, Dominus noster; but they do not listen to me as they ought to, gentlemen: rash, violent men, full of pride and anger, quaerentes quem devorent. Are we not told that bloodthirsty and deceitful

149

men shall not live out half their days? But the angels were not angry with me."

None of the three visitors had moved from his original position by the door. Hawte said aloud, like a man at the end of his strength : "Christ !"

Harry of Windsor heard him and blessed himself again.

"In Him only is our salvation," he said. His vague eyes turned on them and showed momentarily like the eyes of a sane man, aware of what they saw. "But you are not angels," he said slowly. "Why do you visit me?"

Lord Anthony gulped for words. His tongue and throat were perfectly dry and the roots of his hair wet. Again it was Sir John Fogg who got command of his voice first.

"We have come to hear you say your prayers."

Harry of Windsor got very unsurely onto his feet. He was a small man, his back so bowed that he looked dwarfish. He peered from one of their faces to another, pleased, smiling and nodding.

"It is always good to pray, gentlemen. I take it kindly of you: a christian thought to join an old man at his prayers. I have prayed mostly alone these many years back; but it is written that where two or three are gathered together our dear Redeemer will be with them. You are kind."

He picked up the rushlight in its iron stand and went shakily across his prison. His feet slurred and dragged and he went very slowly; paused once or twice to nod and smile at them over the flame of the light, with the look of a dog that knows it is performing the trick wanted of it. Lord Anthony felt as though the thudding in his chest would spring his ribs apart. At that moment, to kill even an armed man with his bare hands would have been easier, he thought, than to give the sign for falling upon this insane, humble little monster, this quite unhuman thing that went, so pleased and obedient, to the shambles, and so feebly, with such patience in its feebleness, lit candles at the feet of the holy images, sparingly pinched out the flame of the rushlight, got down with difficulty onto its knees. The candles were of fine wax and burned up clearly. In their light the cold alabaster trunk of Christ, ribbed and meagre, took a more human colour. A streak of scarlet blood hung like a banner down the pierced side. The head was thrown back in the last pains, and big blood-drops like tears spattered the cheeks.

"Dilexi, quoniam exaudiet Dominus vocem meam . . ." said Holy Harry of Windsor clearly. Sir John Fogg had worked his way round the table and stood over him, the sword clasped in both hands. Richard Hawte, his face as white as paper, was moving with slow steps toward the pair of them. Lord Anthony's breath roared into his lungs. Sir John Fogg's pink-rimmed eyes were fixed on him.

"Circumdederunt me funes mortis, et angustiae inferni invenerunt me . . ."

"Now," groaned Lord Anthony.

Sir John Fogg's sword flashed like a fish in the candle-light. Richard Hawte swiped sideways, not taking aim. There was a miserable thin scream like a rabbit's, and Holy Harry, his hands clutching the ledge of the prie-dieu, tried to stand up. "Again, you fool!" shouted Sir John Fogg, and chopped down at him. Lord Anthony saw a thin hand tossed up, empty and open, like a drowning man's. Then Richard Hawte, with a sob, whirled his sword back. There was a crash as the blade caught and overturned the pricket of candles. Shadows flapped like a blown cloak up the walls of the room and closed into darkness full of Hawte's voice screaming: "Oh God, God!"

God was not there. Lord Anthony, with the darkness pressing itself on his wet face, felt as though God, even the anger of God, had left the Wakefield Tower when the light left it. Only the devil was there now, moving among them who were turned over to him. Lord Anthony felt his close moving presence in the dark, like a cat's presence, and cried out, pushing his hands forward. Then there was red blazing light and, as he turned round, a face in the light as though it were the face of punishment. Duke Richard of Gloucester, holding a torch plucked from the stairs, was looking at him.

Sir John Fogg was by the prie-dieu, his lips drawn back like a weasel's and his sword on guard, blood weeping in slow drops from the point of it. Hawte had his arms crossed on the wall and his face buried in them. Harry of Windsor lay on his back. Lord Anthony saw the black, plaintive gape of his mouth and the twist of one hacked arm. Blood spread from him. Duke Richard saw too. He

151

moved forward, spilling light round him, and found an iron ring in the wall; fixed his torch in it; came back to the body. Without looking at the others he knelt down and, picking up the dead hands, joined them together. He remained kneeling, his own hands folded, his lips whispering; and for a long while the only noises in the Wakefield Tower were Hawte's sobbing breath and the low, rapid sibilation of prayers. Then the Duke blessed himself and got up; came across the room to Lord Anthony. Even in the warm light of the flambeau his face was colourless, and his screwed, narrowed eyes looked out of it like points of swords. Lord Anthony went back until the wall stopped him.

"You have won a great victory," said Duke Richard, "I will not stay to spoil your pleasure in it."

Lord Anthony's eyes fell, and he saw the Duke's right hand with four splendid rings. It was smeared and dribbling with blood from what he had just touched. Duke Richard looked at it. Then his left hand shot out like an adder striking. Lord Anthony felt himself caught by the breast of the doublet and jerked brutally forward.

"This blood should not be on me," said Duke Richard and wiped his hand deliberately, twice, across Lord Anthony's face.

CHAPTER FOUR

MIDDLEHAM

(*England: 1472*)

I will abide till she be ready,
I will her sue if she say nay,
If she be reckless I will be greedy,
If she be dangerous I will her pray:
If she weep, then bide I ne may,
Mine arms been spread to clip her me to.
Cry once—I come: now soul, assay.

Quia amore langueo.

English devotional poem :
fifteenth century.

THE Widow Wrangwysh picked her teeth and debated her recurrent Saturday evening problem : whether to send round the corner for the chantry-priest or shout down the staircase for her little cookmaid. Her Saturday evenings constituted the chief remaining pleasure of the widow's life. Old age had plucked the articles of her faith from her almost as lavishly as it had her hairs. She had never believed in God, and did not now believe in the saints either. But she retained a certain affection for the Blessed Virgin, as a married woman who had known the pains of childbed. Having buried three husbands and thirteen children (her one surviving daughter was in a convent), the widow could appreciate those things, and Saturday being the day sacred to God's blessed Lady, she always over-ate herself on Saturday evenings, and then looked round for entertainment. This, during the past six months, had taken one of two forms. If she felt like talking bawdy, she would send out for a flagon of claret and the chantry-priest. If she wanted to discuss politics, she had up a half-gallon of pudding-ale and her little cookmaid.

The weekly debate between these two prospects gave her Saturday suppers a new relish. She even caught herself wondering whether perhaps our Lady herself might not have guided the little maid—her name, oddly enough, was that of our Lady's mother, Anne—to knock on her door asking for work and lodging. She had been, she said, in the kitchens of the Duke of Clarence's house—which was a recommendation—and one of his pages, whom the widow knew, had suggested her home as one where she might be able to find quieter employment. The Ducal kitchen was too rough and rowdy for her. She certainly looked a delicate little thing, with her mousy ways, her pale face rather flushed over her cheekbones, her light-brown soft hair and her short upper lip. The widow, who was not straitlaced, overlooked the very odd informality of her application and took her on for fourpence a month and all found. But young Anne—nobody ever learned her second name—had not been in the house a week before it became patent that she was no more a cookmaid than her mistress was an Abbess. In the first place, she knew precisely nothing at all about cooking. If hers were a fair sample of his household's skill, then the Duke of Clarence was more indifferent to the pleasures of the table than the widow, who had seen him, had any reason to believe. Again, her hands were small and almond-white; did not at all give the impression of being accustomed to sossing and possing in greasy water, scouring trenchers and drawing fowl. Her speech was too clear and gentle for a plain woman; was by a long way more courtly than the widow's own : and she knew French. A lousy Breton pedlar had arrived at the door one day, jabbering ten words of French to one of English, and little Anne had answered up to him as pat as a clerk. The fellow was delighted; jabbered faster than ever; packed out all his gaudy trash ware, and finally said something that, judged by his grin, was an impertinence. What followed astonished the Widow Wrangwysh as much as if her pet cat Gib had metamorphosed himself into a crocodile. The mousy little Anne appeared to grow six inches taller. Her eyes narrowed and she said something that sounded like the swish of a sword in the air. The grin fell off the pedlar's face and left his mouth gaping. He stammered what was evidently an apology, and got two more words that sent him backward through the door sweeping the dust off the step with his bonnet. Anne did not wait to see him go. She turned her back and marched off with her small chin jutting. The Widow Wrangwysh was fat and lazy and inclined to tipple, but she was not a fool. She barred her maid's way.

"And where did you learn French, my girl?"

Anne's face changed all over again. She reddened. Her eyes were big and unsure and she twisted her fingers together, stammering.

"Why—I was in France, mistress—with the Duke's household."

"Hum," said the Widow Wrangwysh, "come up into the solar."

She grunted her way up the stairs into the sun-parlour on the first floor, Anne following, and lowered herself into the best chair. Then she folded her hands on her stomach and looked hard at her.

"What your trouble may be that makes you hide here, I don't know," she said, "nor who you are nor where you come from. But one thing's certain. You've no more been in the Duke of Clarence's kitchen than I've been in King Edward's bed. Now I don't say I'll be unkind to you, but you'll be best to tell me the truth."

Then, with hesitancies and lip-biting, but without tears, it all came out. She was not a cookmaid; came of gentry, a knight's daughter, and had been one of the maids-in-waiting upon the Duchess Isobel, the Duke's wife. There was someone at Court, a great person, so powerful that even the Duke of Clarence could not offend him, and an evil liver. She had been frightened. There seemed no escape from him; and she had run.

"The dirty hound," said the Widow Wrangwysh perfunctorily; "but hadn't you a mother and father to go to, wench?"

"My mother is in sanctuary in the West Country. My father—was killed at Barnet Heath."

"Ah, Barnet Battle," moralised the widow, her interest in politics getting the better of her, "a sad bloody garboyle. I went to Paul's after it to see Kingmaker's body while it was on show there. Lying on the pavement, he was, all naked down to the middle. He made a lovely corpse."

"Don't," said Anne. The widow looked sharply at her.

"Why, what's amiss?"

"I knew him."

"You knew the great Earl?"

"My father was—was of his household."

"Christ," said the Widow Wrangwysh. It was dawning slowly on her that she was now to enjoy those intimate glimpses of the great world for which she had hungered all her life.

After that there was no longer any pretence of Anne's working in the kitchen. She continued to eat and sleep with the other servants and to do a few light jobs about the house; but her real business was to entertain her mistress with gossip of the Court and the nobility with tales of King Edward and his brothers Clarence and Gloucester, of Holy Harry (whose funeral procession, with more glaves and staves about the bier than torches, the widow had seen dragging its slow course to St. Paul's last May), of Queen Elizabeth and her swarm of haughty relatives, and of the great Lancastrian Lord, the Duke of Somerset, whom it seemed Anne had known also. "He was a blackbrowed man," she said of him, "with a grim face. They say he was very cruel and always for blood-letting; but he was kind to me." On two subjects only, the widow found it difficult to get much out of her. She would never hint at which of the great nobles about Court it was whose lust had made her run and hide, and she would never talk of Kingmaker. "I did not know him well," she said.

For the widow, it was all magic and the blowing of trumpets. Curtains of noble arras were swung back before her. Mirrors in ivory frames were held up to show this world in which people washed several times a day, in which a hanging was a thing to order rather than to run and watch, in which ladies who swore and talked bawdy were not looked askance on, as she was by her primmer neighbours, and in which it was considered vulgar and provincial for a man to beat his wife. It was a world that had always twinkled and beckoned at her from the distance. Though she was seventy-four and sometimes (generally on Sunday mornings) felt every year of it, she had never missed a procession, a royal wedding or christening or funeral. Born in the year that Harry Bolingbroke put down and murdered Richard of Bordeaux, she could remember, as a tiny girl, hearing the London bells peal for the death of Hotspur at Shrewsbury. Ten years later, only a month or so before her first marriage, she had heard the babble in the streets drop suddenly to a whisper as the rumour spread out in rings from Westminster Abbey that Harry IV—that tubby, melancholy little man with the neat beard and the tumour at his jaw—had been seized with the pains of death at the very moment when he was kneeling to ask God's mercy on his manifold wickednesses. She had seen his brown-haired long-nosed son, Harry of Monmouth, ride down Cheapside to be crowned; but it was only later, after her first husband's death (he was an old man, and did not last her long), that the real fun began : bells banging and crowds cheering for the fall of Rouen; the same bells tolling slowly and the same crowds standing bareheaded in the November rain when the victor of Azincourt came home for the last time, a painted dummy in royal clothes lying over a thin corpse sheeted in lead; years of bad news, and broken men home from the wars, cursing and looking awry as they heard that Orleans was relieved by witchcraft, Talbot was made prisoner by witchcraft, Rheims was taken by witchcraft : and then the same bells banged and clanged again and drunken men shouted to one another that the witch had burned, burned, burned at Rouen. In the years after that, politics, that since Azincourt had been mostly rumours from beyond the Channel, came suddenly home again and a mob fired London Bridge and shouted a new name : "Mortimer." Mrs. Wrangwysh (she had just married her third, a Yorkshire woolman settled in London) gathered that Mortimer was the family name of the Duke of York and that many held he ought to be King in place of Holy Harry of Windsor, who was addled anyway. She could hardly have foreseen, though, that Jack Cade's commotion was the egg from which so many of the large public happenings that spiced her life were presently to hatch. The battle of St. Albans took her completely unawares. Nothing had given her or her husband any cause to anticipate it. Simply one morning the news came that the Duke of York and the Earl of Warwick had put on their harness and killed the Duke of Northumberland, the Duke of Somerset, the Earl of Stafford and Lord Clifford, and brought the King back to London as a prisoner : and so in a moment, the War of the

Roses, with its inexhaustible banquet of funerals, executions, progresses, coronations and grand marriages, was spread out for her enjoyment. She was so engrossed by it that she might hardly have noticed the death of her last husband, had not the formalities of mourning most annoyingly prevented her from going to see the Rose of Rouen—certainly the handsomest of the four Kings whom she remembered—crowned at Westminster after the battle of Towton.

To have so much stirring coloured stuff about her in her old age was good : but to be able, through Anne's eyes, to get such intimate glimpses of the harnessed and silk-dressed people whom she had seen riding in processions was intoxicating. She learnt with a warm thrill that King Edward's favourite oath was "By God's Blessed Lady," as it was her own; that the Duke of Gloucester was ridiculously fond of strawberries; that the Queen, who had been nothing but a poor knight's widow till the King set eyes on her, was now so self-pleased that her own mother had to kneel in her presence on the cold floor.

The widow re-settled herself in her chair and banged on the table. She had less difficulty to-night in making up her mind than usual. There was a letter from her young brother-in-law, Thomas Wrangwysh of York. Anne had read it to her once that day, but there were parts of it she wished to hear again. As someone moved below-stairs, she shouted :

"Send Anne up here, and a half-gallon."

Anne's step was always very light and delicate. One would not have thought she weighed more than a bird. She came into the room now with a walnut mazer and a tall, iron-hooped wooden jack.

"You wanted me?"

"Sit you down, dear : sit you down and we'll have a crack."

"I'll fetch my embroidery, then."

"Do, my dear soul. It helps a body talk better if she's got her hand moving. Pour me a sup before you go."

The syrup-thick black beer swished into the mazer with a soothing noise. Blessed Virgin, thought the widow, where would we all be without ale? Ale and somebody to crack with and have a bit of a laugh and hear the fine things there are doing in the world : it's not much I want.

Anne was back again with her broidering-frame. She lit the rushlights, and the worn, painted cloth on the solar walls, the good stonework of the fireplace and the fine pewter on the buffet came to life. The table bore the hacked remnants of the widow's supper: a roast leg of pork stuffed with garlic, a veal lèche, a dish of candied quinces and a green-ginger tart. The widow pointed to it.

"Have a bite now. I've left plenty."

Anne shook a meek head.

"I supped with the others."

"Well, you could do with a morsel more, a growing wench. It's good: better than you could cook, dear God knows. See here." She spread her considerable bosom over the edge of the table, leaning to cut a wedge of tart and give it to the girl between her fingers. Then she took a fistful of quinces; bundled them into her own mouth. "When you've done, read me brother Tom's letter again. It's a nice letter."

Anne brought the thick-scrawled sheet from the buffet and held it to the rushlight; began in her very clear, gentle voice to read:

"To my sister Jonet, dwelling at the Silver Pack in Eastcheap:

"DEAR SISTER,

"I greet you well, letting you know that I am in good health, loved be God, and I shall send you presently some good dried eels, I think you have none such in London; and dear sister, if you can by any means purvey me a piece of good bawdekin cloth sufficient for one gown, cheap, I pray you that you do so for love of me, and I shall pay you.

"Item: that the Duke of Gloucester is come among us in these North parts and dwelling at Middleham, and men say he shall bear rule in all these North parts for the King, and he is worshipfully accompanied and doth promise a good rule and amending of felonies and such great riots as have of late been in these parts, as men say. I pray God it be so.

"Item: that there are many here in York that grudge sorely at the great landlords, and in especial the Abbot of St. Mary's, for their fishgarths and traps that they set

159

up in the rivers for taking of the fish, whereby many poor men, fishermen and other, are deprived of their bread; and in truth it is a great shame as ever I saw; and they say they shall go up to the Duke of Gloucester and complain of such traps which were never allowed of old custom. But I know not what shall befall.

"And God speed you, my dear sister,

"written at York with the hand of your brother,
"THO. WRANGWYSH."

"That's a nice letter," said the widow : "news in it. The Duke of Gloucester, I saw him when the King came back from Tewkesbury field. Riding on a white horse, he was : a little fellow."

Anne had sat back from the rushlight. She said in the dreaming, lazy voice that, her mistress knew, marked the beginning of reminiscences.

"So he's at Middleham."

"Did you know the place, dear?"

"He was a child at Middleham," Anne's voice continued, "in my Lord of Warwick's care : very small, but hardy. He liked a big horse and a heavy spear. I think he was a little ashamed to be so tiny; wanted to show us that he was not weak with it. He could unhorse boys bigger than himself."

"Lord now, and you knew him when he was a child. Fancy that, now. Go on, dear."

"He liked Middleham; told me so. I'm glad he's got it for his own now. Do you suppose he remembers the old times there?"

"Nay . . .," the widow was uncertain how to deal with the question, "you say he was there when he was a little one. He'll remember it. Well, God's flesh, I could find my way about Canterbury streets myself now, me that's not been there since before I wed my first."

"He liked the country. It's dour land in Yorkshire, and there is much rain, though it never seems to make the fields green."

"Aye, so my husband said. I was never in Yorkshire. They say they're a riotous stubborn lot in those parts. The Duke now : d'you think he'll redress the grievances they have?"

Anne laughed very quietly.

"Redress grievances? It's his one thought. When he was

little he told me : 'We think too much of greatness, Anne, as though it were a thing for ourselves. The great are only God's tools and instruments to amend what is displeasing to him.' "

"Now, what a blessed thing to say," approved the Widow Wrangwysh.

"No wrong that Dickon sees will be left unaltered. Those hard landlords with their fishgarths: they don't know what's upon them yet, what a cat they've got among their pigeons."

"And him only young, too."

"Yes, we're both young. I forget that sometimes. But, then, steel's full-grown from the day it leaves the furnace, and when it ages it is only into rust. Dickon is like steel. I always thought that from when I was a tiny girl : steel, anything cold and spare and clear. Nothing will turn his point."

"He sounds a monkish sort to me. Give me a warm man that can laugh, I say."

"Oh, Dickon can laugh : mostly at little things, though. He likes watching birds and puppies, and when he makes a joke he doesn't smile himself."

"Then he'll do well in Yorkshire. My man was the same, and so's his brother Tom. Those Northern folk, they do their laughing with their mouths shut."

"He reads books, too, and remembers them. He used to tell me tales out of old chronicles of Sir Percivale de Galis and Randulph of Chester, and he is fond of singing and music."

"I like a good bawdy song myself," said the widow.

"Not bawdy, but rondels and madrigals and church-singing."

"Ah, well, there's a deal of comfort to be had in sad singing. I mind when I was a girl I always cried at a sung Mass. But he doesn't sound a gay companion like his brothers, Duke Richard."

"He doesn't drink so much as them or play cards or dice; but he's the best dancer at Court next to Edward, and his hands are always cool and he has a gentle voice, not loud."

The Widow Wrangwysh helped herself to ale and narrowed her short-sighted eyes at the girl. One thing was becoming increasingly apparent to her. Whoever was the great personage who had made speeches to young Anne, it

161

was not the Duke of Gloucester. If it had been, she would not have run away.

"Well, he's none the worse for being an honest liver, I hope, God amend all. Some might be the better for following him. There's a fine new tale I heard about the King the other day, a very rusty one. Mr. Shore, the mercer at the sign of the White Hart, must be wishing Holy Harry was on the throne still: God's blessed Lady, yes. He's got a pretty wife, and our good King Edward knows it. When he went to Windsor the last time, they say he took her with him, *malgré* the Queen and all. Was there ever such a bold whoremonger? They say the little dagget-arsed boys in the street make horns with their fingers whenever Mr. Shore steps over his own threshold: and fancy the King of England and a mercer's wife. Oh Lord, I was born too soon and that's the truth of it."

"Edward was always a wencher."

The Widow Wrangwysh started. She was free-tongued herself in her comments upon the doings of great men, and was used by now to Anne's simple assumption of familiarity —almost of equality—with them: but even so, she was unaccustomed to hearing the foibles of an anointed King dismissed quite in that tone of indifference and distaste, as though one were discussing the habits of the cat or the parish priest.

"Lord save us, girl!"

"He always was, though."

"Well, I've heard tales myself. There was talk of the Lady Elenor Butler, long ago, before he married. Did you know her too? Nay, you'd be too young."

"I heard her spoken of. They say he dishonoured her and she married one Lord Sudeley to cover her shame up, and is dead."

"Poor soul! God's blessed Lady have pity on us women, I say; and she ought to, being a woman herself."

"Amen."

"But I must say I'm surprised the Queen doesn't take order with him. Christ, I'd 've liked to see any of my three —god rest 'em—taking their whores on a journey. I'd 've had the hair off them."

"Queen Elizabeth," said Anne in a voice that came from the back of her throat, "was a poor knight's widow until

162

Edward married her. If she thinks she can please him best by sitting mumchance whilst he has his sport, I'm sure she'll do it."

"And I've known some wives rule their husbands very cleverly that way. Those whorson Wydvylles, though: I never liked them. Taxes and tallages have been higher ever since he married amongst 'em. That's true as the Mass: and they're very cruel, too. There was poor good Sir Thomas Cooke, was my last husband's friend, that they made up a moonshine charge of treason against. The old Lord Rivers and Sir John Fogg seized his goods and houses and put him in the Counter in Breadstreet; and there he must stay, poor soul, until he paid eight thousand pounds—think of it, child, eight thousand pounds!—for a fine: and over and above that, may God wither and rot my tongue but the Queen claims eight hundred marks from him as a gift or a privilege or I don't know what. Robbery's what it was: and he was as much a traitor as I'm the Pope. But the cursed Wydvylles had some like of a spite against him, and King Edward listened to them, and there was a poor honest man, and my kind friend and my husband's, beggard and broken."

Anne did not say anything to that immediately. Her hand flashed back and forth at her embroidery. Presently she shrugged.

"Richard was right. We think too much of greatness, as though it were a thing for ourselves; and most of all if we were not born to greatness, but come creeping up to it."

The Widow Wrangwysh took a fresh pull of ale and nodded her head.

"You talk as if you were a Princess yourself, child, but by God's holy body and blood you're right. There's more poor folk than Princes and Lords in the realm of England, but the Princes and Lords never heed it; and there's the trouble."

Middleham Castle woke up at dawn: servants with tousled hair coming out from their quarters in the East Ward, crossing the moat by the bridge into the Inner Ward and getting about their business. It was a clear Northern dawn, blue and cold and with birds singing. Horses stamped loudly and whinnied and cocks crew from the East Ward.

The night-watch from the gate stumbled up the narrow stairs, spitting and yawning, and the day-watch came down to take their place. There was a crackle and flash of sun-gilt wings from the dovecote on the Keep. A flight of pigeons shot out across the battlements, made a wide circuit above the wakening village of Middleham, and came back again. In the bedchamber at the South end of the Inner Ward two grooms of the chamber and two pages set about their morning function of awakening Duke Richard of Gloucester, Warden of the West Marches against Scotland and Steward of the Duchy of Lancaster beyond Trent.

They brought two silver basins of warm water scented with ambergris, armsful of warm linen napkins and a lidded silver tankard topped with the boar that was Duke Richard's cognisance. One groom drew back the arras of the window and set the shutters wide. The other went on tiptoe to the bed, which resembled a pavilion : a great scaffolding of painted and gilded wood with escutcheons of the royal arms differenced for cadency and surmounted by ducal coronets. Its hangings, that closed it in completely, were of green velvet worked with coroneted cyphers of RG. alternating with silver boars and complex scrolls of the Duke's motto : Loyaulte me lie. The groom made the sign of the cross very perfunctorily and drew the hangings on the side nearest the window. The Duke of Gloucester was discovered with his head resting on a frilled pillow of silk and swansdown five times the width of his small shoulders.

He was already awake; pushed his long hair out of his eyes and smiled drowsily at the groom, who said in a hushed voice :

"Your Grace is served."

"Good," said the Duke.

He sat up, naked, the linen sheets dropping down his spare, youthful body to the waist. His skin was almost dazzlingly white and hairless. There was no fat on him, and the narrowness of his hips made his chest, by comparison, startlingly broad. It was noticeable that his right arm—the arm with which he plied the battle-axe—was more developed than his left, so that its greater weight of muscle seemed to have dragged the shoulder down a little. The groom swaddled him in a loose heavy bedgown of squirrel's fur reversed with miniver and turned the cloth-of-gold counterpane and linen sheets back. Duke Richard smiled again, swung his slim boy's legs out of the bed and suffered a page to put his feet in slippers. The second groom served him, kneeling, with his morning draught of small beer in which rosemary, thyme, borrage, hyssop and vervain had been bruised. He drank about a third of it and crossed to the cushioned stool that had been set for him. The elder page presented his ewer of scented water and the younger towels, sponge and Castille soap. The Duke washed his head and body and wiped himself down while a groom rubbed his hair dry. The early light shone, as on ivory, on the separate points of his spine and the bosses of his shoulders. The second ewer was presented, with clean napkins and a silver-gilt box containing a powder of lye, borax and pumice. Dipping a napkin first in the water and then in the powder, the Duke cleaned his teeth, spat vigorously and took another pull from the tankard. His silk shirt was now put on him and laced to the throat. The pages drew his plain green hose over his legs, pulling and stroking so that not a wrinkle showed. There was a discreet tapping at the door and a groom let in the barber. The Duke's beard was of the slightest, hardly more than a boy's down. The barber left his face glass-smooth; trimmed the hair at the nape of his neck with a great pair of shears; scented, combed and brushed his long, straight locks; bowed himself out. A green doublet with silver ouches in the form of boars, tall yellow leather boots and a yellow leather baldric with a long hunting-dagger finished the toilet. The senior groom un-locked a small nail-studded coffer and produced a tray of rings. The Duke chose seven of them and was ready for Mass.

His quick feet sounded along the hautpace, the wooden bridge that joined the bedchamber and the keep. Its un-glazed windows let in the sun and morning air, and the little Duke paused halfway across to take a breath or two; then went briskly into the Chamber of Presence, where the gentlemen of his household were assembled. He met them with his coldly charming smile, talked for a moment with his Secretary, Mr. John Kendal, a blue-eyed Yorkshireman with a mouth like a trap; and on the first clang of the bell led them through the Great Hall into the small second-floor

Chapel, where the candles burned and the chaplain and his acolyte were robed and ready.

The sacrifice was conducted with neither unseemly haste nor drawling slowness. There was no shuffling and whispering among those who watched it. It was a known fact that the Duke actually regarded an impertinence to God as seriously as an impertinence to himself. On "Ita, missa est," he led them out again. Breakfast was served in the Great Hall; but Duke Richard, attended by one groom and one page, took his in the Privy Chamber. A sparing eater, he was content with a pint of small beer, demain bread, a cold game pie and a fistful of cherries. He did not speak once during the meal and, the moment it was over, muttered a short grace and retired across the West hautpace to the Garderobe Tower. No one followed him.

Meanwhile, the Chamber of Presence was filling up again. The Auditor had his weekly accounts to present. The Secretary had letters for signature. A tagrag of people had petitions and reports. The Chamber of Presence had been glorified throughout by the Earl of Warwick only a year or so before his end. Each joist of the high ceiling terminated in a bear clutching a ragged staff with one paw and supporting with the other an escutcheon of one of his innumerable quarterings : the Neville saltire, the Newburgh chevron, the Montacute lozenges, the Beauchamp fess, repeated in order down either side of the long hall. The walls were not hung, but panelled, each panel carved and painted with a device : bear, eagle, ragged staff, pied bull, dun cow. For some reason, Duke Richard had made no move to replace all these with Yorkish bearings, but took his seat each day under the copious blazonry of the man his troops had killed in last year's fog at Barnet.

A door clicked. The gentlemen who had been sitting about the long, carved table on the daïs came to their feet. The commoners standing below uncovered. Duke Richard walked quickly to his chair; sat down and at once beckoned to his head verderer. He meant to kill some driven deer that morning. The man reported three good harts in Sunskew Park. Duke Richard glanced up at the painted Flemish clock on the wall.

"Three hours from now," he said curtly and invited the steward of the household to report on the final preparations for that night's banquet. Noble guests were coming: the great Northumberland on his way back from London to his own marches, the Lords Howard and Lovel, two young men of whom the Duke thought highly, Sir William Parr and Sir James Harrington, Lord Scrope of Bolton, the Duke's next neighbour, and his brother-in-law, Sir Richard Ratcliffe. The steward had a great deal to say for himself. The eels which he had ordered specially from York had not arrived yet. Could a man be sent out along the York road to meet the carrier? Yes. Would my Lord Scrope and Sir Richard Ratcliffe require a bath when they arrived—there were hardly enough bath-tubs? Then they must go without. How many followers would his Grace of Northumberland bring with him? At least a hundred.

"Then I must have another ox killed," said the steward dolefully.

"Do not let that stern necessity weigh too heavily on you," said the Duke, with one of his quick smiles, "and give them plenty of ale. But on no account let any of our servants be drunk till after supper. Have you more?"

"No, your Grace."

"You are excused."

The steward made way for the master of the pages, asking leave to whip a page who had made up a most offensive rhyme about him. What was the rhyme? The master hesitated; hemmed; repeated it in a low voice, his eyes on the floor. Mr. Kendal, the Secretary, suddenly bit his pen, and the Duke passed a ringed hand over his mouth. Then he turned his curious pale eyes on the man and said gently:

"If we punish such little taunts, we acknowledge that they hurt us. It would not go with your dignity to whip the boy. You are excused."

The master bowed and went out, not looking pleased. An old woman from Middleham village took his place. She was very dirty, very shaky, very frightened of everything around her; curtsied several times; muttered. The Duke leaned forward.

"Louder, mother," he said, "I must hear you if I am to help you."

The tale came out under his prompting. She had borrowed a mark. She had borrowed it in desperate need from Mr. Raglan, one of the Duke's stable-grooms, who was a warm man. That was a year ago. Now Mr. Raglan told her that her debt, with interest, was two marks, and if she did not pay by Sunday he would ask leave of the Duke to throw her into the road and take her cottage and her two speckeldy hens and her goat. Christ knew she had no two marks, and she was an old woman. The Duke played with his ring until she had finished and was crying. Then he said simply :

"Call James Ragland."

Mr. Kendal and the Auditor exchanged looks. Unseen by the Duke, Mr. Kendal pulled the corners of his mouth down and jerked his thumb over his shoulder. A red-faced fellow with bow-legs came in, pulling his cap off his head and bowing. The Duke's voice was as remote and gentle as wind murmuring in a cave.

"James, what does a servant deserve who has disgraced his master?"

James looked simple.

"Your Grace?"

"Do you know that woman?"

"What, her? Why, your Grace, has she been so brazen . . .?"

"Mr. Auditor, pay this man one mark and let the steward see that he is out of the Castle before nightfall. Mother, if you will go to my almoner he shall give you something. Next time you are in need, come to me, who am your natural Lord, and not to some cruel man."

James Raglan was on his knees.

"For God's sake have pity on a poor man, my Lord. I've been a good servant to you these many . . ."

"Be silent."

The Duke spoke, though still in a low voice, with such violence that those near him started. He raised his face and voice a little and went on :

"Listen, all of you. There is one sin that Holy Church detests above all; and it shall never be suffered where I am master. Usury is hateful to God. Look at this whore's bastard who would stretch out one miserable mark into two even if he had to break a poor woman's heart with it. Now he will pay for it with his place. Get out, man. Do not let me see you again, or I shall take order with you."

James Raglan rose from his knees and went like a man

168

who has been struck dumb. His fellow-servants made way for him. The Duke signed to a page to lead out the old woman, who was sobbing again and blessing him by many saints. He bowed to her as gravely as if she had been a nun, and was listening, before she was well out of the room, to a man who wanted compensation for damage done to his garden by the deer. Mr. Kendal pointed out sharply that his garden had no business to have spread itself out into Westwood, which was Castle property, though the Rector of Middleham had rights of pasturage in it.

"If a man steals meat from my spit," said the Duke gently, "I do not compensate him for his burnt fingers. Be on your way, my friend. That cock won't fight."

The village ale-taster presented a list of four names of men who had brewed ale without payment of their proper dues. He was told to raise the matter at the next Court Baron. Then came a dispute. Thomas Oakroyd had sold a goose to Edmund Taylor for a shilling on the feast of St. Thomas Martyr, and the money had been paid him across the tomb of St. Alkelda in Middleham Church. It had been further agreed between them that he should have a sitting of eggs from this goose before the last day of August. But now the goose was dead, and Edmund Taylor hung back from the bargain, saying the bird must have been sick before he bought it and Thomas Oakroyd had deceived him. Let the Duke judge between them.

The Duke heard the quarrel out for twenty minutes by the clock on the wall, his face lowered over his joined hands whilst he slid a ring up and down one finger. Then he asked when the goose died. Last Wednesday, if it pleased him, it had been found in the morning, stiff and stark without a wound on its body : most unnatural. The Duke looked at sweating and earnest Edmund Taylor and asked how many geese he had kept in his time.

"Never one before this, your good Grace, and may St. Anthony's fire burn me if ever I keep another. Of all wanchancy fowl that . . ."

"Then I judge the bird miscarried by your ignorance in tending it. Thomas Oakroyd deserves his eggs. Pay him the market price of a sitting across St. Alkelda's tomb and keep hens for the future : and Thomas, see you buy a gallon of ale for you and Edmund out of the money he gives you, so that you part friends."

The two cottagers pulled their forelocks and bumbled out, disputing the number of eggs to a sitting in strong whispers. The Duke leaned back in his big chair and sighed. His pale face was corpse-like, without a vestige of expression, so that it was impossible to tell whether his morning's work intrigued or bored him.

The knot below the daïs had shrunk. The Duke accepted with a smile and a polite word a seigneural tribute of two capons from a married couple who had settled on his land, and declined briskly to give judgment in a case of assault which ought to come before the Court Baron. Then the servants stood back and he attended to his letters. There was a dull screed from Thomas Rotherham, the new Bishop of Lincoln. It was concerned with a fine point of ecclesiastical jurisdiction and written, for reasons known only to the Bishop, his secretary and his God, in Latin. Duke Richard, when Mr. Kendal began the introduction: "Carissimo in Christo filio nostro, illustrissimo principi Richardo duci Gloucestrie, Thomas, permissione divina . . .," held up his hand asked for an abstract of the rest. Having had it, he required Mr. Kendal to look up the law of the matter and draft a suitable answer. "In English," he added. A letter from the steward of Pontefract Castle reporting an outbreak of mange among the hounds there made the Duke frown and pull his lip. There were three letters for his signature: a request to the Mayor and Aldermen of York to investigate a complaint of selling cloth by short measure that had reached Duke Richard's ears, a promise to a small knight of Derbyshire, Sir Richard Revell, to find his son a place at Court if it were possible, and a formal report to King Edward on the state of the municipal artillery of the City of York. They were signed and sealed, and for the next hour the Duke played with his dagger and listened to the Secretary, the Chaplain and the Auditor wrangling over the weekly accounts. A mysterious entry, "to rabbits for the Chaplain, 2/4," threatened to cause friction at one point, the Chaplain, who was also the almoner, explaining that he was not consuming these in secret but distributing them, on the Duke's orders, to needy men.

"Rabbits for God's poor," he said, would have been a more seemly choice of phrase.

Outside the Keep, the business of making ready for the guests went on. New arras was hung and, despite the clear autumn sunshine, perfumed fires were lighted in bed-chambers some of which had been unused since King-maker's day. Bath-tubs, freshly scrubbed, were fitted with new silk curtains. Hens skirled deliriously in the East Ward as the poulterer waded among them, wringing neck upon neck. The eels arrived, and the master-cook, who had already lost his temper for the day, left off work for five minutes to tell the carrier who his father and mother had been. The chief butler was fidgeting on the stair of the Keep, waiting to get the key of the gold-plate chest from Mr. Kendal. In the whole Castle no one was quiet or at ease, and down the sloping village street heads popped from doors at every footstep in hopes of seeing a fine company go by.

The first guests actually arrived well before noon. They were Lord Scrope and his brother-in-law, who had ridden over accompanied only by one squire. Lord Scrope was a dark, cumbrously-built man, just middle-aged. Sir Richard Ratcliffe, rather younger, was red-haired, hard-jawed, blue-eyed, with a bleak look and a rough manner; did not talk much. Both wore plain hunting-dress. Servants took their horses and others ran up the stairs into the Keep to warn the Duke. He met them in the Great Hall; gave his cheek to Lord Scrope, who was his cousin, and his hand to Rat-cliffe; guided them into the Chamber of Presence; called for wine, demain bread and sweetmeats. He had meant to hunt shortly, he explained, but they would perhaps like longer to refresh themselves. Both shook their heads, tossing down malmsey; were ready when he was. They were short-spoken men and looked very rough and large beside him.

The hunt clattered out under the Gate-Tower and swung round below the Castle walls. The brown water of the moat was smeared with blue reflections, and a pair of swans moved proudly and slowly on it. Another, standing on the bank, hobbled with black feet, arching its wings and bending its neck, as the horses passed it. The Duke pointed out to Ratcliffe the mass of the round Drum Tower at the South-west angle of the building, asking what he thought of it.

"Fine strong place," said the guest; "take a deal of winning."

The Duke shook his head.

"Not now," he said, "not with artillery: I tell you, Sir Richard, the day of strong castles is over. I would rather camp in an open field with two great guns than be besieged in the stoutest castle of England."

"Earl of Oxford doesn't think so," grunted Ratcliffe.

That Earl, who had blundered into disaster at Barnet, had since turned pirate and recently seized the strong fort of St. Michael's Mount in Cornwall, from which King Edward's soldiers had not yet dislodged him.

Duke Richard smiled.

"Give me the guns I had the ordering of at Tewkesbury, and in three days I would not leave John Vere three courses of stone to hide his head behind."

"Then I wish you might have them, your Grace. It would be a better world for us with Oxford out of it."

"I see no great harm in the man. He is alone; can do nothing but make a little feeble trouble somewhere on the coast."

"He can join with Henry Tydder in Brittany."

The Duke put back his head and laughed.

"This whispering of the name of Henry Tydder: a bastard not twelve years old and descended by double adultery! I shall never fathom it. Why, there are a good half-dozen English noblemen of our own party who have a better claim to the crown."

"The Welch would follow him," observed Lord Scrope.

"To destruction: my Lord, can you conceive that a Welchman would ever be permitted to hold sway in England?"

They had come to the green place where the deer would be driven out. The Duke had no time that day for a full hunt to hounds, but the prickers and beaters had been at work since before dawn, edging the quarry up into a moderate-sized copse, where they were now surrounded. The huntsmen with their leashes of hounds, the two or three mounted gentlemen, the Duke and his guests spread themselves in a semi-circle. Squires handed round the splendid six-foot yew-wood bows and long hunting-arrows. The Duke, Lord Scrope and Sir Richard Ratcliffe dismounted.

From beyond the copse rose suddenly the shrill babble of those driving the game. The Duke strung his bow with a quick jerk. It was more than a foot taller than himself and made him look vaguely absurd. He tried the wind with a damp finger and waited. There was a crashing and plunging in the copse. A hound gave excited tongue that ended in a yelp as the whip stung it. The crashing stopped; began again. Suddenly, a hart was out of the bracken and bounding diagonally across their view. Lord Scrope, a passionate archer, like all Yorkshiremen, drew his arrow to the head. But before he had loosed it he heard the sharp *plunk* of Duke Richard's bow. The hart leapt with all four feet from the ground and crashed sideways. There was no need to loose the hounds at it. Its legs shivered once and it lay perfectly still. Lord Scrope opened his mouth, but before he had time to speak his congratulations another hart was in view. He sighted, loosed and saw the beast stagger and run on with his arrow in its haunch. He cursed :

"Hell and damnation!"

Sir Richard Ratcliffe planted an arrow in its neck and it stumbled and went slowly down onto its knees; tried twice to rise; dropped flat. A huntsman ran up and slit its throat, keeping a wary eye on the copse in case the appearance of another hart should start the arrows flying.

"I bungled that like a tailor," said Lord Scrope bitterly, "but by St. Hubert the huntsman, your Grace, you're a most marvellous shot."

"Luck," said the Duke shortly.

He had not loosed at the second hart.

"It went over as it had been hit from a crossbow," added Ratcliffe. "If you lay your ordnance with as straight an eye as that, my Lord Duke, I don't wonder you believe in artillery."

"I never lay guns with my own hands," said the Duke, with the twitch of a smile. "I remember the fate of King James of the red face who blew himself up to heaven—or so charity would have us think—at the siege of Roxburgh."

"What is your favourite weapon, your Grace?" asked Ratcliffe. He was older than the Duke by perhaps fifteen years, but he asked like a boy.

"An axe," the Duke told him : "one so seldom has to hit twice with it."

The third hart was long in breaking cover. It came at last, and was bowled over by Lord Scrope. Ratcliffe went wide of it, and again the Duke did not shoot. There were no more, the beaters said. Duke Richard apologised shortly for not showing his guests better sport.

"Come again and we will hunt over Jervaulx way and sup with the Abbot. He keeps a noteworthy cellar."

They rode home without much talking, and were met at the gate by the news that Sir William Parr had arrived and was in the Chamber of Presence. The Duke went up the great stair of the Keep, and his guests, following him, saw that he took the man who had fought by him at Barnet in his arms and kissed him on the mouth. Sir William Parr was wearing a fine new suit of orange velvet and a tawny-coloured gown furred with beaver. He glanced a little oddly at the Neville blazonings on the roof and walls.

Dinner was served in the Chamber of Presence. It was a light meal of bream stewed in white wine, cold roast capon and a sugared pastry stuffed with goose-giblets, with cherries and sweet wafers for dessert. Sweet Touraine wine was served with the fish, Burgundy or claret with the capon and hippocras with the dessert. The Duke mixed his Burgundy with water and refused hippocras. He did not seem to relish Sir William Parr's talk of Barnet and what happened there; turned the subject. He hoped for news, he said, when the Earl of Northumberland arrived, of the King his brother's projects for a war with France. The Earl would know all that was going on. England, handfast to Charles of Burgundy, was bound by honour as well as profit to send letters of defiance to Louis Valois. The Christian King had had a long run and a long tether; should feel the rope jerk at his neck soon.

"For nearly sixty years," said the Duke, "we English have prated of the day of Azincourt. My royal brother intends to hold such a meeting with Louis that Azincourt will be a skirmish to it. 'A hen's turd to a dunghill' were his exact words."

The others spoke up eagerly: "We should get Normandy and Maine at any rate, all Anjou perhaps." "All Anjou, Christ help you? We should get Poitou and Guienne, aye, and Armagnac." "Burgundy'll have to have Champagne, of course." "Not a doubt: but we ought to get the Bourbonnais."

The Duke said: "There is an old rhyme, gentlemen:

> He that France would win
> Must with Scotland first begin.

That looks like work for us here in the North parts."

"All the better," said Lord Scrope: "God damn and confuse all Scots, anyway."

They drank to that.

"There is the matter of Berwick," went on the Duke. "I long for war with France as I long for—well, for few things. But still more do I wish to see that English stronghold in English hands again."

"By God," said Sir Richard Ratcliffe, "now I see we've a governor over us in the North who thinks as we do."

"I am pleased to hear you say it. War with Scotland—unless they keep this last treaty, which I do not think they will—seems certain one day. Sir William Parr, you and I may ride together in a charge again."

"I ask nothing more, your Grace."

A servant was bowing at the door of the Chamber. Mr. Wrangwysh of York had ridden over with a letter of credence from the Mayor and Aldermen and most humbly implored the favour of an audience.

"Take him into the Privy Chamber. Say I will see him presently." The Duke smiled at Lord Scrope. "The City of York courts me these days. They seem to have forgotten an occasion last year when my royal brother and myself had difficulty in getting them to open their gates to us."

"Disloyal scum," said Lord Scrope shortly.

He was a sincere Yorkist, as all his house had been since the judicial murder of their kinsman, Archbishop Scrope, by Henry Bolingbroke. Duke Richard shrugged.

"No, my Lord, not disloyal, only frightened: these have been hard years for the small folk of England. How were they to know which side to hold by when their betters changed sides every day?"

"By God's bones, but that's true. Was there ever such a country as England for turncoats? When I heard that Kingmaker had betrothed his daughter to Marguerite's bastard . . ."

175

The Duke got up quickly. "You'll excuse me, gentlemen. I must attend to the worthy Mr. Wrangwysh. Treat my Castle as yours if you love me."

Mr. Thomas Wrangwysh awaited the Duke of Gloucester's pleasure on the extreme edge of a chair in the Privy Chamber. This room was as large as the Chamber of Presence, which it adjoined, and fully as splendid. The arras of its walls was bright French work showing hunting scenes and fine ladies amusing themselves among arbours of tight little flowers. All the furniture was of the grandest —tall oak buffets, many cushioned chairs and painted coffers. The ceiling was red and blue with golden suns encircling silver roses. The floor was not strewn with rushes or even flowers, but entirely covered by a thick silk carpet. So much softness and richness disturbed Mr. Wrangwysh and made him look nervously at his boots to see if they were clean. The plate on the buffets was all silver and silver-gilt —massive cups, embossed dishes and candlesticks worth, if Mr. Wrangwysh was any judge of such matters, every last groat of two hundred pounds. There was a large press of books, too, bound some in silk and some in coloured leather with jewelled clasps. On a table near Mr. Wrangwysh's chair a book was actually open, displaying bold lines of black writing and pretty initials of blue and red. Mr. Wrangwysh got up to look at it more closely. It was not written, he saw, but printed in the new German fashion : a Psalter. "Judicabit," he spelt out at random and with difficulty, "afflictos populi." He shall judge the hapless among the people. He hoped the words might prove an omen.

"You care for books, Mr. Wrangwysh?"

The Duke had come in so quietly that he had not heard him.

"Your Grace, pardon me !"

"For nothing." The Duke held out his hand. Mr. Wrangwysh kissed it. He had been told that the Duke, whom he had never seen before, was small and pale : but he had not expected anyone quite so tiny, with a face quite so bloodless or with such strange lines about his eyes and mouth. Confused, he broke into a babble about condescension, intrusion and kindness. The Duke perched himself in a big chair and waved a hand on which four rings shone. "You may be seated, sir. It's a long road from York."

"Your Grace is too kind."

"You were looking into my Psalter. It is from Mainz, where they have the new engines for making books : not such handsome work as a good scribe can do, but there's no question that the device will multiply books and spread learning, and that is a very blessed thing."

"Yes, indeed, your Grace."

"The craft is practised in France and Burgundy now. I hope the day will not be long before we see it used in England."

"I hope so, your Grace. If your Grace will forgive me for intruding a matter upon you, there is a letter of credence I have from the Mayor and his brethren."

The Duke glanced through the letter, a formal request to accept the bearer's word as that of the Mayor and Aldermen, and asked Mr. Wrangwysh whether he had dined.

"Oh yes, your Grace, many thanks."

"Well, you will take a cup of hippocras with me whilst you tell me your business."

He rang a silver bell beside him. A servant, much better dressed than Mr. Wrangwysh himself, came in.

"Hippocras, fruit, wafers," he was told.

Mr. Wrangwysh blinked. He knew that bad manners were out of fashion among the nobility nowadays, but he had not expected the Duke's courtesy to go further than offering him a chair. When he had drunk, the Duke, who had been sliding his hunting-knife up and down in its sheath, smiled in an expressionless fashion and asked his errand. Mr. Wrangwysh drew a deep breath and began to talk about illegal fish-traps.

Half-an-hour later he was still talking. An hour later, Mr. Secretary Kendal was sent for and Mr. Wrangwysh invited to state his case all over again. When he had finished, the Duke stood up. He walked the length of the room, head down, his hand at his knife again; turned round and faced his visitor.

"Mr. Wrangwysh, we must not be precipitate. What you tell me shows that these garths and weirs fill rich men's pouches and empty poor men's bellies. That is enough. They must go. But we must be sure the law is with us. Mr. Kendal will search the records and advise us how we are to set about our work. I must go back to my guests now. You shall sup here to-night, and we will find time to talk of this again. Attend to him, Mr. Kendal."

The door shut after him. Mr. Kendal and Mr. Wrang-wysh looked at each other.

"Lord," said Mr. Wrangwysh.

Mr. Kendal gave a bark of a laugh.

"Five years' work you've put on my plate, Mr. Wrang-wysh. There'll be the confusion of hell before we get the rights and wrongs of this settled. Probably it'll need to go to the King. But you may tell the Mayor of York that the day of unlawful fish-garths is past its noon. I know the Duke."

Duke Richard found his guests in the bowling-alley in the East Ward. Sir James Harrington had arrived. The Duke kissed him; apologised for business that had kept him away; stood by impassively whilst they finished their game. Then he joined them in a fresh one. The woods clicked and trundled happily about the smooth turf. Birds twittered in the mulberry-trees that over-arched the alley, and from the smithy they could hear a musical and regular cling-clang of hammers. It was four o'clock when a trumpeter on the Watch-tower suddenly spilled a long chain of notes down through the greying air. The Duke dropped the wood he was aiming and straightened up.

"My Lord of Northumberland is in sight. We can play again to-morrow, gentlemen."

Middleham village saw the pageant it had been waiting for since morning. The last sound of the trumpet from the Castle was crossed by a faint ironical lilt of pipes. Four pipers appeared up the sloping village street, blowing on the small, sweet-toned Northumbrian bagpipes. Behind them rode twenty mounted men-at-arms, with sallets, breastplates and demi-lances. Some were badged with the Percy crescent and others with the Lovel dog. Henry Percy of Northumberland, Lord Francis Lovel and Lord John Howard rode together on smooth-coated hackneys. North-umberland's great charger, sheeted to its fetlocks, so that it looked like a walking bail, was led behind them, and at its tail rode a dozen gentlemen and pages, and the Earl's confessor on a white mule. Thirty sumpter-horses, each led by a groom and carrying their Lordship's baggage, two falconers with their hawks, four leashes of mastiffs and greyhounds and forty men-at-arms on foot closed the procession, which had been straggling its way North from London for the past month.

In the Castle they were received with ceremony. They entered between two files of spearmen in the crimson-and-silver livery of Gloucester. Pages and grooms ran forward to take their horses. The senior gentleman of the Duke's household held the Earl's bridle as he dismounted. Duke Richard was waiting for them on the steps of the Keep, his other guests grouped behind him and more spearmen lining the steps up to the door of the Great Hall. The Earl of Northumberland had been a guest at Middleham more than once when Kingmaker was its lord; but he could not remember being received more pompously.

The newcomers were served with claret and demain bread in the Chamber of Presence, to recruit them a little after their journey. Meanwhile, their horses were being unsaddled, their mails unpacked, and their followers lodged wherever room was to be found for them—in the East Ward, in the basement under the Chapel, in narrow and inconvenient chambers in the three great towers. The drawbridge joining the two Wards sounded under the hooves of their sixty-seven mounts. Men staggered beneath kegs from the brewhouse and trays from the bakehouse. There was great shouting and chivying and contradiction, quietening slowly as the froth crumbles and quietens on a pot of beer. Pages appeared to lead the guests to their chambers and the baths prepared for them, and in the great vault below the Chamber of Presence naked kitchen-lads tended the fires, whose glow reddened their breasts and arms and was reflected in bright trickles of sweat zigzagging down their flanks.

In his own chamber, the Duke of Gloucester suffered his grooms to strip him out of his green hunting-suit and draw back the white silk curtains of his bath. He sat in perfumed water, soaping himself leisurely from neck to heel, whilst Mr. Kendal, squatting on a stool outside the curtains, reported his preliminary research into the law concerning fish-traps. Swathed in warm sheets, he moved across to his own stool before the fire and continued the discussion whilst a page, trained expressly in the business, pared his nails with a sharp knife. His festival clothes were gayer than his common wear. His hose were of fine violet silk and his purple shoes embroidered with gold thread. Over a purple velvet doublet sewn with six rows of pearls and amethysts he wore a magnificent gown, very full in the sleeves, of violet silk embroidered with golden suns and silver bars. It was reversed with ermine and its short skirts were tucked into a jewelled belt. When his hair had been combed and scented, a groom hung the Yorkist livery-collar across his shoulders and set a purple velvet bonnet, trimmed with ermine and pearls, at a slight angle on his head. A page slid his jewelled gloves and his gold rosary into their places in his belt, and he was ready for Vespers.

The little Chapel was packed, for none of the guests cared to offend a notably pious prince by absence. The tapers made much of a thick clot of double velvets, brocades, satins, coloured cloth-of-gold picked out with jewels. The Earl of Northumberland wore a superb new gown of tawny silk embroidered—rather incongruously, for he was a meagre-faced little man with nervous eyes—with true-lovers' knots in silver. Lord Lovel's black sleeves were lined with thick white bear's fur to emphasise the slimness of his wrists. All stood and knelt patiently through the office, and came out at a sober pace, after the blessing, onto the stair-head. It was dusk now, and the stairs were lined and the Hall door flanked by servants with wax tapers. A trumpet announced supper, and they moved in due order into the Hall, the pages and gentleman-attendants trooping up the stairs and turning in behind them.

The wall behind the high table was hung with a cloth of estate and the guests sat, on one side of the board only, facing down the Hall. The Duke had the Earl of Northumberland on his right and Lord Lovel on his left. The Secretary, the Auditor and Mr. Wrangwysh, who looked nervously happy, sat with the Earl's gentlemen at the lower table. As leisurely as a snake, the complex ceremony of the meal unfolded itself. The high table was spread with white linen of Rennes. Silver-gilt candlesticks alternated down its length with bowls of marchpane, blanched almonds, ginger and candied fruits. The daïs was thick, under the guests' feet, with strewn flowers. The senior gentleman of the household, bearing a white wand, appeared from the pantry, heading a procession of servants with damask napkins on their shoulders and gold salts and silver knife-baskets in their hands. Ewers of rose-water came in, and the guests rinsed their fingers. The Earl chatted to the Duke about the dogs that he had bought in London, and the Duke spoke with annoyance about the outbreak of mange at Pontefract Castle. Grace was sung. Sack came in crystal glasses, and the Earl spoke of a cure for mange that his kennelman used and the prayer to St. Hubert which must be said before applying it. Trumpets bawled, and pages served two kinds of broth, one of chicken flavoured with coriander-seeds and one, porridge-thick, of venison and raisins with sweet wine. The pantlers sliced fine white bread and dealt it round on their long knives. All crossed themselves and began. From the screens at the South end of the Hall a procession of covered dishes made its way. Roast eels, carp stewed in white wine with bay-leaves and rosemary, and pike stuffed with chestnuts and garnished with a sauce of almonds and seagull's eggs were the fish-service. The butlers poured Rhenish from enormous conical wooden jacks. The Duke drank to his guests in turn, and asked Lord Lovel what was the news from Cornwall.

"Why, have you not heard, sir? John Vere's taken."

"Taken? That's very good. How was it contrived?"

Lord Lovel chuckled. He was a thin-faced, handsome boy, with very red lips.

"It's an old saying that a castle that speaks and a woman that will hear, they will be gotten both. The King's officers parleyed with Vere's men and promised 'em pardon. They surrendered. I hear the King's Grace means to pack Vere over to Calais or Guisnes and lock him up there."

"It is better than extreme measures."

Trumpets brayed again for the entrance of two roast peacocks, dressed in their full feathers, tails spread wide, nodding and shivering with the steps of the grooms who carried them. Behind them were borne grebes, dressed likewise in their plumage, capons stuck full of almonds and stuffed with apples and quinces, and a dish of partridges stewed to rags with ginger, cinnamon, saffron, sugar and plums. The servers carved whilst the butlers made their rounds again with the big wine-jacks.

"The new Princess—she that was born in April—is sickly, I hear," said the Earl.

181

The Duke raised his eyebrows but did not speak.

"The Prince of Wales grows like a tree, though."

"Loved be God."

"His Grace says he has a certain assurance, on which he relies, that his next child shall be a son."

"A certain assurance?" said the Duke interrogatively.

"Those are his words." The Earl dropped his voice a little. "By prophetic arts," he explained with a certain look of deprecation.

The Duke again lifted his eyebrows and said nothing.

"Who was the prophet?" asked Lord Lovel coolly.

Northumberland shrugged.

"Friar Bungay, I suppose. I know nothing of such things—less than nothing."

"That big-bellied mountebank: God send he's speaking the truth for once in his bad life."

"Amen," said Richard of Gloucester.

"What like of a man is he?" asked Lord Scrope. "I never set eyes on him."

"A great fat hog of a friar," said Lord Lovel warmly, "with the insolence of a hound, and thievish with it. He may be a prophet, but it's hard getting fair water from a foul pipe. I think he hides cropped ears under his hood."

"Can he transmute metals?"

"No, that's Mr. French's mystery. He's the fellow that's forever cracking about toads and phoenixes and the Mouth of Choleric."

"Whorish nonsense."

"Can we be certain?" said Duke Richard. "My brother Edward is not a fool. He has studied alchemical and geometrical arts, and the casting of horoscopes, and he does not find them nonsense. If we make brass from copper and tin, why should we not make gold from sulphur and mercury?"

"But that's near to . . ." Lord Scrope chewed his lip ". . . to witchcraft, devilishness."

"It is not. If it can be done, it is done by skill and art, as books are imprinted or caps fulled in a fulling-mill. Witchcraft we all know of. To doubt that men and women can, if they are so mad, make an alliance with the fiend"— he crossed himself—"is heresy. But this alchemical art is another matter."

"It would be a blessed day for this realm, certainly, if gold could be made like glass."

"It would be the worst day we ever saw."

"Nay, why? To be the richest . . ."

"We should not be rich. If gold could be made like cloth, then it would be worth no more than cloth, and my brother's rich crown would have no more to commend it than a cadger's bonnet."

"By God," said Lord Scrope when he had thought a little, "but that's true. To hell with alchemists, then : I'd hang 'em all."

"And witches, too," agreed Ratcliffe.

"Witches should burn. God's blood, think of it : to damn your soul to all the devils of hell for the sake of craft and cunning. It's horrible."

"Aye, but what crafts do they get from the devil, when all's said?" asked Sir William Parr.

Lord Lovel took a drink of Rhenish and leaned forward.

"A Frenchman told me of a beastly fellow they burned at Cambrai some ten years ago. He had a familiar devil that foretold the future and helped him to get goods as a prophet and to brew love-philtres to seduce honest women. He was so swollen with sin that when they ordered him to do penance he threw down the blessed crucifix and broke it."

"They did well to burn him," said the Duke. "But I do not think all prophecy is devilish. When a thing is certainly coming to pass, then a wise man may see the tokens of it by science."

"That I believe," said Northumberland. "In my country they tell a strange tale of James I of Scots, him that was murdered by the Earl of Atholl. They say that when he was crossing the Water of Leith a prophetical woman of Ireland called to him : 'My Lord King, if you pass this water you shall never turn again alive' : and that was true, for Atholl stabbed him two days after. And they say that Atholl had heard a prophecy, too, that he should be crowned in the sight of all Scotland; and so he was. When they had him on the scaffold they set a crown of white-hot iron on his head."

"Now, that," said the Duke with interest, "was certainly a devil's prophecy to deceive Atholl into the sin of murder

183

and then mock him with the outcome. The devil is very cunning in such sleights, giving gifts with one hand and taking them away with the other, and the soul with them. I have read of an old heathen King who inquired of an oracle if he should invade the realm of his enemy. He was told that if he did he should break down a mighty kingdom, which was true, for his enemy defeated him and took all his realm."

Again, a loud sennet of trumpets broke the air. The roast meats were coming in. A young boar stuffed with march-pane and sugared chestnuts and garnished with sausages and blood-puddings stood upright in the first dish, its brown flesh turning golden under the flare of cressets and tapers. A whole roast lamb, coated with almond-paste, knelt in a meadow of green jelly stuck with candied flowers. A Norwegian bear's ham drowned in a thick sauce of red wine, treacle, white ginger and nard followed; and behind came the exotic titbit of the feast, a roast porcupine stuffed with garlic and truffles. The butlers brought in flasks of Burgundy and white Gascon wine. Pantlers, servers, pages and grooms made haste about the Hall. The Earl of Northumberland helped himself to a pinch of blanched almonds and related how the strange people of Iceland, dwelling in the North of the world, sold winds to sailors.

"And I've heard," he added, "that in those parts they are able to catch live devils and make them do useful work to men, as rowing boats and sweeping out stables : but I do not believe it."

"Neither do I," said Duke Richard.

"But men can be killed by devils if a witch desires it," said Lord Scrope, "and that I do know. The witches make a figure of wax or lead and burn it, and the man wastes away."

Duke Richard beckoned a server and told him to carve a slice of the porcupine and carry it to Mr. Wrangwysh. The yellow-haired Yorkshireman got on his feet, bowing and blushing at the compliment. The Duke nodded and raised his cup to him; turned to the Earl.

"And what is the talk at Court about the French journey, my Lord?"

"The French have recalled the troops they sent to Normandy, thinking we should land there this summer; can see for themselves we don't intend to. Lord Rivers is still in Brittany, trying to tie Duke François down to some sort of alliance. If he'll succeed or not, the saints know. You'd 've thought that damned Duke would be willing to do something definite after we'd sent him two thousand archers."

"My Lord Rivers," said the Duke reflectively, "is always out of England these days. Last year it was a pilgrimage, and now an embassy."

"Strange about the pilgrimage," said Lord Scrope, finishing his portion of lamb and beckoning to a server to bring him some roast pork : "he left almost as soon as he was back in England, you might say. Just after Harry of Windsor died, I think it was. Someone told me there was a matter of his private conscience that he wanted to purge."

"For my part," said Lord Howard, "he may stay abroad as long as he likes."

Duke Richard gave him one of his slow, level stares that might mean anything or nothing.

"I heard a bad report of those archers who were sent to Brittany under Lord Duras," he said. "Have you heard anything of them?"

Northumberland coughed and stroked his chin.

"There were people saying that so many of them are dead of the flux and other epidemics that the remnant should come home. But then I daresay it's not true."

The Duke lifted his cup. His pale eyes were fully open for a second, like a surprised cat's.

"Gentlemen, we'll drink to a meeting with Louis Valois and a hunt through all the parts of France till we blow our horn and relieve our hounds."

They drank.

"All the same," said Lord Lovel, "we'd be best to drink to the Parliament next month, now that we're drinking. Money we must get out of 'em somehow. The King's Grace himself was saying this would be the costliest French war ever waged from England."

"It will be repaid," said Duke Richard.

There was a pause now in the service of dishes. A single trumpet sounded a queer drawling theme, and through the screens at the South end of the Hall appeared Duke

Richard's jester. He was a tall man with a dark face and thick, restless eyebrows; walked with an air. He wore the conventional fool's motley of two-coloured jerkin and hose and hood with ass's ears, and carried a gilt bladder strung from a stick, but there was a lute slung on his shoulders. He lounged up the hall, one fist on his hip, his bauble tapping his calf, his dark lizard's eyes flicking; then, with a sudden standing jump and a whoop, landed himself neatly on a cleared space in the middle of the lower table; glanced round him, dignity recovered, like a nobleman, and burst into a quick string of patter. He seemed privy to all the happenings of the day; spied the master of the pages near the end of the board and hallooed the rhyme the page had made up about him that morning; bounced his bauble off the Auditor's head and asked after his rabbits.

"Rabbits for God's poor, marks for God's poor : if you'd keep your place here never lend a mark to God's poor, I give you warning." His eye found Mr. Wrangwysh and he bent down and kissed him mercilessly on both cheeks. "The Yorkist from York, gentlemen, as I live by bread, the Yorkist from York : here's a man, pretty gentlemen, that lives in York and loves the white rose. Who'd 've believed it? Kind Mr. Yorkist, lend me a mark and I'll teach you to set a trap to catch porcupines. Don't listen to that strong thief beside you that calls himself a Secretary. I'll tell you a thing. Never repeat it. He's a Scotsman. Holy saints and all charity, I forgot the grand noblemen!" He shaded his eyes with his hand toward the high table. "Oh, oh, oh, I see you well enough, but that I'm a trifle gravel-blind and suffer with sore eyes. Wait till I get my spectacles on. Now wait, will you? Don't be off. It'll be fine presently. Ah, ho, yes, I see you. I see you. God have pity upon me, I see you. Oh blessed charity, look at my Lord's bonnet." With a bound he cleared the heads of those sitting at the lower table. Another got him into the daïs, where he bowed and broke instantly into a spate of budge verse.

"The great Lord Percy came riding down
With true-lovers'-knots all over his gown
To kiss all the women of Middleham town.
Oh-ho, Middleham town!

"But the sweet Lord Lovel beside him came.
At sight of his lips every Middleham dame
Cried : 'Jesus, oh tell us the little lad's name.'
Oh-ho, Middleham town!

"Sir Richard Ratcliffe is stout and grim.
If a maiden cast amorous eyes at him,
Cock's body, he'd eat her up limb by limb.
Oh-ho, Middleham town!

"Lord Scrope of Bolton he hunts the deer,
And he's hunted 'em now this many a year,
And his shafts afright 'em they fly so near.
Oh-ho, Middleham town!

"The great Lord Howard's is ancient blood.
His folk were in England before Noah's flood,
But where were they whilst Adam was still in
    the wood?
Oh-ho, Middleham town!

"Sir William Parr is a white-rose man,
He kept the rose when the cowards all ran
As close as he keeps his gob to the can.
Oh-ho, Middleham town!

"Stout Sir James Harrington holds by Sir Will
So long as they've rebels and traitors to kill
Or pottles to empty or bellies to fill.
Oh-ho, Middleham town!

"Amen, pour charité."

There was great laughing. Lord Lovel opened the
embroidered pouch at his belt and threw the jester a half-
royal. The man caught it in the air; kissed it; made it
vanish between his fingers and found it again in Sir James
Harrington's sleeve. Sir James took the hint, giving him a
handful of groats and pence. Other coins were thrown him,
and with a twinkle of legs he was gone from the daïs and
leaning on the shoulder of the Auditor, demanding to have
his money reckoned. Mr. Auditor was simple enough to
comply, and the jester immediately emptied his wine-cup
for him, swept the money from the board, sprang back to
the daïs and unslung his lute.

187

"A French journey, sirs, I hear babble of a French journey. You must all learn to speak French fairly and clearly after the manner of Paris, my little Lords. Godon! Brolanbrigod! Baisemecu! Still, still, be still there. I shall school you. Oh, you'll be scholars presently, I promise you. You must first understand that in France they have the Free-Archers, brave, honest, sober souls as ever robbed a henroost. What, have you not heard the epitaph of honest Pernet, which is sweeter than the sweetest verse of my Lord Rivers?

"Ci-gît Pernet le Franc-Archer
Qui ci mourût sans démarcher,
Car de fuir n'eût oncques espace,
Lequel Dieu, par sa sainte grace,
Mette aux cieux avec les âmes
Des Francs-Archers et des gens-d'armes—
Arrière des arbalestriers."

Lord Scrope's yell of delight made the flames of the tapers wince. Lord Lovel clapped his hands. Even the Duke chuckled, though he had heard the rhyme before. Everyone at the high table knew the municipal regiments of Free-Archers, established by Charles the Well-Beloved, for the most useless rabble in the French army. But before the laughing had stopped, the jester, with a long swing of his arm, sent his bauble flying down the Hall and began to tune his lute. His face changed and became sad and sleepy. He tried the strings, cocking his head from side to side; began to sing in a startlingly sweet pure tenor.

"Oh, the white and goodly may,
Oh, it is a goodly tree,
And oh, when wilt thou return
My own true love to be?"

No one moved or said anything. Duke Richard had dropped his chin on his jewelled chest. His mouth was tight and his hands, joined on the board in front of him, were busy with his ring.

"Oh, the thrustlecock sings sweet
And he sings both soon and late,
And oh, when wilt thou return
For to be my own dear mate?"

188

There was a moment's silence before the applause. The Duke did not move. Light caught the pearls in his cap and the gold and silver on his gown. His eyes were contracted into slits no wider than the edge of a dagger. Presently, he motioned a butler to give the bowing jester wine; joined his hands again in front of him.

The next course was trumpeted into the Hall: hares stewed in spiced malmsey and milk-of-almonds and stuck with cloves and mace, a fowl-custard, yellow with saffron, served in a sugared tart, an enormous pie with the Percy crescent and the silver boar in icing on its raised crust, full of snipe, plover, woodcock and larks. They were followed presently by a host of little dishes: cockscombs in batter, soused herrings, sausages with almond sauce, quails in aspic, ducklings powdered with sugar, frogs' legs, spiced lambs' tongues, snails with garlic, slices of sturgeon with green sauce. The guests' cups were charged with malmsey or black Cyprus wine. Lord Lovel, after a glance at the Duke's profile, began to talk with his neighbour, Lord Scrope, about the fortunes of the campaign Charles the Hardy of Burgundy had been waging that spring on the East borders of France. More details were to hand now. It seemed it was a dirty, ugly kind of war. At Nesles-en-Vermandois the Hardy had strung up the French garrison like fruit on a tree and cut both hands off those few that he had left alive: a vile business. Lord Scrope asked whether it was true that King Louis' brother, the Duke of Berri, who was known to have Burgundian sympathies, had died rather opportunely and mysteriously. Young Lord Lovel shrugged. Quite true: the Hardy swore that Louis had poisoned him, and that was very likely.

"Sooner we take charge of the realm in France the better for everybody: I mean, holy Mary, we're honest. That Louis is simply a tyrant; leaves no place for right, justice or religion. Murder, treason, poisonings: it's horrible."

"And yet the strange thing is," said Lord Lovel, with a straight face, "that the poor, deluded people of France have some affection for him. When Charles of Burgundy invested Beauvais this spring, the very women of the town joined with the men to beat him off the walls. They must somehow have misconstrued what he did at Nesles-en-Vermandois."

"Burghers and commoners," said Lord Scrope, "what do they go for?"

Duke Richard seemed to wake up from his abstraction, come to life again.

"They go for a great deal," he said expressionlessly : "more than we even think. My Lord Scrope, why am I here, away from my brother in these North parts? It's not to hold down a land that's hostile to the house of York. You and my Lord of Northumberland and our other loyal friends would do that. It is to end the hostility itself. I know. You were for telling me that there is no hostility. But there is; and whilst there is, my brother will not be content. He has not forgotten how the commons of his own Duchy of York opposed him last year, to his intense grief. I am here as his ambassador to the North to show these very burghers and commoners you despise that the rule of York is a good rule, and one against which there is no need for them to rebel."

"If the proud-stomached swine were taught that rebellion is a sin, we should do better. I'd like to see the good Statutes of Labourers in full force again. The commons to-day are too rich and they're too proud. Take their wealth and you take their insolence, I say. Things were never merry in England since Jack was as good as his master."

The Duke laid his knife on his plate.

"I have heard that talk before. Those who use it care little indeed for the good of the realm of England. Our might stands on our archers, who are no rich men. If they were made poorer than they are, how should we resist our enemies? As for rebellions, when risings have been made in this land by the commons, the poorest men have been the greatest causers and doers of them, and thrifty men have hung back for fear of losing their goods. What do you suppose it would be if all the commons were poor? By St. Paul, this land would be like the realm of Bohemia, where the small folk, for poverty, rose upon the nobles and made all goods to be in common. Give me a realm with every man wealthy in his station. Nothing can make a people revolt but lack of goods or lack of justice; and when they lack goods they will most certainly rise, saying they lack justice. With God's help, I will see to it that the people of the North shall not want for either. Until they are secure in

190

that, they will not know—certainly *know*, not simply believe or hope—that my brother is the best King England has seen since Edward the Great: and until they know that, my work is not done in the North."

"That's a noble way of talking, your Grace. Aye by God, noble, that's what I call it. But if we're to teach these crofters and fullers and woolmen and candlemakers that the King's Grace wants nothing better than to see 'em all wealthy as ticks—God's body, think of the insolence they'll put on."

"My Lord Scrope, I was a little boy when my brother, your cousin, was crowned King of England; but I've learnt the words of his first speech to Parliament by heart. He said: *If I had any better to reward you withal than my body, you should have it.* Those words were spoken to all England. Our Lord Edward offered his body, like our Lord Christ, for the service of all. Holy Church will tell you that your soul and mine and Hick the hackneyman's are as even in God's sight as three peas in a peascod. I tell you that a good King—and do you doubt my brother is that?—rules all to serve all: burghers, commoners, knights, clerks and nobles, every christian soul breathing in his England."

There was a moment's silence. Then Lord Lovel said gaily:

"It will be a good England: justice from my Lord Richard for the North, clemency from my Lord Edward for the South. John Vere goes to prison at Calais instead of to the scaffold. At this rate the King's Grace should have no trouble raising money from Parliament."

For the last time, the trumpets assaulted the warm air, The subtleties were being carried in: great piles of cunningly delicate sugar-work shining like Bruges enamel. There were three of them: an argosy in full sail with St. George's cross displayed, a tower with a man-at-arms on it and, largest of all, the Duke's silver boar, tusked and bristled with gold, having the motto, Loyaulte me lie, on a collar round his neck and a scroll in his jaws bearing a distitch of kitchen-verse:

Behold ye mighti bore yt can orthrowe
Al rebels & fals traytours att oon blowe.

The confections were more admired than tasted. Each one was ceremonially broken into and the guests served from it; but their appetites were buried and drowned. They picked and toyed at the jagged lumps of sugar; sipped the hippocras which was poured out for them and scarcely reached their hands towards the bowls of oranges stuck with cloves and preserved fruits in syrup that were served to end the meal. Silence overcame them and they moved ponderously in their chairs. Sir Richard Ratcliffe smothered a belch. Fresh water was brought and they washed their hands; after grace went burdenedly, stretching their backs and yawning, across the hautpace to the Privy Chamber.

Here there was plenty to entertain them: chess, checquers and brightly-painted cards. Most of them settled down sleepily to these diversions, and presently Duke Richard, Lord Lovel and Lord Howard were alone at the far end of the room. The Duke asked Lord Lovel if he had seen much of the King.

"A good deal, all his business considered: I hunted twice with him at Windsor."

"He's finding time for sport, then?"

"When did he ever not? He says he must do something to subdue his fat. It's rich living in England after Artois: and by God, Richard, Westminster's not the only place where a man can burst like a sheep in clover, it seems. That supper's given me a belly like a Prior's."

"The porcupine was very choice," said Howard. "I never ate better."

"I am glad. Will you take a turn in the Chamber of Presence to digest it?"

They went out. The long, emblazoned room was empty, and they walked its length and back in a silence only broken by the clicking of Duke Richard's dagger in its sheath. Finally, in his remotest voice, the Duke said:

"What is this I hear about the wife of some London merchant?"

"It's all true," said Howard, after a silence. "Jane Shore, her name is: a pretty woman, nothing in her body you'd have changed, unless to wish her somewhat taller."

"The devil take her body," said the Duke unemphatically. "Is Edward making a public scandal with her?"

"Well, she comes to Court. She goes to Windsor with him."

"And what does the Queen say?"

"The Queen's Grace," said Lovel in his pleasantly ironical voice, "seeks in all things only the comfort and good pleasure of her sovereign liege and most dear husband. I may add that Mrs. Shore has considerable acquaintance among the family of Wydvylle, who seem friendly disposed to her."

"So: then there are two Wydvylle women at Court instead of one?"

"You might say so, yes."

Lord Howard fiddled with the jewelled chain about his neck.

"Your Grace's brother of Clarence speaks very decidedly on that topic."

"He does?"

"He said to me not long ago that when he broke his oath to his great father-in-law it was to help his brother, and not a pack of jumped-up country knights and common whores."

"I hope it was only to you he said it."

"It wasn't," put in Lovel. "He's been saying it to everyone in hearing whenever he gets a pint of malmsey under his belt."

"St. Paul, is he drinking again?"

"Like a sponge."

"I could wish he had a bridle in his mouth. Some loving friend will go tattling to the Queen about him if he talks at that pace."

"That will have been done already. The Court's a whispering-gallery of Wydvylles these days. What from Sir John Fogg—blessed Mary, how perfectly I hate that filthy fellow!—and Hawte and their new Welch friend Sir Thomas Vaughan, you can't spit but the Queen hears of it. Hastings is angry about it. He has his own spy now, too: that little clerk, Catesby."

"A clever creature," said Duke Richard.

"Hastings finds him useful. You know, of course, that Marguerite's old friend Morton, the Rector of St. Dunstan's, has been pardoned and made Master of the Rolls?"

"Yes, yes, I'd heard that. Is he a safe man? Stanley was very urgent with my brother to take his head off."

"Safe he may be," said Howard. "Sly I'm sure he is. The Queen takes notice of him. She'll have him of her faction before she's done."

The Duke's hand came away from his dagger.

"Do not use that word faction. We're at peace now. It has too much of a sound of the old days."

"I'll tell you one thing about Morton," said Lovel. "It was he and the Wydvylles between them contrived the undoing of the Archbishop of York."

"That is a story I should like to hear at large. I knew Edward meant to take order with George Neville, but that is all."

"It's a pretty tale. After Barnet fight and his two brothers' deaths, the good Archbishop buried his plate and treasure; had no great wish King Edward should have the use of it. Then time goes by and our Lord Edward makes no move, so George Neville pokes his head out of his burrow and says: 'What, am I alive still? This is a clement King': and he curries favour. The King receives it all with a smile and a clap on the back, and it seems to George Neville as though the good old times were come again. Then one day the King sends him a message that he will come to hunt and sport with him in his manor at Moor. George Neville, very glad, digs up his fine things and borrows others; arrays his manor as richly and pleasantly as he can. But the day before the King's Grace was to come he is ordered suddenly off to Windsor and there—by God, it was a cruel joke even though it was a good one—arrested and impeached for high treason on a charge that he'd helped the Earl of Oxford. He's in the Tower now: and that's not the best of it. Edward took every parcel and particle—coin, plate, jewels, tapestry, the devil knows what—of all the stuff that he'd got together at the Moor; took it simply, borrowed or not. He even broke the Archbishop's mitre, that was full of rich stones, and made a crown for the Queen of it."

Duke Richard did not say anything to this immediately; finally asked:

"You say the Queen's kinsfolk and Morton were behind this?"

"I am sure of it. Morton supplied the evidence—forged it, for what I know—and the Wydvylles had most of the gain. Why not? Archbishop Neville's not the man his

194

brothers were. If he's forfeited his goods, you may say what was got with sin is lost with sorrow."

"And there's the last of the house of Neville," said Lord Howard, "except for its womenfolk."

"It is time we rejoined the company," said Duke Richard.

The company were more than half asleep. Under the brightness of candles the strong colours of the Privy Chamber only mocked the tiredness and surfeit in their faces. It was past ten o'clock. Lord Scrope, at the moment they came in, made a silly move and lost his queen to Northumberland; pushed the ivory pieces, clattering away over the board. "My wits were in bed an hour ago. I'll yield the game."

Linkmen came to answer a tinkle of the Duke's bell. The company kissed each other good-night. Duke Richard escorted Northumberland courteously over the hautpace to the door of the chamber he was sharing with his personal grooms. Lords Lovel and Howard had the room next to him. At the door of it Duke Richard put his hand on Lord Lovel's wrist, emerging delicately from the immense furriness of its sleeve :

"Come with me for a little."

Two linkmen and two pages attended them back, with tired, careless feet, over the hautpace, through the Privy Chamber and Chamber of Presence, over a hautpace again. The Castle had gone suddenly dead, sordid. There was a stink of snuffed candles and wine, and the air from outside did not refresh them; only made them more aware of headache and bad flavours in their mouths. Patterns of moonlight had a look as though they would have been significant if the mind had strength to concentrate on them and secure their meaning. It was cold.

In his own chamber Duke Richard dismissed the attendants and sat in a painted chair, not troubling to have it brought nearer the fire. His hair was a little disordered by now and he had the expression of a man studying something. Two triangles of the dark appeared to have settled like moths under his eyes.

"Well?" asked Francis Lovel softly, after a long while.

Duke Richard put the heels of his hands into his eyesockets; pushed upward slowly, disordering his hair more;

then tidied the locks round his face as though he did not know he were doing it.

"Is there any news, Frank?"

Not certainly knowing either why he did it or whether it would be permitted, Lord Lovel sat on the arm of the Duke's chair and kissed his smooth, tight-skinned cheek. The Duke turned his head away a little; made no other gesture.

"No, Dickon, no news at all."

"You spoke to George?"

"Twice, alone, and once to Isobel." Lord Lovel jerked up from the chair-arm and went to lean on the stone mantel, feeling the fire against his silk-sheathed legs. "Dickon, Clarence is hopeless. Forgive me, but it's half drink and half ugly cunning. He grumbles. Nothing is right for him and nobody loves him. He sees an affront where his worst enemy would not have meant it : and for this matter, he swears she walked out of his house when he was the last person who expected it and that he's hunted her high and low for no purpose ever since. I can get no further than that with him, drunken fool's-head, and when I pressed him, he went all flaming and asked if I was calling him a liar. I think he is one. Forgive me, Dickon. I do. Isobel's frightened of him. I'll swear she knows nothing. But Clarence is hiding something. If he doesn't know where she is, he knows why she left him. So God help me he does; but I can't get farther with him. Jockey Howard and I tried the Sanctuaries : no sign of her. She's not at Beaulieu with her mother. She wasn't with her uncle George, or we'd have heard when he was seized. I'll renounce God if I know where to look for her now."

"Have you tried Cock's Lane?"

"Oh Christ!" Lord Lovel banged the carved overmantel with his slight hand. "For God Almighty's sake don't take it so hard, Dickon. It's not as bad as that. She can't have come to that much harm, I tell you. Don't think of such things."

"How can I know?"

"Dickon, stop putting yourself to the brake like this for all the hallows of England's sake. She's safe somewhere. We'll find her. There's you with your wits and me and Jockey, and we've men, and we're rich nobles. I promise we'll find her one day. You know yourself we will. Only leave hurting yourself."

"Right now : leave that now."

"But you mustn't think such things, man."

"Leave it. Leave it, will you?"

"Very well : how does your work prosper in the North here?"

"Clever Frank : I could almost talk about that even at this hour of the day. Frank, do you know these people here in my father's own royal Duchy barely know that there is such a word as justice? I could tell tales. We nobles in the South-country have no understanding of what goes on here : and yet they're good folk, true folk. I tell you, Frank, if I can have my way with this North a year or two, long enough to show 'em there's a difference between two words, rule and oppression, by St. Paul I'll found such a loyalty to the white rose here—and it's here the best fighting-men are bred, you know—that neither John Vere nor Jaspar Tydder nor his little nephew shall ever dare think the name of Lancaster. This wicked folly—it is as foul as a heresy, a great lay heresy—of people and princes, that the people are for the use of the prince, not the prince for the use of the people : if I can once break it out of their slow, North-country minds, show them their rulers are not their enemies, we shall have a province to tell tales of, here in the North. Most of them hate me now; hate everyone who wears cloth-of-gold. I shall cure that. But it's a lonely work."

"You'll do it, Dickon. Tell me more of how you go about it."

The Duke's smile was only a shrewd grimace of one refusing a gambit. It showed his upper teeth.

"Go to bed, Frank. You've cured me for now; and God bless you."

"God have you in His particular keeping," said Francis Lovel seriously as he went out of the room.

Parliament had been prorogued to February next, after a hard day of it. It had voted the cost of fourteen thousand archers to aid the King's Grace in recovering his lawful land of France, now usurped and misruled by the tyrant, Louis of Valois. It had taken and acknowledged the young Prince Edward, who had first seen daylight in Broad Sanctuary, to be the very and undoubted heir to the crowns and realms of England and France and to the Lordship and land of Ireland. It had prayed its sovereign liege, King Edward, that the statute made against riots, maintenance and oppressions might be duly executed; and it had confirmed by common consent the release of a sum of five pounds yearly, formerly paid for the issues of bread and ale by the Chancellor and scholars of Oxford.

Through most of the proceedings, George, Duke of Clarence, had sat with his chin on his chest and looked straight ahead of him into his own imagination, thinking how near he had been, only two years ago, to the style and dignity of George King of England, first of that name since the Conquest, and to having the petitions of Parliament humbly addressed to him, to smiling and touching his hat when he rode among cheering mobs of people. I should have been loved, he thought. I should have been a kind King. I would have left all the business of statecraft and alliances to Warwick, but I would have seen the people liked me. God bless King George : they would have shouted that. Richard is cheered in the North, and Edward everywhere : only no cheers for George. A man has a right to be liked, not everywhere and always to play second-fiddle.

After the prorogation he left the Painted Chamber alone. There was a great bustle in the streets of Westminster and on the river stairs. He did not immediately find his barge, and whilst his footmen were still yelling for it, another small procession—liveries of scarlet and silver—clattered down the stairs, and someone touched his arm. He looked round and down. His brother Richard, a white, pointed face between a jewelled black bonnet and a black-and-silver doublet reversed with miniver, was standing by him; gave him a thin-lipped and faintly deprecatory smile.

"A seat in your barge, George?"

"If you're going to the Strand you may. What do you want there?"

"Only to pay my respects to you and your lady wife."

"Very kind of you : Ralph, God damn your eyes, how much longer am I to be kept waiting?"

"No time at all, your Grace : the barge is pulling in now."

"And time, too. You're very friendly all at once, Dickon."

"Not all at once," suggested Duke Richard : "I have been

busy since I came to Westminster. We may call this a very satisfactory Parliament, don't you think?"

"I suppose so: why aren't you with Edward?"

"Because I have two brothers, George: I have seen Edward. Now I wish to see you."

"Edward's getting fat."

They climbed into the painted barge that bore the black, gold-horned bull of Clarence at its prow. The rowers settled themselves; dipped their long oars; struck off. Behind them the wedge of ripples folded over on itself; made living, intricate patterns inside the framework of its own shape.

"You're looking hale yourself, George."

"Meaning I'm fat, too: well, I'd rather be fat than have a corpse-candle colour on me like yours. Yorkshire's not put any red in your cheeks."

Duke Richard, lying back on the silk cushions, twiddled a ring on his finger and did not appear put out. He said:

"It's lonely up there, George."

Duke George laughed; was feeling a little more himself now. Since they were children he had never wholly been at ease with his younger brother. He was afraid of Edward, his immovable mastery of other men even when they were cleverer than he was, his killing tempests of anger; but he was comprehensible. One knew what he would say. Richard said and did nothing that was expected of him, as though he left matters coldly to one's own conscience. Where Edward bellowed, Richard only looked, and not angrily or contemptuously, but with a serene and penetrating inquiry, seeing through one. Why do I always think of how they look when they are displeased with me? George wondered. Why can't I think of the good days we used to have? Richard is easy and friendly now. Let me be.

"Want me to come up to Middleham with you and hold your hand?"

Richard smiled dumbly and shook his head.

"Because we'll all be holding each other's hands in France next year, if it comes to that. Look, Richard, Edward should give us French titles if it falls out well. He should make me Duke of Normandy and you Count of Aquitaine."

"Hardly, George."

"Why not, pray?"

"Those are both crown titles."

"Well, he'll be King of France then. What more's he want? Must he have everything?"

"In any event, I question whether it will be next year, or even the year after. For one thing, we'll want more than fourteen thousand archers. For another, we must have good firm treaties with Burgundy and Brittany. Charles the Hardy can put eighteen thousand in the field, and if Duke François could be relied on for twelve and we for twenty, why, then ..."

"Then God have mercy on Louis Valois."

"Even so : fifty thousand should cook his goose as Harry of Monmouth never cooked it. We'd not leave him so much as Dauphiny to call his own. But we must have that wavering Duke François with us for sure."

"Rivers seems to 've done no good there."

"Rivers has most damnably wasted his time, if all I hear at Court is true. What induced our brother to send him on that errand? Hastings was the man : the most skilled ambassador since Kingmaker's day."

"Twenty thousand devils, Dickon, but you've become a silly Yorkshireman if you don't see the fly in that milk. Edward would have sent Hastings, but the Queen's Grace stopped it. If such an honourable mission was going begging, then her precious brother was the only man for it. By the Sacrament of the altar, when I think of the labour I've been at to put a yellow-haired whore—two yellow-haired whores now, by Christ's cross—back among silk cushions ..."

Duke Richard lifted his hand sharply.

"Watch your tongue, will you, George? If you must talk like that, do it in your chamber with the door locked."

"I renounce God if I will. It's time Edward himself heard some plain speaking on that score. He'd listen to me, after all I've done for him, everything I've sacrificed. I've been making investigation in the matter of these same Wydyvlles, Dickon. Some fine tales I've heard. You remember the heading of the Earl of Desmond in the year 'sixty-eight. Well, I'm credibly informed that Edward never ordered it. The Queen heard Desmond was offended at her marriage, and so she forged a letter to Tiptoft of Worcester ordering his head to be taken off, and when she and Edward were in bed, she rose early and took the Privy Seal out of his purse and signed it with it: and that was the end of Desmond, our father's intimate friend. A sweet story, and not the only one: I've had a glimpse of something darker, something so very strange you'd hardly put faith in it."

"Not here, George, for the last time: you've said too much now. I'll not listen to you."

"Have it your own way, then: but I'll surprise you in the end."

"How is your Lady wife?"

"Well enough, but our little son's loss is a grief to her."

"Surely; it was a grief to me, George."

"You're very kind. Well, we've time yet. I'll show Edward he's not the only one who knows how to plant his garden."

The barge was tying up. Evening fog had closed over the river and torches preceded them to the door of the Duke's mansion.

"I'll take you up to Isobel," said Duke George, and they climbed a narrow stairway to the solar, where the Duchess of Clarence sat over an embroidering-frame among her women. At the sight of the two royal Dukes she got to her feet, thick velvet skirts swirling, a flush on her face.

"Dickon!"

"Isobel, dear Lady."

They kissed fraternally. The Duchess was happy and talkative, sending her slow-footed West-country girls scurrying for wine and wafers, tidying away a strand of hair under her coiffe, dabbing the cushions. There's never this babblement when I come home alone, thought Duke George. His wife gave him a quick, mustering glance under her eyelids, and he knew she was looking to see whether he was sober.

"What good wind blows you here, Dickon?"

"To see my brother and sister, what else?"

"It's good of you. You'll be busy, this Parliament-time."

"Parliament's prorogued and I've come for a gossip. Is this malmsey? Then I'll take water with it, by your leave."

Now I must water it too, thought Duke George, or Isobel will stare at me; and I'm poxily thirsty. If Edward gets a skinful—and he does often enough, by God—the Wydvylle bitch daren't look askance at him. They pledged each other formally and sat down before the pinecone-scented fire.

Duke Richard helped himself to a wafer and ate it in small nibbles.

"I'll send my women away," said Isobel of Clarence cosily, "and you shall have your gossip."

The finely-dressed girls sulked out of the room with backward looks at the small figure of Duke Richard. Duke George guessed they had heard stories of him—his courage and unholy luck in battle, his work in Yorkshire—and were curious of him. He has that whey-face and mim-mouthed look that legends grow about, he thought. Some fool once asked me was it true he was born feet-first with teeth in his mouth.

"And when is the French King to be taught his lesson?" asked the Duchess.

"Not for a year or two, in my opinion, as I was telling George. It will want long preparing. But we'll do it."

"I never liked the slyboots," said Lady Isobel.

Damn her, thought Duke George; need she remind Dickon of when we were at the French Court with her father? He had a sudden vision of the Christian King's long, yellow, foolish face and his shabby dress. It would serve him right to lose his kingdom, shambling, shuffling, hypocritical dog-fancier.

"We'll show him a thing," he said aloud.

"That we will," agreed his brother. "Whether he poisoned the Duke of Berri, as they say, I don't know : but the murder of Jean of Armagnac's enough to damn him. I seriously think it is God's will that we should punish his crimes."

"I had a letter from our sister Margaret," said Duke George. "When Charles of Burgundy heard how Armagnac had been done to death at Lectoure he came near to having an effusion of blood. He's getting more choleric than ever, she says."

"Lord," said his wife.

Duke Richard gave a twitch of a smile.

"That's hard to credit, if he's still outside the Bedlam. It must have been a sad stroke to him, though, that clever counsellor, de Commynes, slipping over from him to Louis as he did."

"Bribed, of course, the dirty rat."

"Of course, but I think he felt Charles was too fond of bidding him run risks as well."

"Coward, then."

"Certainly that : well, God made us all."

"You're as much of a theologist as ever. Always half a priest, weren't you, Dickon?"

Duke Richard pursed his eyelids and looked ahead of him.

"I think," he said deliberately, "that if I had not been a prince I might have been very happy as a monk."

"Not you," said the Duchess, "you'd be wanting an axe in your hand."

"That's only habitude," answered the Duke quickly. "I learnt war as a child, and now I love it. If I had never learnt it I'd be content enough : and that puts me in mind that I've been doing christian work. Your mother, Isobel . . ."

Damnation and devils, thought Duke George, what's in the wind now? He's been sniffing around again : first Anne, now my mother-in-law, damnation and devils.

"Oh, Dickon, yes?"

"She has been more than a year in Beaulieu sanctuary."

"I know, Dickon, and she's petitioned the King and so have I, and I thought George might have done something, but it seems he can't."

"Edward is rather bitter in the matter, but I have done what I could. In time, I think—only in time—he might be brought to show her grace. Edward is not malicious : no man less so. But these last years have made him very wary. Still, I promise you that I'll do all I can."

"Oh, Christ bless you, Dickon."

"You're very kind," said Duke George in a voice that he hoped did not sound as shaky as it felt, "to take such care for the poor outlawed creature."

Duke Richard continued to look at Duchess Isobel. He used his gentlest voice.

"You well know, Isobel, that whatever has happened to divide us, I have always felt kindness and nothing but kindness for the Nevilles."

The Duchess, to her husband's extreme exasperation, began to wipe her eyes.

203

"You're a good man, Dickon. Few people would have thought of poor mother, if they were in your place."

"I wish I could do more, and not only for her. Isobel, I would give all my castles in England to know what has become of little Anne."

There it goes, thought Duke George, just as I thought. He made a final and only half-hearted effort to control his temper; lost hold of it.

"Thank you, Dickon, grand merci. I know why you came to see me now."

"That wasn't the only reason," said Duke Richard, with the atrocious frankness that infuriated his brother even more than his customary two-edged manner of talking. "You are my brother, and I'm very fond of Isobel."

"Yes, and you're still fonder of Anne, and you're fondest of all of those castles in England that you were gabbling about. Middleham and Pontefract: that's all I've got to say to you, my dear little brother who ought to 've been a monk. They're Neville property, and they'd be mine now if everybody had their own. You've filched them, and by God you think if you marry Anne you'll be able to filch some more. You're right. You ought to 've been a monk. You ought to 've been a damned great fat-bellied, land-grabbing thief of an Abbot. That's what you ought to 've been."

"George!" said his wife.

"Don't George me. I know Dickon and his soft-handed ways. I'm not his brother for nothing."

He was feeling wretched now. In a moment Richard would answer him and make him ashamed, laying cold words one beside the other like stones in a wall, showing him what a boor he made of himself. Damn him, damn him, thought Duke George. He's younger than I am. Why can he make me feel like a boy letting his breeches down for the rod? Why can't he and Edward leave me alone with the castles I want and the land I want, and we can all be friends again? If Edward had given me my due in the first place and made much of me, instead of giving everything to those damned Wydvylles, I'd never have listened to Warwick or turned Lancastrian: and now Dickon's even trying to gowk me of half I got out of that.

"George, I often wonder how you're my brother, you talk such trash. Will you forget whatever painted Vice in a play

204

you've concocted out of me in your foolish imagination and remember I'm Dickon? Will you do that now?"

It was not the line of approach Duke George had anticipated; and his brother's smile was real. He felt silly, but not as ashamed as he had expected; muttered:

"Well, what?"

"This"—Duke Richard leaned forward in his chair and began reckoning like a schoolteacher on his fingers—"imprimis, supposing her mother to be outlawed, even, half of the Warwick lands belong, under the King, to Anne, married or not married, and never to you. Secundo, the girl's not your enemy, and if you are hiding her—as, to speak the plain truth, I think you are hiding her—then you are treating a helpless virgin very unkindly, and that's not the tradition of our house. Tertio, we are brothers and very good friends, George, and I love Anne. Will you not help me to her?"

To speak the plain truth, I think you are hiding her. To speak the plain truth, I think you are hiding her. The phrase repeated itself over and over again, with great rapidity, inside Duke George's head. But I am not hiding Anne, he thought. That puts me in the right of it. I have said I am not hiding her, and it is true. I don't know even where she is. I am telling the truth there, but he won't believe me. Me, Clarence, the turncoat, people will not believe even when I am telling the truth. Every word I say, if I say that it rained yesterday, is suspect. They look at my words when my back's turned, fingering them as a Jew fingers a pledged garment, peeping for holes in them; will never believe what I say, lies or truth. He hurled himself out of his chair like a man stung; stood clutching his two hands together, bleeding with wounds of humiliation and defeatedness.

"Now I do perfectly understand you," he said in a thick voice. "Because I once turned Lancastrian and then turned back again, you think you've a licence to disbelieve every dying word I ever tell you. You think you can call me a liar ten hundred times a day. That's what you think. Well, you're wrong, you clever fool. You're wrong from the letter A. George the liar is telling the truth this time. I don't know where she is. Do listen carefully, in case you shouldn't hear me right. I don't know where she is. I don't know and I don't care. I don't know whether she's alive or dead. I don't know whether she's in England or France. She can be in the seraglio of the Sultan of Syria for what I can tell you : and by God's passion, if she were in the next chamber to this I'd rather have my tongue torn out than give you news of it. Brothers and very good friends of mine, Richard. You and Edward always despised me : Edward the great, grand eldest brother, the King of England; Richard the clever little boy, so loyal to his big brother. Not much room left for brother George? By the five wounds of Christ, if ever I injured either of you you've got your cursed selves to blame."

The Duchess had dropped her embroidery, and was fixing her husband with the cold, spear-point Neville look that usually clapped his mouth to like a box.

"You're making a spectacle of yourself, George," was all she threw at him.

"You shut your damned mouth, you trollop. Hell and thunder, am I the Duke of Clarence or not? Be silent when princes of the blood royal are talking. You listen, Dickon, and remember I'm older than you and I'll say what I please. I know what's always in the back of your mind when you look at me. You say to your prim heart : He's a traitor—he betrayed Edward. Well, if I did, it was Edward's own fault. If he'd treated me as I deserved, as the first nobleman in the realm—and that's what I am, you can't deny it—I'd not have betrayed him. I can be as loyal as you. I can. We all know Loyaulte me lie 's your precious holy motto; but I wonder how long your loyalty would 've bound you if you'd always been slighted the way I was, and I didn't betray him in the upshot. I left my great father-in-law to stand by him. I fought at Barnet and Tewkesbury as well as you, even if I didn't have a ward of my own to command, and what do I get for it? Two good castles that ought to be mine filched off me and given to you; you preferred over me, set above me : and then you think you can ask me to find your damned wench for you when it means leaving half my inheritance. You think you can play with me as you please. I'm only the turncoat, the tool. Do what you like with me. Well, I've fooled you this time. It's you and Edward, always despising me, made a turncoat and a schemer out of me. Then, by God's passion, I'll be a turncoat and a schemer, and the whorson pair of you can make your market for it. Now go on and call me what you've a mind. Go on. I defy you. Call me it : turncoat, turncoat, turncoat. Call me it, you undersized little prig."

Sobs made an end of his spech. The tears, he suddenly discovered, were pouring out of his eyes so fast that he could barely see. All his self-mistrust had disappeared in a thick bog of misery and need of pity and encouragement and certainty that he would never get it.

"I don't call you turncoat, George, and if anyone else presumes to do so in my hearing he will need very strong harness to protect him from the consequences."

Duke George sat down again and began wiping his eyes on the edge of his sleeve like a schoolboy. Talking to Richard brought one into a waking world of nightmare; was like clambering onto a continually rolling ball that turned beneath one, shooting one off again.

"But that's what you think I am. That's what you all think I am."

The Duchess Isobel got up. She gathered her velvet skirts round her in a way that seemed to send a draught through the whole room.

"You may have patience with May-games of this sort, Dickon," she said. "I am too accustomed to them. George will start swilling presently. He always does when he has been talking of his wrongs. If you can anyhow discover what he's done with Anne, for God's sake let me know. If not, and if you've any kindness left for the wretched pair of us, stay with him till he's drunk enough for the servants to put him to bed."

She went out.

Duke George clasped his hands to his face and wept again. He tasted his new humiliation luxuriously, licking it as a man licks a painful tooth. Presently someone jabbed his shoulder and pushed a cup into his hand.

"Drink that and be cheerful," said Duke Richard vaguely.

Duke George drank; wiped his eyes again; saw Duke Richard sitting opposite to him and eating a wafer.

"Are you restored?" he asked.

"It would draw anyone's tears," said Duke George defensively.

"Anyone might weep who was as injured and outraged

207

as you think yourself to be, George, Duke of Clarence, first prince of the blood royal of England, Lord Lieutenant of Ireland. But you mayn't. You aren't injured. Oh, you silly man, why must you hate yourself and then blame Edward and me because you hate yourself, and so injure us and then hate yourself worse for having injured us? You're not as tall or as old as Edward and—to speak the perfect truth you're not as clever as I am. But you're a man, and a very proper one. Leave it so. Stop putting yourself to the brake —someone told me that not so long ago—and remember our Lord Edward and I are your brothers."

"You don't trust me."

"We would do if you would but allow us. I swear, as I hope for salvation at the high doom, Edward has no malice against you; and I have less than none. Can't you be easy again?"

"You can talk."

"By St. Paul, if you weren't my respected elder brother, I'd do more than talk. George, I love you, and it sours my belly to see you turn into a wine-soaking, morose fool and a creature of grudges. Pure silly jealousy's the root of it. Leave coveting what's not yours—the crown you once aimed at, Kingmaker's lands you want to swallow the whole of— and take pride in what you have and what you are. It's ample, surely. Leave blaming yourself and then thrusting the blame into our mouths : and at least purge your soul of one thing now and feel easier for it."

"What thing?"

"Tell me where is Anne."

"There you're at it again. There you're at it. You won't believe me. I'm a liar and a turncoat. The devil damn you black, I've told you till the words stick in my gullet, I don't know. She was here and she ran away, and now I swear by God I don't know where she is."

He was aware of his heart banging like an armourer's hammer, of Duke Richard's stiff, white face, full of ambiguous expression, that conveyed nothing. It is half the truth, he told himself urgently : looked at one way, is the whole truth. I want understanding, want forgiveness from someone after they have known the worst. If he asks me why she ran away, I'll tell him. It might be better if I did. Duke

208

Richard's dagger clicked three times in its sheath, at stretched-out intervals, before he said :

"Then God forgive you, George. You've made my life harder than it need have been. But let's try even now whether we can't wean you of these humours and jealousies of yours and teach you that we don't call you ill names when your back's turned."

"No, it isn't that I mind really. I only just thought that perhaps to-night . . . It's silly of me. I feel lonely, I suppose."

"Oh, aye; well, but you've got your women, haven't you?"

"Women."

"Well then, shall I send Will to keep you company a little?"

"Will : oh, you great stupid bear, when you can see quite plainly that it's you I want."

"My dear love : but I've told you how it is. Parliament's prorogued, and I've ten hundred things to see to to-night."

"Ten hundred hampersful of devils !"

"God's blessed Lady, Elizabeth !"

Edward of England sat upright on the daybed where he had been sprawling and stared at his Queen. She, a stiff Madonna in purple velvet and ermine all flowered-over with arabesques of silver and pearls, stared back at him. She knew that she could stand inspection. Everything that decoctions of milk, turpentine, almonds and English herbs, unguents from the domain of the Grand Turk and the odd and rather evil-smelling preparations sent her in secret by Friar Bungay could do to preserve her figure and complexion had been done. Her hair, though hidden under her large coiffe, was powdered with gold-dust. Her cheeks were pink—not, just at present, altogether with fard—and her forehead white. Her greenish eyes under the plucked eyebrows were brightened by the cunning application of a black Egyptian earth and drops of a distillation of nightshade. She did not happen, at the moment, to be pregnant, but a padded stomacher gave her the fashionably forward and upward-thrusting belly. She was wearing several hundred pounds' worth of jewellery and looking her best.

"What's amiss with you?" asked the King grievedly.

"I forgot my duty for a moment. I ask pardon."

"Nay, nay, nay"—Edward's ringed enormous hand fumbled for hers—"tell me the trouble."

"I'm sorry. I shouldn't have spoken so. I want always to be meek and submissive to my Lord. But it's hard sometimes when you're so secret with me, as though you thought I wouldn't understand, that I'd be jealous."

"Jealous : I'll renounce Mahomet if I know what you're talking about."

"Oh, Edward; and do you really think I believe it's State business that's taking you away to-night?"

"Now listen, Elizabeth. I swear by . . ."

"You're going to Jane Shore : as if I minded that. That's what so hard to bear; you thinking I'll be jealous."

"God damn it, Elizabeth . . ."

"I know you are, and if only you understood how gladly willing I am you should take any pleasure anywhere. Jane Shore's a decent little thing, if she was born in the kennel, and I'm sure it's not her fault if she has such a coarse and rusty way of speaking. If she makes you happy, it's enough for me, and I'll be her bedeswoman as long as I've breath. But it does hurt me to my bowels that you keep secrets from me."

"Now may God so help and save me, Elizabeth, I was thinking of nothing in all christendom, but saving you a little ill-ease. You're a kind woman, Elizabeth. You don't grudge a man a little natural happiness of his body. But a good husband doesn't tell his wife : I'm up and off now to say good-night to my leman."

"So you were going to see her all the time."

"Oh, hell and devils, I said no such thing."

"You keep secrets from me. That's what cuts the veins in my heart. You keep secrets. You're not open with me any more."

"My dear love, it was only for your own happiness. God's blessed Lady, I'll be as open with you as you want, then. Yes, I'm going to Jane to-night. A common woman would be angry if her husband told her that, but I do seriously believe you'd sooner I were open about it. Jane's a good skin—the wittiest whore in my realm, I tell her. You understand, Elizabeth."

"Yes, Edward, I do understand, and the blessed Virgin

knows I try to take it all in charity. You so hard at work, ruling your England: what does it matter, I ask myself when at night thinking of her and you together, what does it matter where he gets his pleasure, so he gets it?"

"But look you, Elizabeth, you never lie awake at night troubling your dear head over me and Jane?"

"I try not to. Oh, I do try. I try to be dutiful and think only of your happiness. But when one loves as I love, Edward, God knows it's hard."

Queen Elizabeth put a kerchief of very fine lace in front of her eyes and turned her face away. Between the elaborate and fantastic structure of her coiffe and the furred yoke of her gown, her long neck, the colour of ivory, seemed almost painfully slender, and the brittle colour of the stones about it enhanced its touching appearance of fragility. Many hundreds of dead men whose quarters and heads had rotted upon public spikes or their bones been shovelled into pits on battlefields might not have recognised their butcher as Edward, in red-cheeked perplexity, came behind her and put his hands on her shoulders and mumbled into her ear:

"Oh, my dear love, you mustn't cry. Nay, you mustn't grieve like that. I can't uphold it. Look, if this is how you feel, I'll not go to her to-night. I'll have no more dealings with her. It's you I love best, Elizabeth. I love you with all my heart and liver. I'll have no more of Jane. I swear I'll not."

The Queen turned round to him very suddenly.

"Edward, beloved husband, I'm an ungrateful, wicked woman."

"An angel, an angel."

"I'm not. I'm a wicked woman and I've made you unhappy. Forgive me, dear, my Lord. Oh, I call all the saints to witness for me I'm not jealous. I'd rather be burned in a tar-barrel than rob you of the smallest pleasure. You shan't give Jane up, never. I'll not have it. You must take no notice of my woman's nonsense. It wasn't her that I was crying over. It's only I've had so much to make me wretched these late times, so much to trouble over. Go to Jane, my dear, and give her my blessing if she makes you happy."

"I'll do no such thing. What's this you've been troubling over?"

211

"No, don't mind me."

"God's teeth, but I will mind you. What's been grieving you?"

"Nothing, dear heart, only that I'm afraid people—people who hate me, people who say you married beneath your dignity——"

"Passion of Christ, if any man's so hardy as to say that, I'll take such measure with him as'll make him wish he'd been born dumb."

"But your own brothers say it."

"Not for their lives, they daren't."

"George of Clarence says nothing else."

"You give me proof of that, and I'll buffet George about the cheeks with my own hands so that he looks like a horn-lantern."

"Then the saints forbid I ever give you any proof. I, stir up strife between you and your own brother : Edward, you must think ill of me if you think that."

"Now, Elizabeth . . ."

"And all I ever said was that now my ill-wishers can laugh at me and giggle into their sleeves and point their fingers at me and say that you don't love me now, and they'll have proof, too. They'll say, since you set eyes on that—on Jane Shore, you've ceased to honour my kindred, and I and my brothers and sisters and your poor stepsons are quite out of favour."

"But God's blessed Lady," said the King, sitting down, "your kinsfolk are as close to me as my own brothers. I've exalted and lifted up the Wydyvlles and the Greys as no house was ever exalted in England since William Conqueror."

"Once, Edward, once."

"Haven't I sent Anthony as my orator to the court of Duke François of Brittany?"

"Yes, Anthony's useful to you."

"And married your sisters to half the old nobility of England?"

"Yes, my sisters; but you used to care for your stepsons too, for my poor darlings. Now I suppose they only remind you I was once nearly as common a woman as Jane Shore."

"Don't say that, Elizabeth !"

212

"But I can't help but feel it, Edward, when you care so little for them."

"Nay, but my love, I call that very hard. I'm as fond of your Thomas as if he were my own get: a good, gracious, well-mannered young man as you'll meet."

"Not gracious enough for you to find a wife for him."

King Edward's blue eyes slowly widened to their full. His girlishly lovely mouth opened in company with them.

"So there's where the shoe pinches," he said in a hushed voice of self-condemnation and relief. "What a cuckoo-witted innocent I am. Oh dear Elizabeth, did you truly think I was neglecting you because I haven't made a marriage for Thomas yet? Forgive me. I'm to blame. I've left the business too long. I see that now. Why, Jane herself—now this'll teach you the kind of woman she is, Elizabeth—Jane herself said to me only the other—said to me not long back she wondered Thomas hadn't found a wife yet."

"Well, and if even she talks of it, it shows you what people think; shows how I'm mocked now."

"I was a fool, Elizabeth. But it wasn't as you think. I swear by the sacrament it wasn't. I've had so much to busy me. Tell me, love, had you thought of a likely wench for him?"

"Not I, Edward: I don't plan such things."

"Now if match-making isn't woman's work, what is, in God's name? Haven't you thought of anyone?"

"Well, she's young yet, and you might think her too good for him."

"Never in this mortal world."

"It was the old Lord Haryngton's daughter, Cecily Bonville."

"Will Hastings' little step-daughter: excellent, Elizabeth, that's an excellent thought! The chit's young yet, but we could contrive it in a year or so. Baroness Bonville and Haryngton in her own right, and a very plump little heiress too: Thomas will be among the clover with her. Excellently thought of, love. And her father was a good white rose man; died by mine's side at the ill day of Wakefield. He shall have her. If she weds any other, it'll be across my body."

"Oh, Edward, my dear Lord."

She kissed him, holding her head sharply backward and

pressing her breasts forward, so as not to disarrange her headgear. He patted her shoulders.

"Does that show you that you're still my most special darling of all darlings, Elizabeth?"

"Oh, my love, you're so sweet to me you can almost make me forget my troubles."

"Forget your troubles? Look you, my dearest, what are these troubles you keep talking of? Tell me. Only tell me. I'm King of England, even if I am your bond-slave. What troubles have you I can't put a stop to? I'll not suffer you to have troubles."

"I won't stir up strife between you and your brothers. I've told you that."

King Edward got on his feet again. His face took on a look of anger that suited it better than its previous sheepishness.

"George?" he asked gratingly.

Queen Elizabeth grabbed one of his hands.

"He means no harm, Edward. I'm sure and certain he doesn't. But he does say such unkind things. He's unnatural, I think, to call his own brother's wife a yellow-haired upstart."

"He said that?" shouted King Edward, his long back bending and his elbows and fingers flexing.

"Something like that, I heard."

"The drunken, babble-tongued, insolent ribald, I'll break his neck."

"Edward, Edward, don't say such things!"

"I will."

"No, no, you mustn't speak like that. Oh, I wish I'd held my peace about it all."

"You should have told me long since."

"I'll be sorry I've told you now unless you swear not to be rash with George. Just because he was a traitor to you once, you mustn't be hard on him. Only if he says such cruel things about me, I do think you might speak to him—only gently—and tell him how much he hurts me. I'm sure if you happen to take him when he's sober he'll understand and be very sorry."

"He'll be sorry."

"No, Edward, don't look like that. He's your own brother. You must promise me you'll be forbearing with him."

"As you please: then I'll promise."

"God bless you, my sweet darling husband."

"Happy now, Elizabeth?"

"Very happy, Edward. Nay, but look how I'm keeping you from Jane. You must make haste."

"Elizabeth!"

"Yes, my Lord?"

"But you never mean I should go to Jane now, to-night, after what you said?"

"Oh, you foolish love, you foolish, foolish love, why would I not do? Go to Jane, poor creature. She'll have joy of your body, but never such joy as I have of your goodness and your kingliness. That is my reserved special pleasure. Poor Jane the merchant's wife, the wittiest whore in your realm, she may take what she can of you. I don't envy her. I'm not jealous. I pity her with all my heart. She'll never know the real Edward as I know him."

"Body of God, Elizabeth, you're a marvellous woman."

"No, Edward, only a loving wife. Go to your pleasure of to-night now. Don't keep her waiting, your witty Jane. I love you so much that I can even spare you from the bed of your royalty to lie in the gutter for a night or two, if you so please."

"Elizabeth, are you sure you want me to go?"

"Sure, sure, and sure. Go now: you mustn't keep Jane waiting."

"Elizabeth, I swear it, no man ever had such a wife as you."

"Nor any woman such a husband."

This time, as they kissed, Queen Elizabeth's coiffe was pushed askew. She straightened it with one hand whilst she waved her husband, who seemed disposed to further talk, toward the door with the other.

"A happy night, Edward, and be kind to Jane. She's deserved nothing else from you, whatever she has from her husband."

"Good-night, Elizabeth, and God bless you for a kind, sensible woman and my dearest wife."

One minute after the damascened lock of the door had clicked behind him, Queen Elizabeth tinkled a gold-and-crystal bell. A page appeared and, still busy with her coiffe in front of the mirror, she gave orders for her jewel-chest. Two pages carried it, their graceful bodies, skin-tight in

215

silk, dragged inward and sideways by its weight. When they were dismissed again, the Queen fished a small key out of her bosom and unlocked the nail-studded, stout box. Kneeling, she disposed its trays around her on the floor. Her broad sweep of purple train made the right background for the loops and curves of glittering stuff that she pulled out and ran her fingers through. There were clusters and clots of diamonds like perpetually-sunned, unmelting ice, dull opals, blatant sapphires and emeralds, long lines of pearls that shamed the commoner ones upon her dress, unshining turquoises and bloody rubies. Many-coloured enamels seemed to purr with satisfaction as the light stroked them. Her whitened hands, themselves startling with jewels, delved in and out, hauling up entangled necklaces, chains, heavy gold bracelets, elaborate ear-rings, and splashing them round her on the silk carpet. She squatted back on her heels and trickled them through her fingers : the record, frozen into hard shapes and colours, of King Edward's conjugal affection. She was picking out a really handsome present for her friend Jane Shore.

Mr. William Colyngbourne of Lydyard in Wiltshire, up in London during Parliament-time, was drinking an evening quart of ale at his favourite tavern in St. Botolph's parish. He was a sober, comfortable yeoman in a black best gown over blue doublet and black hose. His companion, a sharp-faced Londoner whom he had met that evening, listened to him with interest and apparent respect when he told him how he had once held office as Serjeant of the Pantry in King Edward's household and was now in hopes of getting himself appointed by the King's mother, the great Duchess of York, as steward of her lands in Wiltshire.

"You're a true, honest white rose man, I see," his companion said ingratiatingly.

William Colyngbourne took trouble to appear so. His real thoughts about the wars of York and Lancaster were his own business these days. He nodded earnestly.

"By the Mass, yes : d'you know I was in this very tavern, drinking with the loyal men-at-arms, when our Lord Edward had come into his own again last year, and a fellow ran to the door to tell us Kingmaker was lying at Barnet Heath with thirty thousand. That was a night."

"Kingmaker: we shan't see his like again, the great Earl."

"A proud nobleman, too proud for this world."

"A proud house, the Nevilles; and now they're broken as small as chaff: Kingmaker and Montacute dead and rotten, the Countess in hiding, and the Archbishop shut up in Guisnes in a prison where he can see neither sun nor moon, because he tried to serve two masters."

William Colyngbourne did not answer. The fall of the Archbishop had been unpleasant news to him. It was contrived, they said, by Dr. Morton, once a close councillor of Queen Marguerite and her dead son, and now so fatly in favour with the Yorkist Court that he was made Master of the Rolls. If Dr. Morton, the traitor who lined his nest by selling his old friends to new ones, was acquainted with the secret dealings between George Neville and John Vere, then how many other secret dealings could he put a name to? How many more Lancastrians now sitting still and thinking their own thoughts in England could he uncover and throw into the hands of Edward's gaolers and executioners? William Colyngbourne reviewed his past and thought of horrible things: a sledge bumping behind a horse's heels to Tyburne, a rope that choked one, but not to death, a cold knife on one's belly. I'll have no more truck with politics, he told himself.

"It was strange," the Londoner went on, looking sideways at him, "how Holy Harry died when he did—of pure displeasure and melancholy, they say."

William Colyngbourne met that gambit without blinking. He was as certain that Holy Harry had been murdered as he was that there was ale in his mazer; but he was by no means going to lay himself open to an accusation of treason by saying so.

"No doubt it was the news of his son's death at Tewkesbury field."

"No doubt."

There was a silence. The Londoner broke it in a way that sent the blood to Mr. Colyngbourne's heart with a dreadful rush.

"I have wanted for a long while to have some talk with you, Mr. Colyngbourne. I am one of Dr. Morton's household."

217

The mazer in William Colyngbourne's hand tipped so that the ale splashed out of it. His throat clicked.

"Dr. Morton?"

"The Master of the Rolls: he sent me to-night to find you and ask for a little of your company."

"What have I to do with him? I never saw him in all my life."

The Londoner had dipped his finger in the spilt ale and was amusing himself by drawing lines along the table-top. He did not look up.

"He knows your name. He—we—heard that you had come to London, and I was ordered to bring you to him privately. To-night is a good time. He is lodging at Dean's Yard."

"What the devil madness is this? What can Dr. Morton want with me?"

"He would be glad to tell you that himself."

"I won't come. How do I know you're not a thief or a Bedlamite? I'll go and wait on him in the morning, if it must be, but by God I'll not budge a foot with you at this hour."

"I think you should come."

"That I will not."

Dr. Morton's servant smudged out the pattern he had drawn on the table-top and looked thoughtfully at him.

"That is what George Neville said."

William Colyngbourne's stomach seemed to contract as though it had been hit. His lips felt swollen and there was a rushing noise inside his head. He stood up.

"I'll come."

There was a tickling, heavy mist in Dean's Yard. Somewhere above it, hidden now, the spire of St. Paul's climbed up five hundred feet into the autumn air. Lights behind windows were rare and faint, fog-yellowed. Mr. Colyngbourne's guide knocked on a door and it was opened.

"Go up the stairs," he said.

Mr. Colyngbourne went up, feeling as though he left his life behind him in the damp fog.

"In there," his guide told him, a hand on his elbow, and pushed a second door ajar.

The room they went into was not sinister; was not even seemly for an official of the King's Court. Its unplastered beams were low overhead. Its hangings were the cheapest kind of painted canvas. William Colyngbourne noticed a truckle bed, a couple of old chairs, many chests heaped with swags of paper and parchment, two rushlights on a table and a man writing. The man looked up as they came in, showing them a priest's face, round, smooth, secret, with considering eyes and a close mouth.

"Mr. Colyngbourne of Lydyard," said the servant, and went out.

The priest stood up. He was short and middle-aged, with a certain comfortable plumpness of presence. His robes were black and grey satin and struck the only note of spruceness and newness in the room.

"Be seated, sir."

William Colyngbourne found a chair and sat in it. The sinews at the back of his knees were jerking. Dr. Morton came round the end of the table, moving discreetly and softly like a cat, and sat opposite to him. His pale, plump face was benevolent and he twined his short fingers together in his lap.

"Mr. Colyngbourne, I have sent for you on a matter that concerns your well-being."

"I do not know what that can be, sir. I do not know what I have to do with you."

Dr. Morton protruded the tip of his tongue between his lips. The effect of this was only to emphasise the shut, secret expression of the whole mouth. He rubbed his broad nose with his forefinger and then twined his hands again. His dark eyes captured Mr. Colyngbourne's.

"Mr. Colyngbourne, you formerly had the honour to be a servant of the King's Grace in the office of Serjeant of the Pantry."

His voice was low-pitched and insinuating, the voice of a friend offering sensible advice.

Mr. Colyngbourne nodded.

"At the readeption of the late King Henry VI, two years ago, you nevertheless protested to many persons that you were devoted in all things to the cause of the unfortunate house of Lancaster, urging as a proof of this that you had been ready to bear arms on behalf of the Earl of Warwick when he revolted against our Lord King Edward."

"Sir, I never . . ."

Dr. Morton lifted his hand and went on :

"When Queen Marguerite landed in the West Country, you left London to go to your place at Lydyard, saying to many of your friends that you would arm your servants and support her : and indeed you had set out to do so when you heard the news of the Bloody Meadow and the destruction of the Queen's party there."

"As God sees me, since that day I have never spoken nor taken on hand anything against King Edward."

"You openly protested your loyalty to him as soon as he arrived in London. But in private and among your friends you have accused him of necromancy, witchcraft, adultery and other vile crimes. You have drunk to the success of John Vere of Oxford in his invasion of Cornwall. You have spoke defamatorily of the King's brothers, the Dukes of Clarence and Gloucester, calling the one a turncoat and a false Duke who betrayed the Earl of Warwick, and the other a misshapen dwarf. You have said that the old Duke of York was a common rebel with no more right to the crown of England than to your doublet, and that even if his right had been ten times better than it was, it could not avail King Edward, for King Edward was no son of his, but the bastard of a Scots archer called Blackburn with whom the Duchess of York committed adultery. You have said this last even whilst you were seeking employment from the Duchess about her lands in Wiltshire."

Terror swooped like a demented bat about the confusion of William Colyngbourne's mind. He had said all these things that stood up in front of him now like a row of pikes laid at his chest. A clear, dreadful picture was shaping in his imagination. A crowd stood round a gallows with a ladder set to it. There was a fire lighted and a knife and an axe put ready on a block. He could feel the rope biting his neck, the crash of his fall as it was cut to keep him alive, hands dragging his clothes off, the steel in his guts. Dr. Morton's cat-face wavered and went black before him.

"These . . . lies . . ." he whispered, putting a finger between his neck and his collar.

"I can prove them all." Dr. Morton made a slight controlled gesture toward a paper on his table. "Mr. Colyngbourne, I know enough about you to send you to Tyburne."

"Dr. Morton, for Christ's sake, I meant no harm. I

220

talked. I was loyal to King Henry in his lifetime, but I meant nothing against King Edward. I swear it on the cross of Christ."

"You told your friend John Turburvyle of Dorset that if the Earls of Pembroke and Richmond would but land in Wales, you and he might strike a blow for the true blood even yet."

William Colyngbourne wiped the spittle from his chin and stared in creeping horror that was not only horror of the gallows at Dr. Morton.

"Are you a devil?" he asked in a dried whisper.

"That is scarcely a fit question to ask a priest of Holy Church," said the Master of the Rolls primly, "and in all events it is I who will ask you a question, Mr. Colyngbourne. What are you, who call yourself a loyal Yorkist nowadays? I will tell you what you are, sir. You are, and you have always been, whatever offices you held or lip-service you paid, as rank a Lancastrian as, let us say, myself."

William Colyngbourne was beyond surprise; was almost beyond fear. He shook his head like a bear in a cage and did not speak. The large, dark eyes, priest's eyes, of Dr. Morton kept their hold upon his own. The full, close lips moved precisely, shaping and arranging words.

"As rank a Lancastrian as myself, Mr. Colyngbourne, and I think one who, also like myself, knows that in these unhappy times he can best serve the true blood by seeming to serve its enemies : that is the man I take you for."

"But you : it was you who destroyed George Neville."

"Certainly I did, Mr. Colyngbourne, because George Neville was of no more avail to us and because I knew that in every case the King intended his destruction. Necesse est, Mr. Colyngbourne, quod unus pro populo mori, which is in English : needs must that one should die for the folk. I sacrificed George Neville, and I stand so high by his sacrifice that no man now dares impugn my loyalty to the adulterous usurper who calls himself Edward of England. That is more matter than whether that hotheaded blunderer Oxford should have been helped to hold St. Michael's Mount a few days longer. Put such foolish schemes as his out of your mind, my friend, and learn to take a long view of our case as I do."

"Why have you sent for me : and how am I to know you are not laying me a trap?"

"If you are not hanged within a month for the treasons that I can prove against you already, you will know that I play fair, will you not? Let me, in my turn, warn you that if ever one word of what I say to-night passes your lips, you shall hang as duly as the sun rises."

"Why have you sent for me, in God's name?"

"Be easy, sir. I have sent for many part-takers of the house of Lancaster in these last months. I think I may say that there is no Lancastrian of standing in this realm or in Brittany whose name and something of his conditions I do not know. Go into Kent one day and ask the Gilfords or the Romneys—both names should be familiar to you—whether I am the traitor to the red rose that I seem to be. There are lists of names here—I may give you a sight of them presently, if we are agreed together—that you would find very muster-rolls of Lancaster."

"Why do you make them? Why do you talk to me? Is there something afoot, an enterprise?"

Dr. Morton lifted his hand and spoke with the first shade of emphasis that had coloured his smooth voice since the beginning.

"Mr. Colyngbourne, there is nothing afoot, nothing, nothing, nothing. I have told you that I sacrificed George Neville and stirred not so much as a finger to help John Vere, because these petty enterprises, these snatchings of castles and raisings of riots, can do the cause and quarrel of Lancaster no good, but only an infinity of harm. We must face what is, Mr. Colyngbourne. The house of Lancaster bled almost to death at Tewkesbury last year. That blood-drained body of our hopes needs physic and a long rest to recover strength again. There will be no sudden changing of the world for us : but nonetheless, I would see us prepared and ready when the time comes, which, in my true opinion, will not be for these ten years."

"Ten years?"

"Until our last hope, Henry Earl of Richmond, now a child in Brittany, shall be a man and capable of leading armies. We cannot try to set a child upon the throne of England. But when he is mature to claim his own we must strike, not feebly and separately, but as one arm dealing one blow."

"But in ten years the power of Edward will be so rooted into the land that we can never move it."

"Will it so? I am not a devil, as you so uncourteously hinted not long ago, and I have no great gift of prophecy: but I will cite to you one or two things that might befall, ten years from now, and that we might turn to our advantage."

He leaned forward slightly in his chair, his plump, white hands slipping over one another as if they were two pale, swollen fish in a small bowl. For the next half-hour he spoke softly and deliberately, and Mr. Colyngbourne listened.

The Widow Wrangwysh opened her eyes and was instantly aware that she had a headache. Her whole fat body was in discomfort. Her back was stiff and her tongue dry. Her brother-in-law Thomas from York, up in London along with the city's two burgesses for Parliament, had supped with her the night before. She had called in the chantry-priest to make an evening of it, and she had only a dim idea of how she eventually got to bed. She fancied Anne had helped her there. Sun was glinting unkindly through the shutters now and iron-shod cart-wheels made an ear-filling clatter in the cobbled street. The widow swore and shut her eyes again. The earlier part of the evening was pretty clearly memorable. Brother Tom had been full of the doings of the Duke of Gloucester, with whom he was to have an audience at Baynard's Castle in the morning. He was the most courteous great nobleman, he said, that ever was in Yorkshire. He had been surprised how much his sister-in-law knew about the Duke, and the widow had to explain how she had heard it all from her little cookmaid who was once in service—she hoped she had not been moved to put it more explicitly than that—in Kingmaker's household and the Duke of Clarence's. After that, they had all been very merry together, and she distinctly recalled singing Dieu vous sauve, Dame Emme, a song popular in her girlhood, and emptying the dregs of her cup down the priest's neck.

"Holy Mary," murmured the Widow Wrangwysh aloud, "I'm getting old."

The noise of the carts went marching through her head like an army with siege-artillery, and she felt as though the devil were in her mouth. Grunting and exhaling, she heaved herself over in the sordid tangle of bedclothes, spat on the floor and sat up. Whoever put her to bed had had the sense to pull her outer clothes off, she observed, and lay them neatly on a chair. That would be Anne, no doubt. The cook and the two scullery-wenches would never in this world of God have taken the trouble. With a final groan she pushed the coverings away and got on her feet. Dressed only in her kirtle and shift, with her hair over her eyes and her face yellow and blue, she was a sight to rebuke sin, and knew it. She tottered to the window and slammed the shutters back. Cold autumn sun and air struck her in the face like a reproach, and from immediately beneath her the piercing voice of a hawker's boy squalled:

"Hot pies, hot!"

The startling noise, coupled with the bare notion of a hot pie, undid her altogether. She sank back, sitting, onto the bed and banged a chair on the floor, hoping it might fetch someone. Bet, the younger scullery-wench, presently looked in.

"Get me a pint of small ale quickly."

"Yes, mistress."

"And send Anne up here, and hurry, pox take you."

It was Anne herself, meek and almost ghostly, who brought the drink. The widow mumbled at her:

"Did you lay me away last night?"

"Yes."

"What's o'clock?"

"It's past nine."

"Oh Lord."

The widow drank, spat and drank again; felt not much better.

"I'm ill, wench. I'm sick."

"You ought to drink no ale, then."

"No ale? What the devil do you know about it? Ale's what I want."

"You had too much last night."

"And that's why I must have some more this morning. You get me another pint, and none of your damned back-answers. Jesus, what's that?"

There was a loud, imperative knocking on the front-door of the house. The widow put her hands to her head.

"Oh, God's blessed Lady, what's this tormenting gar-boyle? St. Anthony's fire roast them, do they want to deafen a woman? Who are they? I'll heave a bucket of slops on them in a minute. Go to the window, can't you, and see who it is? Oh God, my ears!"

Anne crossed to the window. The knocking was main-tained, burst after threatening burst of blows.

"Oh!"

The cry was so small and desolate, so thin with despair, that even in her peevish stupor the widow jerked her head round. Anne was leaning against the wall, twisting her hands together. Her eyes were enormous, like two skullholes in the white of her face.

"What is it, girl alive?"

"Men-at-arms."

Anne's voice was tiny. She coughed on the words as though they hurt her throat.

"Men-at-arms, at *my* door? The wench is daft. Oh Lord, I shall be daft myself before this morning's out."

She peered down. Anne was quite right. There were men in scarlet, carrying pikes, clustered before the door of the Silver Pack. Horses were held in the street by pages, and a crowd had collected. She stared at Anne.

"He's found me out."

"Who's found you out?"

"The King."

"The King? Holy mother Mary, was it the King that . . .?"

"Yes."

There were steps clapping on the staircase. Bet flung the door open, round-faced and round-eyed.

"Oh, mistress, there's Mr. Wrangwysh here and a parcel of soldiers and a fine Lord in velvet, and they're demanding of you. I never saw the like."

The Widow Wrangwysh gulped twice and felt her morning malaise pressing more heavily on her, tangling her lips and wits.

"My gown," she croaked, "get me into my gown, Bet. I'll see 'em in the solar. I think the world's run mad." She got the choking fustian thing over her head somehow, kicked

225

her feet into straw slippers and stumbled to the door, poking her hair out of her eyes. "My hood, girl," she snapped, and Bet put it on her.

A soft hand closed on hers and she saw Anne at her side. "Don't tell them. For God's sake don't tell them."

"I'll do what I can," said the widow, and pushed past her into the solar, shutting the door behind her.

Two men were there: Thomas Wrangwysh in his bawdekin gown made of the stuff that she had got for him, and another. This was a small man, very richly dressed in black and silver with ermine. He had a pale, pointed face and queerly wrinkled-up eyes under straight eyebrows. The Widow Wrangwysh blinked at him for a second and then gasped. Her fat, tired legs came near to failing her in the unaccustomed exercise, but she dropped a curtsey.

"Sister," said Thomas Wrangwysh, "his royal Grace the Duke of Gloucester has come to ask you about a matter. You'll mind telling me last night at supper how you had a little maid with you was in his Grace of Clarence's household once."

The Duke let him get no further than this. He had been drawing his thin lips tight against his teeth and twisting a ring on his finger; but he spoke in the softest and pleasantest voice she had ever heard.

"Mrs. Wrangwysh, I must ask your pardon for invading you. I have cause to think this maid of yours is a lady I have sought very earnestly for a long while. Will you be pleased to let me speak face-to-face with her? If she is one I think she is, I promise you your kindness to her will not be forgotten."

Round and round in the widow's ale-drenched mind there churned the thought: It is the King she fears. She's always spoken kindly of the Duke. She opened her mouth twice, but no articulate words escaped it.

The Duke was staring at her. He had the brightest eyes she had ever seen: clear grey with pupils that swelled and shrank like a cat's. He took a step toward her and looked up—he was the shorter by half a head—into her face.

"Mrs. Wrangwysh, I do not know what tale this lady may have told you. She is in great fear of injury and has been badly used. But I do promise, on my soul's salvation, that if you will give me the means to come to her she will bless you for it all the days of her life; and I will also."

The Widow Wrangwysh had had three husbands. Her bleared eyes looked into the Duke's and she made a clumsy gesture sideways with her left hand.

"In there," she grunted.

The Duke was past her like a weasel. He was through the door before Thomas Wrangwysh could spring up to open it. The widow heard a small cry of terror from within and, immediately upon it, in a voice that shook with triumph and incomprehension, one word:

"Dickon!"

The widow lifted her own voice then.

"Bet, come out of that."

Bet's eyes were goggling as though they would pop like squeezed orange-pips out of her face. She gave her news breathlessly but very clearly.

"He's kissing our Anne."

"Shut your foolish, flappering mouth," ordered the widow vehemently, "and down with you to the cellar and fetch up the best claret, and take and clean these silver cups my second left me."

"But Anne, Anne, you could never have believed it: not of Edward."

"I did believe."

"But of Edward, Edward that you've known since we were little: how was it anyway possible that he could have intended dishonour to you? How could you believe that?"

"Oh God, Dickon, everything has been possible in these last three years. Only think what things have been possible already. I've been an exile. I've been Princess of Wales. I've been a cookmaid. The whole world has been like a quagmire under my feet, shifting, no ground to stand on: and it was George himself who told me. I thought he could not invent such a slander against his own brother."

"Was he sober when he said it?"

"No."

Anne closed her eyes for a second and saw a picture of the great, sweating, red-faced man who had sat beside her on an oak settle, whispering fuzzily in her ear, blowing a

227

breath of stale wine into her face and telling her what Edward had in mind.

"The saints be thanked for that at least. I do not think I could sleep quiet in my bed again if I thought he had told that lie sober."

"But why did he ever tell it? Why does he hate me so?"

A frigid imitation of a smile moved Duke Richard's face.

"He does not hate you; but he knows I love you, and he meant we should not marry if he could hinder it. He is your guardian, Anne, and you are heiress to half your great father's lands."

"And only for that ..."

"Only for that: Anne, Edward must not hear of this. There is bad blood enough between them. I think he would kill George if he knew."

"I shall not tell him. But how am I heiress, Dickon? Mother is alive."

"Yes, but she will not be permitted to inherit. I fear not. Edward has a long memory, Anne. I can get her pardoned, but that is all. But what does it matter, bird? Whilst we're together there is a home for her."

"Oh, Dickon, I'm a fool. I'm going to cry. Don't mind me. But it's so long."

"Don't cry. Anne, my precious bird, my love, it's all over now. It's all over if you'll have me."

"If I'll have you? Oh, d'you know as little of me as that?"

She looked at him. They were sitting together in the little house in St. Martin's Sanctuary that he had brought her to, armed men in scarlet clanking before and behind them, from the Widow Wrangwysh's home that morning. He returned her look seriously, with intent, wide eyes.

"Think, Anne," his low voice told her. "Think, my love. We are an evil house to marry into."

"The royal house of York?"

"Royal and evil, with the curse of Plantagenet, Black Fulk of Anjou's curse: think of us. George you know. He is our blackest sheep. Edward—I can hardly speak indifferently about Edward. He is God to me, Anne, the god of my idolatry. I would damn my soul for him. But other men have not found him as I have. He has done terrible things: and as for me ..."

He swung round a little in his chair, cocking a knee up and joining both hands round it, frowning and chewing his lip. His face was a puzzled scholar's face, bent over a hard manuscript, weighing and considering scrupulously. Bunched in this way, his body was absurdly small.

"I have my own devils, Anne," he said after a long while.

Anne's mind was moving by tiny spasms, as grass twitches back into position when a heel has crushed it, to a life of years ago : Middleham Castle and children playing ball and Richard sitting with her and telling secrets.

"What devils, Dickon?"

His words were coming more and more slowly, as though dragged with cables.

"I am one of those who will let nothing stand between me and what I see clearly ought to be done."

"But that is what saints are, not devils."

There was something almost haggard about his eyes and brow as he turned round on her.

"I am no saint. I am a man who trusts too much to his own conscience, and that is how men are damned. I tell you that when I choose what I think to be right I'll stop at no wrong to accomplish it. There you know the worst of me. I thought it right, and I think it right now, to support my brother Edward and his title in the teeth of universal christendom : and in supporting him, I helped to kill your father."

She remembered words said to her long ago : "I do not think so, my Lady, I heard it was common men who followed your father into Wrotham Wood." Richard had help to kill the man who said them, too. She put her hand out, but he did not reach for it.

"It was not you who cut him down."

"No, I was not there. But as God sees me, I would have killed him with my own hands if there was need."

She took a deep breath.

"But there is one thing, Dickon, you would not have done. If you had joined him as George joined him, you would not have betrayed him as George betrayed him."

"I did not join him, and so betrayed you."

"Never, never and in no fashion have you betrayed me, my dear heart."

229

He put his hands to his face as though to stop her reading it.

"Think, Anne, think. George betrayed his King and got Isobel to wife. If I had done as much, should I not have saved you from that infamous marriage with Marguerite's bastard?"

"You'd have been no husband for me, Dickon, if you had sold your brother for my sake."

"Most women would prize a husband who cared so much for them."

"Not I."

Duke Richard straightened himself in his chair. His hands dropped from his face and he looked hard at her.

"Anne, that is what I hoped in my heart that you'd say. That is you : Neville pride in you. Whether you take me or not, I do thank the saints you are still the Anne I loved, my Anne of Middleham who'd have no truck with dirty bargains. But, Anne, I've not done my tale yet."

"I might think you didn't want me, you argue so well against yourself."

"But you don't think so," he said certainly, and went on : "I've dipped my hands deep in blood since we were children at Middleham, and some of it was honest blood. Not only in battle : I've headed and hanged where I saw heading and hanging would serve Edward. After Tewkesbury—and I shall never know, to the day of my death, whether Edward really swore their pardon as they claimed he did—I was a butcher. That's not much in itself: but I had no anger to help me. Edward would have been in a royal rage and shouted them to the block. I didn't hate them. The only man I hated died on the field, killed like a coward whilst he was yelling to George for succour. But I headed them for all that, coldly and in sober blood, because it was needful. Anne, I am afraid of myself sometimes. My cold wits let me to the things other men will only do in passion. Even in love : I have never loved any woman in my life but you. I'm not lustful like Edward; don't need something always between the sheets to keep my bed warm. Yet I have had them, coldly, because I wished to be sure how little they meant to me. I've a fine crop of bastards now, and the poor babes were every one of them got without affection either of body or mind, like dolls whittled from wood. That is what I am."

Again, she put out her hands to him.

"And it was that conscience of yours in which you trust too much, and those frozen wits of yours that weigh and measure and probe, that made you tell me all these things too, so that I should be sure of my bargain before I made it."

"That is true. You have understood. That is the perfect truth. Because I am clear-sighted, this same cursed conscience of mine will not let you take me with your eyes shut, my dear. It will not let me deal any way but honestly with you. You must not take me unless you take me for what I am."

"Richard, I know what you are."

"You shall not take me from gratitude, nor from old affection in the days when we were children together. If you refuse me now, I will go out of here and never set eyes on you again : but I will make sure that George shall pay you the last penny of your just due and make no trouble for whatever man you choose to marry. Consider that, and then you shall give me your answer."

She had not thought that she could cry so much, since the time her marriage with Queen Marguerite's son had dried and withered something in her. The tears dazzled her eyes to blindness, but she found him with her hands and held him, not laying her head on his breast, but clasping and soothing his on hers.

231

CHAPTER FIVE

WINE

(France–England: 1475–1478)

> *The Queen was in her parlour*
> *Eating bread and honey,*
> *The King was in his counting-house*
> *Counting out his money.*
> English Nursery-Rhyme, n.d.

THE Christian King was awaiting the summons that he had
dreaded all his life. He awaited it very cheerfully, sitting
on a bench in the room at Croissy-sur-Andelle which had
been rigged up hastily as a presence-chamber for the
occasion. The Sieur de Concressault, the Duc de Bourbon,
the Sieur d'Argenton—his name was Philippes de Commynes, and he had once been in the service of the Duke of
Burgundy—with a great number of other noblemen of
France stood about the room; looked serious; talked in low
voices. The Christian King took not the faintest notice of
them. He had a little spaniel in his lap and was pulling its
ears and telling stories to it.

Philippes de Commynes, Sieur d'Argenton, was less unhappy than the others looked. It was three years now since
he had made up his mind which side to back in the continual quarrel between the nobles and the crown of France
and, slipping quietly at night out of the household of
Charles of Burgundy, had gone to join the King whom he
esteemed the abler man. It was not time yet to regret his
bargain. Louis of France had been in tighter corners than
this and come away from them with his skin whole : and as
for Charles the Hardy, what madness transcending all his
other madnesses led that rash man to sit in siege before the
inexpugnable city of Neuss, at feud with the Emperor, at
feud with the Landgraf of Hesse, at feud with the Arch-

bishopric of Cologne? He should be marching his eighteen thousand Burgundians, his three thousand English auxiliaries and the Italian mercenaries he had hired under that dangerous adventurer, Count Niccolò di Campobasso, westward to the Somme, not eastward to the Rhein, if he wished to achieve the ambition of his life against King Louis. But such is the nature of the man, thought de Commynes. The more he is embroiled, the more he will embroil himself. He edged a little way along the wall and set his ears to discover what the King was whispering to his dog. It was likely to be better sense than what the King's councillors were whispering to one another.

The King had lifted the dog up by its forepaws and was smiling his damp-mouthed smile at the self-conscious way in which it turned its face aside and looked down its nose.

"Listen, Cher-Ami, and I shall tell you a story about a bear which the Emperor—who is a very witty man, although he is so mean and such a coward—told an ambassador of mine not long ago. It is a very instructive story for you to hear, so listen and do not make those foolish grimaces. You are listening very carefully? Good: there were once two men who persuaded an innkeeper to let them chalk up a scot on the slate because, they said, they were going to kill a great bear which lived in the district and annoyed the people, and its skin would sell for a good sum. So when they had dined, they went out to look for this bear; but alas, they found it very much sooner and very much nearer to them than they had reckoned. Then these two poor men were afraid and ran away. One climbed a tree, but the other the bear caught and threw down on the ground, standing over him and thrusting its muzzle against his ear, thus."

He thrust his face into the dog's wavy fur for a second and went on:

"This poor man stayed very still and made as though he were dead, for it is the nature of a bear that it will injure neither man nor beast that does this; and indeed presently this bear left him and returned to its cave. As soon as the man saw himself delivered, he was up and away at a fine pace, and his companion, who had observed this mystery from the top of his tree, behind him; and when they had come up with one another, he who had been in the tree demanded of his friend what it was that the bear had told him when it kept its snout at his ear so long. To which he answered very sensibly that it had told him never to sell the skin of a bear till the beast was well dead."

Precisely, thought de Commynes, and felt a page plucking his sleeve.

"The Herald, Monsieur, he's here."

He nodded, and made his bow to the King.

"If it pleases you, Sire, the Herald of the English is now in attendance."

"Good," said King Louis brightly. He stood up and pushed Cher-Ami into the arms of the Duc de Bourbon, who looked as though he did not know what to do with him; made shuffling haste up to his chair of state; sat in it; coughed twice and composed himself.

A boy's voice called into the silence clearly: "The Herald Jarretière, bringing letters of defiance from King Edward of England."

Garter King-at-Arms was a short man with a dark bony face; shimmered and glistened in his tabard of the arms of England and France, or on azure, quarterly three leopards passants and three fleur-de-lys. He walked alone and the smack of his footsteps sounded through the room, noise of new tribulation coming upon France. The summons King Louis had been dodging for fifteen years now was scrolled and sealed in his right hand.

When he was in front of the King's chair and had bowed, he flicked his eyes once round the room and intoned with a strong Norman twang:

"Sire, be it known to you that the purpose of my coming is to present to you, after salutation, these letters under the hand and seal of my master Edward, fourth of that name since the Conquest, by the Grace of God King of England and France, Duke of Normandy and Aquitaine and Lord of Ireland, by which he summons you to surrender to him his lawful realm of France, appertaining to him of ancient hereditary right, to the end that he may restore the Church, the nobility and the commons thereof to their former liberty, of which they have long stood deprived; letting you know that in case you should deny or withhold this his said right, he is utterly determined to take and resume the same by the way of arms."

234

When he had done, be bowed stiffly again; held out the letter. The King said nothing. One white weak hand made a drooping gesture in the direction of the Sieur de Concressault, who, taking the scroll, presented it upon his knee. The scrunch and crackle as the seals were broken was the only sound in the whole place. De Commynes watched the King, wondering whether he would be smooth or angry. There were moments when that long, mild, milk-coloured face with the drooping nose and the damp mouth changed terribly, the features seeming suddenly to recompose themselves on a new pattern, and the generally ingratiating, gossiping voice slowed and harshened into a growl very like a bear's. This was not one of them. The King read in silence. Once he raised his eyebrows. Twice he scratched his lip; put the parchment aside and blinked for a moment; got up and wandered abstractedly down from his chair and out by a side-door.

The Norman in the English tabard looked thunderstruck. There were courtesies extended to his office which were not waived even when the message he carried was a message of war. But he did not gawp long. Very soon after the little door had shut behind the King it opened again and a valet, a rough country-fellow not of the royal household, peered into the room. It seemed he identified Garter King-of-Arms, after a little consideration, as the man he had been sent to find, for he walked up to him, putting a hand under his elbow, and summoned him out with a jerk of the thumb over the shoulder.

The talk in the room blazed up as suddenly as fire in straw. De Commynes took no part in it. Looked at on paper, this was the end. The French intelligence department was well informed as to the nature of the bargain struck between Edward of England and Charles the Hardy. Charles was to be a sovereign and absolute Prince in his own right, with Champagne and Nevers, Eu, Guise, Rethell and the Duchy of Bar, as well as the Somme towns, to spice his dish with. The rest was Edward's. They had divided the bear's hide. Charles the Hardy, though afflicted by God, as de Commynes seriously believed, in respect of his wits, commanded the most perfectly equipped army in christendom, and Edward of England was a captain who had never lost a battle. There was more to it still. Sixty marks in silver

235

the King had paid a confidential secretary of King Edward's Court for copies of the letters in which Duke François of Brittany boasted that he would perform more exploits in one month against the realms of France than England and Burgundy could achieve in six. It was true Duke François was a shuffler, a little mad, but there was the remote chance that he might keep his word. England was sending three thousand archers again to hearten him in his decision. Four thousand such had piled the road once between Azincourt and Tramecourt with the stripped carcases of the nobility of France.

It would be the end, thought de Commynes, if it were not for the providence of God, who, I believe, must have this realm of France in his especial keeping. This is Charles the Hardy's war, and that beautiful-faced, indolent Edward would not be waging it without him. He must be marvellously discontented with him already, because he sits there in front of Neuss, glorying that the grand army of Germany, with so many princes and prelates—that greatest host which has been seen assembled in man's living memory —cannot budge him. That glory will cost him very dear in the end. He has the real glory of war who has the profit of it. I was right to leave him, that besotted Duke. God has troubled his wits, or how is it to be believed that he would be battering obstinately at the gates of Neuss, when all his life he will never find the English so ready to carry arms over the sea, and when he knows clearly that by themselves they will be as good as useless? There is nothing more maladroit and fat-headed than they when they first cross the sea. They will need his instruction in the French fashion of making war at every turn. But instead of getting it, they will find we have taken Tronchoy and Corbie, Roye and Mondidier and Arras, and wasted and burned all the country of Picardy they will have to march through, and Charles has not detached one single lance from before Neuss to stop us. They will find we have set Sigismund of Austria and René of Lorraine and the free nation of Switzerland onto Charles like three bottles tied to a dog's tail, so that even when he does turn his face from the Rhein at last he will have his hands full. What make of ally will they call him then? Certainly God has guided this man to do in every point what is the opposite to right reason.

The talk dropped away round him as a defeated wave drops downward from the flanks of a coast rock. The King had come into the room again. He was smiling and sliding his hands over each other, as pleased, to all appearance, as a peasant after a good market. No one could have less the look of a man whose prescribed hour had found him out. Garter King-at-Arms, walking a pace or two behind him, carried a pleased face, too. The King stopped in front of his chair of state; did not sit down in it.

"My Lords, gentlemen, you have heard the challenge which our cousin of England has been moved, and we may well guess by whom, to bring against us. His pretended right we utterly deny. To his menaces we respond that our trust is in God and Monsieur St. Denis, as our fathers' has been, who twice drove the English out of France. It is our hope, in eschewing the effusion of christian blood, that some amicable means may yet be found to compose the differences fomented between our dear cousin and us : but should that prove impossible—which God defend—then we must do our best to show him that if he has not forgotten Azincourt, we also have remembered Patay and Formigny. Let us all pray God with a firm heart that so bitter and disastrous a conclusion may be avoided and that our dear cousin may yet be moved, as we are, to consider the great blessings of peace and the hatefulness to heaven of bloodshed. Gentlemen, you are excused."

He bent a long, ringless finger at de Commynes on the last word; took him by one arm, as he came forward, and the Herald by the other.

"Monsieur d'Argenton," he said in his most confiding whisper, "you will entertain this good Herald until a safe-conduct and an escort can be found for him; and do so in such a manner that no one will contrive to talk to him. Cut him a piece of good crimson velvet—thirty yards, say—from the wardrobe as a little gift from us : and let no one talk to him under any circumstances, dear Monsieur d'Argenton."

De Commynes nodded at a job altogether in his comprehension. "I will attend to it, Sire."

The Herald fell into step beside him, and he steered him swiftly and without words to his own room.

"Wine or cyder?" he asked when the door was bolted behind them.

The Norman's face, which was pleased and friendly, wrinkled into a smile.

"You know where I come from. That's not hard to see. Cyder: it's a while since I tasted any fit for a christian stomach."

"What sort of service is it, with the King of England?" de Commynes asked as he filled two cups and found a plate of cheese-cakes on the buffet.

The Norman shrugged.

"I can't grumble. Mine's an honourable office. The pay is good. There's many a gentleman in Normandy would be very glad of half of it: and there are perquisites."

"Quite," said de Commynes, wrinkling his nose over his cyder, "how much did the King give you just now?"

The Herald's face went wooden: a peasant's face.

"The King of England, you mean, sir?"

"I do not."

"Then I don't understand you."

"Oh yes, you do. Come along, man. I shan't ask for a share of it, you know: and I'll see you get your crimson velvet."

"There's nothing in my duties forbids me to accept a gift."

"Assuredly not: how much did you accept?"

"He talked so nicely to me I couldn't refuse it; gave it me with his own hands in cash: three hundred écus."

"And how much did he promise you if Edward consented to a separate peace?"

Garter King-at-Arms put his cup down on the table.

"I know you're a great gentleman, but you've no right to ask me such a question."

Most men know when not to tell the truth, thought de Commynes, bored, but so few know when to tell it. This fellow seems to have lived long enough in England to acquire their national hypocrisy on the subject of money.

He continued aloud: "The function of a Herald as I understand it is to promote the intercourse of Kings to the achievement of their mutual desires. If he is paid by results, I cannot see that he has anything to be ashamed of. Do you find this cyder to your liking?"

The Herald scowled pettishly at him.

"I'm a subject and a servant of the King of England. You've got no business suggesting I'd take bribes. Besides, what can I do? I'm a Herald, not a Councillor of State. I'd be glad enough of peace, especially after what your King said; but how could I bring it about?"

"How much will you get if you do?"

"Well, he did name a thousand écus to me, it's not to say it would be a bribe. It won't be me that makes the peace, but the King's Councillors. If he gives money to them, that's bribery: but I'm not bribed. If anything came of it, it would be only a present."

"I must say you have the tenderest conscience I ever encountered in a Norman. My master is accustomed to give presents to such as serve his cousins and fellow-princes; but if even Heralds in England are so sensitive, he would do well to tie a knot in his purse-strings when he is dealing with King Edward's ministers."

The Norman vented a short cackle of laughter from pulled-down lips.

"He'd better so unless he wants the purse emptied."

"Do you say that now?"

"Splendour of God, I do. The English nobles aren't different from any other, so far as I've seen, and I'm speaking no treason if I tell you the half of them care no more about this war than I do about the Alcoran."

"If you have told our Lord the King that good news, I am not surprised it was worth three hundred pieces to you."

Garter King-at-Arms leaned suddenly forward over the table and opened his hands with the air of a man abandoning a position.

"Well, what good to hide it, when all's said? I'm not one of those dogs that bites his master, and all the gold in France won't buy a word from me that can harm King Edward. But what I told your King I'll tell you, and that's what's common knowledge already on the other side of the water. Edward of England's had four easy years. He's not drawn a sword since the day of Tewkesbury. It's not he that's for making this war now, but his brother-in-law of Burgundy, who took very strict promises from him before he would help him back to his throne."

"No one knows that better than myself. Go on."

"And second in that business to the Duke of Burgundy is our King's own brother."

"The Duke of Clarence?"

"He—never : King Edward will never listen to a word he says : the Duke of Gloucester."

"Oh."

"And besides that, sir, you must understand in England they have their Parliament, which is like the Three Estates of France. The King there can undertake no greater enterprise without consulting his Parliament."

"That seems to me," said de Commynes, who meant it, "to be a very just and blessed thing."

"Yes, sir, and when the Parliament is called he declares his intention and asks for a subsidy. He never raises any subsidy in England except to invade France or perhaps Scotland : and very gladly and liberally they give it him, especially for going into France. It's quite a practice among the Kings of England when they want to raise money to get a subsidy for a three months' campaign and then break up their army and go home with enough in their pouch for the year. King Edward's a master at it."

"I see," said de Commynes. He was beginning to see many things.

"But I warn you," went on the Herald, "this time the King has gone to work as though he were in earnest. The subsidy hasn't sufficed him. It would open your eyes if I told you all the ways he has of finding money : selling of vacant bishoprics, dealing in wood and tin with the Greek merchants as if he were a common man that lives by trade. We never saw such things in France; and the cunningest of them all is the invention of a certain priest named Morton. It's what they call a benevolence."

"What manner of tax may that be?"

Garter King-at-Arms chuckled.

"No tax at all, a free-will offering, a love-gift : this is the way of it. Anyone that's worth so much as forty English pounds a year, the King calls him to an audience, and welcomes him as though he'd known him all his life; and presently he asks him what he'll give out of mere benevolence to help him to conquer France. If he offers a proper sum, then there's one of the gentry in furred gowns ready to make a note of it in case it slips his memory afterward; and if he offers too little, the King will clap him on the back like a brother and tell him: 'Come, come, Monsieur so-and-so, such-a-one, your neighbour, is poorer than you and he gave me twice as much. A sound substantial burgher like yourself can afford not to stint me'. That's the way he brings them up to the mark. Have you ever set eyes on our King Edward?"

"More than once: he is the handsomest prince I ever saw."

"That's right, and the most affable, and I say that without denigration of the good King Louis who has treated me so civilly. I've seen neighbours of my own who were summoned before him, and when they went they looked as if they were going to the gallows; but they'd come back smiling to tell me the King had spoken so benignly to them that he was welcome to their money. They say one old woman, a widow, gave him twenty pounds and he clapped her in his arms and kissed her. It's the English fashion. She made it forty pounds then. It was a long while since a pretty young man had kissed her. There's a new means for filling the treasuries of Kings for you."

De Commynes privately thought that it was the most disgraceful means he had ever heard of in his life. He plucked the enamelled chain round his neck and said dubiously:

"Was the subsidy from his Parliament so small, then?"

"Small, God aid you? In all, they've given him more than a hundred-and-eighteen thousand English pounds, and with benevolences and suchlike shifts it will be a hundred-and-fifty thousand by now."

"But that can mean only one thing," insisted de Commynes, alarmed. "He must intend a most serious campaign, two or three years' war."

The Herald shrugged, flicking his open palms almost at right angles to his wrists, and pouted his lips out.

"It is possible: but he has other expenses. The Queen of England, the Count of St. Pol's niece, is a very luxurious lady and has many relatives. All these spend money."

"Then do you honestly believe that there's the possibility of an agreed peace?"

"I have told King Louis of my King's many expenses. I have told him that Duke Richard of Gloucester desires this

241

war as eagerly as Duke Charles of Burgundy, but that some of the other English noblemen, in especial the Lords Stanley and Howard, who are now serving with the Duke of Burgundy and are familiar with his conditions, are not so eager: and I have promised to do my own poor best on his behalf to obtain a friendly reception for his messengers before my Lord and master. That is the utmost I can say, sir."

De Commynes nodded twice.

"I think you have earned your three hundred écus, then. Do what you can to earn the thousand he has promised you."

The door bounced in its frame under a loud knock, and a voice said:

"In the name of the King."

De Commynes opened. A thin-lipped, over-dressed man with hard, pale eyes and a gross jaw was on the threshold, attended by a servant carrying a big parcel. It was his fellow-renegade from the domains of Burgundy, Oliver Necker, alias Olivier le Daim, alias Olivier le Diable, King Louis' barber-surgeon, valet and jackal-in-ordinary, who gave him a formal little bow and said:

"The escort is ready for the English Herald, and my servant, Daniel here, has his present of red velvet. We are to go to the King at once." He went on in Flemish, making a puzzled mouth: "I've never seen the like of this. He's smiling and joking as though he had been given a present. What can be in his mind?"

"I have no more conception than yourself, Monsieur le Daim," answered de Commynes coldly, in French; farewelled the Norman Herald and went off to find the King.

King Louis was sitting in the embrasure of an upper window that looked out upon the stable-yard. His loose, deathly face was set in an expression of most genial vacancy. Cher-Ami snored at his toes. His new physician. Dr. Jacques Coictier, was running over what looked like a list of accounts—for it was the Christian King's foible that he engaged men in one capacity and used them in another, turning physicians into auditors and barbers into ambassadors—and the Seigneur de Brosse and the Sieur de Concressault were leaning beside the window. Grooms and servants were busy in the yard below, and the sound of their voices could be heard plainly in the little shabby room that

242

had the King's bed in one corner of it. De Commynes bowed.

"I have carried out your instructions touching the Herald, Sire."

"Thank you, d'Argenton. I knew we might rely on your discretion."

"You whorson rogue," added a low, rusty voice behind de Commynes' shoulder, a voice so horribly like the King's own that he jerked round with a suppressed gasp. One of King Louis' playthings, a crimson-tailed grey parrot with an eye full of sin and understanding, was hanging head-downwards on the arras wobbling its misshapen tongue at him. Pleased with the success of its remark, it began to bob up and down as though convulsed with paroxysms of secret laughter.

"Perrette," said the King indulgently, "you are being rude again."

"Get out, you thief," creaked the bird, pausing for a second in its bouncing, and twisting its head sideways.

"Nor ought you to call me a thief, naughty Perrette. Keep that name for the English King who is trying to steal all my broad realm of France. But God is just and hears prayers. Remember that, Perrette."

"The question as I see it," said the Sieur de Brosse as though continuing an argument, "is whether we can by any means trust the Count of St. Pol not to go over to the English. His sister's the Queen of England's mother, and he was always the most time-serving treacherous straw-presser, saving your reverence, Sire, that was ever weaned."

"We can trust St. Pol implicitly," said the King, "to betray us to Edward at the first moment. Or I hope so, because until he does I cannot open up negotiations with him to betray Edward to us."

"Double-dealing blackguard."

"You speak strongly; but indeed I fear I may one day be forced to set aside that mercy I cherish as the very medicine of my soul and make a reckoning with St. Pol. He has done infinite harm to France."

"And to the honour of your Majesty."

"That I can forgive. But France is France. When I received the crown at Rheims I swore by the Holy Ampulla to restore her divided fragments, bind up her wounds. I will

243

make it hard for those who hinder me in that work, and not trouble my conscience over them. My victorious father found his kingdom full of brigands and thieves and poverty and sorrow, stamped flat by the English, a footcloth for looters, simply because Henry of England had won the victory of Azincourt. Now they offer me a fresh Azincourt. But it shall be prevented."

He spoke with quick, sibilant vehemence, his long hands opening and shutting on his knees. The Sieur de Brosse looked sideways at him.

"The situation . . ." he began tentatively.

"Will resolve itself according to God's will. De Concressault, you have seen my cousin of England very often. Would you say he was as heavy a drinker as his brother, that empty Duke of Clarence who married the good Warwick's daughter?"

"Very nearly, Sire, but he has by a great deal the better head for it."

"So, so, and a very affable and beautiful prince, I hear, and as great a lover of hunting as myself : does it not seem sad that he and I must meet as enemies in the field and not as friends over a choice bottle of wine and some good little dishes? Very sad, very foolish : war is a needful but most miserable invention, a cause of uncharity. Bona bucella sicca et tranquillitas in ea, prae domo plena victimis iurgii. This is such a cheap year for wine, too."

A curious feeling of assurance and rest had come on de Commynes in the poky little bedroom with the spaniel and the parrot, as though he were a wounded man under the cool fingers of a surgeon. The trouble which threatened them was that very ill which for years had kept King Louis' father a scarecrow and a shadow-king hanging in poverty onto a few provinces below the Loire : a return of the old awful days of burned villages and wildwood creeping like a sea over the tilth, of wolves bolder than men and men crueller than wolves, plundered churches and ruined castles, desolation with corpses rotting everywhere by the roadside save on the gibbets of the King's justice. They were coming close again, those days of anarchy, like beasts ranging in for a fresh spring. King Louis sat in his window overlooking the stables and gossiped of the price of wine and the folly of war. De Commynes watched him, trustful and perfectly content.

"Well, for my part," said Mrs. Shore, "I rather like Lord Hastings. He's very amiable."

"He may be," said the Queen, "but my brother Anthony doesn't trust him, and I don't either."

The two ladies were in affable converse together in one of the broad windows of the Palace of Westminster. The Queen, in a magnificent summer gown of silver tissue sewn with small rubies, sat on the cushioned ledge, whilst Mrs. Shore stood beside her, resting one plump little jewelled paw on the wall. The Queen's women were withdrawn to the far end of the room, where they were amusing her eldest daughter—a fair-haired, sharp-faced little girl of nine, named after her mother, Elizabeth—with a set of ivory skittles. It was sunny and calm outside, light enriching the metallic green of many trees.

"It's true he's a bad liver," agreed Mrs. Shore. She knew; was the King's concubine, but could have been William Hastings' paramour as well if she chose any evening to say yes to him.

"He's a proud, ambitious man; envies my brother," the Queen corrected her, "and I know he grudged villainously when the match was made between my son Thomas and his step-daughter."

Grudged villainously : Mrs. Shore remembered the words he, habitually careless, trusting, in his talk with her, used on the matter : "I'd thought I was too good a friend of Edward's to be plundered for the Wydvylles' sake, at least; but I was wrong." His stepdaughter, the little Cecily, had been married at thirteen to Thomas Gray, the Queen's son —newly ennobled to be Marquis Dorset—who was in his later twenties and famous for his woman-hunting. A special grace of Parliament had privileged her, as soon as she should reach her fourteenth birthday, to confer all her fortune on him.

"Oh, your Grace," she said, "I'm sure he never grudged. It was an honour for him."

"So it was," snapped the Queen—"more honour than he deserved. He grudged, for all that." She twitched her head back so that her strangely shallow, greenish eyes, eyes bright and unspeculative like the eyes of a hen, caught Mrs. Shore's. "I know how much grumbling and banning there goes up in England whenever my Lord honours me or my kin as we deserve. I know it very well, Jane, and so do you."

"Only a few fools," Jane Shore tempered the truth.

"Too many : my Lord Edward is too easy with them. He should rule, I say; teach them their manners."

"It's below your Grace's station to take notice of what common folk say."

"You need not teach me my station, Mrs. Shore. As to those common folk, isn't it from them we royal persons get money to live according to our dignity? They're monstrously tight-fisted."

"They've given largely for the French war, at least, your Grace, what from taxes and benevolences . . ."

The Queen jerked her head again so that the many chains round her neck tinkled. Her voice took on a note as though she were shouting down some kind of opposition. Mrs. Shore, who saw a great deal of her when King Edward's back was turned, knew the trick well. It was as though Elizabeth Wydvylle, alias Elizabeth Grey, alias Elizabeth of England and France, were still unsure, ten years after her secret marriage with King Edward, that people round her understood she was a Queen.

"The war, the war, the war, I'm sick to my very bowels of the war. Waste of good riches is what I call it for my Lord and his brothers to go tramping lanes in France when we've so many needs at home. Six children I've borne my husband's Grace, and four of them alive still, saints be thanked, and I'm big with a seventh : and must the bread be taken out of their mouths now to feed common archers in Picardy? Tens of thousands of pounds to fight the French, that I'm sure never did us any harm that I can see, and I have all the labour in this world to get a little pension from those Jews in Parliament for my poor midwife, Mrs. Cobb, though what I'd do without her I daren't even think. I mean that solemnly : I dare not even think what I should do without Mrs. Cobb. Much those pickpenny lawyers and little country knights understand a woman's needs : and my wardrobe, Jane, would make me ashamed to my soul to show you, now my Lord's gone campaigning."

246

"I never saw anything so lovely," said Mrs. Shore, "as that Venice brocade your Grace condescended to show me yesterday."

"Yes, to be sure, but can I pay for it, d'you suppose? Caniziani's bill must wait till my Lord's done his silly soldiering."

Quite a number of bills would be presented then, thought Mrs. Shore. She herself did not ask the King for dresses or jewellery very often; preferred cold coin. When Edward of England rode in triumph back to London, she would be ready for another dole; and there was her husband to be remembered. A few crumbs dropped, now and again, from the King's board kept his horns from irking him.

"It's a blessing to talk to you, Jane," went on the Queen, less urgently. "You make no pretence you're better than you are, and you know your place. No one dare say I'm proud—though I know well they'd like to—seeing how I treat you. I've heard of Queens in chronicles would have had you poisoned or bewitched to death: but though you're my Lord's harlot, I treat you like a friend, and a better friend than some of these high-nosed Lords and Ladies about the Court."

Jane Shore took her cue and went down plumply onto her two knees.

"Oh, your Grace, I know I am not worthy to breathe the same air with you, but if I could ever find oratory enough to say what it has meant to me that you should forgive me and . . ."

"There, there, Jane, you may stand. You're a good creature and I've always said it. There are matters I'd sooner talk of to you than anybody, that's as true as the Mass. You know, Jane, I have my troubles just as though I were a common woman."

"If I could give my blood for your Grace I'd do it."

"That's a proper thing to say, Jane. I'm pleased. Oh, Jane, if you did but know what a labour it is to have a family to care for."

"But such sweet young Princes, and the little Princesses as lovely as their mother . . ."

"Ah, no, I meant my brothers and my two sons by my first husband, God rest his soul. Thomas is a Marquis and married well now, malgré my Lord Hastings and all his grumbles, but there's still my boy Richard; such a lovely lad! I must do something for him when the time's ripe, and my brother Ned, too. I wish my brother Anthony were here to advise me, instead of fighting in France: he has such wits: and then there's more to trouble me. You know all I've done for young Henry Stafford, the Duke of Buckingham, making a marriage for him with my sister Catherine when he was in the nursery still and begging my Lord to make those brute beasts in Parliament account him to be of age this year instead of waiting till he's twenty-one and confirm an old grant of money on him so that he can maintain my sister as she deserves: but d'you suppose the haughty little whelp is grateful to me? By God's will, no! My sister Catherine says he treats her most unkindly, no better than a filthy Turk would."

"Lord amend his bad ways," said Mrs. Shore, who did not care the price of a rush about him or his wife Catherine.

"Lord amend him or else punish him for his heartlessness, the evil little wretch. Would you imagine it, Jane, but he's told my own dear sister he wishes to God she'd keep out of his bed and out of his sight too? I thought my heart would burst when I heard it. What if she is older than he is a little. She's borne him a son, poor saint, and now he treats her in this vile way. How I wish I'd my Lord home again to deal with him."

"When he does come home," said Mrs. Shore, who understood that she was being invited to help, "I'm sure the King's Grace will see that he repents. I'm sure he will."

"You're a comfort to me, Jane, whatever else you are. I am not ashamed to say it. You're a comfort to me, especially in this sad time when I see all the treasure that I need at home poured out into this cruel war and my Lord and my dear brother and my precious Thomas risking their blood against the French: though, God be loved, they're at least certain of a great victory since my uncle, the Count of St. Pol, Constable of France no less, is going to aid them, by my own entreaties to him; for I've worked as hard for England as any of them. They could do nothing if it were not for my uncle: but oh Christ, Jane, I can't pretend I like the business; and I believe in his heart my Lord Edward would have been very content to stay at home and be merry with me. But that Duke Charles and a certain other person gave him no rest, poor soul, until he put on his armour."

"A certain other person?" asked Jane Shore.

The Queen jerked her head again.

"His Grace of Gloucester, who talks like a monk and never thinks of anything but bloodshed; I'm sure he has a proud and cruel mind, however sweetly he speaks. Look how he always bites his underlip, and the dagger he carries, he's always chopping it in and out. You can see his cruel nature chafing in his wretched body."

Mrs. Shore was interested to find the Queen taking her place upon an already considerable list of persons: those who, without any cause that they could put a name to, instinctively mistrusted and misliked the Duke of Gloucester. She was not sure that she herself should not be in this list too. She had met the Duke once only, and for a second, but the memory fretted her a little. It had been at one of the informal Court functions which, nowadays, she attended openly. There had been dancing, and in one figure she found herself opposite a youth smaller than herself, with brown hair and a face the colour of milk-of-almonds. He had given her one glance, from eyes so narrowed that it was not possible to identify their expression, bowed very gracefully and handed her down the line as the positions were shifted. The touch of his hand, which was thin and cool, had a very odd effect on her. It was like touching something unexpectedly in the dark. She looked sharply back at him over her shoulder, almost with a gasp, but he was already bowing to her sister, the Countess of Lincoln, and she did not see his face again.

It was curious to know the Queen had the same sentiments; but at the moment Mrs. Shore was interested in other things. The Duke of Gloucester lived and ruled in the remote North and served his brother. The Duke of Clarence was more the object of Jane Shore's curiosity. He lived in the South and, for some time past, had been doing and saying things that seemed obscurely significant, but of which she had not so far found an explanation.

"His Grace of Gloucester," she said tentatively, "has a deeper nature, I suppose, than his brother of Clarence?"

The Queen snapped the bait up without looking twice at it.

"George of Clarence's nature is plain enough and un-christian enough," she began, the words breaking from her in a flow dammed now and then by little gasps, as always when she was talking indiscreetly: "a boorish, drunken, envious man with no kindness in him. He's wounded me to the very quick of my heart by the language he's used about me: and I know why. I can speak with you, Jane. I'd not dare tell Edward, but that turncoat brother of his has never forgotten that he once had wicked hopes of being the King. He's never forgotten them and he envies my Lord cruelly. I know it in my bones."

"He speaks very strangely, so I've heard. I believe he tells people now that he is near to knowing the truth of a great mystery."

"That has a sound of necromancy and conjuration," said the Queen, blessing herself. "I've heard on many hands that he's taken to secret devilish arts."

"I've heard so, too," agreed Jane Shore, "but this matter seems to be a different one. He has been saying—or so someone told me—that the greatest mystery in England, which he has a certain assurance that he will solve, is in the life and actions of the Lady Elenor Butler, daughter to the old Earl of Shrewsbury. He says that if he knew the secrets of that Lady—she'd dead now—he would know a wonderful thing. Good God Almighty, your Grace isn't ill?"

The Queen's face was painted in the most meticulous fashion, but under the paint it had gone miserably white. Her mouth hung open.

Amiens on a wet Tuesday morning in August: Lord William Hastings looked from his tent-door toward the city and wished it were in hell. A faint drizzle, like a cold steam, was crawling down out of the parti-coloured sky and dampening the endless gaudy pavilions that sheltered a hundred-and-fifty-six English knights and nobles and twenty thousand fighting-men. Pennons hung drearily from tent-poles and pitched lances, and the ground underfoot was a wet porridge. Beyond the unhappy waters of the Somme, the towers and defended gates of Amiens could be seen like dejected people standing about and waiting for a hardly probable event. Lord Hastings cursed them briefly and called for his horse. A sense of duty had got him out of bed and was sending him for a morning ride into the enemy's ground, now open freely to him and to all Englishmen by virtue of a truce.

William Hastings had some title to call himself a soldier. he had climbed the ridge at Towton, on that terrible Palm Sunday fourteen years ago, with the snow blinding his eyes and the whole force of Lancaster lying somewhere ahead of him in the flurry; had seen his best men killed at his feet when Oxford charged like a mad lion out of the fog at Barnet; and had commanded his wing and done his share of butchery in the meadows beside Tewkesbury Abbey: but never since the sword had touched his shoulders had he seen a campaign at all like this that they were waging in Picardy against King Louis.

They had sailed for Calais from Dover in May: twenty thousand men, with no encumbrance of pages or camp-women, led by King Edward and his two brothers, the Dukes of Norfolk and Suffolk, the Earls of Essex, Northumberland, Ormond, Arundel and Rivers and the young Marquis Dorset. Five hundred flat-bottomed barges of Holland, lent by Duke Charles of Burgundy, bore them, their horses and armour, their iron and brass guns, their siege-engines, artillery-wagons, ladders and sapping-tools, together with a vast provision of stoneshot, gunpowder, saltpetre and sulphur. Their convoy were the warships *George Howard, Thomas Howard, Trinity, Little Trinity, Trinité, Barbara, Martin, Mary Calday, Gabriel, Katherine, Margaret, John, Janet, Peter, Mary* and *Marie,* and the work of transport took three weeks of smiling weather. No such army had been landed in France within the memory of Chroniclers. With a quarter of that force, Harry of Monmouth won the field at Azincourt and chased King Louis' father South to the Loire. As it was the greatest English host that had crossed the Channel, so it was the most splendid. The King's tent was of cloth-of-gold, divided into rooms like a little house. The small knights were ashamed if they had not two or three remounts with coloured trappings, and damascened armour to wear under silk surcoats. The great mass of archers who made the backbone of this force were every one of them mounted, and on good horses. Day after day the narrow streets of Calais were choked with mounted men, riding superbly with their heads up, laughing and calling jokes to one another in the sunshine that coloured their sallets and basnets and the embroidered work, as rich as on Church vestments, on the armorial banners of their captains, They had pay and sustenance money in their pouches, so that the inns were drained as dry as Sodom and men jostled and fought one another all night before the doors of the stews. With the wages of his army filling their town like a dyke in February, the Calais citizens forgot that they had ever loved the Rose of Rouen less than they did Kingmaker. No ruler of England, since the time of King Arthur, had led such a company to strike a blow beyond the sea.

When the news reached Charles the Hardy that what he had prayed for since the days of the League of Public Good had come at last, and that his allies were on the soil of France, he raised his siege of Neuss and made straight for Calais by forced marches, very slenderly accompanied. This was the first surprise the English had, who had expected him to bring five hundred knights and their retainers. The rest of his army should have been turned against Louis of France three months before; but this he had not done. It appeared that he had troubles of his own in Bar and Lorraine.

In company with the Duke, King Edward moved his great host from Calais. It was the Duke's plan that this army—which was, he said, enough to conquer not only France but Italy and Rome itself—should march on his own territory as far as Péronne and then strike a blow westward in the region of the Vermandois, whilst his troops, having taken measure with Duke René of Lorraine, should invade Champagne, so that King Louis would be caught like an eel in a spear. It would be the easier, because the Count of St. Pol, uncle to King Edward's wife, was secretly pledged to them and would deliver the key-town of St. Quentin into their hands.

It was mid-July now, late for campaigning, the best of the year slipping away. They marched by St. Omer and Ruisseauville; camped two nights then at Azincourt. The Duke of Gloucester and some of his company rode out to look at the ridge where four thousand Englishmen had cracked the chivalry of France like a rotten nut.

At Péronne, a certain Louis de Sainville awaited them with very polite letters from the Count of St. Pol, who would have delivered St. Quentin to them before now, he said, only that by so doing he would have lost all credit and communication in France and so could have served them in nothing further: but now that he saw the King of England so near, he would do all that the Duke of Burgundy had desired of him. King Edward showed great joy at this news. Cold mists at sunrise and a morning sky huddling down close to the earth hinted that the autumn rains would begin early this year. He would want a strong town to base his army on. The King had appeared less than his common self since he arrived in France; talked and smiled seldom; was very angry over trifles. He did not spend much time in company with his brother-in-law of Burgundy; preferred the presence of his other brother-in-law, Earl Rivers, and his debauched stepson, the Marquis Dorset. There was a certain look of softness about his neck and chest now and the lovely boyish line of his face from cheekbone to chin had loosened. He was thirty-three.

They had news that King Louis, after spending a great deal of time on his knees in the Cathedral of Beauvais before an image of our Lady of Peace, had moved to Compiègne with the royal artillery and the Scots Guard. In all, he was estimated to have some fifteen thousand men on the East borders of Normandy, under the command of those very useful soldiers, the Counts of Penthièvre and Dammartin and Tanguy du Châtel; and he had prudently commanded that each of the rich citizens of Rheims should make himself a hand-gun on the German model, at his own expense.

Lord Hastings was among those who attended King Edward when he rode out from the camp at Péronne to receive the delivery of St. Quentin. King Edward was in better humour than he had been for days past, although the sky at which he squinted anxiously was bruised with cloud.

"Charles the Hardy may be my brother by marriage," he told Lord Hastings, "but though I say it to my shame, the man's a fool; has wasted my time and his own with his goddamned unreasonable quarrels in Germany. But for him, we'd 've been in Paris by now. Now, my uncle St. Pol's a horse of another colour. See what a blessing it is to marry a wife who has foreign kin. St. Quentin's worth seas and mountains to us. From there we strike at Beauvais and

Rouen with a secure base. Charles must draw off part of Louis' forces—whether he's done his messing in the Duchy of Bar or not—and then we fight a field."

"Aye, in the rain at this rate," grunted the Duke of Clarence.

If the King's magnificent body had a little coarsened in the last years, the Duke of Clarence was now definitely fat. His face, that had once had strong cheekbones and a pointed chin, was as round and swollen as a tomcat's.

"What of it?" said the King. "We'll be snug in St. Quentin before the clouds break."

"Please God, amen," answered the Duke, mauling his charger's mouth as the beast tried to break into a trot.

The town was in fair sight now : good walls, fat little towers, glimpses of a grand church and pompous hôtel-delville, thick fields of grain about the place. It had a friendly look. The nobles and the main body of troops reined-up and stood to gaze at it whilst a couple of hundred outriders and a Herald, embroidered banners waggling, bright badges of the rose-and-sun or the black bull showing up gaily on scoured steel, trotted anglingly ahead to make formal demand for the rendition of the place. The King was smiling. Lord Hastings wondered about the women in the town and thought it would be pleasant to hear a French girl laugh and give him back-answers again. What was the tavern-song he had heard on the road a few days back? A ballade with an oddly memorable catchline : Il n'a bon bec qu'à Paris : true enough, and at this rate they should see Paris.

The bright outriders dwindled away toward the town. The gates were shut, but in a few moments they would open and a procession come out, carrying the cross and holy water, to welcome the Count of St. Pol's allies in. Lord Hastings distrusted the Wydvylles from the very depths of his guts; but he admitted gladly that in this case their kin-ship with the slippery Constable of France was very useful. He turned to the Earl of Rivers, who sat a tall bay horse beside him. Lord Anthony was in glorious Italian armour of white steel damascened with gold under a surcoat of cloth-of-gold with his arms, argent, a fess and canton gules, on breast and back.

"We shall have much to thank your noble uncle for," he said to him. "This looks a very proper town."

Lord Rivers gave him his infectious smile.

"Then on my uncle's behalf I make you particularly welcome to it. You and I must find some little amusements here before the serious work of the campaign begins."

The outriders were almost under the town walls by now, small dots of shimmer and colour like coloured dust-specks in a sunbeam. Sun dropped on them through a ragged hole in the blue clouds. Then a queer thing happened. A bunch of white smoke jutted out suddenly from one of the little towers. A dull noise as though a door had slammed came up to them, and a sapling past which the last of the outriders was trotting shook and fell over, lifting its roots in the air. Three smoke-puffs blossomed out all at once along the wall. Earth spouted, like water when a stone is dropped in it, among the cornfields. Then the gates opened. It was not the procession with the cross that issued from them. They could see that clearly. The mounted men who burst out in a solid wedge had lances couched and were in armour. A sleepy, far-away sound that was the yelling of startled and infuriated Englishmen came drifting back along the road. The packed sallying-force hit the party of outriders as lightning hits an oak; burst it to flinders. An awful noise, neither a scream nor an oath, came from King Edward. He dashed his spurs against his charger's barrel so that it flung forward and almost slipped. Then they were all galloping toward the town, grabbing at swords or axes and slamming down vizors as they went. Before they had gone three hundred yards they checked, seeing no employment. It was all over. The sortie had emptied a dozen saddles, wheeled and gone through the gates, that shut behind it. The English outriders were pelting back in a mob up the road toward their commanders, one or two of the bowmen halting and turning to discharge futile arrows against the town. The expression on King Edward's face was appalling. He could not speak. The Duke of Clarence was bawling "Treason!" at the pitch of his voice and shaking his hands in the air so that his armour rattled. Lord Rivers was as pale as the argent field of his own arms. "There is some mistake," he said foolishly. "There is some mistake." The Duke heard him and made a whinnying noise like a laugh. "Mistake, my

Lord, mistake : there's no mistake, but that your damned uncle's a traitor like all the rest of your ditch-begotten house."

At this moment it began to stream with rain.

No one knew what happened between King Edward and the Duke of Burgundy in the camp that evening. The Duke of Gloucester, who visited Duke Charles after his private interview with his royal brother-in-law, reported him to be in an impossible temper and preparing to leave next day to join his army in the Duchy of Bar. The English camp was full of angry men. The common foot-soldiers, who had looked forward to the inns and brothels of St. Quentin, were cursing the rain, the war, the Count of St. Pol and, under their breaths, the King. The Duke of Clarence was alarmingly drunk and speaking in the most unrestrained fashion about the Wydvylles and their French kin. The Duke of Gloucester bit his lip and replied shortly to those who wished to discuss the situation with him. The King was invisible, and the Marquis Dorset was talking of sending a challenge to the Duke of Clarence. Lord Hastings could not remember passing such an unpleasant evening since King-maker had chased them all out of England in the year 1470.

Next day Charles of Burgundy took formal leave of King Edward. The King, who showed him something a good deal less than cordiality, attended to no business except to order —as the usual rules of courtesy dictated—that their first and only prisoner, a little valet in the employ of a certain Mons. de Grassay, should have his liberty. The man was accordingly turned loose and invited by his guards to take his rump out of reach of their toes lest worse befall. Before he left the camp, however, Hastings noticed that Lord Stanley, that fat, little-eyed man with the gross hands, beckoned him up and talked seriously to him for several minutes. Lord Stanley had been with Charles the Hardy before Neuss and seemed unenthusiastic about the war.

Then there was rain and grumbling and camp fare, armour rusting though it was scoured every day, banners hanging damply from their poles, men sneezing and swearing under the tent-sides. In council, the Duke of Gloucester asked the King for three hundred lances with their complement of bows and some artillery. With these, he said, he could put them inside St. Quentin. The King had been lolling in his chair with his eyes half-shut, smelling at a scented orange. He dropped the thing, looked at the little white-faced Duke for a moment, then slumped back again.

"No, I'll not move a man or loose an arrow now until Charles of Burgundy's done something better than make promises. Let him invade Champagne first."

"But we are wasting time here. The season's half over and we've done nothing. Are we to wait here until Louis of Valois' armed his whole kingdom?"

"I command this journey and I say we'll wait for Duke Charles. Let's have no more of it."

The Duke twiddled a ring on his finger and did not speak again.

It did not seem, though, that Louis of Valois was in any hurry for a field. A few days later a little, nervous-looking fellow with a shield and tabard of the lilies of France turned up outside the camp. He said he was a Herald, though he did not behave like one, and that he had been instructed by the Christian King to apply, through the Lords Stanley and Howard, for an audience. Lord Hastings remembered fat Thomas Stanley's talk with the released prisoner and could guess the sort of message that he had sent by him. King Edward received the Herald after dinner. This mission, the man said, concerned the desire King Louis entertained to have good friendship with his cousin of England in order that the two realms might flourish in peace. Never, since he had been King of France, had King Louis undertaken wars or enterprises against the realm of England. King Edward arched his eyebrows at this, and the Herald made great haste to explain that whatever had been done in the past for my Lord of Warwick had been intended solely against Burgundy. Further, said the Herald, those who had invited the King of England to come into France at such expense had done it for their own ends. Winter was coming on, too. Would King Edward grant a safe conduct to certain French ambassadors in order that the differences between the two realms might be discussed in amity and reason?

King Edward scowled round his Council. His face had the perplexed, sullen look it had worn ever since he came to Calais. Almost without looking sideways at one another, the Lords Stanley, Howard, Rivers and Dorset and the plump-faced Dr. Morton declared for an armistice and a safe conduct. The King turned to his brother of Clarence.

"You, George?"

Duke George shrugged. "I don't trust Frenchmen. There's a trick."

The Duke of Norfolk nodded. "I say so too."

"My Lord of Essex?"

The old man cleared his throat and blew his cheeks out. "Your Grace, if I may say so—and I've seen wars in France before with your great father—the thing's an insult to us. We're here to fight, and I say fight and be damned to it."

"Will?"

"It's true that winter's coming on and that Duke Charles has disappointed us : but it seems early to talk of truces and embassies."

The King was silent for a long while now, tapping his fingers on his knee and wrinkling his nose. He did not look at the Duke of Gloucester when he asked : "And what do you say, Dickon?"

"You know what I say."

Duke Richard, too, was looking at nobody. His face was as impossible to read as always, but his hands, commonly busy with his dagger or rings, were perfectly still.

"Well, say it, in God's name."

"Unless Louis of Valois is prepared to surrender the crown that's yours by right, then we shall be miserably disgraced for ever if we even think of treating with him : and I do not imagine he is ready to part with the crown yet."

"A safe conduct commits us to nothing," said the Earl of Rivers quickly and gently.

The King stopped tapping his knee and spread his hand out as though dropping something.

"He may send his ambassadors."

The end began. The English commissioners, Dr. Morton, Master of the Rolls, Lord Howard, Sir Thomas St. Leger, met the Bastard of Bourbon, the Seigneur de St. Pierre and the Bishop of Evreux at Dives and asked them for the crown of France. Pull devil, pull baker : the French final offer was seventy-five thousand écus in cash, a stipend of fifty thousand a year for seven years, the marriage of the Dauphin to the Princess Elizabeth with an endowment of six thousand English pounds a year, and a trade agreement.

What King Louis privately paid or promised the English commissioners for their acceptance of such terms, Lord Hastings did not know. He himself had since been offered an annual pension of two thousand écus; had neither accepted nor refused it.

"This gift is by the good pleasure of the King your master," he said coldly to the French agent, "and not of my seeking. If you wish me to take it you may drop it in my sleeve : but you will get no quittance or undertaking out of me. I have no wish to have it said of me : The Court Chamberlain of England is a pensioner of the King of France."

The peace irked him like a bad taste in the mouth; was a betrayal of Charles the Hardy, who, with however little grace, had helped them four years ago when they most needed it. Duke Charles had visited the English camp again, arriving sweating and saddle-sore with only fifteen followers. King Edward seemed disturbed to see him, and more disturbed when the Duke, talking in English at the top of his voice, flung in his teeth the names of Crécy, Poictiers and Azincourt, and called him a disgraced King who had sold the honour of the finest army ever brought to France. The scene was a particularly miserable one, because the tallest and handsomest King in christendom had appeared, for a moment, of less presence than the spluttering Duke with half his teeth missing and white smears at the corners of his lips.

They moved to Amiens, where the Christian King had set up lodging, and the town was opened to them. From his tent-door now Lord Hastings could see an ant-thick column of English soldiery, half-armed, keeping no order, dribbling out of camp and across the Somme. Amiens was the Land of Cockayne, better than Calais. Gascon, Burgundy, Touraine, Beaune, Rochelle, Bordeaux, Champagne : they had their choice to drink, and did not pay for it. When they arrived yesterday, a procession had met them that seemed as numerous as their own : three hundred wagons loaded with hogsheads of Bordeaux, a peace-offering from the Christian King. That was not all. Two great tables were set up by the town-gate, heavy with all such dishes as created the most thirst and with the best wines that could be imagined : no talk of water. Fat, jolly Frenchmen, all men of good family, sat beaming and waving friendly hands, ready to perform the offices of pantlers and butlers for common Englishmen. It was like a coronation-feast or a royal wedding. Ten taverns in Amiens were open scot-free to the soldiers of the invading army, and there were jousts arranged for the nobility.

Lord Hastings wried his mouth to one side and put a hand on his horse's neck. He could not like it. Harry of Monmouth's wars and victories left England only the poorer in the end. Peace on a reasonable basis had more to be said for it than a long campaign : but it seemed too much, too much in some way that he could not clearly formulate, that the Rose of Rouen should have led twenty thousand men out of England only to make them drunk at King Louis' charges, squeezed a hundred-and-fifty thousand pounds out of England only to squeeze four-hundred-and-twenty-five thousand écus out of France.

He would have thought it so himself four years ago, he reflected; has changed since Tewkesbury. Well, God amend all. I'd be best to go into the town and see how our English are behaving themselves.

Someone else had felt a duty on him, it seemed, that morning. As he trotted out of the camp, another rider, attended by two squires, waved and joined him. It was the handsome, thin-faced Lord Lovel, looking very fine in his white German harness and blue velvet surcoat tagged with gold. He gave Lord Hastings a quick, ironic smile and a good-morning.

"You are for Amiens, my Lord?"

"I thought I would ride in."

"So didn't I, until his Grace of Gloucester sent me."

"His Grace of Gloucester?"

"Yes, he wishes to see how the men of his division are comporting themselves with all this French wine at their disposition."

"So : our men certainly seem—pox take you, get out of my road, you oaf : damn the fellows, they're as thick as bees—seem to have wakened with a thirst this morning. You fellow with the red beard, if you can't make room for your betters the Camp-Marshal shall have a word with you.

Christ pity us, my Lord Lovel, I think half of 'em are drunk already."

Certainly, some men were already coming back out of the town and not walking steadily. A big archer was lying in the crops by the roadside, vomiting. Lord Lovel smiled again.

"We must celebrate our victory, I suppose."

"You are using an odd word."

"It's better than an ugly one."

Lord Hastings did not answer that, and they sidled through the thick townward column of men to the bank of the river. The crowd was as close as herrings in a barrel on the bridge, and Lord Lovel sent his squires ahead to clear their way. A gaminerie of little dagget-arsed French boys held dirty palms out to them in the shelter of the gateway squealing: "Anglaish, 'allo, gif me some money, gooday Anglaish, gooday!" They gave them nothing.

Riding down through the mob that choked the narrow street was a man in sober, handsome clothes, youngish, with a lined, strong-lipped face and watching bright-grey eyes full of irony and intelligence. He managed his horse carefully to avoid the English soldiers and had his mouth pursed as though something troubled him.

"I'll renounce Mahomet," said Lord Hastings, "but I've seen that man in Burgundy."

The man appeared to recognise him at the same moment. He whipped his bonnet off and kicked his horse forward, crying in English:

"Milord Hastings, Milord Hastings, you are very welcome."

"God bless you, sir. I've seen your face before."

"That is so, Milord."

"In Artois it was. I have your name—of course, yes: Monsieur de Commynes."

"You flatter me, Milord: but they call me the Sieur d'Argenton now."

"My felicitations on the advancement, my dear sir."

"And mine, noble sir, upon the fortunes of war."

He had me there, curse him, thought Lord Hastings, clear through the joint of the harness. If Louis bought him from Burgundy, he has bought us too. The pot called the kettle black. He presented de Commynes to Viscount Lovel.

261

"And how are our English governing themselves?" asked the Viscount cheerfully, smiling like a choirboy: "not abusing your royal master's hospitality, I hope and trust?"

De Commynes pursed his firm lips more and looked sharply round him.

"To tell you the perfect truth, Milords, I have been sent by his Christian Majesty to find some English captains such as yourselves."

"Trouble?" asked Lord Hastings sharply.

De Commynes raised and shook one hand, rebuking the word.

"No, no, no, never at all: they are, what do you call it, good companions, your English, very jolly. But, well, we think there must be some nine thousand of them in the town by now, and they are not all strictly sober."

"So I perceive," said Lord Hastings. He had just seen a feather-bed drop mysteriously out of a first-floor window higher up the street. It was followed by its occupants, a yellow-haired Englishman and a big French whore. They landed on its softness and sprawled cursing. Red, sweaty faces laughed through the window at their discomfort.

"If you will be so friendly as to come a little way with me, I can show you what it is that disturbs us."

"I suppose we'd better," said Lord Lovel.

Lord Hastings sighed. He liked the new fashion of making war even less than ever.

It was to one of the ten cabarets set specially apart for the free entertainment of the English that de Commynes brought them: a big, prosperous house with carved beams, a green bush over the door and a well-painted sign of a dove with the name Au Sainct Esperit. Lord Lovel's man held their horses. They pushed the door open and went in.

Lord Hastings had an enormous experience of merry-making. As an intimate companion of King Edward, he had attended court festivities at Westminster, Windsor and Eltham that ended with scarcely a chaplain or a kitchen-boy in the whole palace sober. In Burgundy he had sat through nightmarish Flemish supper-parties where the guests disappeared under the table and reappeared an hour, two hours, later to begin the work again. He had dined with the Duke of Clarence. Never in his life, not even in the pictures of hell which one saw in churches, had he known anything

262

to equal the interior of the Tavern of the Holy Ghost. At first glance the courtyard appeared full of corpses. Those who could neither see nor speak had been dragged here from beneath the feet of their fresher fellows in the taproom. They lay among sherds of crockery and broken barrels, filth in their hair. One, a boy of sixteen or so, had a bloody face, as though someone had laid his head open. From the taproom itself an endless senseless din broke out in waves : clash of pots, cursing, singing. The room was choke-full; reeked indescribably of sweat and vomit. Five or six men in the Duke of Clarence's livery were dicing at a table they had cleared of mazers and dishes simply by sweeping them all, full and empty, in a smash to the ground. The drawers, scurrying from side to side with food and wine, had terrified faces. One of them, when he answered a call, showed a raw gap in his mouth where teeth had been knocked out a little while ago. A big, bare-armed man with a beard was in a corner trying to shout down the singers to tell some story of his own. Lord Hastings caught the words : "Our whorson King, the bastard King of England." I'll remember that pig's face, he thought. I'll see him hanged for that. The loudest group was round one of the Earl of Essex's men who sat on a table with a girl some twelve years old sprawled in his lap. Her kirtle was dragged up to her armpits and she was otherwise naked.

De Commynes beckoned to the host. The man was sweating and twitching, glancing always at the girl on the table, who was perhaps his daughter.

"Combien d'additions as-tu déjà ce matin?"

"Cent-et-onze, Seigneur, s'il vous bien plâit. Ca ne fait rien. Notre bon maître, vous savez, va payer tout. Je n'en ai de souci, pas du tout. Mais, Seigneur," he spread his hands, "ces Anglais, ils sont des ours, des fauves. Que faire? Je n'ose pas dire un mot, pas pour ma vie, et on casse partout, vomit partout, fait des cochonneries. Ah très-illustre Seigneur, ma pauvre maison, elle est devenue une Géhenne! Ces sales cochons de Goddons . . ."

"Ferme donc ta bouche, est-ce que tu es fou? On entende." He turned to Lord Hastings. "You will forgive this silly fellow, Milord. But you have heard : one hundred-and-eleven reckonings; and it is not nine o'clock in the morning yet."

263

The Viscount Lovel pulled Lord Hastings by the edge of his surcoat.

"In Christ's name let's be out of here. We can do no good."

They stood in the street to take long breaths, clearing the badger-stink of the place out of their throats. Lord Lovel's face was more serious and distressed than Lord Hastings remembered to have seen it. The gently ironic voice of de Commynes said :

"I confess, now I have seen how peaceably they are disposed, I feel less alarmed : but you will understand that it is, what should I say, disturbing to remember that there are nine thousand like them in the town and more coming, in pure friendliness, every moment. Suppose the wine were to run out. You English are a choleric race. They might be angry and remember feats of arms their fathers did in this unfortunate realm. In fact, my master, the Christian King —though this is the octave of the Holy Innocents, a day on which he generally refuses to transact business—has given me orders to lay the matter before some such captain as yourselves."

"The King's Grace of England shall hear of it at once," said Lord Hastings sadly.

Lord Lovel looked straight at de Commynes. "I shall also attend to that," he said. "For your part, though, Monseigneur d'Argenton, you might perhaps remind your royal master that it was not we who wished his taverns to be thrown open."

De Commynes bowed slightly, with a mere flick of a smile.

"I will remember that, Milord Vicecomte : but in the first place the guests were not invited."

They got on their horses.

"I must return to my master," said de Commynes, bowing more deeply. "He will bless you for your good offices. I hope we shall meet again whilst you are in France. Please to commend me in most dutiful humility to your noble King. You have been very kind, Milords. God requite you and give you a good day. I am your servant."

"God bless you, Monseigneur d'Argenton."

"Soyez à dieu, Milord Hastings, et vous, Monseigneur le Vicecomte."

"À dieu soyez, Monseigneur d'Argenton."

They said nothing until they were through the gate and across the Somme. Then Lord Lovel, with a gesture that went oddly with his girlish face and his gold-tagged clothes, leaned out of the saddle and spat.

"Christ!" he said briefly.

"I know, I know," agreed Lord Hastings. "I think it too. But, after all, they're only lads on a holiday, and not used to strong wine."

"A holiday they haven't earned: holy St. Francis, d'you suppose I'd care if they broke every bottle and every maidenhead from here to the Loire, so they did it as soldiers and not as brigands being paid ransom? God rot and damn and wither and blast to everlasting perdition the soul of Louis of Valois. He's made us the laughing-stock of christendom. What will the Empire, Castille, Switzerland, the Italians, what will the Scots and the Turks think of the English army: an army that's twenty thousand strong and sits on its arse in the rain for two months without drawing a sword, and then straggles into a hostile town with no more discipline than a band of Bohemians, dropping its arms where it pleases, and goes to sleep among the pots, nine thousand at a time, with its head in its enemies' lap? Passion and cross of God, are we Irish or what? Five hundred sober men at this moment could send every one of those hiccoughing sots in there to eternal damnation. There's more shame and dishonour to us in this armistice than in twenty defeats."

Lord Hastings blinked. He had never conceived that the quick-spoken boy sitting beside him had the eyes of a soldier, or that he cared more for the outcome of the campaign than any of the other decorative young noblemen about the Court.

"You speak very roundly, my Lord."

"I was never so shamed in my life as I am now."

"We should do well to keep our shame to ourselves. Remember this armistice you complain of is sanctioned by the King's Grace because Burgundy has failed his promises to us."

"Ride ahead," the Viscount said to his two squires. "We'll follow. When you get to camp say that any man of mine who goes up to Amiens to-day will get twelve hours in the stocks."

The men spurred their big horses and trotted on. Lord Lovel turned in his saddle and looked straight at Lord Hastings.

"Sir, I am sure you are a nobleman to whom I can speak my mind. Duke Richard loves you, and that makes you my friend also."

Duke Richard, thought William Hastings: there's the key. It is Duke Richard has turned this silken boy into a soldier; made him use eyes and wits.

"Thank you, Lord Lovel. Whatever you say to me you say in the confessional."

"I'm glad of that; and here's what I say. You are King Edward's intimate friend. You know better than I do that it is not because Charles the Hardy and the Count of St. Pol have failed us that this truce is proclaimed. You know that four years ago the King would have marched straight on Paris if he had only had five thousand men. He had less than that when he landed at Ravenspur and marched on London."

I had better go very carefully here, thought William Hastings. He looked straight between his horse's ears and murmured :

"That is true, perhaps."

"Then what in the name of the devil has happened to the Rose of Rouen in the last four years? There's some plague on him and half the Court, I think. Stanley and that sweet-spoken Master of the Rolls we have now, and St. Leger and even my old friend Jockey Howard are stuffed as full of French bribes as a sausage with meat. This treaty's been bought. That would not have been a thing even to think of in the old days."

I must forget a purse dropped in my sleeve, thought Hastings.

"What of it, my Lord? These things happen infinitely more often than you suppose, and above all in France. Consider. We may not like the manner in which peace is being concluded, you and I. We may think it does less good than it might to the King's honour in the eyes of christendom. But peace itself is no ill thing. Harry of Monmouth beggared England with his French wars. Peace will be a blessing, and the money—call it tribute—we have from Louis of Valois will enrich England."

"Will one farthing of it go to pay back the benevolences the King has twisted out of his subjects for a conquest of France?"

"God knows."

"Do you yourself believe King Louis will keep his word touching the marriage of Princess Elizabeth with the Dauphin?"

"God knows. My Lord Lovel, I am going to ask you a question now. I have known you as a nobleman who smiled at everything that came his way; was easy. Tell me why you are so hot in this matter. Yes, we saw some ugly things in the town this morning; but Christ defend you, you've seen uglier. Why has this business of the French treaty knocked the smile off your mouth?"

Viscount Lovel looked hard at him. Under the blue-velvet cap he wore in place of a basnet his face was utterly serious and old.

"Because it is breaking the heart of the one man in the world I love."

"Duke Richard takes it as unkindly as that?"

"Lord William Hastings," said Lord Lovel deliberately, "you have known Duke Richard of Gloucester almost all his life. You know that he has never complained of any pain or unhappiness he has suffered. You know he has never looked for any advantage or enrichment of his own. You know his one single and only care from the day he was knighted has been to serve his brother the King, who is his god and his idol. He is not twenty-three years old, but he has won battles, headed and hanged traitors, ruled and pacified the most dangerous province of England, all for the honour of his brother : and now you ask me whether he takes it unkindly that his brother wantonly dishonours himself, sells his subjects, betrays his allies and disgraces his kingdom."

"I see," said Lord Hastings thoughtfully. "At least he can have the comfort that he possesses one loyal friend."

"He possesses a dozen : everyone with wits enough to see through the vizor he wears. I had hoped you were one of them."

"As God sees me, my Lord Lovel, I am. You've spoken very openly : a hundred times more openly than I would counsel you to do to anyone else about the Court. I will be open with you then. You asked me the name of the plague that has afflicted our Lord Edward. I'll tell you. Its name is Wydvylle."

The room in Dean's Yard was better furnished than it had been three years ago. The walls were hung with a very costly Flemish arras which was among the fine things Dr. Morton had brought back from France. Wax candles burned instead of rushlights and there was a Venice carpet on the floor. Dr. Morton had not altered, though. He still wore robes of black and grey, very carefully tended, and still slid his hands gently over one another as he talked. He sat now on one side of a large perfumed fire and looked mildly and intently at Mr. Colyngbourne on the other. This time, there was a third person in the room : a short, stiff woman, not in her first youth, who sat bolt upright, like a statue of tough wood, in a chair midway between their two. The flames gave her face more colour than it would have shown by daylight and touched up strongly her thin lips and black, sulking eyebrows. This was the Lady Margaret Beaufort, Countess of Richmond by her first marriage and Lady Stafford by her second, last survivor of the elder branch of her wrecked house, a woman who had been mother and widow before she was fourteen.

Dr. Morton was speaking in his deliberate voice.

". . . and so I say that on all counts this French journey of the usurper has been fortunate for us. Your particular task in the matter I shall touch on presently, my good Colyngbourne. Let us consider larger matters first. Our unhappy Queen Marguerite, after much suffering, long imprisonment, is at her ease in France again. That insatiable Edward was glad enough to ransom her to the Christian King, and the Christian King, after I had talked with him, was glad enough to pay her price."

"That was blessed work of yours, Dr. Morton," said Mr. Colyngbourne : "our true good Queen in prison all these cruel years."

"I was glad to accomplish it, very glad, you may believe. That is one great stone laid in the tower we are building. Another is that Charles the Hardy hates Edward now as he should hate sin. When our time comes—I say when it comes—there will be no more help for York from Burgundy.

268

They say the Duke was so angry at our composition with France that he secretly offered to the Christian King to fall on us on our way back to the coast."

"Aye, maybe, but Edward has the Christian King himself for an ally now."

"Only for seven years, my good Colyngbourne: you are not so simple as to believe King Louis really intends the marriage of his Dauphin to a daughter of Edward the adulterer and Elizabeth Wydvylle? Make very sure he does not. If I had for an instant suspected that he did, I would have used my best endeavours to see that no question of marriage entered into the treaty at all."

"It was a piece of everlasting good fortune that you were named in the commission for settling the treaty. You have done more work for us than a thousand men-at-arms could."

"I have humbly laboured in a cause that I think pleasing to God; and I shall have further openings still. My work has been commended by the usurper with words that I shall not repeat. I have the key of his ear, and he has spoken to me recently concerning a bishopric. If only our Lord God would see fit, in the issue of time, to call that good man Thomas Rotherham to himself, you might one day call me Chancellor. The abominable kinsfolk of the woman Elizabeth—Rivers who cries peace and bites with his teeth, the fornicator Dorset, all the tagrag of them—are taking more and more heed of me : my good offices for this, my opinion of that. I will tell you a very strange thing, Mr. Colyngbourne."

Dr. Morton's large eyes, with the bistred, scorched-looking skin about their sockets, looked straight in front of him. He thrust out the tip of his tongue between his close-fitting lips for a second and went on :

"There is someone in this realm of whom the Wydvylle rabble are mortally afraid : someone who is very near the King."

"Lord Hastings?"

"No : they envy him. Perhaps they hate him. But they are not afraid of him."

"The Duke of Gloucester, then."

"I had supposed you would say that. Richard of Gloucester with the crooked shoulders : I verily believe he was the murderer who killed our holy King Henry. He was at the Tower that night. A dangerous, bloody-minded beast, and the only one of the whole house of York with wits enough to see where his brother's clever treaty with France really tended : if I were a Wydvylle I should shake in my shoes each time he looked at me, for I believe he hates the pack of them; and yet it isn't he has fluttered their dove-cote. It's his brother of Clarence."

"Not that wine-swilling turncoat?"

"No other : ask anyone but me to read the riddle, but the fact's plain as noontide. The Wydvylles and the Greys and their jackals—Fogg, Hawte, Vaughan, the rest of them —walk in mortal fear of him. I shall tell you everything I know, which is much less than I wish it were, and if ever you should stumble on anything that we can lay beside it, give me your news."

"You can trust me for that, sir."

"I am sure I can. Well, here's my part of it. This fear the tribe have of Duke George has grown up since the King came back to London; and I believe it is because of some matter that the Queen heard whilst we were all in France. Whether the Wydvylle crew themselves know what it is, I am not sure. Elizabeth is that kind of fool who babbles what she should keep secret and makes secrets of what she should talk plainly of. The only thing that I am certain of is that my Lord Bishop of Bath and Wells, holy Dr. Stillington, is in some way party to the business. On my faith as a priest, there's all I've known how to discover. But I want more. You must understand, Mr. Colyngbourne, whatever comes to our mill is grist. There is no quarrel, no secret, no dirty private little shame, that we cannot make use of. Our task for the next many years is such a simple one. We have only to make sure that every disgrace of the usurper's utterly dis-graceful life is known to his subjects, that every act he does, if we cannot make it either foolish or tyrannical, shall any-way appear so, that England under Edward of York shall be weak and not strong, poor and not rich, oppressed and not free, and as day follows night, the time will come when the whole land cries out to be delivered from a cursed dynasty, an unendurable rule : and then, Mr. Colyng-bourne, we shall find the deliverer."

"Quousque tandem, Domine?"

The bitter Latin sentence sliced into Dr. Morton's talk

like an axe. Mr. Colyngbourne, in awe from the beginning of the Lady Margaret whose name was magical to a Lancastrian and who was known, too, for her learning and hard, mannish wits, jerked in his chair. She sounded hideously contemptuous, hideously unbelieving in every act and aspect of what they had planned. Dr. Morton moved nothing but his eyes; said in the same sensible, gentle voice : "What, my Lady," and circled his plump hands one over the other again. The black-browed woman in the middle chair—one could tell her anywhere for a Beaufort, thought Mr. Colyngbourne, snarled like a cat at him.

"How long, Lord God, how long do I have to listen to you fools clacking of what you will do the to-morrow after to-morrow, and the King my son away from me in Brittany and unsure of his life?"

Dr. Morton dropped as softly and certainly as a pouncing owl on the most questionable part of what she had said.

"Unsure of his life, my Lady?"

"Ach!" The Lady Margaret made a furious noise and twisted her head round as though the sight of the Doctor's healthily pale, round face disgusted her. Her foot beat the fine carpet and her hard little breast moved up and down. "You dare to boast of your intelligence about the Yorkist Court and you don't know that the usurper has planned to buy my son from Duke François of Brittany?"

"I knew that Lord Rivers had a commission for it in his embassy of three years ago, Madame, but he failed."

"The thing's on foot again. Edward persuaded Louis of France not to wage war on Brittany; has a claim on Duke François now; can ask for gratitude. He will make an offer for my son. A marriage for him will be the pretext, with one of Edward's daughters : a precious likely story. It'll be the death of my son, whilst you babble about deliverers. Duke François has refused for now; but he'll consent in the upshot, wearied with prayer or vanquished with price. Be certain of it."

"Where have you this story from, my Lady?"

"From a source you'd never guess : Lord Thomas Stanley."

"Lord Thomas Stanley?" Dr. Morton put his eyebrows up and let the tip of his tongue show again. "I thought he was wholly devoted to the usurper."

"So he is, but he has a kindness for me. Ask me no more about that. Out of plain charity he's told me what to fear for my son the King; though King's not what he'd call him. He'd never have told you, Mr. Morton; does not trust you; but he thinks me a harmless woman who have suffered because I was married in childhood to a man I did not choose."

She laughed: a high sound as joyless as a sneeze.

Dr. Morton nodded slowly.

"He should know. He's one of the adulterer's trusted men, one of the Cabinet Council. He might be useful to us again."

The woman glared at him.

"After my son's death is it you mean?"

"Be easy, my Lady, be easy. Don't harp on that string. If you know one secret from me, I make bold to say that I know some from you also. I know who rules in Brittany; and it is not Duke François, who, as I thought you were aware, is half a madman."

"Who does then?"

"His Chancellor, Pierre Landois, a greedy man I have some hold over. Put your heart at rest, my dear Lady Margaret. His royal Grace, your son Henry, the last heir of the house of Lancaster, whom God bless and bring into his own, amen, isn't in any manner of danger. There are a hundred ways to make sure he will never fall into the usurper's hands."

"A thousand to make sure he will, though."

"Never, my Lady: you forget I am a person of some influence about the Court, even if I had not heard of this particular matter. If it were necessary, I could even get myself appointed one of the commission sent to fetch your royal son from Brittany."

"There is always that."

The Lady Margaret had reassumed her pose of a wooden idol, head up, chin down, hands on the big arms of her chair. Her brows bent themselves against the play of flames in the fireplace again, and she appeared already to have forgotten the two men, to be satisfied for now.

"I was speaking of the French journey, I think," said Dr. Morton, "and how it marches in every respect with our needs. One of my fellow-commissioners for the treaty was

Sir Thomas St. Leger. I think I have gained something like mastery over him now, by one means and another, and he might be useful. Then the business of the treaty has made a little strife, the smallest breath of a grudge, between that dangerous Richard of Gloucester and King Edward. That might help one day. I could wish we had more intelligence in the North, but Gloucester has most lamentably perverted the loyalty of the silly commons there. That irks me : what was the best Lancastrian part of England turned Yorkist for the love of a misshapen lad in his twenties. That irks me. Still, this little beginning of a division between him and his brother is a thing to watch."

"If he and Clarence both hate the Wydvylles, sir," suggested Mr. Colyngbourne, looking at the chased silver ring on his finger, "is there a chance they might make common cause against them? I could wish there were. It's an old saying, when two fall out the third rejoices."

"I fear we can have no hope of that. George of Clarence and Richard of Gloucester quarrelled forever on the day Duke Richard found Anne Neville and married her. You surely haven't forgotten how we all hoped it might come to blows between them in the question of her inheritance."

"But that's better than two years ago."

"Richard of Gloucester may have forgotten the quarrel. He had his half of the Warwick lands. But Duke George will never love him again. Duke George does not love his mother or the usurper either. There was a prophecy once— I forget the words of it—touching the changes to come when England should be dealt into three parts. I do not myself think that this realm will be great enough to hold those three stubborn, violent men very much longer. Edward's luxuries are finding him out. The stalled beast grows fat. Duke Richard sits in the North, thinking his own thoughts, and I tell you it is not the white rose they love there, but the white boar. The little man has it under his hand to be another Kingmaker. One day, please God, the usurper will be jealous of him : and Clarence is jealous of them both already. Something must crack, my Lady Margaret, and whatever cracks helps us. Quiquid delirant reges, since I know the next way to your heart is through the Latin language, plectuntur Achivi."

"God make it so," said Lady Margaret Beaufort. "The beasts that killed my uncle and my three cousins : let them kill each other so that I can believe in justice again."

"There is justice, my Lady : the sure and pitiless justice of God who neither delays nor makes haste."

"I will believe it when I see my son, who is the only last true heir of John of Ghent, sitting crowned on the King's Bench."

"You will see it. Now, Mr. Colyngbourne, this is where you can show us your loyalty a little. You have an eloquent tongue; talk well in corners. There must be grumbling over the shameful issue of the French journey."

"By God's passion, saving your reverence, but there is that."

"Augment it, then. Bring fuel to the burning."

"I will, sir, but it burns enough without that. I've heard the precious Rose of Rouen called more hard names in taverns in the past month than in all the years since Tewkesbury. A hundred-and-fifty thousand pounds he's pilled and polled the citizens of—four pounds eleven shillings was the least any man gave in benevolences alone, leave aside taxes—and all that's gone only to get him another eighty-five thousand out of France. What's the profit in that for us? the citizens are asking each other. They know where the money's gone : in jewels for the Queen and gifts for Shore's wife and women for the Marquis Dorset and salaries for Friar Bungay and all the sort of necromancers and warlocks Edward keeps about the Court. Look at the disbanded army, the poor commons who left their work and went across to make a fortune in France. They're back at home now, and one-half of 'em are on the road as masterless men. They're turning robber by the thousand at a time. You know it yourself, Dr. Morton. The roads ten miles out of London are less safe to-day than a bridle-track in Wales was before this glorious and immortal victory. The citizens know all these things without my telling them."

"Tell them for all that, Mr. Colyngbourne, tell them. Rub the wound with that particular salt you have. They say you are gifted in making rhymes. English me this little song they are singing in the taverns in France just now :

"J'ai vu roi d'Angleterre
amener son grand hôte
pour la française terre
conquêter bref et tôt.
Le roi, voyant l'affaire,
si bon vin leur donna
que l'autre, sans rien faire,
content s'en rétourna."

Mr. Colyngbourne grinned, and the Doctor looked gravely and benevolently at him.

"I am glad it pleases you. Let it be sung in England. These must seem trifling affairs to you, my Lady Margaret, not helpful to us who aim at nothing below a crown. But remember that this great London itself, which God grant shall one day be your son's royal chamber, is built simply of bricks laid upon other bricks: and remember above all that to-day whatever harms the state of England helps us."

It was spring weather in Middleham, and Alderman Thomas Wrangwysh hummed a tune as he rode past St. Alkelda's Church and up the sloping cobblestones to the Castle. It was a tune he had first heard there and that had stuck pleasantly in his memory.

Oh the white and goodly may,
Oh it is a goodly tree,
And oh when wilt thou return
My own true love to be.

Alderman Wrangwysh stroked his chin and grinned. Nay, but they'd make eyes at him in York if they knew how much he could tell them of the manner in which Kingmaker's daughter had returned to be the true love of his Grace of Gloucester. He remembered a room in Eastcheap and his sister-in-law Jonet, looking as though she had been dragged by the heels through a dusthole, nearly going off in a swoon when she was told that she'd been having her evening draught served her for the last twelvemonth by the Lady Anne Neville. He remembered the Duke of Gloucester (whom he had thought mad when he first insisted on galloping off to the Sign of the Silver Pack merely because he had told him there was a distressed gentlewoman there who had been in the household of the Duchess of Clarence) coming into the solar with the lady's hand in his; had reason to remember it; had been a made man from that moment. They said of him in York now that he was one the Duke of Gloucester would do anything for.

Certainly he enjoyed his visits to Middleham Castle. The men-at-arms saluted him. If there was a fine new horse in the stables or a room had been repainted and hung with fresh arras from Flanders, the Duke would detail someone to show it to him. There was always food and drink beyond what one dreamed of, and at Christmas-time the Duke, as gravely as though he were speaking to my Lord of Northumberland at the least, would implore him to accept the gift of a haunch of venison or a brace of peacocks, and the Duchess would insist on adding something, candied oranges, bitter honey, for his wife. Invitations to the Wrangwysh table at Christmas-time were much sought after in York.

The Duchess had become almost as much a patron-saint in Mr. Wrangwysh's calendar as the Duke. She was so gentle, so serious and under it, anyone with eyes in his head could see, so blindly, so unstaleingly happy. It was as though she had been in prison and now found it miraculous simply to breathe fresh air and look at flowers and walk. God bless her, said Mr. Wrangwysh to himself. God bless her lovely little face; and she's been as good as bread to sister Jonet. Two whole marks it was she sent her last time, and the Duke said something about some eels. God bless them both.

The rest of the people of Yorkshire, he knew, were of his mind in the matter, if with less personal reason. Everybody knew the trouble his Grace of Gloucester had been to, and was still at, in the matter of fishtraps. Everyone knew the kind way in which he had treated the Austin Friars of York, who deserved it a great deal better than some Friars did. One could trust his Grace to take a plain man's view of a matter, and not to look down on it from the perspective of a grand nobleman's saddle. Early that year there had been riots in York. Grumbling began it. We paid for the King's war, and the King's war paid no one but the King. Rhymes that were being said with a sneer in London had found their way North; were repeated. Then the mob was out, shouting that the King's tolls and fees ruined the city, and only to put strings of pearls round London whores' necks. Alderman Wrangwysh remembered the end of that business: a great mass of men-at-arms badged with the boar or the crescent drawn up outside Bootham Bar and the Duke of Gloucester and the Earl of Northumberland sitting their horses at the head of them. He had gone out with the Mayor and the other Aldermen, who licked dry lips and could not keep their hands still, to do reverence. Duke Richard, not wearing armour, had ridden his big white horse up to them and accepted their greetings as though it were a holiday. "You must know, my Lord Mayor, that the reason of my now coming to your city is for its own honour, the good rule of our Lord the King's people and the preservation of our said King's peace": quite formal and meaningless words, said in a clear, expressionless voice. Then he had ridden into the city, leaving his men-at-arms outside. The rioting stopped, and the Duke issued a proclamation in the King's name, in which he asked for the help of the people who had been throwing stones and calling the King a bastard a few minutes ago to seize and bring to prison any misguided person who might hereafter pick any quarrel or make any affray—which God defend. That was the whole of it. There were no fines and no pilloryings. The men-at-arms stayed outside in the cold and presently were marched home again. Next morning, none of the rioters was able to say exactly why he had stopped throwing stones when he did.

He's a masterpiece, Mr. Wrangwysh thought as he turned his horse over the noisy drawbridge. He's a deep, subtle one: plenty of those in the world if it comes to that, but he's honest with it, and there's your difference.

"You'll find Mr. Kendal in the Auditor's chambers," said the groom who took his horse.

Alderman Wrangwysh, who knew his way about the Castle very well by now, went up the stairs to the right of the great gate and knocked on a door. A sharp voice, as of a man expecting something, told him to come in. Mr. Secretary Kendal had been writing, but he was now on his feet with his hands holding the edge of the table, snapping out:

"Any news, any news yet?"

"News of what?" asked Alderman Wrangwysh.

277

"Eh, you, Mr. Wrangwysh : ask your pardon. God give you good day. I was not expecting. . . . Sit you down."

Mr. Kendal's face was not its usual colour.

"God give you good-day, Mr. Kendal. I hope I've not come at a wrong time. What's amiss?"

"Nothing, I pray God," said Mr. Kendal. "What was your errand. Can I be of use?"

"We're in ugly trouble at York, Mr. Kendal, and need his Grace the Duke's noble guidance that he's always favoured us with. It's a damnable garboyle. Our clerk, Mr. Yotton—you know him yourself—I'd 've thought him as honest a fellow as ever spat : and now he tells us on his own confession he's been embezzling the city's money for years. A strong thief, that's what he is, and nothing better. Now we must petition the King's Grace for leave to appoint another man in his room. The Council made bold to send me to beg his good Grace's kindness in the business."

Mr. Secretary Kendal picked up a quill from his penner; tried to balance it over his finger; dropped it. He was frowning.

"Mr. Wrangwysh," he said slowly, "if you ask me to take you to the Duke it's as much as my office is worth to refuse you. But if you have any kindness for him, don't derange him now."

"That I won't, then. But for God's sake, Mr. Kendal, tell me what's happening in this Castle."

"It's the Duchess," said Mr. Kendal shortly.

"God keep her." Mr. Wrangwysh crossed himself. "Is she ill?"

"Childbed : you surely knew she was big?"

"Nay, not for certain I didn't : God and the Virgin be good to her. Has she got her pains now? Our little Duchess, as good and kind as an angel : may all the saints give her an easy time of it."

"The saints have not done so. The pains began before dawn and there's still no word from her women. The physicians are with her now. She's so very small, Mr. Wrangwysh, so tender; was never strong. But oh God, Mr. Wrangwysh"—he got up and kicked his stool from him—"it's the Duke's Grace I'm thinking of. He was the gladdest man in christendom when we knew for certain she was carrying. None of us ever guessed how much he wanted an

278

heir : but now he is like a damned soul. I've no other language for it : like a damned soul."

"Christ have mercy."

"Amen : he's not a man you can read, not open. There's no weeping or crying out now. I was with him more than an hour, and he transacted just the common business of the day as he always does; signed letters; settled a quarrel between two footmen : nothing out of the rule. But his face: God, it was like watching a ghost you cannot speak to and cannot speak to you. His soul's screaming for mercy inside him. I tell you I was almost crying aloud myself before he dismissed me. He did it with a smile, too. By God's body, Mr. Wrangwysh, there are liars in this world who dare say that he conjoined with my Lady for the sake of the Warwick lands. I wish them a tithe of what's in his face now to teach them to know true love next time they see it."

"There'll be hope yet, surely? My own good woman was most miserably handled with her first, but she's as hale as I am now and nursing her seventh, God be loved."

"God send there is hope. Meanwhile the best master and mistress a man ever had are each in a separate cell in Purgatory and there's not a possible thing that we can do for them."

"Saving your presence," said Alderman Wrangwysh shortly, "but if you'll take me to the Chapel I know what I'll do."

Mr. Kendal looked at him with a kind of sour liking.

"You're an honest fellow, Mr. Wrangwysh, and you remind me of my flat duty. We'll both go."

Doves were purring as always on the roof of the Keep, but except for them a discomfortable silence shut the Castle off from the live world beyond its moat. The grooms and men-at-arms going about the Inner Ward walked quietly and did not speak to one another. The usual scurry and clatter from the great kitchen were tuned down to a mere clinking of pots. The two men climbed the stone stairway, as sullen as the way to a gaol, and pulled back the heavy leather curtain of the Chapel door. The tiny two-hundred-year-old place, with its high traceried windows and its vaulted roof, appeared to be the nexus, the focal point, of the whole silence. Nothing stirred in it. A red lamp burning over the altar warned them that God was bodily present.

Mr. Wrangwysh blessed himself, desolately knowing why the sacrament was kept ready. Then he saw that someone else had brought his trouble here : a puny, boy-sized figure in black and violet, kneeling like a figure in stone. The sight shocked and held him as though he had come suddenly on a snake. The figure, head down and hands joined, made not a quiver of movement; and an enormous feeling of helplessness and pity closed down on Mr. Wrangwysh, like the lead sheeting round a corpse. He laid his hand on Mr. Kendal's shoulder, pushing him gently back through the Chapel doorway. They knelt outside.

He prayed a long while, addressing himself methodically to saint after saint : St. Richard of Chichester for the Duke and St. Anne for the Duchess, for himself St. Thomas Martyr, St. Peter for York, St. Akelda of Middleham. You know, he told them, in your glory of heaven, the difficult time we have, being alive. You remember our troubles. You know that life has been very hard here in the North, what with battles and parties, until we did not know whom to look to, and dues and taxes whoever was master, and fishgarths in the rivers and thieves on the roads and justice far away in London, always very difficult to come by, and trade worse than it was. You understand these things, St. Thomas who was murdered by wicked Lords and St. Peter who was crucified head-downwards by King Nero. You know we had a hard time of it till the Duke came. He brought the King's justice within reach of us and broke down the fishgarths and hanged the robbers. Now he is in trouble, and we who have always shown you respect and remembered your feast-days implore you to help him, by the Virtue of Christ who bought us. A very faint smell of incense, accumulated years of praying, prayers of Duke Richard and Duchess Anne, prayers of the Nevilles from Robert of Raby down to Kingmaker, reached him out of the Chapel. It soothed him, narrowing his consciousness to familiar Latin formulæ, worn and rounded like brook-pebbles, which slid through the mind and helped to smother down the impotence of pity : Gratiam tuam, quaesumus, Domine, mentibus nostris infunde, ut qui, angelo nuntiante, Christi filii tui incarnationem cognovimus, per passionem eius et crucem ad resurrectionis gloriam perducamur, amen.

Someone came up the stairs.

Alderman Wrangwysh, standing, drew a very deep breath and shut his teeth on his lip. He was aware of Secretary Kendal, behind him, cursing rapidly in a whisper. It angered him. Don't curse, you fool. You should be praying. A man in the long robe of a physician dived past them, shoving the leather curtain aside, into the Chapel. There was a terrible little silence, and then whispering. At almost the same instant, jarring the heart and brain like a stroke of a mace, the Chapel bell immediately above their heads broke into ringing. It did not toll but danced and babbled, spilling quick gushes of noise like laughter. The curtain was ripped back again, and for the second time in his life Thomas Wrangwysh saw the face of the Duke of Gloucester thawed into unmistakable expression. This time, too, the look was one of blazing and almost horrible joy.

Lord Anthony Wydvylle, K.G., Earl Rivers, Baron Scales and Nucelles, loved beautiful things. His long, capable fingers, bleached with lemon-juice, crispened in pleasure, almost tingled, as he drew them over the coolness of a little ivory diptych he had brought back with him from Italy, a work of that lamented artist, Messer Donatello. It was an adorable object. One of its two arched panels was crowded with tiny delicate figures, minute but unmistakable : weeping Apostles, the Magdalene with dishevelled hair, the Virgin herself, standing a little aside as though her agony refused companionship, and Joseph of Arimathæa lowering, with a tragic movement, the tired body into the sepulchre. In the opposite panel, the risen Christ, heroic and almost naked, with the breast and carriage of an athlete, triumphed over Pilate's men-at-arms who crouched terrorised in their antique harness. A lovely thing, a thing which only Italy could make : Lord Anthony's fingers, which seemed to him to possess wits and will of their own on these occasions, became sad, stroked it regretfully. He had just decided to give it away.

There was a whole raffle of precious objects spread out on the mosaic table-top : a golden crucifix by that other irreproachable craftsman, Messer Lorenzo Ghiberti, a casket of sumptuous Bruges enamels in gilt bronze, a set of ebony paternosters, an emerald ring, a covered cup of Egyptian

281

porcelain patterned with fantastic designs. Lord Anthony had filled in time, whilst waiting for an expected letter, by choosing a birthday gift for the Duke of Gloucester's infant son, who would be one year old that month. Lord Anthony had never set eyes on the young Edward of Middleham—named after his uncle and godfather, the King—and did not want to. Children meant nothing to him. But he held decidedly that a friendly gesture toward Duke Richard of Gloucester was never wasted. No one knew what that bloodless little prince was thinking behind his broad forehead and narrow eyes; but Lord Anthony felt that, should things turn out as he intended them to do in England, his goodwill—or at least the absence of his illwill—was worth even the sacrifice of a Donatello. The gift might hardly appeal to a baby of one year old, but the father was a known connoisseur and reputedly pious; was said to be planning to turn the parish church of Middleham into a College.

Regretfully but finally, Lord Anthony set the diptych aside from the other objects and began to stroll about the room. It was, he prided himself, a unique room, his Privy Chamber at Mote Manor in Kent, being fashioned on the Italian plan. Its walls were not hung, but lined with cedarwood and divided by half-columns of marble into large panels. A wooden frieze in alto-rilievo, Italian work, ran above the pilasters : knights, ladies, heralds, men-at-arms, all in lifelike attitudes, going in procession to a joust. Each panel was inlaid in mother-of-pearl with Lord Anthony's cypher encircled by a Garter. The carpet was an astonishing affair from Byzantium : stiff-looking people in peculiar clothes worked with gold and silver thread on a silk ground. It was mushy to the feet, being laid over a thick bed of dried lavender and verbena, whose odour filled the place. Lord Anthony's enormous library of French, English and Latin works was arranged in presses of the almost unobtainably rare sandalwood, protected by silver grilles. The manuscripts, superbly illuminated, were bound in Moroccan leather tooled and emblazoned in gold and with gold clasps. The printed books had a press to themselves : the Bible, Psalter and *Catholicon* of Guthenberg, the Sallust and Barzizi's *Epistolæ* printed for the Sorbonne, and the best treasure of all, its clasps studded with rubies, Lord

Anthony's own *Dictes and Sayings of the Philosophers*, just executed by his protégé, Mr. William Caxton. In a niche at the far end of the room, like a saint in a shrine, stood another Italian trophy : a great vase of moss-agate, veritable Roman work with figures of dancing hobgoblins, tailed and goat-footed, carved round it. Cæsar or Virgil might have looked at it with their living eyes, or touched it. Lord Anthony stopped to run those long, possessive fingers round its rim now, looking down the extent of his rich privacy as far as the great bay-window full of painted glass that displayed the French quarterings—the fork-tailed lions of Limburg and Luxemburg, the sixteen-rayed star and fleurs-de-lys of Baux, the bends and rose of Orsini—which he claimed in right of his mother, the Duchess of Bedford. From the coffered ceiling of gold and green hung five gold lamps ornamented with tritons and naked mermaids. At night these and ten great prickets of ebony and silver would fetch up gleams on the mosaic table, the inlaid chairs and benches, the service of gold plate on the buffet, the marble hearth guarded by crowned lions and topped by a huge glazed plaque, fabricated after a secret process by Messer della Robbia, of minstrels singing from open books.

A good place to be home from the wars in : it was not many months since Lord Anthony, who wished to keep out of England for a while after the French treaty, had returned from service with the late Duke of Burgundy. Charles the Hardy had taken a good number of English volunteers into his pay, saying contemptuously that they would be better fighting for him than slitting each other's throats at home. Lord Anthony, feeling that some gesture from him might soften the Duke's anger against his uncle, the Count of St. Pol (it did not : Duke Charles stripped him of all but his life and handed him prisoner to the Christian King, who took the life as well), made one of their number. He did not especially dislike fighting; and though it was only now, looking down the length of his own Privy Chamber, that he admitted it, he had been glad to do something to suggest to Duke Richard of Gloucester that he was not one of those who had crossed the Channel simply for a French pension. There had been something indefinably frightening in that Duke's silences since the day King

Edward had agreed to discuss terms with the Christian King.

Charles the Hardy, abandoned by his brother-in-law of England, had patched things up as well as he might with France and then flung himself straightway into a rather meaningless quarrel with the Swiss. Taking his artillery and a great part of his personal treasure with him, he marched to besiege Granson. Lord Anthony was there. He wrinkled his nose now, thinking of what had happened when the place surrendered. The hardest heart would have felt pity, seeing the wretched garrison strung up from trees in such number that they broke the branches and fell down half-dead. Then there was news that the Swiss, not in great force, were gathering for their revenge. Duke Charles, against the advice of those he consulted, moved out to meet them. Lord Anthony was not at all clear about what happened next. He saw Burgundians running past him in retreat before he even knew they were near the enemy; halted his own company and fell back a little; heard the Swiss horns blaring and was aware of a vast body of pikemen rolling down on him yelling: "Österreich und Bern!" and "Rache für Granson!" He put spurs to his horse and found himself suddenly involved in a general rout. When they had collected themselves again, they discovered that they had lost precisely seven men-at-arms, but that the whole of their artillery, their camp and a large share of the Ducal treasure were in the hands of the enemy, who, Lord Anthony supposed, were the only body of men in christendom more surprised than they. They quartered at Lausanne then, and Lord Anthony read books and talked to such scholars as the place provided until, on a June day, he had a letter from his sister, Queen Elizabeth. It was a letter in her own bad hand, blotted and interlined, and though he read it ten times, it did not make sense. Someone whose name she would not set down was making trouble in England; was asking questions. If he were left to go on as he had been doing he would unbury a secret that would be the ruin of the Wydvylles: but she would not say what. The King knew nothing. She had not dared to speak to him. She was a friendless woman, God help her, and could trust no one. Anthony had been away a year now. He must come home.

Lord Anthony, knowing her for a fool, was in two minds on the matter until events decided him. The Burgundian forces, twenty-three thousand strong, were marched out of Lausanne and set to besiege a wholly unimportant little town called Morat. Again, the Swiss army of relief appeared. Exactly how the Republic had contrived to raise thirty-five thousand men, and among them ten thousand hand-gunners and four thousand crack German cavalry, Lord Anthony did not bother to inquire. Half-an-hour after the battles joined he turned and led such of his English as were alive out of the field; was risking no more blood for Charles the Hardy. The Burgundian dead on that day were guessed at eighteen thousand. Lord Anthony was unsurprised when, at the turn of the year, news came to England of the end of it all. Charles the Hardy had not understood the meaning of defeat. Deserted by the soldier of fortune, Niccolò di Campobasso, having only four thousand men, of whom not more than twelve hundred were in a state to fight, he besieged in midwinter the strong town of Nancy. The Swiss marched. They had cavalry lent them in secret by King Louis. Gleaners, two days after the battle, found what the wolves had left of Charles the Hardy, Duke of Burgundy, Brabant and Luxemburg, Count of Flanders, Holland and Zeeland, naked, hamstrung, the skull split.

Lord Anthony stroked his little scented beard. There would be international complications, so far as he could see, for ten years or a hundred years to come on account of that unnecessary death. God had given the lands of Burgundy, after their long felicity and wealth under the three good princes, Philippe the Hardy, Jean the Fearless, Philippe the Good, a Duke who kept them in continual war. At one stroke he had tumbled down the great and sumptuous edifice, the powerful house which had flourished whilst its neighbours were in distress. God did such things before we were born, decided Lord Anthony, and He will do them again when we are dust. But the wise man takes warning by what he sees. The God who can ruin the Ducal house of Burgundy need not stretch His arm far to destroy the Wydvylles.

He looked round his room again: mirrors in jewelled frames, swansdown cushions, his own portrait by Meister van Eyck. He had got them, and a Garter and an Earldom

and the office of Chief Butler of England and title of King's
Kinsman by nothing but his own wits and his sister's pretty
face. And I wish to Christ, he thought irritably, that all the
wits in the family had not been mine. I wish Elizabeth
might have had some. As soon as he reached England he
had gone to Court. Edward, fuller-fleshed even than before,
welcomed him sumptuously : balls, hunts, banquets,
chamber-music, buffoons, malmsey. He got a morning with
the Queen alone, whilst the King was giving audience to the
desperate ambassadors of his sister, Margaret of Burgundy,
who was holding her dead husband's territories on behalf of
her stepdaughter (she herself had borne no children to
Duke Charles) and whom the Christian King was pressing.
He asked bluntly what had been the meaning of the letter
sent him to Lausanne. It had seemed like Bedlam, he said,
but there was presumably a cause for it. He got an answer
to that : the Duke of Clarence. He had expected it; was
merely relieved that it was not the Duke of Gloucester.

"And what the devil has Duke George been at to throw
you into this panic, my dear sister?"

Queen Elizabeth alarmingly put her head down and
burst into a wild trouble of weeping. She would not tell him,
dare not tell anyone in the world, what the danger was with
which Duke George of Clarence threatened her.

Lord Anthony argued with her for an hour. If she would
not tell him where the trouble was, he could do nothing. He
was not here to guess riddles set by his own sister. Either let
her be open with him, or he would go back to Mote Manor
and she could go to the devil. Queen Elizabeth wept three
kerchiefs into sops, but she fought him off with all the
bottomless obstinacy of a feeble-minded woman. Like a hen
in front of a galloping horse, she tracked wildly from one
side to another, but would not leave her road. The secret
that Duke George was threatening to discover was one
between her and King Edward and she dare not speak of it
to a living soul : but let Duke George once find it, and the
rule of the Wydvylles in England was at its end. The mob
would tear them out of their beds and burn them alive. The
King himself could not protect them. Probably the King
would be deposed and Duke George or even Henry Tydder,
the pretended heir of Lancaster, put in his place. Duke
Richard, that cold-blooded, horrible little man who hated

286

them all, would join Duke George and march his Northern savages against London. Her precious darlings, her dear children, would suffer death or worse : probably worse.

By this time, even assuming that half of what she said was moonshine and May-games, Lord Anthony was disturbed; felt his heart tighten. His sister—he had never realised it more clearly—was the biggest fool on two feet : but she was not a coward; was as little given to meeting trouble halfway as her husband. In the old days she had absolutely refused to see the threat in Kingmaker's hourly darkening sullenness until the stroke fell and her father and her brother John had their necks on the block. During the awful months in Westminster Sanctuary she had never, by all accounts, doubted for a moment that the Rose of Rouen would come riding back like Sir Launcelot in the tale to rescue her. If she was seeing pitfalls in the snow now, then the pitfalls were there. He lost his temper with her.

"Woman, it was well said by King Solomon that there are birches for fools' backs. So God help and redeem me, I could strip and whip you now, though you were twenty times Queen of England, with all the pleasure in life. For the last time before I ride back into Kent and leave you to hang yourself in your own garters, will you tell me what it is that Duke George may discover?"

She would not. King Edward would kill her if she ever breathed a word of it.

"Then if it's as close as that, why in the name of all devils don't you tell Edward that George is nosing after it, and let him deal with the matter?"

"I don't dare, yet—not till I can prove more. He'd say I was jealous of George and meant to destroy him, and Christ knows I have always hated him, drunken treacherous pig, and he's always hated me, and Edward knows it and he wouldn't believe me, and besides he's forbidden me ever to speak of the thing to him since the day when he told me; but it's destruction for all of us if Duke George learns of it. I'm all alone, God have pity on a poor woman, and a good one too, whatever they may say, and you must help me. Anthony, you *must* help me."

"Devils and thunders, you addle-witted woman, how in the name of the Blessed Blood of Hales am I to help you when you won't say what you need?"

"But I've told you, Anthony. Watch Duke George. Spy on him. I'm sure he's conspiring other wickednesses as well as this, and he wants the Crown for himself, and he works black magic. Find proof against him, enough to make Edward suspicious. Make Edward angry with him. Then I could dare tell him what George's real drift is. But you must begin it."

"That's the first sense I've heard from you, sister. That might be contrived."

"You must do it, Anthony, for all our sakes, for my precious children. Duke George must be killed. He must be killed."

"That's as may be. For the last time of all now, will you tell me what the root of the matter is?"

"No, Anthony, I daren't. Not even you : it's too horrible. I daren't."

"Now listen, Elizabeth. Do you solemnly swear to me on your salvation as a christian woman that unless I check George of Clarence he can tell news that will destroy us?"

Queen Elizabeth got on her feet. Tears had made ruin of her planned complexion. Her hands opened and shut at her sides and her mouth wobbled. There was an extraordinary and disconcerting glare in her green, shallow eyes.

"I swear by almighty God and all His saints, by the Sacrament of the altar, if George of Clarence does not die he will ruin us utterly. I swear it by the body of Jesus Christ."

"Very well," said Lord Anthony.

He had gone to work. That had been months ago. At first he had a good hope that the mere thrust and twist of his investigations would worm out, somehow, from somebody, a hint of what the secret was that has turned his shallow sister into a bloodthirsty creature full of fears. He was disappointed. Whatever it was that Duke George was groping after, the secret was well kept. Dr. Robert Stillington, Bishop of Bath and Wells, knew something—Queen Elizabeth had hinted. He cultivated that simple-natured, saintly little man, with his gentle, candid face and his grave eyes, but got nothing out of him. Yet something was in the air. Something was forming. Duke George had been displaying eccentricities of late which were not the eccentricities of a common drunkard. For one thing—and this was fortunate, since it annoyed King Edward—he had been absenting himself more and more, and more and more rudely, from the Court; kept his own state at Warwick Castle; came to London only when summoned, and then showed an extraordinary unwillingness, he who had never refused wine, to eat or drink in the palace. Kind people said that grief for the loss of his wife had made a change in him. Duchess Isobel, elder daughter of Kingmaker, had died in December of last year, just after Lord Anthony came home from his Burgundian adventures. Duke George had given her a pompous funeral in Tewkesbury Abbey, which was in his domains, and laid her away in a good vault at the back of the high altar there. She had not had a very happy life, and perhaps he regretted it. But the real reason for his odd behaviour came out in the end and made a chilly scandal; startled and puzzled people. It was at a supper given to the Burgundian ambassadors : a simple meal, and particularly well chosen. Lord Anthony remembered an exotic dish of quails stuffed with figs and a sweetbread-tart : both good. Duke George sat at one end of the table, his lower lip stuck out; refused to talk. Edward, magnificent and enormous in mulberry-coloured velvet sewn with emeralds, had looked once or twice at him, puckering the side of his mouth in irritation. They brought him a big gold tankard of his favourite sweet wine, malmsey : and then, in front of them all, King, Queen, ambassadors, perhaps twenty Lords and Ladies, he did an unimaginable thing : put his hand in the breast of his black mourning-doublet; fished out a great piece of unicorn's horn on a silver chain; dipped it into the drink. No one was there but knew that the strange twisted spikes of ivory, to be got at a price from the far North, were sovereign against poison; cleaned any drink one dipped them in. George, Duke of Clarence, had announced as plainly as by spoken words that he expected to be poisoned at his brother's supper-table.

Lord Anthony still remembered the little suppressed noise that rippled round the place, the eyes turned on Duke George. It had looked for part of a second as though the King would do something. His face, that had so much broadened under the cheekbones and filled in at the jowl of recent years, turned blood-coloured. His eyebrows snapped down over his eye-sockets and his nostrils stiffened. But a curious lethargy, as Lord Anthony was aware, came between King Edward and the world nowadays. He belched over his food; pushed the plate forward from him; said nothing. But he could hardly have forgotten the incident, thought Lord Anthony contentedly.

He crossed to the tall cabinet by the fireplace that was one of his best-valued things. It was of highly-polished olive-wood inlaid with ivory, and held for the most part little objects of gold and rare stones—cameos of ancient work, ornaments from Byzantium and the Saracen lands— that had come his way : but a sliver of wood along the front of a shelf went sideways under his fingers, and with a sad, thick noise a piece of the inlaid front pouted forward; showed a concealed place. He took out the small wad of papers that he kept there; might as well read them until the newest additions to his file arrived.

Several spies had contributed to the dossier of Duke George. The papers were written, both in cypher and long-hand, in three languages. Sir John Fogg favoured dog-Latin for his reports, which were brief and ambiguous, mere indications of the spoken word to follow later. Sir Thomas Vaughan, a useful Welchman whom Lord Anthony had been at some trouble to attach to himself, wrote French. There were English scrawls from less reputable sources. Lord Anthony sat in a deeply-cushioned chair flicking them over, smiling a very little. There was enough here already to make trouble for Duke George, but not certainly the final trouble he intended. It was a mixture. Duke George was certainly addicted to magic. Mr. Stacy, his clever secretary, had been buying books on the casting of horoscopes and similar matters. That was recorded. A dismissed groom deposed that on a certain evening he had been ordered to bring a white cock up to a turret-chamber in the Castle of Warwick. That room had contained a brazier, an astrolabe and a number of books. The Duke had been there with Mr. Stacy and one Mr. Burdet. The Duke had been pale and excited, but not drunk. Mr. Burdet, of Arrow in Warwickshire, was a queer man. As long ago as the year 1474, Sir John Fogg had discovered, he had used very intemperate expressions about King Edward. The King, condescending to hunt in Arrow Park, had killed a tame white buck belonging to him. "And I wish the buck's head," Mr. Burdet had

exclaimed, "in his belly that moved the King to kill it."
Almost lèse-majesté : Mr. Burdet would repay watching.
Something a great deal more significant was in the next
note. The Duke still kept by him, now in this year of 1477,
an exemplification of the old Act of the Lancastrian Parliament of six years ago, whereby, supposing the death of Holy
Harry of Windsor and the death without issue of his son,
the Prince of Wales, he was declared heir to the throne of
England. That was important; was almost worth retailing to
the King. What did Duke George want with that shameful
memorial of his old treachery, if he was a loyal man now?
In comparison with it, the outcry he made when the King
took Tutbury Castle out of his charge, though Lord
Anthony had a full note of the ill words he used on that
occasion, hardly was important.

There was a knock at the Privy Chamber door. That
would be Sir John Fogg's latest news out of the West
country. He had gone down there to see whether a little
unobtrusive ferreting in Dr. Stillington's own bishopric of
Bath and Wells would tell them anything, and his report
was promised for to-day. Lord Anthony unlocked the door
and took the sealed paper, addressed in Sir John's crabbed
hand, *To my Lord Revieres att hys maner of ye Mote wth
spede,* from a page; locked the door again and broke it
open. Within, the paper was as blank as the moon. Lord
Anthony stroked his scented beard once more; approved.
Only a fool ran risks. He took from a drawer of the cabinet
a flat pewter dish and a small bottle of vinegar; laid the
paper in the dish and soused it vigorously. If, as he supposed, the message had been written with the juice of the
common spurge, it would soon show plainly. It did : one line
in Sir John's particular brand of cursive Latin. Lord
Anthony bent over the dish, wrinkling his forehead, until
the drastically abbreviated words were clear and could be
read: *Mulier' q̄dam p'pheticam ī Bath ī̄veni q̄ sec'ta om'
D.d.C. coḡ'it:* I have found a certain prophetic woman in
Bath who knows all the secrets of the D. of C.

Holding the paper delicately with finger and thumb, Lord
Anthony shook off as much as possible of the vinegar; then
dropped it into the fire that burned, though it was spring,
in the lion-guarded hearth; began to walk the room again.
All the secrets of the Duke of Clarence : that was promising.

That was very promising indeed. What could they be, those secrets that had terrified his silly sister so, that threatened such damage to her and him and their brother and sisters and the young Marquis Dorset and Sir Richard Grey and even the royal children : what black adders of secrets coiled under a stone and ready to bite if the light fell on them? Had Duke George discovered truth in the old wicked rumour that King Edward was none of the Duke of York's get, but the son of Blackburn, the Scots archer? Was that it? But would even Duke George make a harlot of his own mother? Had Elizabeth, in some moment of inconceivable folly, cuckolded the King? No, it was not that, for whatever the secret was, King Edward shared it. Then had their mother, Jacquette of Bedford, really used sorcery to bring about the marriage? She had been charged with it by King-maker eight years ago, and had cleared herself before the Privy Council, but Lord Anthony was not blind to her nature. She would stop at neither sorcery nor murder for a sufficient end. Well, he would know soon now. The prophetic woman must be bribed or blackmailed until she talked. Edward was the difficulty : to find enough to convince Edward that his own brother was a danger to them; must go. For the first time in his long days of power, Lord Anthony found himself regretting the changes that had come over the King. He was easier to rule now; gave with both hands; shrugged off responsibilties onto any shoulder that would carry them. His paunch sagged and his face was permanently red, with little broken veins scribbled over the cheekbones. The old royal rages were no longer in him; had been replaced by a sort of sullenness, a bad temper that growled and smouldered on for days once it was roused. Virtue had gone out of him.

We did it, said Lord Anthony frankly to himself. We needed to do it. We found from the day of the marriage that he was ruled most easily through his pleasures; so multiplied them. Now we have ground the edge of the blade till we can never cut our fingers on it. I was in awe of him seven years ago; not now. He is not royal now. But if the blunted blade cannot hurt us, it is hard, too, to use it for a weapon. He would have struck quickly once, or else refused to strike at all. Now we shall have to work on him : but at last we know

292

that the work cannot fail. Blunt or not blunt, the blade is in our hands for good.

He looked again round the exotic, ordered luxury of his Privy Chamber. Once he had owned nothing but a couple of horses, his clothes and armour, his good looks and wits. Then had come his marriage to the Dowager Lady Scales, widow of a detested Lancastrian Baron whom the London mob had torn in pieces after the Battle of Northampton. That was a beginning, the first change. God rest her soul in peace, he said to himself now. She has been a dull wife, but profitable. His marriage with her had been a kind of omen of the more splendid marriage of his sister. It had been fine horses then, Egyptian perfumes, cloth-of-gold gowns reversed with miniver. He had his Garter, and when the Bastard of Burgundy came over magnificently to the English Court he met him in the lists at Smithfield and beat him both on horse and on foot. The old nobility looked sideways at him; and sometimes that had seemed the best part of all. Let them look sideways. They could not look down. He had earned his place; played pimp to Edward's least honest whims; run into dangers. England was a rogue horse to ride at first; reared; bolted. His father and his brother had been thrown. There had been exile and battles and the one act of necessity that he still kept his memory away from : Holy Harry's mangled little corpse bleeding into the rushes in the Wakefield Tower. Now there was a crown on the work : money flooding in from a hundred sources, his blood mixed into half the noble blood of England, Edward subdued to him finally like a tame lion gone blunt in the claws and blindish. More was coming. Edward talked of a royal second match for him : a political marriage with the sister of the King of Scots. He would have brothers-in-law on two thrones then and, when the Princess Elizabeth married the Dauphin, a niece Queen of France : and Edward would not last forever; would not last as long as he did. His nephew, the Prince of Wales, whose upbringing more and more was in his hands, would be King of England and his puppet. The superb manor-house was round him like a cloak round a magnificent body : outside the locked door, rooms tapestried with the best work of Flanders where people waited for the chance to bow to him as he went past; over his head, the scented bed-chambers with inlaid beds, silk pillows; beneath his feet, the vaults of priceless German and Cretan wines and the locked iron chest, packed up to the lid with little canvas bags of gold, whose secret only he and his secretary knew. There were forty horses in the stable, every one of them a blood, a pack of hounds the Christian King would envy, better hawks than in the royal mews. The aviary that he had built had hopoes and aigrettes in it and strange sickle-beaked crimson fowl from Egypt. It was very pleasant: and there was hardly a man in England who would not give his ears to take it from him.

He knew that; accepted it. He was hated in England. The old nobility hated him for a man of yesterday. The London citizens bitterly, personally hated him for the fashion in which he exercised his office of Chief Butler. The commons everywhere hated him because his fingers were in their pouches, because with each new tallage and benevolence King Edward raised he had more jewels on his doublet and more servants in his house. Husbands and fathers hated him for his nephew's sake, the Marquis Dorset from whom no woman could be protected. His tenants hated him because he never let a tithe of his uttermost dues slip by him.

Give them a scent to bay on, he thought, and they would pull him down. Duke George of Clarence was casting round for the scent now. Mote Manor and all the works it crowned and gathered into itself were too dear and precious for a drunken prince to kick to pieces. I killed Holy Harry of Windsor, thought Lord Anthony, for less than that.

"And who for St. Ninian's stall? Name someone, Dr. Beverley, if you can. I am open to hear proposals."

"With respect, your Grace, Mr. Richard Cutler, whom I believe your Grace knows, is a pious clerk and also a very deserving one."

"Richard Cutler"—the Duke of Gloucester tightened his upper lip over his teeth and almost shut his eyes—"I know the name. Yes, I have him: a Derbyshire man. Well and good; I like Derbyshire folk. He shall have St. Ninian's stall if he pleases: and that closes the list. Have you his name down, Kendal?"

"I have," said Mr. Kendal, sanding a slip of parchment.

The Duke, his Secretary and Dr. Beverley, Rector of Middleham, were discussing details of the College of six canons and a Dean Duke Richard meant to found in Middleham Church to the honour of Christ and his mother and St. Alkelda, and for the offering of prayers and Masses for the good estate of his brethren, himself and his wife and son. Dr. Beverley was delighted with the idea. He hoped he had christian humility enough not to be moved by the prospect of a Deanery for himself : but he loved his little church with its tiny hospital adjoining it and its brand-new chantry of the Virgin that Mr. John Cartmell—might he have his reward for it—had founded : and now, thanks to the Duke, the little place was going to be splendid as the College of the Blessed Virgin and St. Alkelda of Duke Richard of Gloucester in Middleham. He knew it was the Duke's joy at having a son and heir at last which had moved him to this piece of piety, and he felt very glad that he had prayed so hard for the Duchess during her pains last year.

Duke Richard stood up. He glanced over Mr. Kendal's shoulder at the papers on the table, nodded and stepped down from the daïs of the Chamber of Presence. He had been very busy lately, Dr. Beverley understood, over a nasty case of piracy, the seizing of a Dutch merchantman at Hartlepool by that ungodly person, Sir Thomas Lumley. No doubt he had seen justice done. Justice had become almost a matter of course in the North, these days. He turned now to Dr. Beverley with one of the smiles that were more a movement of the puckered eyelids than the lips.

"Well, there's all our morning's business done, sir. Come down and tell me the parish gossip. Any more children for you to make christians of?"

"Only one, your good Grace : Joanna at Westwood's daughter has a daughter of her own now."

"I did not know Joanna's daughter was even married."

"I'm afraid she isn't, your Grace. It would be harvest-time last year, as near as I can reckon, and your Grace knows that harvest-time . . ."

"Surely : see if you can find the name of the man. If he's one of our own people, I'll have a word with him. See my almoner if the family need anything, and mind you give the girl a stiff penance. Harvest-time indeed! Well, we're all sinners."

Very humble and proper in a great Lord, thought Dr.

295

Beverley. He knew Duke Richard kept one of his own bastards, a likely boy named John, about the household. It pleased him that the Duke did not throw up his hands to find that poor men had the same fleshly failings as the nobility.

"And otherwise the parish does fairly well?"

"More than fairly : we may say more than fairly, your Grace; and thanks to you."

"I don't see why you thank me, but I am pleased to hear it : no sickness or no too great poverty?"

"As I am a clerk, my Lord Duke, they were never better."

"Good." The Duke, who had been drumming his fingers on the big mantelshelf of the Chamber of Presence, turned toward Dr. Beverley. His expression was oddly naïf, like a bright child's. A kind of honesty and wonder seemed to be behind the puckering of the eyes and the set of the mouth, as though the thought in his mind were so simple that he expected nobody to understand it. "I want the people about me to be happy," said Duke Richard.

Not summer yet, the Windsor weather was cold at night : big stars in the sky between the rainfalls, a cold little wind going along the ground. Sir John Fogg, accompanied only by two torches and two men who tramped behind him, drew his big cloak of martens round him and cursed the cold. The hard bulk of the Curfew Tower pushed up above him into the air, and lights still burned in many windows of the Palace, telling him other people had an easier time of it. This was a job worth money, but unwelcome on an ugly night.

One of the two silent, experienced men slid past him and unlocked a door at the base of the tower. The other took both torches from the torch-bearers. "Get out of this," Sir John Fogg told them; and they went reluctantly, guessing what was going to happen under the roots of the tower there. Sir John Fogg wished they might have his work to do and learn when they were well off. The steps into the dungeon were narrow, and a cold struck out of the place past anything Sir John could have conceived. He should have questioned the wise woman of Bath, Ankarette Twynyho, immediately, instead of waiting to improve his position with her. He had gathered that she was skilled in peculiar arts, a prophetess, that she had been a chamber-woman to the late Duchess of Clarence, and that the Duke had consulted her in various queer matters and had asked her to resolve some indiscreet questions about the crown of England. That should have been enough for him. He should have threatened to denounce her as a sorceress and got what he wanted out of her. She would be alive now if he had done. It was last month that a body of eighty men, some of them armed, had burst into the unfortunate woman's manor of Cayford, seized her in the name of Duke George of Clarence, dragged her through three several counties to Warwick, charged her at the Guildhall there with having poisoned her late mistress, the Duchess Isobel, and hanged her out of hand on Mytton gallows, although several of the jury, after her apology for a trial, had come and asked her forgiveness for having delivered a verdict contrary to their conscience, to which, they said, they were driven by their terror of the Duke of Clarence.

To Sir John Fogg, the matter was as plain as need be. Duke George had trumped up a charge against the woman to keep her mouth shut; must have learned somehow that she was being asked questions. But holy God, he thought, he must have been drunk when he did it : to abuse the King's privilege, subvert the law of the land, so blatantly. Even King Edward's England, even King Edward, would not stand that. Duke George had played into their hands superbly. The Writ of Certiorari had reached Warwick too late; but there were inquiries on foot now. He had his part in them.

The dungeon beneath the Curfew Tower was an enormous place. Light of two torches was not enough for it. But they showed all that Sir John Fogg wanted to see : the queer black bundle on the floor that had been there six hours. It looked like a kind of box at first; resolved itself then, the torches coming nearer, into the shape of a man kneeling on his hams, but in an unnatural posture, his breast shoved close down on his knees, his arms bent at his sides like the wings of a trussed bird, face on the ground. As the two torturers came up on either side of him, the reason for his position appeared : glints of metal round him in odd places. The man had been crammed into an iron framework that misplaced every joint in his body, crushing his neck down so that his head was lower than his rump, twisting his arms up : the device known, after its detested inventor, as the Duke of Exeter's daughter.

The torturers stuffed their flambeaux into iron holders; brought up the things that had been put ready in the dungeon : a table, stool, brazier, bucket of water, rods. Sir John sat at the table, laying penner, inkhorn and some sheets of paper on it; rubbed his thin hands. The silence in the dungeon was wonderful. The torturers had learned, apparently, to control even their breathing. The man on the floor made no sound. The insidious damp and cold seemed to crawl up the legs like centipedes. Sir John twitched his shoulders.

"God's cross, light that brazier, can't one of you?"

They lit it, muttering and pushing each other's hands aside like children; brought it, crackling, and put it near Sir John's stool. The blue-and-yellow flames, as solid as rags, popped in and out, licking the coals as though they were not sure whether they would make a meal of them. Sir John stretched his arms and breast out to them for a minute; got no warmth yet; was aware of the two men looking at him with dull servants' eyes, waiting for him to do something; said crossly :

"Well, has he still his wits about him?"

One of the men gave the prisoner a little push on the side. Pinned as he was, he rolled over helplessly, eyes and mouth opening in a white face.

"Aye, he has, sir."

"Mr. John Stacy."

"Yes."

The voice coming out of the cramped dummy of a man who could not move anything except his lips and eyelids was more normal than would have been expected; was almost polite.

"I ask you whether you are prepared to give me the information I have required of you."

"No."

"You are not, Mr. Stacy?"

"No."

"That is foolish of you. Let me rehearse what you have already said. It might help your memory. You are John Stacy, a Baccalaureus Artium of Oxford, and employed as

Secretary by his Grace the Duke of Clarence. Well, Mr. Stacy, that is true, is it not?"

"Yes."

"You have found his Grace a good master?"

"Yes."

"Are you loyal to him, Mr. Stacy? I ask you that. Are you loyal to him?"

"Jesus, would I bear this . . ."

"Are you loyal to him?"

"You whorson devil, isn't this proof enough? You're killing me."

"So it is for your master's sake you obstinately refuse to answer?"

"I never said it."

"Oh, you did, Mr. Stacy, but plainly. Come now. Isn't it that you know some small thing envious people might misuse against his Grace, God defend him? Isn't that why you are silent? You've told me as much. I admire you, Mr. Stacy. You are a brave man. As God sees and judges me, you're a very brave man. But the folly of it : we mean nothing against his Grace. Look you, I'm King Edward's commissary. Is it likely that our Lord King would contrive anything against his brother? It is for the Duke's own sake, to quell these mischievous slanders against him, that he has ordered this inquiry : so that the Duke may clear himself. Now, Mr. Stacy, you are a learned man and the Duke's friend. Will you not help us?"

"God damn you."

"Mr. Stacy, why was the woman Ankarette Twynyho hanged?"

"She poisoned my Lady."

"She poisoned the devil's grandmother. Why was she hanged?"

"I've told you. You bastard, may you rot in hell. You're killing me."

"Why was Ankarette Twynyho hanged?"

"I had no part in it, Jesus Christ help me. I had no part in it. For God's love, Sir John, let me out of this brake. I'm dying."

"Why was she hanged?"

"I don't know. I don't know."

"Then it was not for poisoning the Duchess?"

"I tell you I know nothing of it."

"Mr. Stacy, if you will answer me this one question you shall be taken out of here. You shall have a room with a bed and a fire, some wine. Was not Ankarette Twynyho hanged because the Duke of Clarence had spoken to her of a matter of which he should not speak?"

"No."

Sir John Fogg looked at the torturers. They stood just on his side of the thin grey film dividing the torchlight from the dark.

"Strip his back."

One of them stooped, pulling Mr. Stacy to his knees again, and began to drag his shirt and doublet over his head as far as the iron bands of the brake would let him. The other took up a rod. It was not a birch, though of the same shape and size; was made of long iron wires bound together at either end, the handle-end being wrapped in cloth to give a grip.

"Mr. Stacy, I am asking you one last time whether the Duke of Clarence asked Ankarette Twynyho to prophesy if he should be King of England."

Mr. Stacy, bunched and clamped on the floor, blood oozing from his nose, as it did often with men kept too long in his case, did not make a sound. Sir John Fogg looked sideways at the brazier. It would brighten and begin to warm him soon. He shuffled his feet on the cold floor and nodded to the man holding the rod, who touched Mr. Stacy very lightly on the back with it and then swung it up behind him to the full stretch of his arm.

He brought it down almost slowly, with a long, smooth movement suggestive of great power. The sound of it striking Mr. Stacy's flesh was like the splash of a bucket of water thrown at a wall. He immediately lifted his arm again and brought it down again. At the third stroke, a noise like a cat's mew came from Mr. Stacy. Sir John Fogg held up his hand.

"Did the Duke ask Ankarette Twynyho to prophesy whether he should be King of England?"

There was no answer. Sir John looked at the torturer with the rod.

"Use your strength, fellow. He's not felt you yet."

After each blow, the same mewing gasp came from the

man on the floor, until the tenth. Then there was silence. The torturer struck five times more. Mr. Stacy's back was covered with short deep cuts. Blood streamed from them.

"Mr. Stacy."

There was no answer. The other torturer kicked the kneeling man in the ribs, knocking him sideways again.

"Swooned," he said.

Sir John Fogg held his hands over the brazier. It had grown hot. He twisted his upper lip in boredom. This was going to be a long job, difficult : stubborn pig. It was not easy to do work of this kind at all in England. In France he could have strapped his man to a bench with the poire d'angoisse, the hollow wooden gag, between his teeth and poured water, bucket upon bucket of water, down his throat until he talked : or in Germany he could have hung him by dislocated shoulders from the ceiling with stone weights on his feet; burned the hair on his belly and under his arms with pitch. But torture was looked sideways upon in England; was used only where the charge was one of witchcraft or high treason. Its very lawfulness was rather more than questioned. Sir John Fogg's only warrant, he was aware, for laying so much as a finger on his prisoner was the old mandate of Edward II directing torture to be used on the Knights Templar, "without mutilation or permanent weakening of any limb and without violent shedding of blood." If the man should happen by ill-luck to die on him, he would be not much safer than a murderer.

"Take him out of the brake," he ordered.

The torturers began fumbling with the locks of their device. There was a clang as the iron arms dropped apart, and Mr. Stacy fell on his face, slack-limbed like a dead body. Sir John felt in the deep sleeve of his gown and brought out a little leather bottle of German cordial. He drank some, shuddering as it warmed his throat and chest, and passed the bottle to the men.

"Give him a sup of it."

One of the torturers went on his knees, lifting Mr. Stacy's head into his lap, and the other pushed the bottleneck between his teeth, tickling his throat to make him swallow. Mr. Stacy coughed and rolled his head from side to side; then began to moan.

"Now, you stubborn mule," said Sir John harshly, making

his voice intentionally threatening, "now you have a taste of what we do to traitors. You know what else we do to them : hang them like dogs and draw them like rabbits and quarter them like sheep. Save yourself while you can, fool. Tell me what you know. Your master the Duke has aimed at the crown. I can prove it. You have done devilries with him, invoked devils. I can prove it. You and Mr. Burdet of Arrow in Warwickshire have plotted with him, and I can prove that also. Tell me what you know, before we send you to the Guildhall to be tried for your life."

"Oh-h," screamed Mr. Stacy, as the blood began to run back into his arms and legs, "oh God, Mary, Jesus."

"A little cramp?" asked Sir John. "You'll have something worse than that, my friend, if you won't unlock that mouth of yours. Now tell me why the Duke had Ankarette Twynyho made away with so suddenly."

"Sweet Saviour, let me die. Oh, take my soul quickly. Let me die. Oh God . . ."

"All in good time : what did the Duke promise you if you would make him King of England by magic?"

"Nothing : oh, saints and angels kill me. Jesus take my soul."

"Damn you for a stubborn beast!" Sir John got on his feet, banging his hands on the table. "I'll oil your tongue for you. You men, off with his hose : he's feeling cold; wants warming."

The men dragged the long hose off Mr. Stacy's legs. He groaned and cried out from the pain of his cramped muscles, twisting his haunches from side to side. He was still not able to bend his limbs. One of the torturers took a length of cord and tied his ankles with it. Sir John sat down again.

"I am patient with you, Mr. Stacy. It is no pleasure to me to see you mishandled. Will you not be wise now? The King's Grace is merciful. A confession could save you; might save your master too. Tell me what Duke George said to you touching her Grace the Queen. Has he never slandered her to you?"

"Never, I swear it by the glory of God, never."

"You liar."

"It's true, I'll swear it on the Gospel."

"Confess that you and your master practised witchcraft

302

against her and I'll take you out of this dungeon. I'll have a physician to you. You shall be put in a bed, no chains, and I'll send you a good supper from my own rooms. I promise you. Don't be such a stubborn martyr, sir. I beg you, for your own sake, confess and help yourself. I'm your friend. I want to help you if you will but let me. Think of a soft bed, Mr. Stacy, linen sheets, roast capon and demaine bread, a good coal fire. That's better than the Curfew Tower and the brake. I have a splendid Cyprus wine in my chamber. I'll send you up a bottle of it. Only tell me why Ankarette Twynyho was killed, whether the Duke has slandered the Queen and her kindred, whether he was aiming at the crown. I'll make it easy for you if you'll tell me. I'm your friend."

He had got up again and was standing above his prisoner. Naked from the waist downward, Mr. Stacy was lying with his head in his torturer's lap, his arms limp on the floor, palms of the hands uppermost. His attitude recalled pictures or carvings of the descent from the cross. Round his ankles the flesh was ridged and blue, puffed up by being held in the Duke of Exeter's Daughter. His hands were swollen. He lay with his head turned a little to one side and chest heaving laboriously, like a tired runner's. His face was absolutely white except for the dark crusts of blood round lips and nostrils, and his short black hair, filthy from the dungeon floor, dragged on his forehead. His eyes were shut. A sudden irrational thrust of anger to see anything so hurt and brutalised and so obstinate, like the annoyance a man might feel in the company of an invalid, overcame Sir John Fogg. Stooping forward a little, he kicked him with all his weight.

"Put his feet in the brazier."

The hand-organs blared up, heaving full, quivering notes toward the roof, and the choir broke into singing again. The royal procession swung in a huddle of colours out of St. Stephen's Chapel and down the main aisle of the Abbey. The King and Queen went first: Edward, heavy and enormous in the new-fashioned clothes he had devised, very tight hose clean up to the groin and a voluminous gown, hiding the shape of his belly, with amply pendant sleeves like a monk's frock; Elizabeth in a gown of green cloth-of-gold sewn with pearls and moonstones, the train furred

303

with ermine and carried by four pages. The bride and bridegroom walked behind them. They were six and four years old : the little daughter of the great Duke of Norfolk, newly dead, and the young Duke of York, whom his royal father had just now created, in virtue of his bethrothal, Duke of Norfolk and Earl of Warenne, hereditary Earl-Marshal of England, settling on him (it was presumed to have been the Queen's idea) half the estates that the Dowager Duchess of Norfolk might reasonably have hoped to enjoy in peace until her death. It was the second time the Wydvylles had carried out a raid on the Mowbray lands. Sir John Wydvylle, at twenty, had been married to the old Dowager Duchess of Norfolk, aged eighty, to the scandal of England, but had not profited much by it. Kingmaker had had his head off. Now it looked as though the job were really done. Lord Rivers, in cloth-of-silver spangled with rubies, walked on one side of the wedded pair like a farmer bringing a sound cow home from market. Young John de la Pole, Earl of Lincoln, supported them on the other side. He was King Edward's nephew, a fresh-faced boy who looked as though he thought poorly of his present occupation. Duchess Anne of Gloucester walked behind them at her husband's right hand. Duke Richard's lined little face, between its glossy falls of brown hair, told no more than it ever did : but he had said to her plainly enough in private that he feared this wedding of babies was meant to be of advantage to the bridegroom's mother and married aunts more than to him or to the crown, and that he was sorry with all his heart for the stripped Dowager Duchess.

Behind them trod the nobility of England, new and old together : Suffolk and Buckingham, the Marquis Dorset, Northumberland and Westmorland, Essex, Huntingdon, Arundel and Kent, the Viscount Lovel, the Lords Hastings, Stanley, Howard and Scrope, and a whole rabble of smaller Barons and Knights, jetting it superbly in their best clothes and accompanied by their ladies. Only two of the great ones of England were not there. The venerable Dowager Duchess of York, mother of the three Plantagenet brothers, was in her mansion of Baynard's Castle, praying most probably at this moment for the freedom of her son George of Clarence : and George, Duke of Clarence, was in the Tower.

It had begun in the spring of the year that was just now over : rumour of a plot of witchcraft against King Edward's life. Duke George's secretary, Mr. Stacy, was in it; confessed, after unspecified things had been done to him in the Curfew Tower at Windsor. Duchess Anne remembered him from the bad days after Tewkesbury : a tight-lipped, bloodless man, a jackal. She had not liked him; but it was filthy to think that they had twisted and hurt him till he accused himself. Duke Richard had often told her torture had no right to be used in the free realm of England; was a game for Scots and Frenchmen. Mr. Stacy and two others, one of them a certain Burdet, a friend and retainer of Duke George, died at Tyburne in the manner reserved for traitors. Their heads were on the Bridge now. Then it appeared as though Duke George of Clarence had gone mad. He burst into the Council Chamber at Westminster, red and yelling, bringing with him learned Dr. John Goddard of the Friars Minor. Dr. John Goddard was a man noted for his skill in temporal and Canon Law : but he was also noted for having been far too much involved, eight years ago, in the old sins of Kingmaker and Duke George; had no more place in Edward's Council Chamber than the devil in a holy-water pot. Duke George insisted in a loud voice that he read to the Council a declaration setting forth that Stacy and Burdet had been maliciously accused, falsely condemned and tyrannously put to death. King Edward was at Windsor. When he heard the intersting news that his brother had been telling his own Council that he was a tyrant and a law-twister, he flogged his horses, he who so seldom rode now, up to London and, in the presence of the Lord Mayor and Aldermen, ordered Duke George into the Tower.

The news had come North when Duchess Anne and her husband were at supper in the Privy Chamber at Pontefract, a castle that Anne had never liked as much as Middleham. Duke Richard read the letter with a word of apology to her; bit his lip; clicked his dagger several times in its sheath and then told her what it was about, frowning and looking straight in front of him. She saw he was worried, but not desperately so. "The fool," was his last word on the subject, "the pitiful fool : he has insulted Edward beyond bearing. We couldn't have a day's peace in the realm if anyone—anyone at all—were able to behave as he has. I hope

Edward keeps him in the Tower for a year and stints his wine-ration." He had been silent, playing with his ring, for a long while after; and finally they had got up from the table and gone to see the baby in his gilt cradle, who woke and smiled at them. Duke Richard smiled back then, putting his worry behind him. He gave his son a finger to hold and talked nonsense to him. For all that, Duchess Anne could see that something was on her husband's shoulders from the night the letter came. He was one of the two things on earth she studied so that she knew them as closely as a priest knows his books. From the day she had leant against the wall in the Widow Wrangwysh's foul-smelling bedchamber, seeing the door open and seeing the one face she had not dared to hope for, her life had been building itself up again slowly, almost painfully, as a honeycomb is constructed cell by cell, on the sure ground that he had given her. She was whole now again, but through him and for him. Nothing of him escaped her. She had seen the silences and long terms of unawareness, as though his very sight were withdrawn and turned inward onto his thoughts, come on him after the French journey. She had known then he was ashamed. Now the same ill-ease was on him a second time, because his brother George had fooled himself into prison. God damn them both, thought the Duchess Anne with a sudden little explosion of fury, as the procession filed out of the West doors of the Abbey into the February fog. Edward and George, Edward with his money-bags and George with his winepots, God damn them both. Why can't they let him have some ease? First one shaming him and then the other, hurting him, cutting his pride and his heart that's so much softer than any of them know : he's worth the pair of them; is the only one of them who's lived honestly and without a spot on him since the day he was knighted. Why can't they let him rest?

The marriage-feast at Westminster Palace was a great bore : infinitely too much to eat and drink, altogether too loud and insistent music, incalculably too many people with too-voluminous clothes and too-strong perfumes. King Edward and his Queen seemed to be tossing money out of the windows with both hands nowadays. Next to the baby bride and bridegroom—and the Duchess was shocked to her marrow to see those children being given strong malmsey to drink instead of claret or small ale—the guest of honour was the Prince of Byzantium, the Lord Andreas Palaiologos, a person with painted cheeks and extraordinary trailing garments, who had come to ask King Edward's help to drive the Turks out of the city in which he should by rights be Emperor. Naturally, the King was doing nothing about it, but the Duchess Anne heard that he was allowing this epicene piece of royalty, who had nothing masculine about him but his long beard, a pension of two hundred-and-forty pounds a year. Possibly the Queen saw a chance to make one of her daughters Empress of the Greeks.

The royal children were everywhere at that banquet. Anne had the eldest of them, Princess Elizabeth, more generally called the Lady Bessy, sitting opposite to her. At the age of twelve, the Lady Bessy was a precocious child. She could write and speak French, as she was not tired of telling people. Her official title was Mademoiselle la Dauphine, she being affianced to the Christian King's son Charles. Her mother's eyes used to brighten like a bird's when she heard her called by it. Her seven-year-old sister, Cecily, was a quieter girl, but so stuck about with jewelled pins, ouches, pendants, collars and rings that she looked like a miracle-working Virgin on a feast-day. As for Edward of Westminster, Prince of Wales, Anne hoped to all the saints that his little namesake and cousin, Edward of Middleham, would grow up very different from him. He was a lovely-looking child, certainly, tall for his eight years and with his father's long, beautiful hands and his mother's hair : but he had his mother's eyes, too, silly-cunning, greenish and oblique, and her small, petulant lips. His manners were abominable and his voice a high, continual whine. Lord Rivers was his principal governor.

These were all of the royal children present at the marriage feast, but there was another Princess in her cradle and two in their coffins, and the Queen was big again.

The Duchess Anne had been placed, for no reason that was apparent to her, between Lord Rivers and the Duke of Buckingham. I ought not to grudge, she told herself. It might have been the Prince of Byzantium. The Duke of Buckingham had only recently begun to come to Court. He was a pleasant-looking youth, handsome, one would even say, but there was something peculiar in the set of his eyes, which were too wide apart and showed the whites all round the irises. He had good manners and a studied, oratorical way of speaking. Lord Rivers was in excellent humour. He began by talking playfully, with a man's condescension, to Anne; but after one snub altered his drift and discussed foreign politics with a pretty air of deference to her opinion. Things in Burgundy were quieter now. The Lady Marie, Charles the Hardy's daughter, had married the young Maximilian of Austria and they had the Low Countries, whilst King Louis held the western lands of Burgundy as appanages of the Crown of France. His tone was a shade less enthusiastic than his words. Duchess Anne remembered gossip that he had aspired to plan a supreme and final Wydvylle wedding: that of the Lady Marie to himself. Presumably even King Edward had felt that too much.

As soon as Lord Rivers had finished with her, the Duke of Buckingham began. How did her gracious husband find the Scots situation? Was there a chance of war? She thought there might be. Her husband would of course be in command, suggested the Duke of Buckingham, and went on straightway to present her with what sounded like a rehearsed panegyric of Duke Richard and his abilities: his marvellous administrative work in the North, his skill as a soldier, his unselfish devotion to the good of England. It was all pleasant hearing, if a little too like a formal speech before the Privy Council. The feast limped somehow to its end. There was a sung grace. Anne had a headache from too many kinds of sweet wine and a feeling of breathlessness from too much food: but she knew she would have to dance presently. They filed out, trumpets going before them; broke up into knots and groups in the long gallery. King Edward and Duke Richard were talking together, Edward, in purple and silver, still looked magnificent from behind: immense breadth of shoulders, a straight back. But as she watched he turned round, still talking, and she was shocked again by the heaviness and redness of his face, his hanging chops. He looked dull and bearish, too, stupid with food. His appetite, she had noticed, was past all bounds now. In one service of fowl during the banquet he had eaten a whole cygnet boiled in wine and stuffed with Portugal oranges, and the best part of a roast flamingo. His long hands, between courses, had been continually reaching after the comfits and almonds and sugared fruits; and he must have drunk a gallon of mixed wines, chiefly sweet resinous stuff from the Morea, strong enough to stun a Norwegian. He was scowling now. Duke Richard was saying something emphatically to him. He pulled his lip a second; shrugged and made an annoyed consenting gesture with one arm; stamped off down the gallery. Duke Richard looked after him for a second, his hand at his dagger; then came to Anne. He bowed.

"Can you divert yourself without me for an hour, bird? I have a conference with Edward."

"I saw. He doesn't seem to relish it."

"He has drunk too much," Richard's voice was carefully lowered : "this accursed banquet. But I must speak to him."

"George?"

He nodded, chewing his lip, eyes narrow.

"God speed you, then."

"Can I find anyone to entertain you?"

"Yes, for God's sake send Frank Lovel or Jockey Howard."

"What, not my Lord Rivers?"

His face was entirely serious, blank.

"Dickon, Dickon, are you ambitious to wear horns, thrusting my dearest of men into my arms?"

Anne was one of the very few people in England who knew her husband had a sense of humour. She got what she wanted : a tiny twinkle of eyes in his pale, thinking face.

"So I know who it is at last. Shall I challenge him?"

"I wish you would."

The twinkle went out like a blown candle-flame.

"I wish I might. I'll send Frank to you."

He bowed again and went away from her. Before Lord Lovel had come, Lord Hastings was at her elbow. He looked older, too, but was not fat yet. His hair was grey at the temples and his eyes were tired. He gave her his best smile; asked how she had liked the feast.

"Too much to eat, Lord William, and outrageously too much to drink."

He raised his eyebrows, nodding. "Yes, dear God, I sometimes feel I'm too old for these pleasures nowadays : and we've had no time to recruit ourselves from Christmas yet. You kept the feast at Middleham, no doubt?"

"We did, very simply."

"So didn't we. And how is the heir of Gloucester?"

"My Edward? Oh, but he can talk now, quite plainly. Truly he can, and walk a little. He's a forward boy."

"God bless him; that's excellent news, excellent news. Let me tell you a secret."

"Yes?"

"You'll have a new name to call him soon. The King spoke of it to me."

"A new name?"

"Aye, an Earldom: Salisbury was mentioned."

"That's kind of Edward. Oh, that's kind. Salisbury was my grandfather's title."

She stopped then; remembered that her father's title of Warwick had gone to Duke George's son; and Duke George was in the Tower now. It was unpleasant always to be remembering that. I bear him no grudge, she thought, for that piece of silly wickedness seven years ago. I wish him out of his troubles; would do even if I hated him, just for Dickon's sake.

Viscount Lovel was coming up to her now, all impish grins and pretty gestures. He amused Anne because he always talked to her about clothes, as though he were a fellow-woman. He kissed her—they were cousins by marriage—and at once demanded that she feel his apple-green-velvet sleeve and guess how little the stuff cost. It's odd, she thought, how his mincingness is always pleasant; has no harm in it. If it were the Marquis Dorset trying to talk women's matters to me now, I'd want to scratch his eyes out. The music started in the next hall, and Lord Lovel asked her if she would dance.

"God's mother, Frank, I wonder whether I can. You'll find me as heavy as if I were in harness."

"I know, I know," said Lord Lovel, "and I was as slim as a page myself once."

"You are now and know it, you parcel of vanity sewn up in green velvet. Come, then. I'll try one turn with you."

They danced, and were bumped heavily by Lord Stanley. Lord Lovel whispered to her:

"Why was that fat oaf ever allowed on the floor? A gryfon's foot his badge is. It ought to be a bull's foot. If he's split my hose I'll murder him."

"Charity, Francis, charity."

"And for God's love look at the Prince of Byzantium. He'll trip over his petticoats in a minute."

"Or his beard."

"Lord, there's some strange things about this Court now."

"Who's the little man with the hard mouth who looks like a lawyer?"

"Sir William Catesby, friend of Hastings, cleverest little devil between this and the end of a stick : some great ones we won't mention hate him as a cat hates water."

She could feel it suddenly : the prickly hates and mistrusts that were all round the Court. The grand people danced in their grand clothes; smiled like images. That meant nothing. Under velvet and behind smiles there was a life of the mind that was a continual march and counter-march of grudges. England was once York and Lancaster. Now it is York, Lancaster, Wydvylle, Hastings, Clarence. Every one of them in London doubts the other. All doubt my Richard. We, who are England, are only a bunch of faggots bound together with one rope. Edward's the rope, and he is rotting. When he parts we all tumble asunder, and the first-comer can pick us up and break us one at a time over his knee.

She felt again like the little girl who had sat seven years ago by a fire in the Benedictine house at Cerne Abbas. The world was loose and quaking under her feet again, a moving world. *Hora novissima*, she could remember that much of Church Latin, *tempora pessima sunt, vigilemus. Ecce minaciter, imminet Arbiter.* . . . But what judge was coming? Who will bind the faggot firm again, she thought, when the rope parts? Where is there a man of goodwill, someone with power and single purpose, who will be what we once thought Edward was? The music stopped and started again. She danced now with the Duke of Buckingham, and scarcely heard what he was saying. When that dance was over, a voice spoke to her :

"Anne."

It was Richard.

"Dickon?"

"We are going home now."

She knew better than to ask why. Something was very wrong to-night in the Palace of Westminster. She felt her heart shaking. Torches and weapons accompanied them to

311

their barge. When the curtains were drawn round them, Richard found her hand under the thick bearskin wraps. He did not speak for a long while, only held her fingers. She heard the sad splash of the oars and the town-noises from the banks. Then he said:

"George is to be attainted of high treason."

"What?"

She did not believe it; did not believe it at all. The words did not mean that; had some other meaning she would see in a moment.

"He is to be attainted in Parliament to-morrow."

Duke Richard's voice was absolutely flat. She could not see him in the dark.

"But of high treason?"

"Of high treason, of having assembled armed men in Cambridgeshire, of having maligned the King and procured enchanters to bring his death about."

"Oh God."

"There's worse."

"Dickon, I can't bear this. Have we all gone mad?"

"He is accused of having called Edward a bastard."

"A bastard! No, then it's all lies. It's all lies, Dickon. It will be disproved. Even George wouldn't do that. Men don't call their own mothers whores."

"Good God!" he said, "it will be disproved. Do you suppose I thought for an instant it would not? But what has induced Edward, what devil has got into the man, to countenance such a filthy piece of comedy, let it get as far as Parliament?"

"George must have done something foolish, Dickon, and he means to frighten him."

"Frighten him by letting it be said before all England that he called our mother a harlot?"

"Ah, Dickon, but I'm afraid I know whose device that was."

"Thank you. I know myself. Haven't they always hated George? He was a partaker with your father in the heading of old Rivers. They've not forgotten it. But that they should have the insolence to use such a shameful means of getting revenge on him, and Edward should be so besotted as to let them do it—by St. Paul, if I can lay hands once on that pack . . ."

"Why listen to dogs barking? We know George is no worse than a fool. He'll be cleared, and it'll be the more shame to the Wydvylles that they ever drove Edward to this point."

"When dogs piss in the King of England's Court, and on the name of his mother and mine, d'you think it's likely I shan't notice them? A huntsman's lash is what's wanted in Westminster. I've had the heads off honester men than that stinking Rivers for far smaller sins against Edward. Beaufort and the Bastard were angels of God and good friends to my house compared with him. I was thanked for putting them in their graves : but when I told Edward to his face to-night that this attainder was a mere piece of Wydvylle impudence, he cursed me like a water-man. He was not drunk then. As soon as we were alone he went into the garderobe and vomited. I heard him : but he'd scarcely come back when he was calling for hippocras and a cold pasty to cram himself sick again. That's the manners the Wydvylles have taught him since the French journey. Anne, my darling, do you think I'm a fool?"

His voice in the dark had come more urgently, more nakedly, with each sentence. His rather hideous self-control had been put aside for a little, as though it were armour that tired him out. Anne squeezed his hand.

"My dear love, no man in England's less a fool, none."

"Nevertheless, I think I must be one. I must be. Consider. I'm twenty-six years old, a husband, a father. I've ruled a province; been in exile; fought battles. I should know a monk by his frock by this time."

"You do, Dickon, you, the cleverest head of all of them."

"But with that much experience . . ."

He stopped, biting the sentence off with a snick of the shut teeth; then deliberately went on again like a man hurting himself, squeezing a boil.

"But with that much experience I've still loved and adored a fatted animal as though it were King Arthur."

"Ah, Dickon !"

"A fatted animal : one thing beside you and our son I've loved, I've served, I've worshipped, I've fought and told lies for : and look at it. Pitiful saints, look at it : a fool that juggled away his crown once for the sake of a woman no more fit for his bed than a pig for Paradise, a wencher without even the wits to do his wenching with the curtains

313

drawn, a gut-stuffer who'll cram a knight's ransom into his big belly and then spew it up for the pleasure of cramming himself over again, a tradesman who'll pawn the honour of his crown to a Frenchman, and before God, a man who'll have it said that his own brother called him a bastard."

"Dickon, listen. He may really have said it. Think what he said to me about Edward years ago. He'd say anything : and if he did, Edward is right to punish him."

"My lass, he may have said it. Where does that take us. Edward should have had more care than ever not to drag our name through all the kennels of England. He should have taken George in private and beaten him within an inch of his life with his own hands : and he'd have done it once, as I'd do it now. But if the Plantagenets of York are to show their sores to the world like lepers at a town-gate, I know whom I may thank. Anne, I am afraid I have my eyes open, and for the first time since I was weaned. Oh God, I could forgive Edward seventy times seven, as our Saviour told us to : but not every time, not each pitiful time I've given him a chance to hurt me. I trusted him to be the King our father would have been if he had lived : and all he did after Towton was to fool it with one wench after another until your father threw him out of the realm like a dismissed groom. I trusted him to give me honourable work, and he set me to heading men he'd sworn to pardon. I trusted him to help me be a good Lord to our poor folk in the North : and I've had to badger and plead, and sue to clerks and lawyers I wouldn't trust to groom the heels of my horse, to get the few common acts of justice you'd 've thought he'd do without asking. I've served him better than any other three men in his kingdom, and the upshot is I'm the last man of all whose wants he'll care for. He can be sure of me, and so he'll grudge me a smile or a hearing that might be given one of his Greys and Wyd-vylles. I tell you, by the head of St. Paul, there's nothing, nothing, nothing I ever trusted him in where he hasn't betrayed me : nothing, ever. The man I love more than I do the health of my soul, God forgive me, is a fat, sodden, self-seeking playboy who'd break my heart to get a smile from a whore in the gutter : and may the saints have some kind of pity on me somehow, for I still love him."

"Well?" asked Sir Richard Hawte.

"All well, sir," said the gaoler, and coughed.

The Tower was a lake of fog in a verge of stone walls that evening. The fog had followed him like a stray cat up the stairs of the Lieutenant's Lodging and was invading the room. Sir Richard Hawte irritably bade him shut the door.

"What were they doing?"

"The Bishop was praying, sir, and the Duke was having his supper."

"Good: you may go."

The man turned half round; hesitated; put on his bonnet and pulled it off again. "Asking your pardon, sir . . ."

"Yes, what?"

"Have you heard anything more of what's to become of him, like? The Duke, I mean."

"Not a word: now get out of here and shut that door after you."

The gaoler got out. Sir Richard Hawte had been sharp-tempered, and everyone in the Tower had been, since the day, a month back now, when the Duke of Clarence was carried back in procession to his cell from Westminster, the edge of the axe turned toward him, attainted by Parliament of high treason. It had come as a surprise. Everybody had said he would be acquitted. The King, they said, would not see sentence of death and disinheritance passed on his own brother. They had been wrong there.

The gaoler, whose name was Miles Forest, was interested in politics. Plenty of folk had told him how things went that day before the Lords when the Duke took his trial: but, as they said, the mind shrank from dwelling on it, the quarrel between those two brothers, and such brothers, seemed so sad. No one spoke against the Duke but the King and a few witnesses who behaved more as if they were accusers. No one answered the King except the Duke. The rest of the Lords sat with their eyes down; could not bear it when King Edward told the tale of what his brother was supposed to have done. He had cherished the Duke, he said, as tenderly as any creature could his natural brother and had made him the richest man in England, and the Duke had paid him by taking sides with Kingmaker in the year 'seventy. Aye, thought Miles Forest, and so he did; but that's dead and done now. Why would he want to bring

315

that up again? Then the Duke had made a scandal when Mr. Stacy and Mr. Burdet got their deserts. So he had, too, and very silly of him: but was anybody going to believe he had really gone about saying the King was a necromancer, a poisoner and a bastard? No very likely witnesses had been produced to show it. But then, if it weren't so, why had the King solemnly told the Lords that he could not be answerable for the public peace if the Duke were let alone?

I never heard tell of such a thing, Miles Forest decided, not in all my time. Wicked King John that died of the devil in his belly did nothing like this: to stand up and ask the nobility to judge his own brother to death. I don't wonder the Duke of Gloucester refused to be there. They say he's all at work to have the sentence undone again; and God speed him. We never had such doings in England. We don't want them.

Turning the corner of the Bell Tower and going along under the West wall toward the Beauchamp Tower, coughing and spitting, he met a fellow. There was too much fog to see his face, and he challenged without thinking.

"Who goes?"

"Who goes yourself, Miles. Don't be such an addlewit."

"Nay, is that you, Will?"

"It's not my ghost."

"Whorish night, isn't it?"

"Proper bastard: want a sup? I've some claret here."

"God love you, man. Where in the saints' names d'you nip it from?"

"The Constable's butler: here, take hold."

The leather jack was passed to him. He tipped it with a slopping sound and gulped. The wine was sourish.

"May you live long, man. I've just been to old Hawte."

"What's he to say for himself?"

"Get out and shut the door. Damn you. Damn the Duke. Damn everyone."

"Ah, he's always so nowadays. Any news?"

"Oh, him?" He nodded sideways and forward in the dark toward the Bowyer Tower.

"Aye."

"Not a whisper."

"They'll never make away with him, Miles?"

"Well, he's attainted. Lord High Steward passed his sentence. Commons of Parliament sent up a petition to have him ended."

"What in the name of twenty devils did they do that for?"

"Thought it'd please the King, I reckon."

"His own brother: nay, he'll never be put away. It wouldn't be christian. There's never such a thing been done since King Arthur."

"Aye, well, that may be. But it's not King Arthur we've got now, look you. It's King Edward."

"He's a hard master on us, with his cursed benevolences, and subsidies and all manner of devilries. Aye, God's teeth, he's a hard master: but I'll never credit that he'd have his brother's blood on him."

"He had Holy Harry's, didn't he? But I tell you what. It's his other brother'll put a stop to it."

"Duke o' Gloucester?"

"That's your man. Listen, I was talking to a servant of his this morning. Give us another pull of that jack."

"Pox on you, have you a fire in your guts?"

"I'm so dry, Will, I couldn't spit as far as the ground."

The jack was given him again.

"God bless you, Will, and may you never wear horns. Here, I've only taken enough to wet my mouth."

"Aye, but with a mouth your size . . . Jesus be with us, listen!"

A deep, frightening sound, a little like the bark of a cannon, but prolonged, came suddenly over the moat and wall. It was the roar of one of the lions in the dens at the Lion Gate. Instantly, the others answered it, and crash and crash of their voices, thickened by fog, rolled over the ground. They were joined, after a second, by the shriller cries of leopards, miawling like giant tomcats; and then the whole pandemonium was slashed through and through by the devilish screams of a hyena. The outcry did not subside. The men could almost hear the lions draw breath after each explosion of roars to start again. It was as though the fog were populated by noisy demons. After what appeared a long while, the voices fell silent one after another, a single lion closing the tumult with a rolling of short broken grunts.

317

"What's come to 'em to-night, in the devil's name?" Miles Forest said.

"If you'd ask me," Will Slater told him, "I'd say something unholy had just come into this Tower. Beasts know such things."

"The cross of Christ between us and harm." Miles Forest blessed himself.

"Amen: go on with what you were saying the Duke of Gloucester's servant told you."

"Oh, him: he told me when he heard the sentence was passed the Duke was like a man in a fit. Like a man in a fit, he said. He hadn't looked for it any more than the rest of us. He went stiff, he said, and couldn't speak, and his eyes glared to frighten you. Then he yelled for his barge and off to the Palace, and he's been at the King ever since. It's the talk of them all, I hear, the anger he's got against the Queen and the Lord Rivers and the way he's rated the King to his face. He said, this servant fellow, his master's contrived a secret audience with the King to-night, no Queen to be there or none of them, and when that's achieved the Duke of Clarence'll walk out of here as free as a bird."

"And I hope he does so," said Will. "With all my heart I do. I'm fairly sorry for him, and that tale of treason's moonshine, if you ask me. It's the Queen's nasty spite."

"Like enough: eh, I wish I might 've had a word with our King before he ever married the widow Elizabeth."

"Go and rub your arse on a thistle, man; what'd you've said to him?"

"I'd 've said this. I'd 've said: Think on, your Grace, there's them that's born to be ruled like me and there's them that's born to rule like you, and that's the nature of things. But don't go to set up one that was born to be ruled, like your lousy widow, to be one that rules, for the rest of them that was born to be ruled won't love her."

"Aye, you're an orator: and shall I tell you where the King would 've set you up? Over the Bridge on a spike to poison the crows."

"Well, there's many a poor soul as honest as me that he's set up there. He's a changed man since the French journey, Will."

"Ah, God rot and consume that journey. It beggared us all to fill half-a-dozen Lords' sleeves with gold."

318

"Aye, and fill all the roads of the country with robbers : and what do we get for it?"

"Better trade, they say."

"Let them say it. There's none of us London folk'll be any the happier for it, not with the Earl of Rivers as Chief Butler."

"That's a true word. Look you, Miles, what d'you reckon he's gone and clapped up Dr. Stillington for?"

"Ask about. I'm not in the Privy Council."

"To put a Bishop in hold : he must have some cause or other. It's a grave thing to do."

"You're right. It is. All I know is, he's a very decent soul for a Bishop. I looked in there about an hour back, and there he was, God damn me, down on his two knees praying like a holy hermit : and he's as patient as you could wish. I reckon there's good Bishops just as there's good folk of all kinds."

There were steps in the fog and a voice calling : "Miles Forest and Will Slater, is that you clacking there?"

"Aye."

"Then stretch your fat legs the two of you and get on up to Sir Richard Hawte. You're summoned."

"We will, then.'

They went through damp obscurity toward the fuzzy lights of windows in the Lodging, and climbed the stair. Miles Forest wondered why they were wanted; hoped no one had escaped. It could be a pardon for the Duke of Clarence, he thought, if the Duke of Gloucester's had his audience with the King now. That fellow told me it was all over the Palace the King was only waiting to be sued to a little more to reverse the sentence.

He knocked at Sir Richard Hawte's door and was called in. Sir Richard had his back to the fireplace and his hands under the tail of his gown; was biting his lips. There was another man in the room. Miles Forest stared at him. A friar's dirty habit sloped forward and outward over a huge belly and hung thence straight down. A hood, drawn in close, made a frame round a broad, glistening, snub-nosed face like a brass mask, yellowish and abominable. Miles Forest remembered Will Slater's saying that something unholy had come into the Tower. It had. There was an abysmal wickedness in those hanging, sweaty jowls, that

319

wide mouth with a set between a smirk and a sneer. Below the broad, menacing forehead, the eyes were like two black rats peeping from holes in a haystack. The friar stood with his hands in his sleeves, rocking comfortably from foot to foot and missing, it could be seen, nothing that was said or done.

Sir Richard Hawte's face was a little paler than when Miles Forest had seen it last. He spoke in a quick voice.

"Forest, this is Friar Bungay, from whom you will take certain instructions."

The name explained everything to Miles Forest. Friar Bungay was a legend. It was said the old Duchess of Bedford had found him first and he had helped her by necromancy to get her daughter married to King Edward. Now he assisted the King in his search for the Philosopher's Stone and, so it was hinted, in the construction of wax images and the concoction of foul potions and the conjuration of those whom a man invokes only to his loss and never, in the last upshot, to his gain. Few people had seen him : but the hangman was known to tap on the door of his lodging after dark, bringing him things he needed from the gibbet : and old country women of bad repute sold him baskets of herbs and toadstools that were not good to eat, and adders and spiders that would make better ingredients for poisons than for medicines. Some people claimed to have seen him hanging about churchyards at night, repeating sentences that were not the Office of the Dead.

"Pax vobiscum."

His voice was something between a creak and a squelch. Miles Forest did not answer; would have liked to cross himself. The black, moving eyes in the yellow face considered him for a moment and the voice went on :

"You are keeper to his Grace of Clarence, dear son?"

"I am that."

"Then will you take him a little present from his well-wishers?"

"If I'm ordered."

"A little tonneau of the best malmsey wine," the friar smacked his gross lips and nodded, "it is waiting below. Take it to him at once, my son."

By God, thought Miles Forest, but I smell smoke. He looked at Sir Richard Hawte.

"Is that right, sir?"

Sir Richard jerked his shoulders and did not look back at him. A sort of tension thickened between them for a second. Then he answered: "Quite right, man."

"What'll I tell the Duke, then?"

"Tell him, my son," said the friar, who had not ceased to rock from foot to foot, "that it is sent by friends who know of the labours now being made for his pardon to the King's Grace and who wish to give him some cheer during these hours of wanhope whilst he is still in doubt. His good Grace of Gloucester is not the only man who concerns himself for your prisoner. Those who send this small gift by royal authority—royal authority, Sir Richard Hawte—have also an interest in his fate. So take the wine to him, my son. Take it quickly before the King's pardon is announced, as we all pray and believe it must be. The tonneau is below stairs: and God be with you, my son."

He finished with a grin so impudent that Miles Forest wondered the roof did not crash in on him. The whole look on his sweaty, wide face was of a hypocrite who deliberately willed his hypocrisy to be blatant, to offend rather than to deceive. He almost winked. I'd best not think of what he means, Miles Forest told himself. It's money in pocket for us, I shouldn't wonder, and know-naught was never hanged. He nudged Will Slater, and they went down the stairs together without saying good-night.

"Christ," Will grunted as they were hefting the little cask between them, "that was a rogue."

"If you want to keep the house clean," Miles Forest told him, " 'ware monks, friars and pigeons. It's an old saying, and it's true."

"What d'you reckon to this business, Miles?"

Miles lost his temper. Trying to make me a party to Christ knows what, he thought.

"I reckon nothing, and if you've more sense than your mother had when she listened to your father behind the barn, then you won't either. Poor men can't keep consciences. Now shut your gob."

It was fortunate that they knew their way: across the Green, skirting St. Peter ad Vincula's Chapel, and so to the North wall. They were as remote in space as two demons carrying a soul to hell. The whole fortress was gone, wiped out in fog. They could hear voices, faint and from unsure directions, but saw nothing. Soldiers, yeomen, gentlemen, grooms, servants, mint-workers, prisoners, horses, lions, were crowded round them in the small area of Tower Royal, but the damp visible breath of the Thames isolated them as though a spell had been put on them until their job was done. They say that damned friar raised the mist at Barnet, thought Miles Forest. This must be his work too. Holy St. Peter look down on us and help us. Remember we are poor men and can't pick and choose like rich ones.

They were at the door of the Bowyer Tower.

Miles Forest set his end of the little cask down to find the key. The Duke of Clarence was allowed no servants since his condemnation; was alone in the small turret, locked in one room. They humped the tonneau up the very narrow stair to his door; unlocked that also. Five candles burned, one before a crucifix and four on a large table spread with a good damask cloth, and in that light the round face and big body of the Duke was seen, stooping a little forward above the broken meats of supper on the table, blue eyes looking hard at them under frightened eyebrows, the top teeth showing. The Duke had lost colour in his nine months' imprisonment; was stouter. He looked older than twenty-eight. When he was put in ward first he had been in unabating rage; threw dishes at the servants' heads; cursed everyone. He fell sullen next, like an adder that has struck and missed until it is tired. He ceased to dress himself properly or use the barber; lay the whole day in bed, refusing visitors; and since Parliament had declared him attainted in blood and issue, unworthy to live, he had asked occasionally for a priest. Miles Forest, from being in awe of him, despised him next for a bellowing calf; came finally to be sorry for him. He's a man in trouble like any other, he thought. It was a merely silly face that looked over the table at them : whitish puffed cheeks with a day's rust of beard, hair with the curl gone out of it. The fat had subsided under the small chin and around the throat, and left the skin in bags. The lips were a bad colour and sagged downward. The whole look was that of an out-at-elbows gentleman who had drunk himself into the gutter; was not even sure now of his welcome in low company. The Duke of Clarence was completely tamed.

"Good evening to your Grace."

"Hey?" The Duke got on his feet. He wore a furred bedgown over shirt and hose with the points untied. The size of his stomach showed. "Hey, what have you got there?"

"Cask of malmsey wine for your Grace."

"Malmsey for me : what's this?"

"I think it's from the Palace, your Grace."

The Duke came round the table to them, his face pinkening. His eyes were open wider than they had been before.

"God," he said in a quick voice, "who sent it, you fool? Don't you know?"

"The man that brought it," said Miles Forest, looking past him, "said something about cheering your Grace whilst your Grace's pardon was being sued for to the King : but I don't know. I don't know anything at all, your Grace."

"Splendour of God, but I do, though." The Duke's voice had a different pitch now. He was smiling, and it was possible to distinguish under the flabbiness of his cheeks the fine bony structure that had made him handsome once. "Go on, set it on that trestle there. It's ready tapped, isn't it? Malmsey, by God : who says George of Clarence has no friends? It's long since I tasted it : and here's to tasting it again outside of this mews. Here's to an end of this fool's comedy. You fellows, I think there'll be a message for me to-night. I'm sure of it. See that I have it at once, even if I'm asleep : at once. Reach me that cup off the table, one of you. Whether I'm asleep or awake, mark you. The man who brings me the news I want will have a half-royal for himself."

They had a last glimpse of him as they shut the door. He was standing up to his height, the pewter cup in one hand and the other on his hip. His head was thrown back and he was laughing, giggling and gasping with laughter like a man who finds that what he thought was a wolf padding behind him in the dark is only a stray dog. The candles touched up the yellow of his hair.

"Poor whorson," said Will Slater as they were locking the lower door. The Tower was dead and wicked still, fog pressing its shapeless face to theirs. Between St. Peter's Chapel and the Devereux Tower, they separated, not saying anything. Miles Forest was on duty. He could not go to

323

bed; marched down past the White Tower to the King's Lodgings; marched back again. He thought for a foolish moment that he would go to Dr. Stillington's cell and talk to him for a little. Nay, I must keep my mouth shut, he told himself. If I'm a tattler there'll be trouble either way. He coughed and walked, thinking of a reward. When, an hour later, he stiffened himself to look into the Bowyer Tower again, he saw what one half of his mind had expected from the beginning. George Duke of Clarence lay on his back under the trestle where the tonneau stood. His teeth and the whites of his eyes showed frighteningly in the candlelight against the colour of his wrenched, horrified face, which was between black and purple. He must have died at the very instant of drawing himself another cup of wine, for the cock of the tonneau was still open, and drops of malmsey fell with a thick, regular splash upon the body, whose clothes and hair were already flooded with it, soaked, sodden, as though drowned.

CHAPTER SIX

HEROD

(*England–France: 1483–1484*)

So that the man is over al
His owne cawse of wele and wo.
That we Fortune clepe so,
Out of the man himselfe it groweth.

John Gower : *Confessio Amantis.*

"WELL, I say all it'll mean is new taxes and nothing to show
for them, the same as it did before."

"And I say it won't, then, and I'll tell you for why :
because our Duke'll have the guiding of it."

"Nay, he won't, man. King'll go himself."

"Ah, you can say so, but I saw the King when he came
to York five years back. I saw him. I went to York city on
purpose and I saw him, and he was a fat man."

"Well, what in the devil's that to do with it, man alive?"

"I say he was a fat man. He rode in the like of a litter
with fellows to carry him. He won't go to the war."

"Aye, but that was just because he was a King, like. He'd
ride in a litter because he's a King, don't you see? But he'll
go across and make war on the French for all that, and
then he'll ride on a horse."

"Well, now, I'm asking you somewhat. Did he go and
make war on the dirty Scots?"

"You don't understand . . ."

"Nay, but I'm asking you. Did he go to make war on the
dirty Scots?"

"No, but . . ."

"No, he didn't : well, then. Our Duke made war on the
Scots last year, didn't he?"

"Aye."

"And he went to Edinburgh and made 'em sign a writing
that they'd do as he bid, didn't he?"

"Yes, but what I mean . . ."

"And he took Berwick that the wicked old Queen sold them before Towton battle, didn't he?"

"I'm not denying he did."

"You'd best not, lad, because my son Ned was there at the siege of Berwick himself, as you very well know : and I say our Duke'll have charge of this war too, and it'll be a proper war."

Thomas Oakroyd and Edmund Taylor were discussing the prospect of a new French war in the alehouse of Middleham village. Being very old and rather silly, they did not know much about it : but they had heard rumours of how the French King had insulted King Edward by arranging to marry his son to a foreign heiress although he was plighted to the Princess Bessy. It was said King Edward had fallen down in a fit when he heard the news. Perhaps it was all lies anyhow, but it made something to talk about. Except for the Duke's war with Scotland last year, there had been nothing to talk about in Middleham for a long while. The Duke had come riding home, white-faced and small as always, and had been met at the foot of the village street by his six-year-old son. He had swung the boy up on his saddle-bow to kiss him, and the boy had snatched the reins and guided the white charger, his father's hands on his wrists and the two of them laughing, and everybody had cheered. That was the only kind of sensation there was in Yorkshire nowadays, where there had once been robberies and hangings and fights between noblemen. The Duke had altered things.

"Well, and if he does have charge of the war, there'll still be taxes," said Edmund Taylor.

"Aye, aye, but it's the King raises them," Thomas Oakroyd explained to him. "King takes the money and our Duke fights the war."

"Ah, but there'll be money taken, choose how, and that's the devil in it."

"Oh aye, it's we must pay : and if we don't it's King comes near on us. Duke's got to do what King bids."

"I'd wish he might go his own road about it. He's the master for me, the Duke is."

"Aye, well, so he may be, but he's afraid of the King, same as the rest of us. He has to do as he's told."

"Our Duke afraid: don't talk so daft, man. He's afraid of nothing; and he's the King's brother."

"And look what King did to his other brother: drowned him; drowned him in a barrel of wine, they say."

"Devil take that for a rhyme. I never did credit that London clack. What'd he go to drown him in wine for? Have they no ponds down London way?"

"Well, he was a Duke, see. They'd never go to drown a Duke like a common fellow."

"I don't believe it, Tom; never did. Nay, God's body, it'd be as bad as old Adam's two sons the Friar was telling a tale of that was here last week."

"I never heard him. What'd he say, then?"

"Nay, I couldn't rightly make it out: something of two brothers killed each other. It'd be a long while back it happened: something in Holy Writ."

"Ah, there's all manner of bloody wickedness in Holy Writ, I believe. But he's a right hard one, King Edward is. Hundreds and thousands of men he's killed."

"That'd be because he has to be King. Kings have their own consciences, I uphold, and they answer to Almighty God in their own way."

"Happen they do. Happen that's gospel."

"And we don't have the garboyles and battles nowadays as we had in Kingmaker's time. Things are better in that way, so how it is."

"Duke stopped that, Edmund. See how he punished the whorson Scots when they tried making commotions. My son Ned says they were that afraid of him they never even stood and made a field."

"They're all scum, the Scots are—muck. That Scots Duke our Duke had guesting with him, Albans, Albany, what his name was: he wasn't what you could call the make of a real nobleman. Our Duke was a kitten to him, go by their build; but he was the master, man, I tell you. I saw 'em riding together plain as how I see you. Scots Duke, he was a big bastard, red hair; ran through hell with no bonnet on, like they say. He sat up on his great horse, talking and babbling and telling what a grand one he was, the like of a tumbler at a wakes: no decent quietness about him. Our Duke, he looked little, all drawn up in himself, like, the fashion of a hawk on a cadge, and smiling as sweet as you could ask. But I

saw him looking under his eyes at the red fellow, as good as
to say : You're not worth two groats, and I know it, so you
may babble. He's a deep mind, our Duke has."

"Aye, he has that. That's what I was saying. I uphold as
he'll fight this French war. King Edward . . ."

Daaarr:

a deep, sad note, final and startling as the fall of a headsman's axe, jarred the air they sat in. It seemed to come like
a presence into the alehouse and march through it and out
again, going away into the park and fields.

Daaarr:

it was repeated after flat silence : the bell of St. Alkelda's
Church tolling for death. The two old men looked at each
other. A murmur of puzzlement and question grew up
gently in the street and doors were opened. Feet tapped the
cobbles.

"Nay," said Edmund Taylor foolishly, "nay, but there's
no one sick I know of."

"It's sudden death, then," said Thomas Oakroyd, "we'd
best go and hear."

Daar

Daar:

they got out of the alehouse, wondering, going over names
in their minds. In the uncoloured April light, women and
old men were peering out of windows and coming together
on the cobbles, beginning to straggle up like nervous cattle
in ones and twos toward the church. They chattered, and
the slow, unpardoning voice of the bell repeated its phrase
over their talking heads.

Dr. Beverley was standing for them in the lych-gate. His
canon's scarlet robes were part of the surprise and question
of what was happening. He had the look on his face of a
man whom something altogether unthought of has frightened. When they saw him they all slowed a little and came
up almost unwillingly.

"Who is it, doctor?" "Who is it, Canon Beverley?" "Dr.
Beverley, who's gone, rest their souls?"

Dr. Beverley lifted his chin a little and tightened his
mouth, staring out over their heads. His voice came between
two strokes of the bell, solemnly giving an order :

"All good people, pray for the soul of our Sovereign
Lord, King Edward IV of gracious memory, whom it has

pleased Almighty God to call to himself by the path of sickness."

My Lord Duke and Brother

I grete yow well, letting yow to witte y^t my Lord Prince is to go vp from y^s place to London y^s Thorsday next ensewing, to be Crowned: and he wil go in my charge. My Lord Duke and very trew Brother, it is so y^t owr Lord Kyng Edward of fulnoble memorye deceas'd, on whose sowl Jhesu mercie, did in his life-tyme point ye Duke of Gloster to be Protector of ye Reaulme in ye infancie of my Lord Prince, in soch fashion as Humphrey Duke of Gloster, Unkle to Kyng Harry ye Sixt, hadde y^t Office aforetyme, and ye said Duke is riding incontinent vp to London, wth but a slendre company, to take vppon him ye ordering of al things within ye Reaulme. So, at y^s sadde tyme, I ask yow hastily, who are my Sister's husband and whom I ever cherish'd as kindly as in my powre was, whether it be better one man, and he lytyl lov'd and less known in y^{se} South Partes, shuld have rule over vs al, seeing there be some amonge vs he doth lytyl cherish, or whether it be not a more natural thing, and surer for owr safety and ye common wele of y^s Reaulme, y^t my Lord Prince shuld rather be in ye guidaunce of his Mother's kindred. And y^s I ask ye more, for y^t I am creditablie informed how ye said Protector (as we must for ye present cal him) purposes a hard rule and ye vndoing of soch as he loves not, wch might be to ye jeobardy of vs al.

My very dear Brother, for ye rest I pray yow give credaunce to Sir Tho. Vaughan, bearer of y^{se}, who shal trewly deliver yow my entyre mind herein. And I wold have you know y^t I have longe thoghte how y^r Grace shuld have some great Office of State, by favour of my Lord Prince, ye Kyng y^t now is, and y^t I have made diligent labor to him for y^t ende: and if in anything I can serve yow, my dear Brother and good Lord, I shal do it wth al my powre, and so God keep yow and bring yow to a good decysion.

Wrytyn at Ludlow, y^s XXIJ day of Aprile wth ye hand of your frend   A. REVIERES

To my Lord of Bukynghame, good Grace, in his Castle of Breknok.

329

Henry Stafford, Duke of Buckingham, read Lord Rivers' scrawled letter through : lowered the paper a little between his hands and looked over it at the Welch face of Sir Thomas Vaughan : a face with high cheekbones and thinned, white hair, the skin stretched tightly on it and its black eyes attentive.

"This is a most extraordinary writing, Sir Thomas," he said with a careful air of being stern, "and I am in two minds what to think of it."

Sir Thomas Vaughan, whose black eyebrows, in contrast with his hair, gave him rather the appearance of a mountebank, made a little grimace.

"My Lord Duke, I am here to interpret it so far as my poor wits will allow me."

"Very good : then let me ask you, Sir Thomas, why my Lord Rivers dreads and hates the Duke of Gloucester?"

That will knock him out of his saddle, Duke Henry thought as he said it. That will unhorse him : a direct question when he expected covertness. Sir Thomas Vaughan took the buffet without flinching; leaned forward as though pleased to have the game played in the open.

"Because we live in a changed world, your Grace, and the case is altered with us."

"The case is altered." Duke Henry leaned his elbows on the oak table that separated them and joined his hands under his chin, using his eyes, which he knew had the facility of startling people, in an attempt to break the Welchman's guard : "How is it altered? Le Roi est mort, vive le Roi. Why is the world changed so fearfully?"

To his annoyance, it was the Welchman whose spear slipped inside his now.

"Your Grace, you are familiar with the affairs of Court. You know the private hates and grudges which the virtue of our late master, whom God assoil, kept within measure. They are all broken loose now. Our new King, your nephew, is a child, not crowned yet; and I who know him tell you that he is a child that can be ruled by the bend. Someone must govern the realm, and the question my Lord Rivers asks you is : Shall it be Richard of Gloucester?"

"Why, sir, should it not be that virtuous Prince, richly endowed, I may say, by Heaven with all the skill and courage necessary for the guidance of a kingdom, a prudent and valiant nobleman and the one surviving brother of our late Lord Edward, God give him peace?"

"Why you know that too, your Grace : because the Lord Protector hates the Queen's Grace and my Lord Rivers and all their affinity beyond words or measure. My Lord Duke, why play a game with me? You know. You know that since that day five years ago when you were created Lord High Steward of England for the sole purpose of condemning Clarence to death when they attainted him, there's been no room in the same world for Gloucester and Wydvylle. I say you know it : and you know that now King Edward's gone to God things have come to the crack. Your Grace is allied in marriage to the house of Wydvylle. If Richard of Gloucester reaches London next week and is acclaimed Protector, then there's an end of the power of your Lady wife's kin. The Duke won't eat by day or sleep by night until they're stripped, broken, dead for what I know. He hates them as the devil hates charity. You know all this. The Duke of Gloucester is a dangerous man, your Grace, and we're in dangerous times. Why should you pretend to be deaf—I speak without offence—when you can hear as quickly as any man?"

"I've heard a great deal : perhaps too little, perhaps too much," the Duke answered carefully. "Our ears are as treacherous as all our senses, and many an honest man has gone to ruin, or run into great dangers, through no more than listening. What you say is true, or for all I know it is, but how does it concern me? Answer me that, Sir Thomas Vaughan. You have come to me, God knows, without my seeking, and have talked dangerously. Our Lord King that was appointed his noble brother to be Protector of the Realm and guardian of our Lord King that is. Am I to cavil against his dying commandment, spoken at that dreadful moment we must all know one day, when the soul makes ready to quit her earthly lodging? God forbid."

Sir Thomas Vaughan uncrossed his legs and crossed them again; bit his lip with dirty teeth. He looked as though something had slightly but not seriously annoyed him. He said patiently :

"My Lord Duke, we ought to see things as they are. Richard of Gloucester may be a virtuous Prince and our late master's brother, but with our late master's death,

Christ have mercy on him, the world's turned upside down. Everything's now possible, look you : and it's a Trojan hate there is between him and the house of Wydvylle, and has been since the death of the Duke of Clarence that you passed sentence on."

"As an officer and not as a judge."

"You passed it : and Gloucester's never forgotten or pardoned his brother's taking-off, as you very well know, and you're married into the house that took him off at the very time when Gloucester was softening the King to pardon him.

The impudent bastard, thought Duke Henry parenthetically. Sir Thomas Vaughan went on :

"Now, your Grace, I bear a message from your brother-in-law, my Lord Rivers. Here's what he says. This is the time, he says, between a King and a King, where scores will be paid. He knows a score that's owing to him from Duke Richard, and owing to his sister the Queen and you and all of us, my Lord Duke. Why wait for it to be paid? he says. Why not strike first and let us have no Protector, but a Council of Regency of which your Grace will be one, he says, and all of us secure and England merry again?"

"Murder?" asked Duke Henry as casually as he could contrive.

Sir Thomas Vaughan leaned over the table to him, looking pleased.

"We hope not, your Grace. We mean nothing extreme unless we're forced to it : but the Duke of Gloucester must never reach London. The house of Wydvylle are unloved there. Once he's in London and has the mastery of our Lord Prince, we're shent. So he must not come as far. Somewhere on the road we must prevent him; charge him with treason, rebellion, witchcraft, anything. He must stay behind. Either as a prisoner or a corpse he must stay behind, and then we ride to London with our Lord Prince and tell our tale there."

"That is a perilous scheme, as God sees me, that you are talking of now. How many men has the Duke?"

"Not more than six hundred, your Grace, reckoning priests and pages, and he moves slowly; stops in every town to order Masses for his brother and have the notables of the place swear allegiance to my Lord Prince. It'll be Sunday before he's even as far South as Nottingham. We have two thousand at Ludlow, and arms. We'd 've had more but there's been trouble in London."

"How, trouble?"

"Lord Hastings: he never loved my Lord Rivers since my Lord tried to have the Lieutenancy of Calais from him. He told the Queen's Grace that if we came up more than two thousand strong he'd retire to Calais and arm the garrison there. He's frightened."

"What plans have you for London? You may tell me everything, man. By my faith I am not one of those who would go about to destroy men that put their simple trust in me. I am open with those who are open; give plain answers; and the answer I give you now is: I will not forget the tie of wedlock between me and my Lord Rivers."

"Loved be God, your Grace. That's sweet hearing, yes indeed it is! We have our plans for London, your Grace, you be sure. The day we leave Ludlow, the Marquis Dorset will seize the Tower. Sir Edward Wydvylle, my Lord Rivers' brother, will take charge of such shipping as he can find. We shall have the Treasury, too, and the Queen herself will take charge of the Great Seal. We've negotiated with my Lord Chancellor Rotherham for that. Why, your Grace, nothing whatever at all can stand against us if we go the right way to work."

"And what part am I to play, then, in this scheme? It seems you have everything so perfectly arranged that there is no need of helpers."

Sir Thomas Vaughan showed his bad teeth again. He seemed very cheerful and cunning now, flashing his black eyes at Duke Henry and sharing secrets with him.

"Your part, your Grace, is to muster as many tall fellows as you can, defensively arrayed, and join us on our road to London. Northampton would be a good place. There we shall wait, or thereabout, until his good Grace of Gloucester comes up with us. With your men and ours, it will not be hard at all to have the better of him. We will send him to Ludlow to cool his heels. The coronation is for the fourth of May, and once our Lord Prince is crowned and we've held a Parliament and set up a Council of Regency, we might let him go again: why not, indeed? His teeth will be drawn then: and look you, my Lord Duke, we shall all be rich. England's a fat prize, for sure : something for all of us."

To Duke Henry's utter astonishment, the table that was between them had begun very slowly to move toward him. He stared at it for a second, wondering if his eyes were affected; then realised that he had clenched his right hand with all his strength on the leg. Had the Welchman noticed anything? He had not. He opened his hand, feeling an aching welt on his palm; rubbed it secretly against the silk of his hose and said :

"I take it kindly that my Lord Rivers has been so plain with me. I'm a young nobleman, far from his experience in great affairs. It is generous of him to promise me advancement through his kind offices. You have my answer already. I will not forget the tie of wedlock between me and my Lord Rivers. Tell him that, and that I will be at Northampton with three hundred men."

"By God's mother, your good blessed Grace, that's very excellent hearing indeed. We . . ."

The Duke lifted his hand, enjoying the sense of authority and power the gesture gave him.

"Leave me now, if you will. I shall have a great deal of business, and that must be my excuse for not entertaining you as I should otherwise delight to do. You are riding back to Ludlow to-day?"

"Yes indeed, your Grace, immediately."

"Command everything in my Castle, if you love me, sir. Go with God."

"God bless and prosper your blessed Grace."

"Good day."

"God give you good day."

The door shut after him. Henry Stafford of Buckingham stood up. A sensation was coming over him that he had felt once or twice before : a feeling of lightness and constriction in the head and commotion in the midriff. Something as warm as blood was bubbling and rising up in him, shaking his belly and making his lungs prickle. It was laughter. Laughter clutched at his throat and prised his jaws open. He had to throw back his head and let it out, burst after burst of it, until he thought it would conspire with the tightness round his brain and kill him. He belonged to a strange house, very old, inheriting the blood of Plantagenet and Bohun; sometimes thought there was a curse on him. His father had died in the brawl of noblemen at St. Albans and his grandfather had been cut down before Holy Harry's tent outside Northampton. Himself had been a book-lover and hater of battles ever since he could remember; had crept down passages of stone castles, close to the wall, with a big manuscript under his arm, and found a sunny place on the leads of a tower, pigeon-visited, reached by a forgotten trapdoor, where he could read. This was the life from which, when he was twelve years old, virgin, King Edward and the Wydvylles had called him up to do their injury to him, marry him off to Katherine Wydvylle, twice his age, so that she, being the new Queen's sister, might be Duchess of Buckingham. He had not thought about marriage, one way or the other. They were welcome. But being Duchess of Buckingham by name was not enough for Katherine Wydvylle. A boy's untaught body and his fears had been a new excitement for her.

The loud, rattling laughter stopped with a click when he remembered it, and he began to knuckle his forehead with both hands. He had always to make some such gesture when he thought of his wife Katherine. God damn her, God corrupt her body, God wither her skin, he repeated under his breath his invariable impotent litany. God consume her and all her kind in horrible hell. He sat down presently, his arms shaking a little; jangled the old-fashioned brass bell on the table and continued to jangle it until Ralph Banaster, his personal gentleman, scratched very demurely at the door and came in.

"Ralph."

"Your Grace?"

"Have you seen to that fellow Vaughan? Has he gone off yet?"

"Not yet, your Grace. He asked for food and that his horse should be saddled in half-an-hour."

Ralph Banaster was small-nosed, short, with a somehow impudent mouth and tow-coloured hair. He wore his smart clothes badly and held his shoulders stiff, letting his arms droop.

"Get pen and paper, Ralph. I'm going to write a letter. As soon as the Welchman's gone, Persal or one of the others must ride day and night, kill his horses, until he gives it into the hands it's meant for."

"I'll see to that, your Grace. Whom would it be for, your Grace?"

Duke Henry felt the laughter forcing itself up inside him again. He had to squeeze it down before he could say :

"Duke Richard of Gloucester."

Like an enchanted spear driven into the road to stop an army, Queen Eleanor's Cross stood up and told Lord Anthony he was near Northampton. Delapré Woods, on his right, were dusted over with greenish-yellow of buds and patches of full leaf. There was a lark grinding out its rattle of song, mounting higher and higher on the spiral of its own voice. The fields had revived from winter. Lord Anthony, who had left the Prince fourteen miles farther on the London road, at Stony Stratford, and was riding back to Northampton to meet the Duke of Gloucester, settled the pin of his cloak and sighed. The Duke had gained on them, his southward and their eastward paths to London intersecting here : but the Duke of Buckingham was in Northampton with three hundred men and Lord Anthony had five hundred. It would be enough. They would talk courteously to Duke Richard for a night; seize and arrest him on the way to Stony Stratford the next morning.

They rode on up the gentle ridge past Delapré Abbey until they were looking down to the green links of the River Nene, where there had been a notable Yorkist victory twenty-three years ago. Lord Anthony thought of the men who had had part in that victory and were dead now : the old Duke of York, borne down and cut to rags at Wakefield; Kingmaker, left cold by the side of his horse in Wrotham Wood; Edward Earl of March, the Rose of Rouen, Edward IV of England, who won his spurs there and whom they had buried pompously at Windsor eleven days ago. Remote on the Welch Marches with the new King, he had not said good-bye to Edward of England; had simply heard one morning that he would not see him again. At the beginning of April, too fat for other sports, the King had gone out fishing; had caught a chill. He coughed and wheezed and swore and took wine to drown it; complained of a devil's pain in his side. They put him to bed; let blood; purged him; let blood again. He suffered from shortness of breath and they suffumigated him with crushed amber. That was fatal, and priests began at once to crowd into the room where the King lay like a whale driven ashore by storm, a vast and magnificent monster suddenly pushed, in the midst of its unsuspecting lustiness, into a strange element. He made a good end. When they had heard his long confession, assured themselves of his penitence to God and charity to men, they anointed him, not as at his coronation, but with the oil that cleans and closes the gateways of physical sense, making way for the soul to go out and be met by angels and archangels and all the host of heaven. But the King would not die. He wanted his courtiers round him now, after the priests had done what they had to do; had something to say to them. Dorset with his silvery-yellow hair, Hastings, crying unashamedly, fat Stanley, John Howard, Francis Lovel, Sir Edward Wydvylle, handsome John de la Pole of Lincoln, Arundel, William Bourchier, Sir John Fogg: they all came in, and King Edward, propped up on many pillows, spoke to them. They said, those who were there, that a frightening change had come on the King after he had been given absolution, that the gross face, blue with death, had fined down to something nearer what it used to be. He made a long speech to them, gasping between words, talking of things he had never shown an instance of caring for in his lifetime. They hated each other, all of them. The Court was split with jealousies: the open loathing, as it was now, between Lord Hastings and Lord Anthony, the contempt of Howard and Lovel for almost all the Court habitués. He told them they must be friends now, for his son's sake, lest their quarrels pull England back into the old swamp of blood that he had ridden through from Mortimer's Cross to Tewkesbury. No one who remembered the Bloody Meadow could have expected that he would cry out, putting his fingers up to his blued lips like a terrified child: "If I could have foreseen; by God's blessed Lady, I would never have purchased the courtesy of men's knees with the loss of so many of their heads." Perhaps he was thinking of swords in the Wakefield Tower or poisoned malmsey in the Bowyer. His last sensible words were: "For the love you've borne me, for the love I've borne you, for the love that our Lord bears us all, each of you love the other." The Rose of Rouen, who had never taken kingship seriously whilst he was on his feet alive, had spared a good half-hour of seriousness to it now he was dying.

His last words might come in useful, Lord Anthony considered. One could hint that the King had foreseen trouble from the Duke of Gloucester; and that would give them all a plausible reason for serving him as the Beauforts, in Harry of Windsor's day, had served the last holder of his unlucky title. On the face of it, a few months' honourable imprisonment on a charge of conspiracy, just until the Coronation was over and the Council of Regency allowed by Parliament, would be enough. He could be turned loose then. No danger that he would ever get office or favour under the young Prince : Lord Anthony had taught the forward little boy too much about his uncle of Gloucester's grim ways and merciless ambitions for that. He might go back to his North parts—lopped of some of his castles and nearly all his offices, though—or they could even send him over to Ireland as Deputy-Lieutenant, to reside there. That should be enough, so far as the mere policy of the matter went : but with a little juggling, thought Lord Anthony, trotting his horse down to the bridge in the thin April sun, with a little juggling a more satisfactory end could be put to the business : an end on a scaffold. Treason was a much easier charge to bring than to disprove. It could be said the Duke of Gloucester had written secret letters, even before his brother's death, to stir up the old nobility against the Queen and her relations; that he was aiming at the throne.

Why am I frightened of him? Lord Anthony, the speculative philosopher, asked himself. Why shall I not be happy until he is under the ground? Because I killed his brother, used the royal warrant to put him away quickly before he softened the King's pliable heart? A little, to be sure : because of how he looked at me that infernal night with Holy Harry's blood dropping off his fingers? That's more of it. But I have never lied to myself. Neither of them is the true final reason. I hate him because I dread him, and I dread him because I could never be his master. Well, he shall go. There is not room for both of us in the realm of England, and I have climbed too high now to climb down again. I will be Constable and Admiral myself, before this year's turned; and there should be pickings from his estates as there were from Clarence's. I might have the wardship of

338

his son, too. Thomas is making a fat matter out of Clarence's children. Treason, my Lord Duke Richard of Gloucester : who would have thought that both King Edward's brothers, one after the other, would be guilty of high treason? Who would have thought it, my Lord Duke? Middleham is a fine Castle, I am told, and it is time I had a seat in the North. Or shall it be Pontefract? They say the country there is very lovely. What was it you said to me when you heard that George of Clarence had died so suddenly? My Lord Rivers, I begin to think I owe you a debt. That was all you said, very politely, with your snake's eyes on me. You fool, you shall pay your debt, I promise you, to the last groat : but in coin of my choosing.

The inn where the Dukes of Gloucester and Buckingham were harbouring that night was easily found. It was the largest in Northampton, and packed with followers. The two Dukes were waiting politely for Lord Anthony in the courtyard.

As he saw the man he had decided to end, Lord Anthony had a moment of queer surprise. Duke Richard was dressed from top to toe in mourning black, unrelieved by the least hint of colour. Even the jewel in his cap was a great square of Irish jet set in black pearls. Lord Anthony could not remember his face otherwise than white : but it was now ghastly, face of a corpse. The queer lines at the corners of his mouth had sagged and deepened, pulling his lips down. His narrow eyes were not a snake's eyes; had something dumb and terrible in them. It was misery dressed in black damask that stood in the inn-courtyard bowing, sweeping its black cap from its head. Great Christ, thought Lord Anthony, the little manikin loved his brother. I never guessed it.

"You are very welcome here indeed, my Lord Rivers." Duke Richard was coming forward, bowing again. Behind him, like a gaoler behind a prisoner, stalked the Duke of Buckingham, tall in comparison with his smallness, his black clothes touched with crimson and silver. Aye, there you go, thought Lord Anthony, with your fate going behind you. Three hundred Stafford knots in the town and my five hundred lads : we can show your six hundred in their black clothes all the force they need. We'll make you prisoner on the road to-morrow, between here and Towcester, where

ll be no scandal. You have won a great victory. I will
ay to spoil your pleasure in it. Do you remember saying that to me in the Wakefield Tower? No doubt you do.
Well, my Lord Duke, I have won a victory indeed; killed
one of your brothers because he threatened me, and befooled
the other: and you will certainly not stay to spoil my
pleasure in it.

Supper that night was, annoyingly, the most abominable
meal Lord Anthony had eaten since he campaigned in
France. Two Dukes and an Earl in his house had been
altogether too much for the innkeeper. He served them
river-fish with an unforgivable sauce, lampreys sodden with
grease, burnt capons and raw mutton. The Duke of
Buckingham complained furiously. He was a rather stupid
young man, Lord Anthony decided, and the promotion
he gained over this business had better be all he ever did
gain. They had had no opportunity to talk alone yet. The
Duke of Gloucester said very little, beyond inquiring
closely after the young Prince. You think you are to have
the rule of him soon and want yourself advised for it,
thought Lord Anthony, answering his questions. My good
Grace of Gloucester, if you knew how much I have taught
him to fear the sound of your name already.

He slept that night in a big, comfortless room, alone. It
was agreed that they make an early start in the morning.
Stripping off his clothes and regretting the absence of a
mirror, he allowed himself a faint quiver of laughter. It
went well. The Duke of Buckingham had whispered five
words to him on the stairs: "My three hundred are ready,"
and he had given one word back: "To-morrow." To-
morrow would be the last rung on the ladder he had
climbed so long. Two great men in England, to dispute the
rule of England, to-night: there would be one to-morrow.
I've climbed so very long, he thought, sliding his bare body
between the covers. I shall rest soon. All my life I have
had one intention. Now it comes near. I see its colours
now. I feel the warmth of it like warmth of a woman's
flesh near mine in the dark. Anthony Wydvylle, K.G.,
Earl Rivers, Baron Scales and Nucelles, King's Uncle,
Chief of the Council of Regency, Lord High Constable of
England and Lord High Admiral to keep the Seas, Lord
Chief Butler of England, Premier Earl of England, Steward

of the Duchy of Lancaster beyond Trent : I will be all of that in a month's time from now. Gloucester gone, I can deal with Hastings; break or bind him. I'll have the Lieutenancy of Calais, malgré his cheeks. Kingmaker will be small to me. God, how white he looked to-night, my little enemy. A face like a tortured man's, his lips shut to keep his yells in : he did not welcome Edward's death, and if they ever see that face in London they'll know it. So it shall not be seen. Ludlow or Brecknock will do for him until we end him. His widow, Kingmaker's daughter, the little Lady Anne with the high chin : her father always hated me; had my father's head. After widowhood for a year or two she will know better how to treat those who have the power in the realm; might welcome a marriage. Brother Ned has no wife yet : and marriage is after all the surest way to fortune. Wydvylle blood has mixed with Plantagenet and Stafford and Bourchier and Mowbray : why not with Neville? Blessed saints, what an abominable supper that was. Let me live to see the last of my kin well married; see all the old nobility tackled to our house with the bonds of matrimony, and I'll say Nunc dimittis. We shall be sure then. Our line will go on and on. God damn Louis of France for disappointing us over the Dauphin. Still, I'll find a better match than ever for little Bessy : Spain or the Empire. By marriages and a shrewd blow at the right moment : that is how we work. Young Henry of Buckingham is a fool, but none the less to my purpose for that. Father, you died, and my brother John, to lay the foundation-stones of the tower we build. Rest in peace now. To-morrow the coping-stone will be put on it.

The knocking was rude and continuous; hammered into Lord Anthony's dreams so that he was conscious of it before he woke. He sat up, dazed for an instant, taking in the only half-familiar details of the frowsy bed-hangings; then pushed them apart to call angrily :

"What the devil is this?"

"My Lord, my Lord !"

It was his page's squeaky voice. He recognised it.

"Come in, boy. Don't stand hammering out there."

The boy came in, big-eyed and clamorous.

"My Lord, we're locked in ! My Lord, I just wanted to go out in the courtyard, but there's two of the Duke of

Buckingham's men at the door and they say no one's to go out unless the Duke lets them."

Devil take that fool Henry Stafford, thought Lord Anthony in fury. He'll spoil everything. I don't want Gloucester seized till we're out of the town. He said:

"God, boy, what of it? It's only for fear of thieves. Now get soap and water and my perfumes quickly, and quietly. I must get up. You ought to be whipped till there's no skin on your buttocks, making such a pestilent garboyle about nothing. Hurry, will you, you brat?"

He made a quick toilet, not stopping to bleach his hands or polish his nails. It would really be devilishly inconvenient if the Lord Protector were to discover that the Duke of Buckingham was having the inn guarded. Why couldn't the young fool have let well alone? He strapped his sword round his waist as an afterthought, and came down the stairs two at a time to discover the Duke of Gloucester eating his breakfast in the hall.

The Duke did not look as though he had found anything in the place amiss. He was still terribly haggard, but was talking, with more animation than he had shown last night, to two of his Yorkshire retainers: the short-spoken Sir Richard Ratcliffe, and Sir James Tyrrel, a cold-eyed, young-old man who had conspicuously distinguished himself in the Scots campaign. Lord Anthony noticed that their voices dropped and died when they saw him; but there was nothing remarkable in that. He sat down to cold pigeon-pie and a tankard of small beer, wishing them good morning. The Duke left his fork on his plate in order to fiddle with a ring as he said:

"A very good morning to you, too, my Lord Rivers: you've joined us at a most fortunate moment."

"I am rejoiced to hear it, your Grace. How am I to serve you, then?"

"Ah, you'll laugh at us, my Lord, I am afraid. We were discussing poetry."

"The saints forbid that I should laugh at anyone for that."

"It was a poem which concerns you closely, my Lord."

"Not one of my own poor rhymes, I hope."

"No: but a poem which celebrates one of your greater

342

services to my late brother's crown, Jesus, Mary grant peace and perpetual light to him."

"Amen."

Lord Anthony noticed that Sir Richard Ratcliffe and Sir James Tyrell were looking a little surprised. The Duke had his grey, unhappy eyes on him with the expression of a man's genuinely searching for information. The upright cleft of a frown on his forehead was more noticeable than ever.

"It was that ballad that was being sung through all the lanes in London just after Tewkesbury. Crude stuff to a poet like yourself, sir, but there were verses in it extolling your exploits against the Bastard of Fauconberg. How did they run, now?

> With guns they were beat, that some lay in the mire.
> They asked wage of the Bridge:—they paid them their hire.
> Ever among, they had the worst. Then wakened their woe ...

What was the next line, my Lord Rivers?"

He's mad, thought Lord Anthony suddenly. His mind's snapped. God and good angels, how much easier that makes it for all of us. Duke Richard was still looking at him, puzzling with his eyes, trying to find something out. He repeated his question:

"What was the next line, my Lord?"

Lord Anthony shrugged his shoulders. Indulge him.

> "Ever among, they had the worst. Then wakened their woe.
> False men must be punished, the will of God is so.

Poor budge stuff, in my opinion."

The Duke looked at his friends.

"I told you so, gentlemen. That was the line."

"Yes, your Grace."

Sir James Tyrrel spoke in a very unsure voice. He has noticed it too, thought Lord Anthony. I was right. The man is mad.

The door of the inn hall opened. Duke Henry of Buckingham came in. He was dressed for riding, his black wool cloak already slung on his shoulders. In his hand was a bunch of keys. He walked straight up to the table, saluting nobody, and threw them down.

"The keys of the inn, my Lord of Gloucester."

Lord Anthony was not conscious of getting up; only heard his chair crash backward on the flagged floor behind him. A hand seemed to have shut inside his body and to be squeezing his guts. Duke Richard was looking at him, not puzzling now, but with the eyes he remembered from the Wakefield Tower twelve years ago.

"Your Grace of Buckingham, my Lord Protector, great God, what is this folly? Keys of the inn? What is this?"

"Be easy, my Lord Rivers. My cousin of Buckingham has closed the inn by my orders. His men guard all the doors to it, and mine are posted on every road out of the town."

Lord Anthony could see everything in front of him very clearly. There was no cloth on the table. The wood of the top had been scourged into ridges. There was a wedge of bread lying near an empty tankard. A little bit had been broken off from it and lay about an inch away. He could see the place where it would fit in, if one moved it back again. His heart was kicking and kicking in his chest like a caught rabbit. Sir James Tyrell's hands rested on the opposite side of the table, with a big emerald ring on the left thumb : a lovely stone, he thought, but a mistake to set it in seed-pearls. A dog in the yard outside was yelping. He hoped no one had kicked it; hated to see animals ill-used. His mouth was so dry that he might just as well not have had that drink of the small beer, which was bad and werish, an offence to the palate. He heard himself saying, speaking very well and slowly :

"My Lord Protector, I cannot understand you. What is this comedy? Are you afraid of an attack by someone? This is not the wild North. They are all good, peaceable, loyal folk here. There is no need for locked doors and guarded roads. On my faith, this is all very foolish, and not consonant with our dignity."

"My Lord Rivers, why have you tried to set a distance between my nephew the King and me?"

You have won a great victory, my Lord. I will not stay to spoil your pleasure in it. My Lord Rivers, I begin to

344

think I owe you a debt. Why am I the best-read man in England, thought Lord Anthony, when there is no book that tells us that the voice of calamity is neither thunder nor trumpets but a small voice, a sound like a sigh?

"Your Grace, I think you are unwell this morning. I do indeed. Your grief for your royal brother's death, on whose soul God have mercy, has unseated your nerves. You are talking strangely. I have set no distance between the King's Grace and you."

"You have set out to bring me to confusion, Lord Rivers. But it shall not lie in your power, whether or not it be better one man, and he little loved and less known in these South parts, should have rule over you all."

Lord Anthony put his hand out. He took the broken morsel of bread and fitted it carefully back into the place that it had come from. Then he looked up.

There was no anger in the sad, bloodless face that stared at him. There was nothing human. The lines round the mouth, the wrinkles under the attentively-narrowed eyes, were not made by passions he could understand. Something better or worse than a man was sitting and judging him, something outside his experience and horrible as an idiot or a viper was horrible, obeying its own laws. The Duke said very gently:

"False men must be punished, my Lord Rivers, the will of God is so. You are arrested for high treason."

The noise was sudden and frightening. Men were stamping into the room. They were dressed in black with the badge of the silver boar, and they carried halberds. Lord Anthony could not move any part of his body. He felt hands round his waist, unfastening his swordbelt.

He looked round him. Something was wrong in the business. Something was unreasonable. It was all over certainly, and he was a ruined man; was perhaps dying: but it did not make sense. Then, above the head of Duke Richard, he saw the face of Henry Stafford of Buckingham, the well-shaped lips wet and writhing and the eyes glaring like the eyes of a horse. His voice broke out of his control into a shout so angry that the halberdiers crossed their weapons in front of his chest.

"Devil, Judas, what did I ever do to you?"

Something terrible appeared to be happening to Duke

Henry. He was in the strangle-hold of an excitement that made him gulp and grimace like a poisoned man before he could control his voice and say :

"I might have asked you that, my Lord, when you thrust your bitch of a sister into my maiden bed."

Hard hands on his arms told Lord Anthony that he must go now, and leave everything behind him. The Duke of Buckingham's mad face, and the feel of their grip, cleared his mind. The broken fragments of the world that had spun round his head fell into place again and there was order and reason. He could understand; could smile, it was necessary for his dignity as a philosopher that he should smile, at the thought that the house of Wydvylle had risen by marriage and fallen by the same way.

Supper that night was no better than supper the night before. Shall I eat decent food again one day? the Duke of Buckingham asked himself. It had been a strange, triumphant day for him. They had locked Lord Rivers in his room under guard and ridden to Stony Stratford to find the King. Duke Henry had not had many moments of presence and commandment in his life. This had been one of them. He had ordered everything, Duke Richard, the first nobleman in the realm, walking or riding silently beside him. When they reached the King's lodgings he had said, as authoritatively as any experienced captain : "Go before, gentlemen and yeomen : keep your places," and had been obeyed. They had made a very handsome procession when they came into the presence of the twelve-year-old half-Wydvylle boy who was now King of England and France and knelt humbly down in front of him. He had received them pleasantly, though Duke Henry noticed the way in which his eyes crept sideways to the Duke of Gloucester, as though he were frightened. It was then that another of the Duke's great moments had been granted him. He saw Sir Thomas Vaughan's white head and fox's face in the crowd and pointed a stiff finger at him. "Arrest that man." Again there was such unquestioning obedience as he did not get in his own castles, unless his wife were away. Two men fell in, one on each side of Sir Thomas, and took his sword off. They seized Sir Richard Grey, the Queen's younger son by her first marriage, and Sir Richard

Hawte at the same moment, by the Duke of Gloucester's orders, Duke Henry supposed. The yellow-haired, girlish child whom they were taking to London to be crowned began to shout:

"Uncle, no, what are you doing? You shan't. What are you doing?"

Duke Richard took charge of the matter then; explained —Duke Henry, even with the wild excitement of laughter bursting up in him as it always did when he was happy, was impressed by the quietness and tenderness of his voice —that Sir Richard Grey and the Marquis Dorset and Lord Rivers had plotted to rule both him and his realm and to subdue and destroy the old nobility, to which end the Marquis Dorset had seized the Tower and taken all the King's treasure out of it and sent ships to sea. All that was true: but the yellow-haired Prince, his face crimson with temper, had found enough maturity to answer:

"What my brother the Marquis has done I cannot say: but I can answer for my Uncle Rivers and my step-brother here that they're innocent of any such matters."

Duke Henry had had his chance then. Kneeling once more, with great reverence, he said in a sure deep voice:

"They have kept their dealings in these matters far from the knowledge of your good Grace."

It was true, too, but the boy naturally had not believed it. They rode back to Northampton again, Duke Richard silent, and the new King, as might be seen in his face, sulky and frightened at the same time. England, reflected the Duke of Buckingham, could find two hundred thousand fighting-men if the need were great enough. She is the seat of two Archbishops, and Calais, Ireland and Wales are vassals to her. Her royal revenue is almost one hundred thousand pounds a year: all in the hands of this brat when he shall have reached sixteen.

They sat at supper now, and Duke Henry beguiled himself by imagining what the cook's expression would be if he were suddenly arrested for high treason in having attempted to poison the King and his two premier noblemen. The presence of the new monarch in person had finally unhinged the landlord and all those about him, so that the Duke of Golucester's retainers had had to take charge of the business, rigging up an old altar-cloth bor-

347

rowed from the nearest church as a cloth of estate, begging
or stealing waxlights from the same source to replace the
rush tapers; appealing at once to the loyalty and christian
charity of the Mayor for some drinkable wine. They had
made a fair job of it; but oh God, thought Duke Henry,
might they not have taken charge of the kitchen as well?
The meal was in every respect a nasty one. King Edward
V sat in the raised chair that they had placed for him,
with his uncle of Gloucester on his right and his cousin of
Buckingham on his left. He was a handsome lad, Duke
Henry saw, with his long, delicately-boned face and lovely
hair, but the viciousness of his mouth and the cunning cock
of his eyebrows were not reassuring. He had been kept,
during the last years of the Rose of Rouen's life, embosomed
at Ludlow in the thick of his Wydvylle kin like a young
Turk in a seraglio, Lord Rivers' transparent excuse for the
game being that, the Welch Marches having grown wild,
the authority of the Prince's presence would restrain ill-
disposed persons from the boldness of their former outrages.
Everyone in England but the King had recognised this as a
device for keeping him wholly under the influence of his
mother's family : and to all appearances it had been a
successful one. The boy was Wydvylle to the ends of his
hair, if obvious pertness and slyness were signs to go by.

A dish of pigeons was the best thing on the table to-
night; at least did not taste as though the Northampton
cooks belonged to the same guild as the Northampton cord-
wainers. He bent politely forward toward the King.

"Has your Grace deigned to try these birds yet? They are
very tasty."

The boy's too-small blue-green eyes flicked sideways at
him with a look between fright and dislike. His cheeks
flushed.

"No, they're not."

"As your Grace says."

"Nothing's tasty in this horrid kennel. We had good food
at Stony Stratford."

"Indeed I fear the fare at this poor inn is not worthy
of your good Grace."

"Well, then, why did you bring me here? Why have
you come and spoiled everything and meddled and taken
my Uncle Anthony away?"

"Alas, my dear liege, it was necessary for the welfare of your realm to do these things. Your Grace will understand and thank us one day. We shall convey your Grace up to London as soon as may be, and there you shall have everything that becomes a King."

"I want my Uncle Anthony, and I'll have him, too. You daren't stop me. You'll be sorry for this when you get to London. If you're taking me there, why have you brought me back to this hateful town? It's a dungheap. It's a dirty dungheap."

"It is a poor place, I know, your good Grace, but for your own sake it was necessary that you should pass to-night here."

"And I wonder you dare to show yourself here, my Lord of Buckingham. I've heard this is where your old traitor of a grandfather was killed fighting for the Lancastrians against my father the King."

Christ, thought Duke Henry, if for five minutes this brat could cease to be King and for those five minutes I could have a birch in my hand. Duke Richard of Gloucester had been sitting quite silent during their talk. Now he turned toward the King to say in his persuasive voice :

"But all the same, your Grace has not tried these pigeons yet and they are really very good."

"I don't want any."

"You are very right not to over-eat, nephew. Never eat more than your belly asks for, however good the food is. Though God knows, the food's poor enough here. Sir James Tyrrel"—he crooked a ringed finger toward the thoughtful-looking young man at the lower end of the board—"Sir James Tyrrel, take a dish of pigeon up to my Lord Rivers, if you please. Salute him from me and tell him he must not despair. All will be well enough, yet."

Sir James Tyrrel bowed and went out, followed by a servant with a heaped plate. Duke Richard spoke to his nephew again :

"Your Grace, I know you are angry with me and your cousin of Buckingham, because we've had this ugly duty of arresting men who are dear to you. You are right to be angry at first. It is a Prince's duty to protect his friends. But my dear nephew, won't you believe me, your uncle,

when I tell you that we have only done what we must do?
You can see now I bear your Uncle Rivers no malice."

"No, I can't."

"Think a moment, nephew. You have a good wit of your
own. Use it like a King. Kings must know how to read
their subjects' minds by their acts. If I had any malice
against your Uncle Rivers, I could have done what I
pleased with him this morning. I could even have taken
his life."

"You couldn't. You'd 've been afraid of me and my
step-brother at Dorset. When we get to London he'll
punish you. I'll tell him to punish you. I'm the King."

"You are the King, your Grace. You are my liege Lord,
the King of England and France, Lord of Ireland, Prince
of Wales, Duke of Lancaster and Cornwall, Earl of March.
Do you know what that means?"

The boy hid his face behind the rim of the vast silver
cup, big as a helmet, that he was drinking out of. He had
insisted on taking the rough heady Burgundy that was the
mayor's best liquor, and had had the cup refilled twice.
He took another gulp and said:

"Yes, it means you're my subject and I can punish you."

"It means that, certainly, nephew: but it means more
too. It means that tens of thousands of very brave men
have died terribly—shot with arrows, stabbed, crushed,
broken to pieces—in order that you, at twelve years old,
may sit at the head of this table under your cloth of state.
You do not remember your grandfather, my father. I only
just remember him myself. He was a small man, as I am,
but with yellow hair. He was a wonderfully brave captain,
and he was killed fighting in order that his children and
grandchildren might have the crown that was rightfully
theirs. The old Queen, Marguerite of Anjou, and Black
Clifford besieged him in his Castle of Sandal. My father
could have stayed safe behind the walls until your father,
God rest his soul, came up from the Welch Marches and
rescued him. But instead, he chose to fight in the open, and
was killed. My brother Edmund of Rutland was killed with
him. Almighty Jesus, grant them and all my brethren who
are now passed unto thee the light of thy mercy."

He spoke the last words in a quick mutter; crossed himself and went on:

"But that was only the beginning. English blood was shed in seas and rivers before the white rose of York could flower. You have been told, perhaps, that I am a captain who loves a field. God forgive me if that is true. Those who have seen fighting know what fighting is, and I do swear by St. Paul it was never any happiness for me to see dead Englishmen, whether they were Lancastrians or Yorkists. It is a miserable thing when men of one race kill each other. There is no glory in it, nephew. When you are a man you shall fight the French or the savage Scots. For a King to punish his people's enemies and protect his realm from them is honourable and according to God. But these civil battles that we have had too many of in old England : they are of the devil. It's right enough that the leaders and chief doers, the false noblemen who rise against the King's dignity, should be punished for their treason. But think of the common men, nephew, who follow a great Lord's banner, perhaps not even knowing whom they are to fight or for what cause : the twenty-seven thousand dead of Towton and the poor souls the great Warwick captained to their undoing at Barnet. They were your father's subjects, your subjects now. Have you never heard, have they never taught you, the noble words your father said to the commons of England at his first Parliament?"

"No," said the boy sulkily, "I never heard them."

"Then hear them now. *For the faithful and loving hearts, and also for the great labour, that you have borne and sustained towards me in the recovering of my right and title, which I now possess, I thank God with all my heart; and if I had any better to reward you withal than my body, you should have it: the which shall always be ready for your defence, neither sparing nor letting for any jeopardy.* I know these words of his by rote, nephew, and you certainly should know them. Those were your father's words, Lord Jesus rest him; and that is what it is to be a King : to defend with your very body, and whatever more than your body you can anyhow command, the peace of your subjects."

The boy shifted in his chair, scowling, his mouth drooping.

"What then?"

"This then : an infinity of good English blood has been

351

ut to make you King. See you to it. See that no
...eeds to be poured out to keep you King. Let no
...ion of yours, no hatred of yours, begin a civil tumult
...n. Defend your realm against its cruellest enemies of
...: the wicked men who would take advantage of your
callowness, for their own private profit, to stir up discord.
Your Grace, I have told you I mean your Uncle Rivers no
harm that can be avoided. But he and certain other persons,
God amend them, grudge because your father made me
Protector during your infancy. They have plotted—and my
Lord of Buckingham can give you proof of it—to start the
old madness of civil war afresh, to kill me and the other
noble men of the old blood and to throw this realm back
into the miseries of Henry of Windsor's day. They told you
nothing of it. What did you know of the Marquis of Dorset's insolence in seizing your own fortress of the Tower
Royal, of the barrels of harness hidden in the very baggage
that came up with you from Ludlow? Your Grace, I tell
you that yesterday, though you, the King, were as ignorant
of it as a monk in a cloister, your realm of England was on
the edge of civil war again. You are King to no other purpose but to prevent that. You are to prevent it, at whatever
cost to your own affections, as your most sacred duty to
God and your father's soul."

Duke Henry of Buckingham almost shouted applause.
Eloquence and the fitting together of words were the chief
interest of his days, and he could admire them in another
as well as in himself. Duke Richard's soft winning voice had
kept him so attentive that the food had congealed on his
plate. If any man can put an honest purpose into this brat,
he thought, then it's his uncle. Can even he, though? The
puppy's been so guided by his mother's relatives that he talks
and acts as though he were five, not twelve. No will, no
wits : and in four years he'll be of age. The saints help
England then. The boy was not flushed now; was pale and
looked more frightened than ever. He opened his mouth and
shut it again without speaking. Then Sir James Tyrrel was
bowing at the Duke of Gloucester's elbow.

"Your Grace, I conveyed your message to Lord Rivers
and he thanked you, but required me to carry the dish to
his nephew, Sir Richard Grey, with the same message for
his comfort. He thinks he has more need of comfort, as one

to whom such adversity is strange : but he himself has been inured to it all his life and can bear it better."

Duke Richard nodded : but then the young King's voice broke out, as shrill as a yelp.

"You see, dear uncle, my Lord Anthony knows you too well. He's not blinded by pretty talk. I suppose he thinks you meant to poison him."

Duke Henry gasped. Sir James Tyrrel, standing impassive as an image in his black mourning-clothes, tightened his lips. But Duke Richard twisted a ring on his finger and smiled sideways at his nephew.

"And so sends the poison to his nephew to swallow? That's a bad uncle. No, your Grace, I do not think Lord Rivers is so silly or so unchristian as to suspect me of poisoning."

"Who are you to call your anointed King silly and unchristian?"

The boy was nearly crying with temper. There were tears in his eyes. This time Duke Henry could not control himself.

"Your Grace is not anointed yet."

"But I shall be : and then you'll all be sorry. I'll take your titles away from you. I will. I'll have you beheaded. You're both traitors, traitors, traitors."

The tears had left his eyes for his cheeks. Duke Henry turned his face away; was blushing. The whole scene had become horrible with embarrassment. The King of England, he repeated over and over to himself, turned twelve and howling like a baby, only twelve and drunk in full sight of his servants : Lord God, what sort of a realm will England be in his time? Wouldn't I be serving my country if I put my dagger into him at this moment? Harry of Windsor's reign will be the Age of Gold beside what he'll bring on us. For the first time that night he heard the Duke of Gloucester's voice with an edge like a sword's on it.

"Your Grace is making a spectacle of himself in front of his subjects."

There was a gulp and a shuffle, very loud in the silence that had descended on the inn-hall. Duke Henry could not bring himself to look round yet.

"Fill me another cup of wine."

353

Duke Richard's voice was persuasive again.

"Your Grace, you have drunk all you need. This Burgundy is very strong stuff. Try a little claret and water or some syrup."

"Fill me a cup of wine. Do you hear, groom? Fill me a cup of wine, damn you to hell."

He was shouting at the top of his voice again. Duke Henry heard a stir behind his shoulder and saw a groom lean forward unwillingly with the big wine-jack. He was about to pour from it when Duke Richard's hand stopped him.

"Take that wine away and bring some cordial syrup," he said evenly.

Then it happened. The King's face was flushed crimson now. His greenish eyes goggled, swimming with tears of temper, and his teeth showed. He grabbed for the wine-jack with both hands, rising in his seat, but at the same moment Duke Richard's one hand caught it whilst his other motioned the groom away. They were posed in a strange group : The young King in his blue velvet and jewels tugging and wrestling with both hands against the one hand of the Duke, who sat rigid in his chair, his fingers round the neck of the jack and his narrowed eyes fixed on his nephew. Every muscle in his face showed under the blenched skin and his whole stiff, small body jerked slightly in its seat with each tug of the infuriated boy's arms. As he struggled with him the King was shouting in a voice that must have carried beyond the room :

"God damn you, you whorson, God damn you, God damn you. Traitor, pig, you conspired with Clarence against my father. You damned dirty hunchback, I think you had my father poisoned. You're a traitor, hunchback, bastard. You're a bastard."

Duke Henry of Buckingham was on his feet too. He swung his hand back to the stretch of his arm. In another second, King Edward V would have taken a whirret on the ear that sent him flying. But he let go the jack in time and, with a concluding sob of "Hunchback," flung himself down the hall and out of sight up the stairs.

There was entire silence, so that rain could be heard prattling in the puddles and gutters of the courtyard. Everyone in the room was looking his own way, avoiding

354

others' looks. Duke Henry lowered himself into his chair again. The sinews at the back of his legs felt weak. After a very long while he said in a voice that he hoped might sound comforting:

"Only an impudent boy, your Grace, frightened out of his wits: drunk too."

Duke Richard did not answer. His puckered eyes and lips were barely marks in his shrunk face. He was staring at his own hand on the table in front of him. Wine had been splashed on it and trickled from his jewelled fingers in drops like blood.

It was quite dark in the room where William, Lord Hastings, entertained Jane Shore, whom he had lusted after for ten years. Curtains of double velvet shut out the London street over whose cobbles traffic no longer battered. A scent of musk and powdered violets thickened the unlit air. In the baffled exhaustion of spent appetite he moved his hands toward her under the sheets; touched her skin, which was smoother even than he had imagined it; with a tensed finger traced the miraculous line of her backbone from neck to buttocks; cupped a hand round her knee, pulling the leg towards him. She gave a small sigh, like a dog, and her head bent to his shoulder so that he could feel the harsh silkiness of hair. He had fallen like Lucifer. Ten years ago he had seen the yellow-gold hair and small firm bosom of Shore's wife, King Edward's concubine, and something had rolled over in him like a wheel. He knew that she would be what the other women, the dozens and scores of them, had not been. Even whilst he walked behind the six-horsed chariot that carried the dead Rose of Rouen from Westminster to Sion House, he had been thinking that Jane Shore would want a fresh protector.

Like Lucifer: the news came last night, a mud-splashed man hammering him out of his sleep to say that the Dukes of Gloucester and Buckingham had uncovered a plot. The Earl of Rivers was at the head of it; had been sent North to prison with his confederates. The Queen even at that moment was flitting, with her daughters and younger son and all the valuables she could lay her claws on, from Westminster Palace to Broad Sanctuary: proof she had something ugly on her conscience. The Marquis Dorset and Sir

355

Edward Wydvylle had bolted like rats from a threshed rick out of the Tower and ridden God knew where.

He stood in his bedgown, shivering in the sharp May night, and heard the best news told in England since the day of Tewkesbury. The detested house was down, gone at a breath. The Wydvylles, who had flourished like the bay-tree, were pulled up, and less blood spilt in the business than would have come from a cut finger. He breathed loudly. Somewhere in the cold North, with his legs bound to his stirrup-leathers, his continual enemy was jogging away from power and worship into oblivion. Somewhere along the Thames, in the London dark, the Queen he abominated was flapping and scurrying like a frightened hen; had got a whiff of the fox at last. Everywhere in England profound sighs of well-being would go up and men would stretch and smile and look each other in the eyes again. It was a tardy miracle, all the more marvellous because, after nineteen years of impotent loathing, a dozen headings and four bloody battles, it had come suddenly and without sword-strokes.

His first act was to send a messenger to the Lord Chancellor, the doddering old Archbishop of York, who was certain to fly into a feeble panic and do something stupid. "Wake him if he is asleep," he told the man, "and say to him that there's no fear. All will be well, I assure him." Even whilst he spoke, a cold, heavy feeling began to come on him, drugging his lungs and bowels and making his heart go heavily. All would not be well. Somewhere in the involved thicket of his soul an infernal horn was blowing, winding the mort for his honesty. He was sure already that the part he would play in this changed world was not the clean part that he wanted, the cleaning of England, from the damage of the Wydvylles. Fate gave two gifts at once, cleverly, so that they annulled each other. When Jane Shore waited on him early that morning with a message from the Queen, her friend, he had known before she spoke what she would ask him to do and what price she would offer; and that he would close with the bargain.

Crosby Place in Bishopsgate had been bought by Duke Richard in the year King Edward drove his bad bargain with the Christian King. It was the tallest house in London, a great pile of gables and carved ornament. Sir John Crosby had been rich. Duchess Anne sat in an upper room, waiting for her husband to come home and thinking about her son. He was seven years old now, as high as his small father's waist, and was beginning his Latin. She thought of his small, frank forehead and the seriousness of his eyes under it. They were grey, like Richard's. He would be like Richard; never shouted or chattered and very seldom cried. He could say sensible things, too. When his father told him the story of St. Nicholas and the two children whom the wicked inn-keeper killed and hid away in his powdering-tub, he amazed them both by saying: "I suppose God let him kill them so that St. Nicholas could work the miracle." They repeated the tale to Dr. Beverley, who said that the child had a better wit for theology than some whom he could name that wore mitres.

If he were here now, thought Duchess Anne, if we had him here with us in this London, things would be plea-santer; but Richard was right. The air of this place makes sickness: so many crowded together, sweating and hating each other, brawl and din and no clean winds coming over the place to freshen it. She remembered the Sign of the Silver Pack with dust swept into corners and pigs guzzling offal by the doorstep and the Widow Wrangwysh throwing fishtails on the solar floor for Gib the cat. The cottages of Middleham village were dirty, but the wind scoured them. Here fog sat above the town like a devil sitting on the lid of a creelful of the damned to squeeze them into small compass. Below her, as far below as though she were on the leads of the Drum Tower at Middleham, people jostled each other in the narrow jarnock of a street and the voices of hawkers came up, small and shrill, crying wine and rosaries and salves against disease. Lepers were forbidden, under forfeit, to come inside the gates, but she had seen several since she arrived a month ago: bladder-like faces, silvery-grey with criss-cross of red lines that might be veins, lips rotten, frogs' hands, sometimes short of a finger.

There had been no peace since she set foot in Crosby Place. The day after her arrival Richard had been all morn-ing at a Council meeting; came back to dinner with more lines in his face than ever; said nothing except that Queen Elizabeth, who was still in Broad Sanctuary and refused to

357

come out of it, was more trouble to the realm than France and Scotland together. He had been in Council almost every day since. Writs were issued for a new Parliament; ships commissioned to chase and catch Sir Edward Wydvylle, who had fled from the Tower only to steal one of the royal vessels and turn pirate; new appointments made. The Duke of Buckingham, who seemed never to be away from Duke Richard's side now, was made Chief Justice and Chamberlain of North and South Wales, Captain of all their castles and keeper of all their chases for life, with other powers during the King's minority.

"He's a rash creature, God knows," Richard had said to her, "but I owe him something, and I must have the affairs of Wales out of my hands. As I see it, I shall have trouble enough in England."

That looked likely. He had broken Lord Rivers—now a captive at Middleham, in rooms Anne had got ready for him before she left—and all his pack between finger and thumb as though they had been rushes, not ambitious men. London mobs had cheered him for it when he rode into the city in his black clothes with the boy King beside him. The watchword of the taverns had been that it would be as good a deed as almsgiving to hang the traitors : and so it would, God make better men of them, thought Duchess Anne resentfully. My father was in the right about that pack, rest his soul. Though they were broken, the Marquis Dorset and his uncle Sir Edward were still loose, and the Queen was squatting in Broad Sanctuary like a witch (perhaps thought Anne, she is a witch?), clutching her younger son to her and doing all that her power reached to discredit the Protector's government. She was a poor lorn widow and mother of orphans, and her unnatural brother-in-law was after her life; had privately murdered her brother Anthony and her dear son Sir Richard in some horrible dungeon in the black North; was aiming at the crown. Torrents of her malevolent hysteria gushed out of Westminster like dirty water and trickled down the obscurest gutters. When her son, Edward V, at his own wish, had been moved from the Bishop of London's Palace to the State Apartments in the Tower, the unbalanced harpy had cried out that the Protector was imprisoning him in the place where, all the world knew, he had piteously murdered

Harry of Windsor, and that she should never see her darling again.

Edward V, his mother's son : when she thought of him Anne put down Sir Thomas Malory's book of King Arthur she had been pretending to read, and walked about the room. She had heard things that made some part of her, deep down in her body, go heavy with fear. What had they taught the boy at Ludlow to make him hate and dread his uncle so much beyond reason? There was more than Lord Anthony's arrest behind it. That was certain. She knew some of the silly tales told of her husband in the South : how he was a hunchback born feet-first into the world with teeth in his mouth, how he worked magic. Had they frightened the boy out of such wits as he had with market-clack of that sort? If so, what kind of a King of England would he make who believed fairy tales when he was twelve years old? The child was a menace. There were times when he reminded her, for a horrible second, of her first husband, Marguerite's son who had been cut down squealing for quarter at Tewkesbury. Another lie had grown from that, propagated, she would take her oath, by the ingenious Wydvylles. It was said Duke Richard had stabbed the Prince in cold blood after the battle so that he might marry her. I should not blame him if he had, she thought with a shiver, but it's a common slander. Clarence and his men-at-arms killed him whilst he was trying to cross the ford. All these lies were being stirred up, like mud settled at the bottom of a pond, since the Rose of Rouen had died and Duke Richard had the Protectorship. That did not matter now. The Wydvylles might spin what tales they pleased : let them make one move toward armed trouble and Lord Anthony and Sir Richard Grey should kiss the block. But in four years Edward of Westminster would be of age to rule. Protectors seldom prospered in England after they left office. Five had miscarried in the past two centuries : Thomas of Lancaster, leader of the Lords Ordainers, headed without trial by Edward of Caernarvon; Roger Mortimer, murderer of Edward of Caernarvon, headed by Edward of Windsor; Thomas of Gloucester, imprisoned and murdered by Richard of Bordeaux; Humphrey of Gloucester imprisoned and, they said, poisoned by the Beauforts; Richard of York, her husband's father, surprised and overcome at Wakefield.

Two Dukes of Gloucester: it was a common byword that that title brought no luck with it. We can count on just four years, she thought: four years in which to put some honesty into England again; and Dickon's reward at the end of it will be a King who hates him.

There was a sound on the stairs. The door opened and a voice said:

"My Lord of Gloucester."

Duke Richard still wore his mourning, and for the hundredth time it pinched Anne's heart to see how deathly the black cloth made his face.

"Alone, Anne?"

"Yes, Dickon."

"Loved be God." He dropped into a chair and drew the palms of his hands over his face. "I am so tired; and there's the Bishop coming to see me before supper."

"Bishop—what Bishop?"

"Stillington of Bath: wants an audience on something secret and vital; won't tell me what."

"Lord, more trouble?"

"I fear so. Stillington isn't a fool, that I've noticed. My guess is he's stumbled on some new device of the Queen and wants to warn me."

"That woman: I could scratch her eyes out."

"I'd rather you cut her tongue out. D'you know her latest drift?"

"No."

"That I am only waiting for her to give up the little Duke to have him and his brother murdered."

Anne had perched on the arm of the big chair her husband sat in. She got up, stiff on her legs, her hands shut.

"Now may God punish the lying old viper as she deserves."

"He will. What's Purgatory for? But I can't send her there."

"You could send her brother there, and he deserves it."

Duke Richard bent his head until his chin pressed the low collar of his doublet. The dagger at his side clicked regularly like a clock marking off seconds of silence. After a long while he said:

"Anne, do you remember what I told you years ago in St. Martin's Sanctuary when I asked you to marry me:

that I let nothing stand between me and what I see clearly ought to be done?"

"Yes, Dickon."

"Bird, I'd give the health of my soul to punish Anthony Rivers. He is the only man in the world I hate. He murdered one of my brothers and corrupted the other. But I must not do it. Alive he's my hostage against the Queen, my pledge that there'll be no civil war, no new field of St. Albans. Dead, he's a martyr, something the Wydvylle scum can make their reason for taking arms against me and putting poor England back where she was when my father died."

"You're right, Dickon. You're always right. But I wish the whole pack could be brought to heel, the Queen and all of them."

"The Queen is creating an abominable scandal, keeping the little Duke in Sanctuary; and that I'll stop. By St. Paul, I will. If he's not in my hands before the next Council, I'll ask the opinion of the Lords Spiritual on taking him out of the Sanctuary by force."

"Isn't that sacrilege?"

"I don't know. Sanctuary is for grown men who are in danger of the law. The Duke's a child and in no danger. I can't see for the life of me that the right of Sanctuary extends to him at all. Buckingham is going to argue the matter to the Lords Spiritual for me. He's got more eloquence than I have."

"He's got an unmercifully long tongue, if that's your meaning. I don't think I like that young nobleman very much."

"I owe my life to him, or next door to it, but I know what your drift is. He's very raw, very hot and ambitious, perhaps even a little odd in his mind. But he has his uses; takes work off my hands that I can trust him with and leaves me free for what I have to do myself: and God knows there's a great deal of that. Anne, you wouldn't conceive the state the government is in. It's frightening. I've been taking a view of the Exchequer and its workings to-day. Small wonder my brother needed those damned benevolences to raise money; there are debts outstanding to the Crown over the last five years. Officers in the Exchequer are holding places in the Receipt and tother way on. The accounts seem to be audited when and how God pleases—accounts of the Crown estates aren't audited at all, that I can discover. Crown lands are farmed out to men who can't sign their own names—friends of the Wydvylles mostly. Any fool with ten marks to spare can buy himself a place in the Exchequer over the heads of the under-clerks, which is a sweet encouragement to them to do their work honestly. It's the confusion of hell. I see a year's work for myself straightening it."

"Ah, Dickon, do you see anything at all ahead of us but work and trouble?"

"No."

"Shall we never see Yorkshire any more?"

"That, yes : as soon as Parliament's sat. I will not stay an hour longer than I need in this pestilent London : this place of fogs and stinks and quarrels. I hate it. After Yorkshire it's like a Purgatory, as full of wickedness as we suppose Purgatory is. I tell you I trust nobody in London. There isn't a Cockney born who wouldn't cut your throat for a rotten apple. Anne, I've made another ugly find, or I think I have."

"Oh God, what now?"

"I believe on my soul there are still Lancastrians in the world. I've caught looks out of the corner of my eye; heard whispers. If the Wydvylle woman were to succeed in her plans and start an armed rising against my Protectorship, d'you know what I think would happen? I seriously believe there are some men about the Court who'd try to bring over the Welch bastard from Brittany."

"It can't be. I can't conceive it. Lancaster was dead and buried at Tewkesbury."

"I pray you're right, Anne. But I can't be sure. I can't be sure. Morton—you know as well as I—was Marguerite's right hand. Has he so utterly changed colour as we thought? I don't know. I wish he might not have been made Bishop of Ely. It's too high a place for a doubtful man. Then there's Stanley. I believe he was a faithful friend to my brother. I won't question his loyalty. But he's married Margaret of Richmond, Henry Tydder's mother, and all I hope is she does not talk politics to him."

"I'd swear to Stanley's honesty. He's too gross a fat fellow to be anything but open."

"He's not without wits for all that. But I don't doubt him: only his wife. What does he want with a woman that age, a widow twice over?"

"God knows."

"He knows. I'm being foolish, seeing shadows in corners. By St. Paul, Anne, but I shall be doubting myself soon, I think. Will you believe that I've even caught myself wondering whether Hastings had not a secret of some kind? He's taken the strumpet Jane Shore to bed with him, you know, almost before Edward was in his coffin: something less than decent, that. These women: you and my mother and yours are the only three I ever trusted. Why are men such fools? Why must they play the comedy of the apple over again each time they see a pair of plucked eyebrows? I've no charity for that kind of weakness. Once let a woman get her teeth in a man and she'll suck his honesty like a stoat. My brother and the Wydvylle bitch, Stanley and Henry Tydder's mother, Will Hastings and Shore: I wish I could have a Court of eunuchs round me. Lord, I'm tired. My heart aches: work without end, and no satisfaction if there were an end."

"Except the work itself."

He looked sharply up at her and held both hands out.

"Anne, come here to me. Kiss me. Oh, bird, you're the only one with any wits of them all. You know. You do know. The work pays itself. Enough if we're allowed to do it, build up England: we'll build such an England, Anne. What does it matter if we get hurt a little? We've the stomach for it."

She was on the arm of his chair again now, her hand on his shoulder. He leaned his head on her thigh and looked straight in front of him.

"Reforms everywhere: they're wanted. The useless mouths put out of office, benevolences abolished— that must be done—the Exchequer reformed: God, we shall make enemies. There are complaints in the shires of corrupt juries, sheriffs selling injustice for what it will fetch. We can amend that: and there are towns, Anne, honest old towns all over England, like our own York, that owe dues to the Crown that they can hardly pay. I wonder does my authority extend far enough to remit those? It's a wanchancy thing, a Protectorship. No one seems fairly to know what I may do and what I mayn't: sovereign power without sovereignty. But there's room for plenty. We can break many extortioners and restore many impoverished people in four years, bird. We can make a happier England of it."

"For that brat."

"Don't think of him, Anne. We don't do it for him. We do it for the people of England, all of them, and for . . ."

He waited a moment and went on:

". . . for Edward, God rest his soul in peace. Work he ought to have done and didn't do: so we do it for him. Masses aren't enough—God forgive me if I'm talking heresy—I have the belief that it will go better with him where he is now if I can undo some of the errrors that woman led him into. Whether it's sound doctrine or not, the saints know: but I believe it."

Anne felt her eyes pricking. Her right hand went round to Richard's hair and began to stroke it. But I must say what I believe, she thought, for all that. That's what he taught me himself.

"And if that boy destroys it all when he comes to his own?"

She felt him move slightly under her hands.

"That's with God. We can do nothing for that. Whatever happens, I have four years. I can build high in that time. He may kill me at the end of it. To tell the truth, I think he will . . ."

"Dickon, don't!"

"We're better to see it plainly, love. The child hates me beyond anything I would have thought possible. I've seen him turn haggard with fright and malice when I came near him. He may serve me as Richard of Bordeaux served Thomas of Gloucester. He would to-day if wishes were horses. No, bird, I don't think I shall live to make old bones."

"Dickon, my own sweet, I can't bear this; indeed I can't. It's too pitiful: Edward's son, your own nephew."

"I never think of him as Edward's son. He's Wydvylle, Wydvylle all through, and the worst of the crew of them: nothing of Edward but his looks, and those corrupted with his mother's abominable cunning. Blessed St. Paul, that that should be all the Rose of Rouen's left us to remember him by."

"He's left us you."

"Aye, he's done that. He didn't send me to join George, though his son may yet. Well, we shall do what God lets us : straighten a few tangles; punish a few extortioners; fight a few battles, perhaps."

"Battles?"

"The Scots are certain to create some garboyle, now Edward's gone. I half wish they would. A Scots journey would at least take us North out of this miserable London. I could enjoy to have an axe in my hand and get my legs over White Surrey's back again."

"Dickon, did you mean what you said when you talked about Henry Tydder?"

"The Saints know, Anne. There are Lancastrians in this country yet. But I can't believe that Welch milksop who never saw an army in his life would dare to come over. Intrigue he may. Fight I'll take my oath on the sacrament he won't. No, I think we've greater dangers nearer home than Henry Tydder."

There was a light tap at the door. Duke Richard smoothed his hair, calling :

"Come in."

John Nesfield, one of the Duke's favourite personal gentlemen, opened and bowed.

"Yes, John?"

"The Bishop of Bath and Wells asks audience of your Grace."

"Let him come up here."

"Your Grace."

"I'll go," said Anne.

"That you'll not. You'll stay with your liege husband. I need you more than many Bishops, bird."

Dr. Robert Stillington, Bishop of Bath and Wells, was an old man. He had a priest's brown, watchful eyes in a thin face, the colour of standing cream. There were lines from his nostrils to the corners of his lips, which were as sensitive as a girl's. It was a good face, an attractive face : not at all a strong one. He moved slowly, but more as though from nervousness than from infirmity, and Anne noticed that his long, exquisite hands were continually wandering toward his gold cross, twiddling it as Richard twiddled his rings or his dagger. The man's frightened out of his hide of something, she thought. Oh Lord Jesus, what bad news do we hear now?

"You are very welcome, indeed, my Lord."

"Your Grace, my Lady, good day. You are kind to receive me : very kind. I give you good day."

"You're tired, my Lord. John, a chair for his Lordship, Burgundy, wafers, fruit, quickly,"

"Oh no, your Grace, I'll drink nothing. I thank you. Your Grace is kind, but . . ."

"My Grace is obstinate. You're tired and you shall follow the precept of St. Paul as touching wine on pain of my displeasure. Be seated. Your business will wait till you're refreshed."

He's putting the old man at his ease, thought Anne : but he's wondering himself what fresh trouble's beginning now. Oh, Edward of Rouen, you fool, why did you marry that harpy and leave such a coil for us to straighten? Did you once in your life consider anything but yourself?

John Nesfield brought the wine and served it; went out. The three formally pledged each other. Anne noticed that the cup wobbled in the old Bishop's hand and that the cross on his chest winked as though he were breathing quickly. Duke Richard sat in his chair again like a boy, one leg pulled up and his hands round the knee. His chin was sunk and his eyelids pursed tightly.

"Well, my Lord, what do you wish to say to me?"

The Bishop locked his fingers together.

"Your Grace, I have come to purge my soul."

Duke Richard gave no answer whatever; did not move.

"Your Grace, I am a priest; but I have sinned against my priesthood. From the weakness of the flesh I have taken God's holy name in vain. I have told lies."

There was still no answer. Bishop Stillington's pale tongue explored his lips. His eyes were pitiable. Anne would have liked to stroke his hand.

"I have come now to beg your forgiveness; beg all England's pardon for the wrong I did. I cannot keep silence any more. Your Grace, in the teaching of Solomon I have found it written : Vae tibi, terra, quod rex tuus puer et principes tui in mane comedent. Beatitudines tuae, terra, quod rex tuus filius heroum. Woe to thee, oh realm, that thy King is a child and thy nobles feast in the morning. Blessed

366

art thou, oh realm, when thy King is a son of champions."

"Where are you leading to?"

The Duke's voice was unencouraging.

"Your Grace knows that at the time of the pitiful death of your brother Duke George, Lord Jesus have mercy on his soul, I was made a prisoner and put in the Tower? Your Grace remembers that?"

Duke Richard took his hands from about his knee and said: "Yes." He leaned forward a little.

"And that I was afterwards released because I took oath —mea culpa, mea maxima culpa!—that I neither knew nor had spoken anything contrary to the dignity of his late Grace, King Edward?"

"Yes."

With an oddly touching little gesture, the Bishop stretched out both hands towards the Duke.

"Your Grace, I was lying."

"All men are liars," said Duke Richard inexpressively. "What did you know or do against my brother, God rest him?"

"This: that the marriage between our Lord and master King Edward and the woman Elizabeth Grey, calling herself Queen Elizabeth of England, was no marriage, and that the children born of it are bastards begotten in adultery."

"What?"

Anne heard herself almost shriek the word. It was as though gunpowder had exploded around her heart. She felt an atrocious pain in her hand where she had banged it down on the carved arm of the chair. The room was tilting like the cabin of a ship all round her and there was a thin devilish humming in her ears. Richard was on his feet. She saw his face as a blob of whitewash above the black of his clothes. The Bishop's voice, big and sure now, rode in over the private clamour of her surprise.

"It is true, your Grace. I denied like Peter, and may I be forgiven like Peter, but it is true. I swear this to you on my priesthood. The marriage was bigamous, if indeed there ever was a marriage, for there were no witnesses. But a hundred witnesses could not have made Elizabeth Grey the wife of Edward of England."

"Why?"

"Because, your Grace, two years before he ever set eyes

on the Widow Elizabeth I myself solemnly betrothed your brother to the Lady Elenor Butler, daughter of the old Earl of Shrewsbury."

Richard had his back to both of them now. His voice was his own again : soft and explaining none of his feelings.

"I knew that my brother dishonoured Lady Elenor. Lord Sudeley married her afterwards out of charity. There was a child."

"The child is dead." The Bishop's words seemed to be coming from a distance. "So is she. So is her husband. They are all in God's hands now; but she was not dishonoured. I hallowed her conjunction with your brother by all proper rites. While she lived, she was his only wife to God, if she was never his Queen. Afterwards, Lord have mercy upon me, a sinner, I was silent because he commanded me. I was afraid : and she herself would never bear witness against him, poor Lady. She loved him. Lord Sudeley himself never knew she was an honest woman."

"Who knows it now?"

"I do, your Grace, and I believe the woman who has been called Queen knows. There were no witnesses at that betrothal either. I consented to it, because your brother swore that he would make it known in time and crown the Lady Elenor in the sight of England. God forgive him, and me."

"You say that Queen Elizabeth herself knows this : that her children are bastards?"

"Your brother, God have pity on his soul, when I protested—oh, I did that much of my duty, your Grace—when I protested in the name of God against this pretended second marriage : he told me he had warned her. He said she would rather be a Queen and his concubine than an honest woman and a plain widow; and he told me that if I ever spoke of the matter to one living soul he would cut my tongue out of my mouth."

There was a quick scuffle of Duke Richard's feet as he whipped round and stooped over the Bishop's chair like a stooping hawk. The Bishop shrank back on himself and half lifted an arm as though he meant instinctively to hide his face behind it.

"Bishop Stillington, why was my brother George killed?"

"Your Grace, your Grace, I could not have saved him.

Stand away from me, your Grace. I'm an old man. He had found it all out for himself; knew it already. I implored him to say nothing. For the mercy of God, your Grace, don't look at me like that. I swear to you he found it all without me, the Saints know how. I've sinned, I know I've sinned, but I'm doing what I can to make restitution. Oh, take your eyes off me. Take your eyes off me."

"Dickon!"

Anne had his arm and was pulling at it. The Bishop was moaning and whimpering like a child with night-fears.

"Christ!"

It was Richard's voice, but raised for the first time that she had ever heard it raised: a shout going up to the rafters. He was off down the room, tearing his arm out of her hand; got to the wall and came back again. She saw, as though she were poring over the delicate complications of an initial in a manuscript, that there was blood on his lower lip where he had bitten. If he had shouted again she could have borne it; but he had come back to himself.

"I beg your pardon, my Lord. I have distressed you. It was not meant."

"Your Grace, I begged him to do nothing rash. I went on my knees."

"I do not blame you in any way, my Lord."

"I swear I——"

"I do not blame you. My Lord, swear this. Do you believe that my brother George of Clarence was put to death, with my brother the King's consent, because he knew this secret?"

Bishop Stillington got his gold cross in his hand. It slipped between his fingers, which were jumping like mice, and he grabbed after it; brought it to his lips as he stood up.

"As I believe that our Lord God died on this cross to save me, I believe that the most noble prince, George of Clarence, on whose soul, Jesus, mercy, was condemned and killed because he could have told the world that the marriage of King Edward and the Widow Elizabeth was a false marriage: so help me God and his hallows."

"I believe you."

Duke Richard crossed himself: began to speak under his breath. The Bishop stared at him for a second; then, as though remembering what he was, prayed too. Anne knew that she was crying because she could feel the wet on her cheeks. Her mind formed words that did not get as far as her mouth. Blessed Mary, Mother of God, intercede with your Son for them: Edward and George. Let him have mercy on their foolishness and forgive them their sins. They were very wicked men, but they did not mean it all: and let him have mercy on Richard my husband and help him out of this trouble, amen.

Twilight had got into the room. The high, fretted, roof-beams were almost out of sight, and the leaded window-panes were blue. It was the Bishop who spoke first, gently and gravely, as though for the moment it were he who commanded the business.

"Your Grace realises fully what this brings about?"

Duke Richard sat in his chair again.

"I realise that my nephew, Edward of Westminster, cannot be crowned King."

Thank God, thought Anne. Thank God. He will take it as he must take it. He will see it as work to be done, not as a betrayal of his big brother. She listened for what he would say next.

"The child of that unhappy Lady who should have been Queen Elenor of England is dead: so that the heir of the Plantagenets of York is my other nephew, Edward Earl of Warwick, son of my brother George."

"Oh, God, no!" Anne called out. He's never going to let it slip from him now, she thought: now, after it's come so near.

"Attainted, your Grace: the children of Duke George are attainted in blood."

"Yes and you know best with how much justice they were attainted. Parliament passed the attainder. Parliament can annul it; and shall. Make your market for that. If I have any authority in this realm, my brother George shall be cleared of what those cruel devils blackened him with. As for themselves: I needed Anthony Wydvylle as a hostage before. I do not need him now. Remember him in your prayers, my Lord."

"Your Grace, I will speak and will not be silent."

"Well then, speak. You've brought me good news so far. I shall listen cordially to you, my Lord Bishop. You've told me my brother Edward was—there's no name for what he was—but you've told me I can save England from being ruled by his son. That's much. What have you to say, now?"

"George of Clarence's son cannot be King of England. Only Parliament can release him from the ban Parliament put on him; and Parliament can only be summoned by a King. Your Grace, you are a better christian than I am. I, a Bishop of God's Church, say that. You have the blessing of humility, as I, who hoped I had always gone humbly in the sight of God, have not. But I am a man of law as well as a priest, and I tell you that I have burned my wick down to the oil these last nights weighing the law of this question : and I have a plain answer."

"Then what is this plain answer?"

"The true King of England and France, descended without any defiling in law from King Harry II, is Richard Plantagenet of Gloucester. We have no other King in England. The laws allow us no other King : and I, who speak for many of us, say that we want no other King. When will it please your Royal Grace to declare yourself and be crowned?"

"You speak for many of you?"

If a whip talked, thought Anne, it would talk like that. Oh, Richard, Richard, take it. Don't ride your high horse now. The Bishop was brave again. Anne had to remind herself that he had been wincing and crying out in his chair not long ago.

"Yes, your Grace, I foresaw your scruples, which do credit to a christian prince but harm to this kingdom. I guarded against them. It was my duty, your Grace. I have let terrible sins be done because I kept silence. Before I came here I told the most trustworthy noblemen I could find that you were King."

"Who were they?"

"The Lords Lovel and Howard, the Duke of Buckingham."

In the increasing dark, holding the chair-arms with both hands, Anne heard her husband's dagger click and click in its sheath. Eventually he said :

"My Lord, I shall ask you a question of theology."

"Theology, your Grace?"

371

"Can there be true repentance without restitution?"

"No."

"And without repentance we are not saved?"

"No, we are not. That is certain."

"Even in Purgatory, as souls, after we are dead?"

"Your Grace, I don't understand : and the question's too deep for me. How can a soul make restitution from Purgatory? It can repent, but . . ."

"If restitution were made for it, for its express benefit, on earth?"

"God's mercy is infinite. Whatever is done on earth with a sincere intention will be so received by him, or why do we offer the sacrifice for the dead as well as for the living?"

There was a long emptiness, no one moving. Then Duke Richard got on his feet again. He dragged the back of one hand over his forehead very slowly, as though he were tired out.

"Anne."

She was beside him at once, close to him, getting her fingers round his that were as cold as iron and as dead as his voice when he told her :

"Anne, you know what I must do."

"I know what you've said to me twice, Dickon. You'll let nothing stand between you and what ought to be done."

She pressed herself against him hard; got her arms round him. I can warm him; with my body and heart warm him; can make him remember that the work's happiness as well as duty. It was from her arms that he spoke to the Bishop, saying flatly and formally :

"My Lord, we your King command you, on your allegiance, to tell no one of our right and title to the crown until the time when we shall require you to declare it publicly to our subjects."

But it is mortal sin, Jane Shore repeated to herself over and over. It is mortal sin. We could be hanged and damned for it. When I tell it in confession, the priest will look white and cross himself, and if I die before I've confessed it, I shall be in hell.

The cellar would have been a place of smells and shadows even by daytime. Now, at midnight, with the brazier glowing inside the triangle and circle that had been traced with ashes on the dirt of the floor, it choked her. Even in her fright, it was odd to her that Queen Elizabeth of England, who had walked for so long on Byzantine carpets spread over dried flowers, should be here to-night in a filthy kennel of Broad Sanctuary, trysting with a dubious Friar and her late husband's mistress to ask help from the Devil.

But it is all needless, thought Jane : a crime we don't need to be guilty of. Will Hastings has given me his promise and will keep it. That's more of a weapon against Duke Richard than any secret wickedness in a cellar. She remembered his unhappy face with greying hair round it and his final assurance.

"I'll do it for you, Jane. I can't help myself. But I hate the business."

"Will you even kill him if nothing else works?"

"God help me. If there's no other means to make him release Lord Anthony and accept a Council of Regency I'll do that."

They had it well planned : William Catesby, Lord Hastings' intimate friend, to be a spy on the Protector; Dr. Morton, Bishop of Ely, to forge them legal arguments against the Protectorship; Writs of Supersedeas to be sent down to all the shires in the Queen's name so that no Parliament should meet to approve Duke Richard's title. It was all smooth and sound; held water. They did not need the Devil. It was the Queen who brought him into it. Jane looked sideways at her, trembling a little. She was dressed in black with a black hood. A little tent of flame grew up suddenly over the mottled charcoal in the brazier; lighted her long neck, the forward thrust of the small jaw and the pursed, painted lips. Her face had altered since King Edward died; taken on purpose. Under the careful fard the muscles round mouth and nostrils were stiff with decision, and the green eyes were hard as pebbles. It was as though a goose had turned into a cockatrice.

The tent of flame broke up and the light shrank again. The stink of rats and ordure in the cellar fought with the thin sourness of the burning charcoal. Nothing was audible from the road above their heads, and nothing they did down here would be heard in the world. If the darkness were to thicken into some abominable shape, if the flames sprang up again to cast suddenly on the wall a shadow with curving horns and wings, no one would hear her screaming. She was alone with the Queen and her set hatred, and the Queen's necromancer, and with whatever company these summoned.

There was the sound of a door being bolted and Friar Bungay walked out of the shadows beyond the brazier. His swollen body was draped in a white alb and a chasuble of smoky red embroidered in black with Hebrew letters. There was a tall parchment mitre painted with a five-rayed star on his head, and he had a drawn sword in his hand. He looked ridiculous and terrible. His face shone greasily, like a great larded copper pan in front of a fire.

"It is time now," he said with a kind of sickening casualness, as though he were talking about an appointment or a journey. Something like a round hard ball was rising in Jane's throat. Her kneecaps were jerking. Oh Edward, Edward, why did you die and leave me and the Queen to this? Why aren't you alive now and we safe, with no need to dabble in abominations and put our souls in danger : or why didn't you kill Richard when you killed George, instead of leaving us to call in the Devil against him? She tried to speak, but her throat clicked twice before she got the words out :

"Your Grace, must we—must we go on?"

Queen Elizabeth looked full at her. The poise of the head on the long throat, that was looking skinny in spite of daily washings with milk, was viperine.

"We are going on."

"You have nothing you need be afraid of, Madame." Friar Bungay's voice was that of a midwife heartening a frightened mother. "The spirits will not come visibly; but they will hear us. Remember this is white magic. We control them with holy things and names. Only for your life you must not step outside the circle."

He picked up a holy-water stoup and aspergillum from a litter of small things near his feet; sprinkled drops rapidly, talking under his breath; threw something onto the brazier. A blue flame whisked up and disappeared again and an atrocious smell invaded the air.

"Now," he said happily.

The round ball was rising in Jane's throat again. She

could feel sweat streaking the paint on her face. The inside of her body was one hollow in which her heart went backward and forward like a pendulum. Friar Bungay held the sword straight upright, reflected fire veining its blade. His fat, squelching voice became suddenly brazen; blared like a bell.

"Adonai, Eloim, Jehova, Sadai, Ariel, Sabaoth, very God who commandest all spirits, who hast given power also unto the demons, and that for vengeance, of thy grace be favourable to our enterprise. Elh roceban hor agle goth ioth venoch aubruth. By the terror of thy names be the spirits of air obedient to us. Amen, amen, sela. Per aquam consecratam, signum crucis, gladium conterentem, in nomine magno exaltato valde Jehovae, Adonai, Eloim, adeste principes tenebrarum regni. Adeste, adeste! Io, io, io! I straitly adjure you, foul spirits, wicked angels, stirrers up of murder, authors of incest, masters of sacrilege, teachers of heresy, begetters of all uncleanliness, in his name that cast you out of heaven, to be obedient to me. Come, you wicked ones. Come, you powerful infamous ones, whether out of the air or out of the fire, out of the water or out of the earth. Come to me, by the power of the names of him in whom you believe with tremblings. Agla, tagla, mathon, oarios, almozin, arios."

The blare of gibberish ceased, leaving a faint after-echo to creep like a worm round the stone walls. The sword-blade swung down into the fumes of the brazier, and the gross red-and-white figure turned slowly and ludicrously on its own axis, directing the point to the three corners of the triangle they stood in. The left hand scrabbled the air with crosses and the lips moved in a wet whisper. Jane's skin was twitching on her flesh like a horse's. He had called them. They would certainly come, stirrers up of murder, begetters of all uncleanness. He had said they would not see them : but if they did? Or would it be a worse, a subtler danger, if they did not? Devils could take innumerable shapes. They could show themselves as cats, bears, goats, men riding on horses. They could crawl as pieces of blackness, like huge slugs, or float in the air as a dark cloud. Bodiless, they could make themselves what bodies they pleased; could appear to poor people as gentlemen with full purses, tempting them to ask alms of hell; could hide even

375

in the carvings of church-walls listening for women to tattle during Mass or penitents to make a bad confession. At every deathbed they were secretly present, jumping and grinning like dogs watching a supper-table. Hell washed like an unlimited sea around the thin walls of men's lives : one crack, and it was in. Here, with smoke and shapeless words they were busy as though with crowbars, prizing apart the frail stones of their own safety, opening a gap for the flood to come crashing in on them. Soon it would come, the tumble of waves of damnation, the utterly hostile, bitter and destructive element in which the soul no longer breathed, in which the familiar handholds of ordinary life and wickedness floated out of reach, leaving them to gasp helplessly, and drink present and eternal death, and drown. The Friar's voice was blaring again :

"Messias, Soter, Emanuel, Sabaoth : by these terrible names I summon you, rebellious and contumacious spirits, powerful princes of sin. Why will you tarry? Why will you disobey? Make haste to the summons, by sword and cross and holy water and by the power I have over you. Parinosco, estio, dumogon, davocon, casmiel !"

With a quick, toad-like squat he dropped to his haunches and snatched up something from a cloth at his feet; heaved upright again brandishing it as though threatening invisible people. A jagged thrust of nausea transpierced Jane's body. The thing was a rotten human hand, brownish, with a white end of wristbone showing. She could smell it. Sweat was tracking down the Friar's broad, Neronian face in streams. His voice loudened enormously; became frenetic.

"I have power, I have power, I have power ! See, you rebellious ones. See, you hostile ones. With his hand, with this sword, with power that is in me, with the awful names, Sadai, Ariel, Eloim, I compel you. I prevail over you. See the hands that bind you. Tremble at the names that command you. Sint mihi patifactae portae regni tenebrarum. Io, io, io ! Satana, princeps aëris, Lucifer, signifer infernorum, Asmode, negotium perambulans in tenebris, Belzebuth, Belphegor, Barabam, Astarot, Azriel, Belial, adeste in subito. Adeste, adeste, adeste !"

A scream struggled up into Jane's mouth and died there. The darkness seemed to be bulging in over the brazier like a blown curtain. The air had turned to sand; could not be breathed. She imagined rustlings of leathery wings, scrape and scratch of feet, sniggers of infernal laughter. In a moment the curtain of the dark would break and the composite and distorted forms of hell jump through it : bird-faced and snake-tailed monsters with goats' loins, abortions whose bellies and rumps and knees were grinning faces, claw-footed creatures with wings of bats and heads of owls. Friar Bungay, in the apex of the triangle, had turned round on them. His swollen chest heaved with his breathing. He said, panting, in his normal voice :

"They are here. Give it me quickly."

Queen Elizabeth stooped, a black night-bird dropping down on a victim; scrabbled among the cloth-wrapped things on the floor. Was it a child she had in her hands? Jane thought. Oh Jesus, it must not be a child. It was a dummy of wax, child-size, a Ducal coronet on its head.

The Queen lifted it on her two palms. Her head was thrown back, her mouth open. Her eyes reflected the glimmer of charcoal like lumps of glass.

"This is Duke Richard of Gloucester, ordained to be consumed at the instance of Elizabeth, the Queen of England."

The thing was thrust at her. She stayed rigid. Feeling and life had gone and she was only a shell of fear. They were there, listening, watching her. Devils were looking at her. Clawed hands and mouths full of long teeth were open, just on the other side of the dark, gaping and ready.

"Take it, you fool!" the Queen's voice stung her. "Say the words."

The wax was frighteningly cold against her fingers.

"This . . . Duke Richard, ordained to be consumed . . . the Queen of England."

Her palate was dead in her mouth. Large, wet hands snatched the puppet away. Through the swirl and confusion of her fright she could hear Friar Bungay's voice again :

"Great princes of hell, monarchs of all evil, destroyers and corrupters of man's body, as I pierce this image with the sword, let him be pierced. As this image melts and withers away so that there remains nothing, let him melt, let him pine, let him be undone. Let the skin part from the flesh and the flesh from the sinews and the sinews from the bones and the bones from the marrow. As this image dwindles and is consumed, let him fall, let him be struck

377

down, let him consume utterly away. Swift and sure death come upon him. Instant destruction lie in wait for him. Blasting and blindness without light overtake him. In the eyes and in the breath, in the heart and in the head, in the belly and in the breast, let him be smitten, let him be consumed, let him perish utterly."

The Queen's voice, shrill as a boy's singing, chanted back to him:

> "Let him lie in his bed, let him lie there sick
>   and sore.
> Let him lie in his bed, let him never rise up
>   more."

His full bellow confirmed her.

> "He shall lie in his bed, he shall lie there sick
>   and sore.
> He shall lie in his bed, he shall rise up never-
>   more."

The image of Duke Richard, spitted upon the Friar's sword, was melting. Great drops like tears ran down the face. One side crumbled suddenly, so that the figure appeared crooked and monstrous. The Ducal coronet withered from the head. The features grew blurred, unrecognisable. The brazier, fed with molten wax, flared suddenly. A great gout of yellowish fire roared out of it; wrapped gustily round the tormented image; sprang up from it, lightening the whole cellar, and mushroomed out under the low ceiling in a spread of smoke. With a tiny sound, the flaring core of wax dropped from the sword-point onto the charcoal and disappeared instantly. An intolerable stink filled the whole place.

She did not clearly remember how they got her out of the cellar; was not in her full wits until she was sitting on a dirty bed in one of the rooms of the place, choking over a glass of German cordial with the Queen's hard, green eyes on her. Friar Bungay, taking no notice of her, was mopping his broad face and talking.

"It will do what is needed. Have no fear for that, your Grace, no fear at all. The charm of the wax puppet is infallible, absolute. To be all the safer, I'll tell the Office of the Dead for him to-morrow. Said for a living man, it kills like a lance. Or has your Grace heard the Mass of St. Cæsarius? That's sure and good. We shall have no need of my Lord Hastings and his men-at-arms : indeed no. More powerful helpers are taking our part."

Oh God, thought Jane, shuddering from the sting of the cordial, nothing can ever help us now. We have destroyed ourselves. We've done the sin against the Holy Ghost that Christ won't pardon. Devils we called and we can never send them away. They are all round us; will go with us when we got out of this place; will slide down the street beside us and pluck at our skirts. They'll be always with us. Oh God, oh Jesus, oh bright Mary, why did we do it? Why did we do it at all? We've destroyed ourselves. We can't prosper now.

One of the bars of the small window halved the sun's dropping disc exactly; split it in two segments the colour of red-hot iron. Lord Anthony changed his position a little to see past it; wanted to fill his eye with the whole picture this time. Beneath him, from the footings of the Castle, Pontefract slid down steeply in a tumble of mottled roofs and wisps of smoke; spread out toward the green links of the Calder and the Aire : a pretty town.

Lord Anthony drew his hand curiously round his neck, inside his collar. Sunset : it was queer to think, a little hard to believe, that before the hurrying sun had come back to the place where it stood now, the axe would have gone through where his hand stroked; his brain, the best of all his possessions, would not belong to him any more; would have been separated from his body, blinded and deafened, left with no voice or hands to carry its schemes out. Before sunset to-morrow he would be in Purgatory. It would be a long penance : many hundreds or thousands of years. Thou shalt not murder : Holy Harry, with his mouth open in a silent shriek, dead in the Wakefield Tower, blood on him. Thou shalt not commit adultery : women, so many of them, in such soft beds—easy game, not worth the expiation they would cost. Thou shalt not bear false witness : George of Clarence, blue-faced with poison, his life lied away. Thou shalt not envy. He had envied many men, but not for himself alone; for his family too, for the house of

Wydvylle. Perhaps that would be taken into account. His own neck was warm and firm under his hand. He fingered the muscles; probed to find the hardness of bone at the nape; stroked the big veins. All those the axe would have to go through : at one cut, please God, a clean finish. They would leave him to the last, and he would watch and say prayers whilst Sir Richard Grey and Vaughan and Hawte were made an end of. The axe would be blunted when it came to his turn; but if it cut the bone at the first stroke it would be enough. Two days ago, after he had been moved from Middleham to Sheriffhutton, they had condemned him. The shifty-eyed Percy of Northumberland was his judge, mumbling the sentence as though it were an apology, and then Richard Ratcliffe had brought him here, to the four-towered Castle springing from live rock where Richard of Bordeaux had been murdered by Henry Bolingbroke a lifetime ago. It was his sister, Elizabeth the silly Queen, who had brought the end on him. Poor fool, he thought, she will be like my body without my head when I am gone. Her feeble plot had hardly been formed before it was quelled. Ratcliffe, kind to him after a gruff fashion, told him the news : how the Lord Protector, sitting at Council in the White Tower, had suddenly ordered the arrest of Lord Hastings and the Bishop of Ely; had played the comedy of Northampton over again, telling the appalled conspirators to their white faces just what they had done and what they had planned to do : witchcraft in cellars, Writ of Supersedeas to forestall Parliament, murder if need be. Lord Anthony could see and hear him doing it, with his expressionless corpse-face and his small voice. Lord Hastings, the dark-eyed, affectionate man who had hated the Wydvylles when it would have paid him to love them and embraced them when it was too late to help them or himself, did not last even as long as he had. They kept him in the Tower a week; tried him after a fashion; headed him early one morning on a convenient log of timber on Tower Green. William Catesby, his most trusted follower, had been the one to betray him and the whole design. Trust no one, thought Lord Anthony. I learned that too late in the day. We fall by our friends. Buckingham or Catesby : there was never a plot that someone wouldn't sell. Jane Shore had been turned over to the Bishop of London to deal with as a common trollop. Learned Thomas Kemp was not one to let his eye spare an adulteress, but she was lucky for all that; better a public penance with a taper in her hand and her feet bare than the death that was assigned to witches. Queen Elizabeth had been forced to render her younger son up out of Sanctuary. The house of Wydvylle was shattered as though a mine of powder were sprung under it.

Too many blows dulled the mind so that the greatest shock made the least tumult. Now that everything was strange and fading, in this last stopping-place before death, Lord Anthony found he took the wildest news of all without any amazement; might have expected it. Blind man I was, he thought, with my eyes in the ends of the earth and not in my head. We were not as cunning as we supposed when we brought Edward to the altar at Grafton Regis. Married already: I should have guessed it. The Wydvylles have not profited so very much by their marriages, after all. Pitiful to think of Elizabeth plotting so gaily against Richard, of all men, when he had that in his sleeve to crush her with: poor silly woman, she should have told me the truth, and I would have warned her not to draw a dagger on a man who had a sword at her throat. She has killed me now, and perhaps the children. Bastards or not bastards, if Richard wants a quiet throne he'll make an end of them. Richard of England and France, third of that name since the Conquest: that is what the grave is called into which all the pride and devices of the house of Wydvylle go down and are buried. Richard of Gloucester, Richard of England, both unlucky titles: Richard Lionheart spent his best years in prison and died of an arrow. Richard of Bordeaux was starved to death somewhere in this place. He starts with the stars against him; would be best to run no hazards.

The sun's lower curve rested as though balanced on a shoal of slate-blue clouds. With a sudden scatter of cries, a flight of rooks began to drift over the town toward the Castle. Lord Anthony leaned his shoulder against the embrasure of the window and continued to look out. The axe to-morrow: not another sunset, even through bars, not another flight of rooks, no more sight or sound. He would not ride a horse again, or drink wine out of a gold cup, or run his long, possessive fingers over the surface of his moss-agate vase. He had loved beauty, and would be blind. That did not matter. Beauty was everlasting. In Italy, after he was gone, men would still carve and paint and build most wonderful things. In London, Mr. Caxton's creaking engine would still stamp wisdom on paper. French cathedrals would sound still with the golden music of Ockeghem. A hundred years hence his own poems, his translations of Christine de Pisan and the old philosophers, might still be read. Beauty was for eternity, and in the eternity he was bound for it became perfection. It was not that loss that grieved him as he rested himself on the cold stone and saw the clouds crawl slowly and unrecallably up the face of the sun. It was the work to which he had given the best of himself that would go down forever; would die when he died. The house of Wydvylle that had grown like a cedar from his father's and his brother's graves would be cut down to make his coffin. So many schemes and sins, such plotting in corners, such clever reading of men's hearts was wasted. He had ridden his high horse and seen the blood of his enemies: the King's kinsman, Anthony Earl Rivers, Baron Scales and Nucelles, Chief Butler of England : and in a moment of time, from the least dreamed-of quarter, Fate had broken all of it into nothing; had shown him fragility where he depended on strength, hatred where he was sure of loyalty, as though the cup in his hand turned suddenly into a rotten skull or his own dagger leapt out of its sheath to stab him.

So much, such single-hearted labour instantly wasted : Fate was too clever; only gave to take away. The fool lifted up his voice and wearied God with his indignation when he found worms in the fruit he had climbed high to pick. The wise man recognised destiny and covered his mouth. But it was sad that a whole life with which he could have done so much should have been poured, down to the last drops of cunning and courage, into the sieve of the Danaïds : all given, all offered from a free heart, all wasted. A man could not be blamed for regretting that a little. Lines of poetry came into his mind : a ballad he had begun composing on the cold ride, leg-bound, from Sheriffhutton, unfinished yet. The cadence pleased him; seemed to chime with the cawing of the rooks whose last stragglers were passing now over his head.

Somewhat musing
And more mourning
In remembering
Th' unsteadfastness,
This world being
Of such wheeling,
Me contrarying,
What may I guess?

Guess nothing more now. The world wheels too quickly for us, and it is by the world and not our own feebleness that we are vanquished. It turns and slides us off, tilting us out of the light into confusion, and nothing that we do can steady it in the end. Guess nothing more. The time for guessing is over. Time is. Time was. You guessed cleverly then. But time shall be no more. That is not your fault.

Lo, in this trance,
Now in substance,
Such is my dance :
Willing to die . . .

And this is true : as well now as twenty years from now, so that we die by fortune, with which no man can quarrel, not by our own fault. The axe is nothing. The mercy of God is very great. It is no shame to die of a blow in the dark : and the mere act and mechanism is easy: the gabbling chaplain, pikemen staring with their mouths open, the rough fellow in the black frieze jerkin dropping down on one knee to ask pardon for what he is to do. There is nothing to be afraid of there.

Willing to die,
Methinks, truly,
Bounden am I,
And that greatly,
To be content,
Seeing plainly . . .

How did it go now, the reason, the resolution of the discord : the why and wherefore of dying without anger or resentment or the knowledge of failure? Why was defeat not defeat?

> Seeing plainly
> Fortune doth wry
> All contrary
> From mine intent.

The edge of cloud was half-way up the sun now. Behind him the stone room began to swim with shadows. Content, content, content : his mind said the word almost aloud. To be content, having lost the game only by fortune, by no folly or feebleness on one's own part : it had been played hard and well. Richard was not the winner, but destiny, the mistress of booby-traps, the eternal inventress of odd surprises. He might lose to her himself one day; and if he did not lose, if he lived forty years as King of England, it would not matter. What mattered was that Anthony, Earl Rivers, was not the villain of his own tragedy; died having climbed high enough to make fortune jealous. It was no hardship to see one's work smashed in a storm and to be killed in the ruins. Only to know it had fallen through one's own heedlessness, for want of care one could have given it, was the pain of loss. He escaped that.

Suddenly, with a single decisive movement like that of a raindrop falling from a leaf, a quatrain added itself to the poem in his mind.

> My life was lent
> Me to one intent.
> It is nigh spent—
> Welcome, Fortune.

He had not failed that intent whilst he was alive; had earned his epitaph. He repeated it, leaning his cheek against the stone and watching the steady and continual accession of the night.

"My Lords, temporal and spiritual, and you, the commons of my realm, and you especially, my Lord Chief Justice and all the Justices, Barons and Serjeants of the law; you have now heard me, in this place which is called Court of King's Bench, take the oath administered by old custom to the Kings of England when they begin to rule, that I will be a good and gracious Lord to my realm of England : and it may be that you have wondered why I should choose to make an oration to you here and not to go at once to St. Edward's Shrine, as the usage is.

"I shall make this plain to you.

"My Lords and commons, and you my Lord Chief Justice and your brother-judges, you know what is my title to the crown. That has been rehearsed to you, and because you found it good you came to me yesterday at my mother's Palace of Baynard's Castle and by the mouth of my cousin of Buckingham you petitioned me to be King. I need not recall to you the tenor of your own words. My brother's children are adjudged bastards by sentence of Holy Church. We leave them there. But before you spoke of any such matter, you alleged another on which I must dwell with you for a moment. You spoke of a time when the Kings, my progenitors, feared God and were zealous for the indifferent administration of justice. Then, you said, the land was at peace, the malice of enemies was resisted, the intercourse of merchants was largely used and poor people labouring for their living were spared any miserable or intolerable poverty. You told me next of a later time when insolent, vicious and avaricious persons turned your felicity into misery and confounded the order of policy and the laws of God and man, so that no man could be sure of his life, and or livelihood, or of his wife or daughter. All these things you urged to me as reasons why I should be your King.

"My Lords, commons and Justices, as touching kingship, I have stood near to a throne all my life. I am not one of those of whom it is said in Holy Writ that they come out of prison to be crowned.

"To men who are subjects, there appears nothing happier than to be a King. My Lords and Commons, I wish to make no longer oration to you : but be sure of this : that if I had much regard for my own happiness I should not sit in this seat.

"This seat, the King's Bench, has been from of old a seat of judgment; and the kings of England are accustomed to begin their rule here because a King is also a judge. Learned grammarians say that in Latin a King takes his name from *regere*, signifying *rule*, so that he has the name but not the substance of kingship who is crowned but does not rule indifferently according to the law. My Lords and commons,

385

and you most particularly, my Lord Chief Justice and your brethren, it is for this reason that I have chosen to speak to you sitting in this marble throne of the King's Bench. Indeed, it is for this reason that I am willing to speak to you in any place as your King.

"This is the place of law; and the law is above all of us, for it is the whole marrow of the old liberties of this land to say : The King is not above the law, but the law above the King. Therefore, for all these distresses of which you have complained to me, there is a remedy in the law administered without fear or prejudice or affection and now I speak to you, my Lord Chief Justice Hussey, to you Judges of the King's Bench and the Common Pleas, Barons and Judges of the Exchequer, Mr. Attorney-General Kidwelly, and all you men of law, straitly willing and commanding you justly and duly to administer my law without delay or favour. My law, the old law of England, is for all men. It is the refuge of the broken and the strong castle that the righteous run to and are safe. See you to it that that castle is guarded and not betrayed. As to you, my Lords temporal, see the countries where you dwell well guided, and that no extortions are done upon my subjects down to the very least of them. Do this, my Lords and Judges, and fear nothing, for the whole might of England is on the side of justice now. Rather than that you should see a leper or an Irishman oppressed in my realm, and want power to help him, I will send you a thousand men-at-arms to protect you in doing justice.

"Have a particular care that no money be wrung from my subjects by unlawful means, even though it were in my own name. I remember how the commons of this realm have been put to great exactions by a new imposition called a benevolence, which forced them against their freedom to pay large sums of money to their almost utter destruction. It is my wish that at the next Parliament this device of a benevolence shall be damned and annulled forever.

"Yeomen, call for silence at the end of the hall there. I will have no cheering.

"You judges and Lords, your business, I tell you again and with all the oratory at my command, is to do justice to all men. Let me not hear that officers of the courts have seized on the goods of accused men before they have been found guilty by law, as has been done lately to my knowledge. Let the Justices of my Peace not be too hardly induced to grant bail or mainprise to such as are accused, for by our law no one is criminous until twelve men of his own shire have found him so : and now I come to speak of these twelve men. See you to it that they, whose oaths can free a wrongdoer or bring an innocent christian to the ladder, are always men of good name and fame, not things of straw to be bought by some Lord to protect a scoundrel or hurt an honest man. That is another charge I lay on you.

"Now I am coming to the end of what I am to say. I am not eloquent and would have been glad to say less than I have done. My Lords, commons and Judges, you know that since the death of my dear brother, to whom Almighty God grant peace and perpetual light, amen, I have put five noble persons of this realm to death; and of this I shall not attempt to make any concealment. Lord Rivers, Sir Richard Grey, Sir Richard Hawte and Sir Thomas Vaughan died by the consent and agreement of the whole Council because they had attempted my destruction and to seize the person of my nephew who was then called King. As to Lord Hastings, I can only say this to you, that he intended my death, and that I wish I might have died before I found him, whom I always loved, a traitor. May God have mercy on his soul. These men died because they broke the law. Pray for their souls as I do : but remember that their sin was rebellion, which Holy Writ tells us is like the sin of necromancy. I have told you I will not suffer extortion. Neither will I suffer that devilish wickedness of civil war which has filled England with widows. I will stamp it out utterly. There is no nobleman in the realm who would not be better to starve than to arm Englishmen against Englishmen whilst I am King. If he were the dearest friend I have, I would not dine until I saw his head off.

"Silence at the end of the hall there : I am grateful for your cheers, but keep them till I have spoken. I have almost done.

"But if I condemn civil bloodshed, I must give you your example. It shall never be said of me that I taught others to exercise justice and good which I would not do myself.

"Those who were prime enemies of their own country I have punished already. Presently I shall call before you a man whom I have no reason to love, but whom I think powerless to hurt the state now, one Sir John Fogg. Those of you who best know him best know what he deserves : but I shall take him by the hand and pardon him in the sight of you all, as a sign that King Richard of England has forgotten the enemies of Duke Richard of Gloucester.

"When I have done that, we are to worship at the shrine of our great Saint and King, St. Edward the Confessor. Let us pray that by his intercession God may be pleased to grant each of us the virtues most requisite to his station : to you, my Lords temporal, courage and loyalty to put down forever this curse of armed faction, this sin of rebellion; to you, my Lords spiritual, zeal to see virtue and cleanness of living advanced and vices repressed; to you, Judges, conscience to administer my laws indifferently to all men, without delay; and to me, your King, grace by God's infinite mercy to rule well in England."

The reindeer stared at de Commynes, and de Commynes, not particularly impressed, stared back at the reindeer. It was really very much like any other kind of deer, he thought, except that it was longer and lower in the body and had finer antlers. He had just counted fifty-four points on the head in front of him, and that was certainly impressive. Whether it justified the Christian King in paying forty-five hundred German florins for a herd of six of the creatures was a question : but doubtless it was better for him to amuse his dying fantasy with jackels from Tunis and elks from Denmark and dogs from every inhabited quarter of the world than with his other pastime of making and breaking men simply to prove that he could still do it.

Those who did not know him thought he was mad now, crouching behind the spiked grilles and drawbridges of Plessis-les-Tours like an hysterical cat in a tree-top. He was not mad, de Commynes knew, only beyond words afraid : of his nobles who might restrtain him and take the guidance of affairs in their own hands; of his subjects who might break down the iron gates of his hermitage and murder him; of his neighbours and enemies who might drag France into the dirt again during his son's minority; above and beyond all, of an old servant of his who suddenly threatened to become his master, of death whose very name he had forbidden to be spoken in his hearing. Tormented with hæmorrhoids, drained white with dysentery, his body numbed and ruined by frequent strokes, King Louis of France was trying to buy life for himself as he bought peace for his kingdom : ten thousand écus a month to his physician, foul-mouthed Dr. Jacques Coictier, who bullied him like a schoolmaster, offerings to the value of above seven hundred thousand francs to all the saints in Christendom from St. John Lateran to the Three Kings of Cologne; even acts of mercy, for he had released Cardinal Balue, the traitor, from the iron cage in which he had been kept for fourteen years. All the world watched his long campaign against dying. Frederic of Aragon sent him, at his entreaty, a holy man from Calabria who had lived in a cave since he was twelve years old and ate neither flesh, fish nor butter. The Pope lent him relics of great sanctity. His fear still stalked through Plessis-les-Tours like a visible thing, breathing coldly on the necks of those who lived there. The place was like a frontier-fortress. From where he stood, de Commynes could see one of the guard-turrets of solid iron from which the Scots archers had orders to shoot without challenging whoever came within sight of the walls at night. The King received no one. The veritable Grand Turk, Sultan Bajazet himself, had sent an embassy offering a fortune in coin and all the relics in Byzantium if the Christian King would oblige him in a little matter. It was refused an audience. The King had seen his own son once in the past four years.

A heavy, impatient tread broke de Commynes' reflections. He looked round. Dr. Coictier, the most powerful man in the little iron-barred world of Plessis-les-Tours, was stumping toward him, head down, gown floating behind him, the very image of a surly tup looking to see who intruded on his pasture. He had the tup's yellow eye, too, perspicacious, quick, intolerant. He grunted a species of good-day and stood, his thumbs in his girdle, glaring at the reindeer. De Commynes almost expected him to tuck in his chin and charge it, head-to-head.

"How is he this morning?"

"How's who?"

"His Majesty."

"Him : he's well enough, well as he'll ever be. He won't

last long. All the holy relics in Christendom can't cure a man in his case. I've told him so but he won't listen."

"I don't doubt you have."

"Obstinate man, obstinate : I've no patience. If he'd take more notice of me and less of that damned mountebank he fetched out of Calabria he'd do better. But what's the use of talking? Any news from outside?"

"None that I know : I believe Monseigneur le Daim had a post this morning, but I've heard nothing."

"You never will from that fellow; keeps his mouth shut : wise man."

There was a silence. The reindeer, tired of their company, walked slowly away. Dr. Coictier, whose manners were not pretty, hawked and spat; then wiped his lips on his physician's gown. De Commynes said :

"I thought he seemed somewhat easier the last day or two."

The yellow eyes turned their glare on him.

"You did, did you? Well, my dear and learned fellow-physician, you'll be interested to hear that I, with my poor science, had formed the same opinion. He is easier; and if I could contrive to kill one of the reigning princes of Christendom every month or so I might keep him alive for quite a while yet."

"You mean the news of King Edward's death has cheered him? I thought that too. It's a strange grace God's given him to outlast all his enemies and neighbours : Charles the Hardy and his daughter, Galeazzo Sforza, John of Aragon. He's seen them all out, and I think he's conscious that that's a divine mercy to him."

"You've a little more sense than these other numskulls about here," Coictier told him in an almost friendly manner. "The poor devil would do better if he troubled himself less : worrying about how long he's going to last, worrying about how much Purgatory he's going to get when he is sent for, worrying about what'll come to France after he's gone. Sacrament of the altar, why doesn't the fool take things more quietly? He's only a man when all's said: plenty more like him. I've told you that I'm sick of it but he won't listen. I said to him to his face the other day, I said : You may be the King of France, Sire, but you're a troublesome old fool to all those who are trying to do you good. I've ordered you to keep your mind easy, and if you can't do as you're told I wash my hands of you. That made him think."

"By God, Coictier," said de Commynes, "you go a great deal too far. A man wouldn't use such outrageous language to his servant. You ought to be ashamed of yourself. There was a time when you'd sooner have bitten your tongue out than talk to the King like that. One of these days his Majesty will remember who he is and who you are, and you'll find yourself outside the gates with nothing but the clothes you stand up in : and you'll deserve it."

"Oh no, I shan't, my dear d'Argenton. Our good King Louis isn't as big a fool as all that. He knows very well that he won't live a week after he's dismissed me."

"Then I can only pray," said de Commynes, turning his back, "that the humiliations our master suffers from you will be accounted for him as an expiation of his sins."

Dr. Coictier chuckled.

It was very quiet in the enclosure of Plessis-les-Tours, in this last covert and retreat of the restless King. The servants went about their business avoiding noise. No traffic of the general world passed under the ramparts. Even the sentries of the Scots Guard walked their beats, cross-bows over their shoulders and long swords in their belts, like somnambulists. Their light eyes and freckled, unexpressive faces made them like creatures of another earth, clammy statues animated by the spells of the old dying necromancer whom they guarded. Plessis-les-Tours was on the edge of the sensual world, nearly over it; was a place where emissaries from the far side of the grave were almost to be looked for.

A small door near the Chapel opened; let out a figure in green velvet slashed with gold and silver which came toward them. De Commynes recognised a man he disliked as much as, and respected far less than, he did the Court Physician : Olivier le Daim, the tight-mouthed Flemish barber-surgeon whom France cursed under the name of Olivier le Diable. Whenever the Christian King threshed France with a flail for its own good, Olivier le Daim was there to filch a poke-full of grain for his private profit. He greeted them now with a species of familiar condescension; would be glad if they would come with him to the King.

"Why?" asked Dr. Coictier flatly.

"I have received some intelligence which I am afraid will disturb his Majesty."

"Then don't give it him."

Le Daim peeped sideways out of his cold, close-set eyes at de Commynes as if winking at such unstatesmanlike simplicity. De Commynes deliberately turned his head; would not share a joke with him.

"Alas, my very dear learned Dr. Coictier, I fear I must: affairs of policy."

"What are they?"

Le Daim pursed his lips. Discretion fumed from him like steam from the horse's flanks. Dr. Coictier looked him up and down as though he were a corpse on the dissecting-bench and said:

"Well, if you're dumb, don't ask me to cure you. You need a purge, by the way. Your eyeballs are discoloured and your breath stinks. That's your affair. I'm here to look after the King, not his understrappers. Let's go to him."

The Christian King spent much of his time in a little upper room near to the Chapel; a kind of antechamber to his bedroom. It was here that the country musicians he had assembled used to play at night to keep him from sleep. He had a great terror of sleep now; was afraid that one morning he would awake dumb or paralysed. They climbed the mean little winding stair, guarded by two motionless Scots, and knocked on the oak door and went in.

The ruins of the King who had dragged France back by main strength from the inferno of the Hundred Years' War were piled together in an armchair. King Louis's face was frightful. The skin appeared to rest directly on the bones. The nose was like a vulture's bill and the eyes, heavy and ensanguined like those of an old hound, were too big for the skull that held them. A double bonnet with ear-flaps was pulled down over the high head which de Commynes knew was totally bald. Like his father before him, the Christian King had taken to dress in his old age. His starved body was wrapped in a superb gown of crimson satin, coming down to the ankles and trimmed with martens. As always there was a dog at his feet. The sight of the animal pricked some vein in de Commynes' heart. It was a link with better times, a sign that it was still Louis of Valois, excoriated, moribund, but impregnably himself, who sat and fought day and night against death in the Château of Plessis-les-Tours. I knew him, he thought, in the flower of his age and in his great days, but I never saw him without cares. In nothing, not even the chase, has he had as much happiness as in his dogs. Women he's never meddled with in the time I've known him. Hunting gave him very nearly as much irritation as pleasure, he took so much trouble over it. When he has had war he wanted peace; and when he has had peace he could scarcely endure it. Who could ever say he has known happiness? I am sure that if all the easy days of his life could be reckoned up there'd be a good twenty of sweat and discontent to each of them. He has built up France, and torn Burgundy asunder like rotten sacking; has had its own will with the Bretons and the English and the Spaniards and the Catalans. Could one see a finer example of the littleness of man and of how short and evil this life is?

The huge, cunning and miserable eyes of the King were turned on them. Very slowly and painfully he lifted one dead hand in a kind of greeting and dropped it again onto the fur rug that covered his knees. His head trembled slightly on his neck. He did not speak. Olivier le Daim cleared his throat and made a bow.

"I have news to give you, Sire."

Still the King only used his eyes. His expression was childishly timid now. He did not want to hear anything. Dr. Coictier, lounging impudently against the back of a chair, shouted—he spoke habitually as though his patients were deaf:

"Much better not hear it, Sire, I've told you if you want to keep your soul in your body a bit longer you must not be plagued with things. Listen to your doctor and send this fellow in the short gown about his business."

The lead-grey, pendulous lips moved. A tiny whisper crawled over them.

"Let him speak."

"Much better not."

This is a King, thought de Commynes. This is what being a King amounts to in the end. Le Daim had deliberately placed himself in front of Coictier; said in a voice almost as loud as the physician's:

"The news is from England, Sire."

That worked. The faint tremor of the head stopped and a kind of brightness came into the eyes. The King's voice was still lamentably weak but it was fluent, a voice de Commynes recognised.

"England: we have to thank God for his guidance of the affairs of that country; to thank God and his blessed Mother, le Daim. England ruled by a child is not dangerous. A child can't come and twist money out of me as that Edward did. Tribute, he had the insolence to call it. Think of that, sirs. But God is very merciful to France. A child can't lead armies."

"Sire," said le Daim, "the news from England is very bad."

The King hunched his shoulders pitiably. He looked like a monkey expecting to be struck.

"Bad, bad? No, don't say that, le Daim: not bad news from England. I've prayed so much. God couldn't be cruel now. Don't say Edward's still alive, after all. We must have a child to rule England until my son's a man and can protect his France. We must."

"The news from England is that King Edward's children have been pronounced bastards by the Church. King Edward's successor is his brother, the Duke of Gloucester."

Good God, thought de Commynes, but this will kill him. A shiver and stiffening passed over the crimson-gowned body. King Louis' jaw fell and his thin hands shut slowly in his lap. He sat like an image of death, colourless, dead-eyed, dead-lipped. The clock on the wall noisily dissected time. With an oath, Coictier pushed past le Daim and grabbed for the King's wrist. The dog—it was a pied Italian greyhound—got up from its silk cushion and sniffed his knees. Le Daim's face, ugly, stolid and cunning, did not change. He watched like a man at a play. Coictier talked urgently, his tone less brutal than it had been.

"Compose yourself, now. Compose yourself. Don't listen to any more. I'll send them out. You should lie down for a while."

"Be quiet."

Again it was the King's natural voice, or at least its wraith. The King's chin was up and he was trying feebly to put Coictier's hand from his wrist.

"Now calmly, Sire: let them go. Lean back in your chair."

"Be quiet, man, and stand away from me."

"Belly of God, will you listen to me? I forbid you to talk. I, Jacques Coictier, forbid you."

"Le Daim, d'Argenton, listen."

"At least speak briefly."

"I will. I'll do as you tell me, Coictier. But I must say this. Listen. There is a boy in Brittany, a fugitive. My poor head's going. I can't remember names now. But they say he is the heir of the house of Lancaster. If this Duke of Gloucester prepares war on us, he might save everything. It's a trick I've played before. Tell my son. We must have peace in France. The wounds bleed still. I can hear them in my sleep, the dripping of blood; and widows crying: all because of the English. We must have peace. If this Duke opens the old quarrel, my work's undone. Do you understand?"

"Yes, Sire, and touching that I must tell you that this Duke or King has said openly that the treaty of Pécquigny was a bad bargain for England and that given time and means he will . . ."

Dr. Coictier flung himself on him. He caught him by the shoulders and drove him backward toward the door, shouting:

"Be quiet, you fool. Be quiet! Do you want him to have another stroke?"

Of course, he had a great deal to remember, because such a lot of important things had happened just now, so that it was really rather hard to keep them all in his head.

When he had been a very little boy it had been important that he was called the Earl of Salisbury and not just Ned. That was a long time ago, but he could remember it. Then it was important beginning Latin. Then it was very important being seven years old: and now the really important thing, much bigger than all the others, was being Prince of Wales. He had not been quite sure what it meant, to begin with, but now he had got it all laid out in his head. Dean Beverley helped him with some of it; but he really did most of it quite by himself, just by thinking.

When a person became Prince of Wales he was wakened

up late at night and a lot of people came into his room and knelt down and mumbled and called him Your Grace and My Lord Prince. Ned saw now that he had been stupid to look round the room for the Prince that they were talking about, when all the time it was him : but he explained to Dean Beverley afterward that he would not have done it only he was rather sleepy. That was the beginning of being Prince of Wales, and the rest was mostly hearing what Father was doing and getting used to people's calling him the King's Grace. Everybody in London—nice Lord Lovel and the Earl of Lincoln and all sorts of other people—had asked him would he be King of England because Uncle Edward's two boys had been bastards all the time only they hadn't told anybody; and he had sat in the King's Bench, which wasn't a bench at all but a chair made of marble, and said yes, he would be King if they wanted him.

All that part was quite easy, but when Father came home there were a lot more important things. They had to go to York and show themselves to people. "Our York," said Father, putting his arm round him. One of the nicest things about Father was that he was a sensible size and not so big that a boy of seven, or even nearly eight, couldn't see his face properly. "Our York," he said, "it's our own City where they love us." "Don't they love us everywhere?" Ned asked him. "I hope so, lad, and if they don't we have to make them." "How do you make people love you?" Father smiled his own particular smile. "Why, by being kind to them."

So they went to York, and the Mayor and his Aldermen met them, all wearing scarlet, and lots of other people in red and violet and blue; and when they got to Micklegate Bar there was a beautiful wooden tower painted in all the colours of the rainbow and hung with banners, and minstrels playing outside it, and the Three Holy Kings, Caspar, Melchior and Balthazar, looking out of a window with their crowns on. Caspar (they told him afterward that it was really the Rector of All Saints) made Father and Mother a long speech in Latin. He did not understand quite all of it, but when Caspar said "Gwalliae Princeps pernobilis" he knew it meant him and remembered to touch his bonnet and smile. At Ousbridge there were David and Goliath and a lot of angels. Goliath was very fierce and said : "Ha, sang Dieu !" to show he was French, and David killed him and then made a rhyming speech in English to say he was only small but had killed an enemy and now he welcomed King Richard who would do :

> "Such knightly deeds and fair as never this
>   world saw,
> Wherefore we all may say : God bless King
>   Richard, evermore."

After that there were St. Peter with his keys and St. Cuthbert and St. Adrian and St. Akelda—he was very glad she was there, because it would have pleased everybody at Middleham—and a choir dressed in white singing a hymn. The Mayor gave Father and Mother each a lovely gilt dish full of money. Father smiled and told them that he had refused money in all the towns he'd come through, but that he would refuse nothing in York and they might think the money well spent one day; but Mother only said : "God bless you," and looked as if she was going to cry : and then the queerest thing happened. Mr. Wrangwysh, who was a big man with a deep voice, really did cry and had to turn his face away and muddle about inside his scarlet robes for a kerchief. Ned could not understand that.

Of course, it all seemed very grand at the time; but that was a week ago, and now it really was not anything to compare with to-day and yesterday. Yesterday they went through the streets to see the Creed Play which was played specially for them. It was just like watching the whole Bible from beginning to end. There was God with a long beard on his throne and beautiful angels round him and a terrible Devil who was thrown down into hell and jumped and stamped about in the smoke there wagging his tail and shouting : "Out, haro, I roar !" Then there were Adam and Eve, quite bare until they put belts of leaves on, and Noah with his ship and Christ being crucified. That part was very terrible and Ned would have held Mother's hand if he had not remembered that he was Prince of Wales now. Christ was young and had a pale face, and Pilate and the soldiers made fun of him : but afterwards the stone was rolled away and there was nothing to be unhappy about.

So now the really important moment had come, after so many long prayers and so much singing and tickly smell of incense here in the Minster : and he did hope he would do everything properly.

He was kneeling down with his hands joined together in front of Father. Father stood there, with a great burst of coloured sunlight through the Minster windows spilling over him. He had an ermine tippet on his shoulders over a long scarlet gown, and his head seemed to be on fire with the reflections from all the gold and jewels of the great arched crown with crosses and fleur-de-lys that he wore : the crown of England. His face under it looked so pale and serious. He had a sword in his hand. Now it came up, the long, clean shine of the blade, and Father's mouth went tighter than Ned had ever seen it. Now it was coming down, very gently and quickly. He felt a pat on one shoulder, then on the other.

"Rise up, Sir Edward."

He was a knight now.

People came round him, Bishops mostly, and began to take off some of his clothes and put others on. He stood very still, because if he didn't do anything at all he couldn't do anything that was the wrong thing. They tickled rather, and were not as clever at undressing people as his own grooms. He wondered for an instant if they were going to strip him quite naked like Adam, but they only put a cloth-of-gold tabard and a belt on him instead of his gown, and then a coronet on his head. It was rather heavy. Now they were all kneeling down, one after the other, in front of him and muttering. He heard some of the words : "Acknowledge and repute you, Edward . . . very and undoubted heir . . . mumble, bumble, mumble . . . outlive our said Sovereign . . . bumble, mumble . . . in all things truly and faithfully behave me toward you . . . mumble, mumble . . . God . . ."
He knew a lot of the people who knelt : his old friend Lord Lovel, in grand cloth-of-gold figured with silver, not laughing or making jokes for once, but kissing his hand very solemnly; William Dudley, Bishop of Durham; handsome, serious-faced young John de la Pole of Lincoln, his cousin; Lord Scrope and the fat Lord Thomas Stanley. Ned did not like Lord Stanley very much.

Now someone—it was the Bishop of St. Asaph, he

thought—touched his arm very gently, making him move
aside a little. The Spanish Ambassador, thin-faced Señor
Don de Sasiola, was kneeling to be made a knight now.
Father did not look so serious this time. There was the same
glint of the sword in the coloured light and "Rise up, Sir
Geoffrey," and that was over. Ned felt very wise because he
knew that Father had knighted Don de Sasiola to please the
King and Queen of Castille so that they would help him
against the wicked King of France. He had told Ned all
about it : how Don de Sasiola had stood up in front of him
and all the Lords in Warwick Castle and said that Queen
Isabella wanted to make a good firm league with him
against King Louis and would open all the ports in Spain
to the English and send forty thousand men to help him.
"And the Spaniards are fine fighters," he said. "So one
day, son, you may sit on your throne in Paris." That
would be after Father was dead, and Ned didn't much
want to think about it. So he thought about Father, on
White Surrey, and the forty thousand Spaniards defeating
the Frenchmen over and over again the way Harry of
Monmouth did in the chronicles : and presently they
went out of the Minster.

This was another of the important things, and he had
been told all about it. He had to walk all by himself. His
cousin of Warwick, Uncle George's boy, and his cousin of
Lincoln would be a little behind him, and Mother and
Father with their crowns on would be just in front. But he
had to go all alone and keep the same pace as the rest of
them and be very careful about his coronet : and now he
thought the coronet was heavier than ever and he would
have liked to go behind a wall somewhere just for a
minute, but there was no time for that.

Father's head was very stiff over the wide collar of
ermine. The great golden crown he wore glimmered and
gleamed. Mother's head under her crown was bent forward
a little. They moved slowly. He got accustomed to their
pace after a yard or two; felt a little better. Now the west
doors of the Minster opened and they were out in the sunshine. For a second, his heart jumped right up so that he
thought it would choke him, and he was dreadfully afraid.

He had never heard such a solid, deafening clap of sound
in all his life, though he was really soon going to be eight

years old. It went off with a single bang like a cannon: a crash of people's voices. There had been lots of cheering ever since they first came to York, but not like this. The sunshine made him dazzle and blink; but past the steps that Father and Mother were going down he could see the men-at-arms. They were not standing and facing into the street, which was what they were for, but had turned their backs on the grand procession and got their pikes in both hands and were pushing and pushing. What they were pushing against was a solid mass, to the end of his sight, of people: faces piled one on top of the other and all with mouths open. Red faces in thousands were heaving and cramming and trying to come in over the shafts that the men-at-arms held like rails in a fence against them. He could see their shoulders straining as they pushed them back. It was like being between high walls that were going to fall down.

Oh, he thought, I really am frightened. I don't want to go out. I don't.

This was the first step that his foot was reaching down over, and in just a minute he would be right in between those clamouring walls. I am Prince of Wales and a knight, he said to himself, as my Father is King Richard III of England and France. Being frightened is all right if I have to be frightened: but showing it would be wrong. He took another step down and then another, and then the din soared up to its worst again, and men and women were heaving and surging against the pikestaffs and stretching hands out between the men-at-arms so that they nearly touched him. He had gone several steps between them, deaf and with his nose full of their smell, before he realised that they were making all this noise at him because they were glad that he was Prince of Wales.

The October sky was so low that it appeared possible to reach it with a hand. Northward, it was the colour of an old bruise, blue-black and morbid, paling unwillingly toward the South to a kind of lucid grey. The cold was winterish. It was a sky from which snowflakes might fall. The threat and oppression of it overcame the city as though a host of utterly silent riders charged down on Yorkshire through the air, cold sheen on their harness, their axes swinging for a mêlée and their vizors shut: the devil's weather. The thick concourse of citizens whom the ringing of the common bell had fetched together wore cloaks and shuffled. Alderman Wrangwysh in his scarlet felt chilled and sickly. He had volunteered for this duty because he could not bear to be idle; had to do something under this feeling of calamity and unnaturalness that had descended on them all. He fidgeted and wrinkled his nose whilst the Serjeant of the Mace called for silence; then unrolled the parchment he had in his hand; looked over it at the chilled anxious faces, blockish and a little resentful, that looked back at him; cleared his throat; read:

"By the King:

"Forasmuch as the King our Sovereign Lord Richard III, by the grace of God King of England and France and Lord of Ireland, understands for certain that . . ."

Aye, he thought, I must say it now. It is past belief or anything that could have been feared, but I must say it to them.

". . . that the Duke of Buckingham traitorously is turned upon him, contrary to the duty of his allegiance, and intends the utter destruction of our said Sovereign Lord, the subversion of his realm and the utter disheriting of all his true liege people: our said Sovereign Lord therefore, considering the weal and surety of his royal person, the tranquillity and peace of his said realm and subjects, takes and reputes the said Duke as his rebel and traitor, and charges and commands all his true subjects so to take him.

"Also our said Sovereign Lord charges, and upon pain of death commands, that no manner person, of what estate, degree or condition he be, at the commandment or desire of the said Duke, or any other in his name, arouse, assemble or make any manner commotion other than accords with our said Sovereign Lord's law and peace; but that they and every one of them be ready to attend upon our said Sovereign Lord, or such as he shall command them, for the repressing and subduing of the traitorous intent and purpose of the said Duke.

"And over this, our said Sovereign Lord straitly charges and commands that no manner person, whatsoever he be, in any wise attempt or presume to rob, spoil or hurt any of the tenants, officers or other persons belonging to the said Duke, his rebel and traitor—so that they rise not nor make

401

commotion or assemblies of his subjects against his peace; and if the said Duke's tenants, officers or other do, then they to be taken as the King's enemies and traitors.

"God save King Richard!"

A kind of gritty murmur, like waggon wheels in shale, grew up from the crowd when he had finished speaking and loudened into a crackle of shouts. "King Richard!" "God save King Richard!" He thrust the parchment into the Serjeant's hands and went quickly away; did not want to talk the news over with anyone.

A month ago, after the grand procession when he had knighted the Prince, and a week's more solemnities, King Richard had called the Mayor and Aldermen to him into the Chapter-House. Very small and splendid in purple cloth-of-gold he sat in the Archbishop's throne and reminded them, in his low voice, of the part they had played in his Scots wars. No one had petitioned him for what he did next. *Only of his most abundant grace,* as they told the clerk to inscribe it in the record afterward, he relieved them forever of the annual fees they owed the Crown, so that the merchants coming in from the country would be toll-free now; appointed the Mayor ex-officio his chief Serjeant-at-Arms at a salary of a shilling each day, and promised the city a yearly grant of forty pounds for its relief. That had been his last public act in his city of York. He went on his way then to rejoice other places; was at Lincoln now; and hardly two weeks after he had left they had news that the rabble of Kent were up in arms, making politics, as was their habit, an excuse for setting out to plunder London. Lord Howard, whom King Richard had created Duke of Norfolk, was ready to handle them, and it did not seem that any plant more fruitful than a gallows-tree would grow out of their wickedness. But there was a stranger rumour than that of follies in Kent. It was said the old Earl of Richmond's son, the Welch brat whom a few soured eccentrics in corners still spoke of as the heir of Lancaster, was taking ship from Brittany; was coming—it seemed the ultimate distillation of moonshine, but those who knew best swore it to be true—to claim the throne of England. The Courtneys in Devonshire had risen for him. After twelve years, the ghost of the house of Lancaster stalked out of its grave to trouble peace. The very curse of civil war that

402

King Richard had promised his people he would crush down forever like a nettle had begun to sting.

That was not the worst. Messengers from the King's kinsman, Duke Henry of Buckingham, had appeared in Derbyshire and Yorkshire summoning all well-disposed persons to get into their harness and follow the badge of the Stafford knot. At first, they thought he was raising his forces like an honest man for the King. Now the murder was out. The Duke of Buckingham, the most untrue creature living, had declared for Lancaster against the King whose life he had saved from the Wydvylles, whose train he had carried at the coronation and who had rewarded him with the offices of Constable of England and Chamberlain of Wales and with more lands than any Stafford had owned since the Conquest.

What has possessed the man? wondered Mr. Wrangwysh, walking up Micklegate to his own house in the boding weather. Have his wits been turned? A traitor bringing back all the old troubles on us, the rumours and garboyles we hoped we'd done with forever now : oh, God curse you, my Lord of Buckingham : you to bring this on us just when the sun was shining at last. We were happy a month ago; had got a King we wanted. You did not stop to consider that when you turned the world upside-down. It was not much of a matter to you that we, the middling sort of folk who don't live in London, were drawing breath and beginning to hope for good times at last. We only want what King Richard's promised us, only a little justice, a little security, a little refuge from extortioners and court-understrappers who'd draw blood from a turnip. What does it matter to you, now you've chosen to play at Kingmaker? God punish you the way you deserve.

He turned into his own door in a bitter temper. The strange, cold and discoloured sky joined with his fears to give him a feeling as though the world were on the edge of calamity. Lancaster out of its grave again, as though a rotten corpse should walk; Duke Henry of Buckingham a traitor to his own King and cousin : the world was mad. It was too much for him to understand. He felt as he might have done if his ambling horse had suddenly become a dragon.

Standing in the middle of his great hall he lifted up his voice and yelled for his sons, his apprentices and his wife. Doors sounded and people scurried. He eased the trouble of his mind a little by barking orders.

"Walter, go up to the loft and fetch down my harness. Ralph, where'd we put my sword last time? Don't know? Think, you fool, think. Where's your mistress? St. Anthony's fire burn you, Walter, will you be moving? Miles, get your harness too. You'll ride with me. Ralph, when you've found my sword go in a hurry to Mr. Marston and ask him courteously to step round."

His wife arrived in the long gallery above the hall. She was a tall, fat woman with yellow hair gone grey in the front, and she began to talk as soon as she set eyes on him.

"Swords, harness, oh Lord Jesus, what's to do now? You're never going on a journey, Thomas? Oh God, you'll be the death of me. Swords, he says, harness, he says, as if he were Captain of Calais, and never a word to his wife. Mr. Marston's to hear it all, but not me. You'll break my heart. Are we never to have peace in the world?"

"I might ask that," said Mr. Wrangwysh. "Hold your clack, woman. There's three hundred to ride from York and Ainstey to uphold our good King against the rebels, and I'm chosen Captain: now then."

Mrs. Wrangwysh stopped at the foot of the stairs with her hands on her hips.

"You're chosen Captain," she said slowly, "and didn't shave this morning. You'll go and disgrace the city of York in southern parts: a captain with two days' beard on his chin."

"I will not, woman," bellowed Mr. Wrangwysh, comforted already by the safe, familiar atmosphere of a domestic brawl. "I'm not to set out before the day after to-morrow. I'll shave when I please."

"You'll shave now. I'll shave you. Ralph, put that sword down. It's a razor your master needs now. Fetch it and the lather-bowl. You, an Alderman and a Captain, to be walking the naked streets with that face on you: I'm ashamed to my heart."

"I've no time to be shaved now. I've a hundred things to contrive. How am I to attend to King Richard's business——"

"He wouldn't desire you to in that villainous condition. Cower down on the stool while I get to work on you."

"The devil fly away with the stool and all pestering women along with it."

"Cursing and banning: reach me those things here, Ralph."

Mr. Wrangwysh, feeling almost warm in his soul again, squatted down on the stool. His wife rubbed the lather into his face with the hard edge of her hand. As she worked she talked.

"The bare, shameless notion: sending for Mr. Marston in such a condition, to say nothing of sitting at the Council like a crying disgrace: God knows I've tried to make you value yourself, but pains are clean wasted on you. A woman could talk for a year . . ."

"I do believe it."

"Don't babble, man, or the soap'll be in your mouth and then we'll hear more rusty words. So three hundred are going: and not too many. They should arm us women against that Duke. We'd show him a thing with a besom, the wicked, vile, ungrateful, treacherous viper. We'd show him what it amounts to turning against our blessed King. If it should come to a field and you should come close to him, Thomas, though God knows I doubt if you will, you'll bang him for me. Hold your chin up. Blessed Mother of God, Walter, take care with that harness, will you? That's your master's good jack that he bought in London. The foul thieves to rise against our kind King Richard: but no good ever came from those South parts. Three hundred, you said. How much money are they giving you in hand?"

"Twenty pounds."

"Twenty pounds: it's a deal of money. You must keep it carefully. Miles, you'll see your father takes care of his twenty pounds: and scour your jack, boy. It was a cruel disgrace with rust when you rode to London. If we're to fight great wars and bloody battles we'll fight them decently from this house. God have mercy, Walter, have your feet grown into the floor? Sand and lamp oil and help scour Mr. Miles' jack, or do you want me to lay a strap to your rump? There, wipe your face, man, and you'll do."

"Loved be God."

Miles was examining the leather padding of his sallet. He was a big boy, rising seventeen. He said:

"Where do we meet the King, Father?"

"Salisbury, lad: he's making haste there across England now, from what I hear."

"And there'll be a field?"

"Aye, by God, I think so. That devilish Duke's raised a great army of the Welch on Severn-side and they say he'll cross over and join the other rebels. God mend the world."

"It's a cruel wickedness," said Mrs. Wrangwysh bitterly, "now, when we thought there'd be some decency in England."

Mr. Marston came in, wearing a winter coat lined with budge: a tall, serious-looking man. His face had a deep expression of anxiety and he said his good-days as though he were at a funeral .He and Mr. Metcalfe were chosen as Vice-Captains under Mr. Wrangwysh. Mrs. Wrangwysh bustled him into a chair as though she were shooing a hen.

"Ah, dear Lord God, Mr. Marston, aren't they horrible times? Into this house my husband comes and calls for his harness and sets us all by the ears. No words of mine he'd listen to, but he must be off to-morrow to fight for the King and take our poor boy along with him; and my heart breaking in silence. The wickedness of those rebels who'll turn poor folks' houses upside down: what do they care who's burned when they go about to set the world on fire?"

"You may say so, Mrs. Wrangwysh," said Mr. Marston seriously. "It's the most damnably wicked and senseless uprising I ever knew. The Duke of Buckingham must be mad, I think; and to call in Lancaster, to want to bring this little Welchman over that we none of us ever heard of: it's past understanding."

"But what I can't comprehend," said Mr. Wrangwysh, feeling his chin with his fingers, "is that the Queen's friends have joined him, or they say so. If they'd risen for Edward the Bastard I could find sense in it. But what have they to do with Lancaster?"

"God knows, Thomas. It's a wicked world."

"It is that, William. Is there any more news?"

"I heard someone say Lord le Strange, the Lord Stanley's son, was raising ten thousand Lancashire and Cheshire lads to go to the King."

"God reward him."

"Why are we for Salisbury, Father?" asked Miles.

"Nay, boy, I couldn't be certain. But as I see it, that's a grand middle place to meet the damned Duke when he crosses the water of Severn or the Courtneys if they come up from Devonshire, and break one or tother of them before they can join their forces."

"Aye," said Mr. Marston.

"Then we'll happen fight two fields," said Miles, with his clear grey eyes bright.

"God forbid, lad. D'you want to kill more Englishmen than need be? That's not King Richard's teaching."

"I want to kill all the damned southern traitors who've turned on him; show the South what we think of it. He's our King, King Richard is, and that's why the whorson Southerners want to pull him down."

"There is truth in that, I do believe," said Mr. Marston in his deep, oracular voice. "There's not one hand been lifted against his good Grace North of the Trent and never will be."

"I should kindly hope not," said Mrs. Wrangwysh. "We're honest in these parts."

"We can tell a monk by his frock, too," said Mr. Marston. "Our good King, God save him, he's shown us a blessed disposition. We know he's our hope for fat days and quiet living. He's the one to protect us against the nobles who'll spill the blood of a thousand of us only to advance their own cursed quarrels."

"I heard him in London," said Mr. Wrangwysh, "in the Court of King's Bench before he was crowned. I heard him say to us all : There's no nobleman in the realm who'd not be better to starve than to arm Englishmen against Englishmen whilst I'm King."

"Ah, that's blessed language," said his wife.

"But won't we have to fight two fields?" persisted Miles.

"You'll not rhyme so gaily about that when you've fought one," his father told him.

"We should not need to, from what I hear," said Mr. Marston. "If the King's Grace can but strike one party of rebels before they join with the other, the world's ours."

"God send he does, then."

"Amen."

"Walter," said Mrs. Wrangwysh, "stir your great lazy feet and bring us some pudding-ale. You'll take a sup, Mr. Marston. It's most unnatural weather."

"Unholy, I'd call it. I thank you for your kindness. There was a wind getting up as I came down the 'gate."

"Ah, they're bad times in all ways."

"That's a true word."

Mr. Wrangwysh's faint cheerfulness evaporated again. New wars, he thought, new bloodshed : and there's no one can tell but what it'll be my blood or even young Miles' that is shed this time. God have mercy on poor folk and God save the King who cares for them, says Thomas Wrangwysh.

The ale was brought and poured into the mazers. Miles, who had ridden in harness to London when King Richard summoned his Northern friends to overawe the Queen's following six months ago, and whose mind had been full of soldiering ever since, lifted his bowl and proclaimed extravagantly :

"Long life to King Richard and death to all traitors."

They drank to it with curt grunts of approval; were not warmed by the words. It was all too foolish and too miserable, this sudden unnatural disturbance in the unnatural weather that seemed like a destiny over England.

"Where d'you think the Welchman will land, Thomas?" asked Mr. Marston.

"Nay, I've no inkling : or whether he will land. It might be only a tale."

"I'm afraid it's truth. Please God he'll not have a large power with him."

"Who is he?" asked Miles. "I never even heard him spoken of."

"Son to the Lady Margaret who's married my Lord Stanley now," his father told him, "and grandson to the Welchman that Queen Katherine took into her bed after Harry of Monmouth died."

"Then what right's he got to be King in England?" said the boy angrily.

"None," said Mr. Marston : "he has none."

A faint, unhappy moan of wind sounded outside the house, like a cur crying.

"He has no right," agreed Mr. Wrangwysh: "a Welchman to bear rule over us."

Mr. Marston took a deep mouthful of ale and was silent again. Mrs. Wrangwysh began to fill up the mazers.

"Well, if he does land I hope and suppose our King'll teach him a lesson. I never did like the Welch, God knows. There was a dirty toad of a Welch peddler came to our door two years back. I sent him out of that: and as God sees me and comprehends me, I found him at after behind the wall of the yard with my maid Dorothy. The impudence: I'd a skillet in my hand at the time, as the Saints would have it, and I cracked his crown for him to my satisfaction; and as for Dorothy, I birched her till the blood came: filthying my house with foreigners."

"Aye," said Mr. Marston, "it's old England they're for filthying with foreigners now."

"But never shall," said Miles.

"That's my lad," his mother encouraged him. "If you meet any dirty Welch tykes on the journey you're going—and that bethinks me, I must see to your clean shirts—remember your mother and lay their heads open. I'm only a weak woman and of small account in the world, even in my own house, but you think of my words: and if you love your poor mother, see your father shaves when he gets to Salisbury in case the King's noble Grace condescends to speak to him."

"Leave that, woman," said Mr. Wrangwysh emphatically.

"Leave that, woman: you see how I'm handled in my own home, Mr. Marston, thwarted and trodden on till I daren't open my gob. It's we women have the hard time of it in this world. The great Captains in their harness with twenty pounds in their pouches tramp over us roughshod and we can only . . . God have mercy, hear that!"

The noise of the wind had been rising steadily from a moan to a growl. Now, with a sudden frightening accession of power, it became a scream. A cold draught fluttered the rushes on the hall floor, and in the gallery a door crashed shut. The scream enlarged, repeated itself. Rain suddenly smacked the leaded window-panes like vicious whips. The hearth belched smoke.

"Lord, it's sudden," said Mr. Wrangwysh.

The blare of the wind was orgiastic now. It howled and

triumphed over the roof whilst the rain beat kettledrums of exultation. Shrill squeals pierced the dominant roar where the storm found chinks to whistle in. All the witches in Scotland might have been riding South calling the names of their devils to one another. Mrs. Wrangwysh blessed herself and turned instantly upon Walter.

"Out with you," she shouted, "out and put the shutters up."

The apprentice fumbled a minute with the latch. Then the door was torn out of his hand and crashed against the wall. Rain and cold hurried in like conquerors. Miles jumped up and closed it after him with a long thrust of the arm and they could hear him struggling with the shutters.

"It was bound to come," said Mr. Wrangwysh. "The weather was bound to break."

He felt frightened. The noise was so thick and immense, as though wind were a solid thing like stone that bashed the walls of his fine house and might bash them down. Mr. Marston coughed in the smoke that was still flooding into the hall. The rushes on the floor were dancing up almost to the height of a man's knees.

"Dear Saints, what a todoment," said Mrs. Wrangwysh, "I never heard it so bad as this."

"A night of this and we'll have the floods out."

"And you riding for Salisbury, oh Jesus!"

The door crashed again and Walter was in the room. The boy's clothes were black with wet, soaked-through and clinging to him like a skin. Rain streamed from him. He shook himself like a spaniel, crying:

"Holy Mary, master, it's over shoes in the street already!"

The words were scarcely out of his mouth when the still-deepening note of the storm was split by a crash that seemed to shake the floor under their feet. The wind had prized a chimney loose. Mr. Wrangwysh bounded out of his chair.

"Lord have mercy!"

"The Lord has great mercy." Even in the powlering of the wind, Mr. Marston's deep voice sounded loud and thrilling. "The Lord has great mercy upon England. He has judged between King Richard and his rebels and traitors. Think, man. How will the wicked Duke cross

Severn in this? How will the Welchman put his nose out of Brittany with the sea as it will be to-night? God has shown us who is his anointed."

"I will not see him."

Sir Richard Ratcliffe made no immediate answer. The King's face was bent over a huddle of papers on the oak table. He had not looked up to speak.

But Sir Richard, who knew him, knew that his lips must be pressed together and his eyes narrowed like a cat's pupils when it is watching a bird. He was not like this even when it was Rivers who was for the axe, he thought. The King raised his head suddenly. The cleft between his eyebrows was very noticeable.

"Why are you waiting?" he asked.

Sir Richard fretted with his feet like a schoolboy.

"The Dean of the Cathedral," he said.

"What of him?"

"He only asked, your Grace, that is to say, he only asked me to ask whether, seeing that today is Sunday and the Feast of All Souls, your Grace would be pleased, out of regard to Holy Church, to respite the Duke until . . ."

"I know no Duke."

"Your Grace?"

"I know no Duke. I know only Henry Stafford, a traitor condemned by the Vice-Constable's Court. He dies this morning."

God, thought Richard Ratcliffe, may I never be where Henry Stafford is now : and this man was the kind Duke of Gloucester. Buckingham was never so much his enemy as Rivers or his friend as Hastings : but he condemned those two like a man doing work he hated. Why has he become Nero now? The King's cold voice pricked his questioning as though his thoughts had been read. He spoke deliberately, his hands joined before him on the table.

"You think I am a hard master to-day, Ratcliffe?"

"No, your Grace."

"Don't lie. You have a face like a boy's hornbook. It does not want a clerk to read it. You were thinking that presently I shall be called Bloody King Richard."

"Never, your royal Grace : others can think what they like. I know you're for mercy."

411

The King unclasped his hands and dropped back in his chair. A deep breath moved the jewelled front of his doublet. Automatically, his right hand felt for his dagger.

"Yes, I am for mercy. I've done all in my power to see that not a single innocent or even doubtful soul shall suffer in this business : but I've no mercy for Henry Stafford."

"Yes, your Grace."

The King looked full at him.

"His sin is against England and not Richard," he said in a flat voice. "There is no pardon. He tried to bring the old garboyles of the two roses into England again. Only one mercy will I show him, and you may say as much to the Dean. This is All Souls' Day, as he says, the day when universal Christendom prays for its dead. I will grant Henry Stafford the benefit of those prayers, and that is all. Now go, and when you have seen his head off come back and tell me so."

Sir Richard Ratcliffe bowed and went out.

And he is right, he thought, walking in the black November weather across the Close from the Bishop's Palace where the King lodged. He is right, as he always is. This is the wrong time for mercy. Last month's great gale, which had mown trees and houses down over the length of England, smashed shipping to driftwood in the Bristol Channel and turned the Severn into a howling sea, had broken an unbelievable conspiracy. It was as though all the separate and hostile devils which had possessed England since the death of Richard of Bordeaux had made common alliance against their common opposer, Richard of Gloucester. The plot to which the Duke of Buckingham had openly and boastfully confessed before Sir Ralph Ashton, the Vice-Constable, equalled in unnatural audacity the old alliance of Kingmaker and Queen Marguerite. Bishop Morton of Ely was its leader. He had been given into Duke Henry's charge after his arrest that spring in London; had wormed himself by god knew what devilishness into his gaoler's heart and then propounded a device. Henry Tydder was to be fetched out of Brittany to be King by right of Lancaster. The Gilfords and Courtneys and the rabble of West Wales would take up arms for him. But since they would not be enough against the might of England under such a captain as King Richard, a further, a more audacious

412

subtlety was devised. Henry Tydder, waiving the matter of her bastardy (as why should he not, thought Richard Ratcliffe, seeing his own family are bastards on both sides?), was to marry the Lady Bessy, eldest daughter of King Edward and Queen Elizabeth. What was to be done about her two brothers no one knew, but at least the Wydvylles would share the government of England, after all. The Marquis Dorset, Sir Edward Wydvylle, Sir John Fogg with the ink hardly dry on his royal pardon, Sir Thomas St. Leger, had all joined the plot.

Some of them were in arms still. The little Welchman himself, Henry Tydder, who was said to have lank yellow-white hair and a wart on his chin, was actually on the sea now unless, as was to be hoped, the storm had put him under it, drowned him as it had drowned his hopes. Buckingham's Water they would call the great flood for years after, for it had been the end of Buckingham. Like a rat in a pit, the man who had set out to be another King-maker had ranged up and down the Welch bank of the Severn, trying to find a way to cross to his part-takers. But on the English side King Richard's folk had been before-hand with him and had broken or occupied the bridges, and behind him, the loyal Welch, under Sir Thomas ap Roger of Tretower, had seized and plundered his Castle of Brecknock. Nipped as in pincers, deserted by his men whom he could not pay, with the devil behind him and Severn wide as the sea in front, storm-soaked, agued, the new Kingmaker fled in disguise to the home of his retainer Ralph Banaster of Lacon Hall; was taken and hidden by him, betrayed by him; was brought yesterday into Salisbury with his spurs chopped off and his arms bound; was tried instantly before the Vice-Constable; was going to die.

Sir Richard Ratcliffe's horse waited for him outside the Close. He mounted and rode through the Sundayish, empty streets to the Council House, where a strong guard was. Some of the men wore Lord Lovel's badge of the dog and the rest the gryfon's claw of the Stanleys. In the Council-chamber itself he found the Vice-Constable, the Sheriff of Wiltshire, and Sir William Catesby, now Chancellor of the Exchequer. The hook-nosed, hard-eyed lawyer with his perpetual loose smile was in high favour. It was he who had warned the King of Lord Hastings' compact with the Wydvylles; and it was commonplace that King Richard never forgot a friend. Standing a little aside from the others was a fourth man, gross and powerful, wearing a gown of orange-and-black velvet over black doublet and orange hose: Lord Thomas Stanley. Sir Richard Ratcliffe knew why he was there. His second wife, the Lady Margaret, was Henry Tydder's mother; was inextricably involved in the new plot; deserved (but it was known King Richard would not kill a woman) to lose her head. Lord Stanley's own loyalty was not breathed on. He and his son had raised Cheshire, Lancashire and Derbyshire flockmeal for the King. But doubtless the fat Baron thought it wise to make another gesture still; to be there in person when the Duke of Buckingham was ended. He is not the fool he looks, Sir Richard thought.

The Sheriff, a nervous little man, obviously much daunted by the responsibility of a Duke's execution, edged up to him and asked in a hushed voice:

"Will the King's Grace grant him an audience? He has been asking again."

"No, we are to proceed at once. Have you everything ready in the market-place?"

"Yes, yes, I hope so."

Sir Richard looked at the Vice-Constable.

"I suppose men are guarding the way, Sir Ralph?"

"Yes, some of mine and some of Norfolk's: enough. We'll have no trouble, anyway."

"Surely not. Has he had the Sacrament?"

"He's having it now."

"Oh."

There did not seem much more to say. Sir William Catesby was talking apart to Lord Stanley. The Sheriff exsinuated himself from the room on some errand. The Vice-Constable sighed and looked at Richard Ratcliffe; said almost casually:

"You know he's mad?"

"Who's mad?"

"Buckingham: clean crazy."

"Do you tell me so?"

"Oh yes: he was talking of what he would have done if the flood hadn't held him, boasting. He would have made the Welchman King and then unmade him. He said he and

414

Morton of Ely could rule all Christendom between them. He was to have destroyed the Wydvylles too when they'd served his turn."

"Lord: it was that devil's fox Morton that seduced him in the outset. I'm sure of that. I wish to Christ we could have laid hands on him."

"We shall yet, but where's the use? Our Lord and master would no more head a priest than a woman."

"Where is the King?"

They jerked round as though the voice behind them had been a wolf's. Henry Stafford of Buckingham was in the doorway, one hand on the jamb, a Friar twittering at his elbow and the Sheriff and two men-at-arms behind him. He still wore the coarse frieze clothes of his disguise, torn at the wrists and very dirty. His brown, wavy hair was tangled and hung partly over his face. All round the iris of his eyes the white showed staringly. His chin wobbled.

Sir Richard said:

"You must be patient. I have been to his Grace. He will not see you."

Henry Stafford's head went back and he stiffened his shoulders. There was something terrifyingly wild and commanding about him, standing mad and dirty on the edge of his death.

"Go to the King I made and tell him the Kingmaker demands to speak to him."

"I will do nothing of the sort."

"You servant, do you hear me? I am giving you an order, I who made your little King to suit myself. I can make any King in England. I am Stafford, Bohun, Plantagenet. I showed the world as many Stafford knots as ever Warwick had ragged staves. I broke the Wydvylles. I called back Lancaster into England again to please a friend of mine. Do you understand an order?"

"Yes, and my orders are that we must carry out the sentence passed on you. Will you be patient now, sir? You ought to think of your soul."

Henry Stafford was no longer listening to him; had seen Lord Stanley. His face began to work as though the muscles were being plaited together; went out of shape. He was shouting:

"Why is he here? He disobeyed me. I sent him orders. I

415

commanded him for his wife's sake to help me make his stepson King of England. He failed me. Why is he here now?"

Lord Stanley kept his fat countenance well; only said:

"I did not fail you. You mistook me. I am a Yorkist, and my honour is not on sale."

The loud gasping laughter that filled the Council-chamber abashed them all. Henry Stafford's whole body was shaken by it as though by an agony that made his legs and back bend and then straighten and then bend again. They stared at him. After a long time he pushed his hair back out of his eyes and said breathlessly:

"Everything is for sale in England."

"Sir," said the Vice-Constable, "if you have nothing else to say, I must tell you to make ready. It is time now."

Henry Stafford did not look at him. His voice was a shout again. He threw his arms apart, ranting at them.

"For sale, for sale: you madmen, who talks about honour in England after civil war for thirty years? You're mad. Why can't you understand? Honour's dead. It was killed with my father at St. Albans. There's no honour now."

"That is enough," said the Vice-Constable. "You must——"

"If there were honour in the world, who'd be more honourable than Henry of Buckingham? I've betrayed everything that was put in reach of me: and you all would. This is England where there are only perjurers. Look at that fat man, your loyal Yorkist. Hug him. Kiss him because it's profited him now to stand by King Dickon. Henry Stafford of Buckingham with his feet in the grave tells you that he'd sell King Dickon to King Harry for a Scots groat if he were sure of the payment. Remember that in season."

"Is there any need for us to listen to this?" asked Stanley moderately.

"There is not." The Vice-Constable beckoned. "Here is your prisoner, Mr. Sheriff. Do your office."

Henry Stafford did nothing whilst the men-at-arms closed round him; let them bring him into the street. There were more people about now. Faces gaped over the pikemen's shoulders to see the Duke of Buckingham, who had tried to play Kingmaker to King Richard, receive his wages. The scaffold had been set up before the Poultry Cross: a small platform. Two men were waiting on it. They had vizors of black frieze with eyeholes pulled over their faces, and their arms were bare. It was awful weather. Over the Salisbury house-tops the lower sky was as black as midnight. A pale, wretched light dropped like snow from the zenith, silvering the jacks of the men-at-arms and showing the vapour of their breath. The still crowd, waiting for its treat, looked unreal, a picture. A miracle might happen in weather like this, thought Richard Ratcliffe; the end of the world come. He heard the two headsmen, on their knees, ask for forgiveness. Their man looked at them as though what they said puzzled him.

"It does not matter," he told them. "The foxes are killing a hawk for raiding the poultry-yard."

The Friar took him by the hand now.

"Kneel down, my son. Pray. Ask all these others to pray with you."

"I'll pray alone," said Henry Stafford.

He did not kneel; put his hands together and looked down. The others on the scaffold pulled off their bonnets. Some in the front of the crowd crossed themselves. Presently he lifted his head again.

"Now I am ready."

A dry, precise voice surprised Richard Ratcliffe. It came from Sir William Catesby, who was peering forward a little like a lawyer making a point.

"Will you not ask the King's forgiveness for having contrived against him?"

Henry Stafford's eyes were like those of a wild horse again. He spoke so loudly that Sir Richard was afraid the crowd might hear.

"If the King I made had given me an audience I would have stabbed him to the heart. I am Buckingham. My house does nothing by short measure. England is the kingdom of traitors, and I would have been the greatest traitor of all. There is nothing for forgiveness in that."

One of the masked men laid hands on him; began to pull open the collar of his doublet. He took no notice; went on, still loudly:

"Look at your conscience, William Catesby, and tell me if it is not true. You are only another Englishman. You betrayed Hastings to Richard when Hastings betrayed

Richard to Elizabeth. There is no honesty anywhere. Honesty bled to death in the wars before I was grown. Tell your King Richard that I made him King of a nation of perjurers and he must not blame me if I was no better than my fellow-subjects. Tell him it is a rotten carcase he has to rule. The soul went out of it when we were young. Now leave me in peace."

He turned to the block as the headsman took his hands off him. It was a high piece of wood, black-painted, with a hollow for the chin. Without crossing himself, he knelt down and caught hold of it by the two sides.

The Friar slipped round in front of him, holding up a crucifix. From somewhere, the other masked man had produced his three-foot axe. The huge triangular blade glimmered like lead. Henry Stafford was smiling drunkenly.

"This England is too much for any man's conscience," he said, and crouched over the block.

"Proficiscere, anima christiana . . ."

Gripped by two hands, the axe heaved slowly up against a background of roofs and clouds. It rose higher than the uplifted crucifix; quivered for half of a breath; swooped down. A loud crash shook the silence round the Poultry Cross. Henry Stafford's hands dropped from the sides of the block and at the same instant the Friar flinched backward with a yelp. A great crimson spurt had stained the front of his habit.

The headsman stooped, groping for something on the far side of the block. His hand came up with fingers in the hair of the head, whose lips and eyelids shivered and from which blood pattered like thaw-water from the eaves.

"This is the head of a traitor."

He spoke the formula in turn from each quarter of the scaffold. Sir William Catesby stared at the tall block that rose, like a black promontory in a sea at sunset, out of a widening puddle of red. Presently he said in his dry lawyer's voice :

"He was mad, of course."

"Oh, yes," said Sir Richard Ratcliffe, "he was quite mad."

Dr. John Warkworth, Master of St. Peter's College in the

418

University of Cambridge, drew his hands from his sleeves to make a negative gesture.

"No, no, my days of writing chronicles are over and done."

His host, Dr. Robert Wodelarke, Provost of King Henry of Windsor's College of the Blessed Virgin and St. Michael, smiled.

"Does a man leave the inclination of a lifetime as easily as that, Domine? You have been a spectator of the great affairs of the world as long as I've known you. Are you going to content yourself suddenly with Aristotle and Alexander: no more annals, no more strangeness?"

"None whatever, Domine: as much of my little chronicle as I thought it wise to preserve was written out and given to the library of our poor house, not to be removed on pain of anathema, a year ago. I do not meddle with news now."

"But you must still hear stories."

"The world was full of gossip as soon as God took Adam's rib out of him. I don't run after it any more."

"I could wish almost that you did."

"I know, Domine, and I know why. But if you wish these things recorded you must find someone else for the task, a young man who will write a fine book for Mr. Caxton in London to imprint. You and I are too old for vanities."

The two dons were taking their ease in the solar of the Provost's lodgings. It was a cold March afternoon over the Fenlands, wet and unsure. Cambridge, snuggled in a blanket of mist, was recovering from its greatest season of excitement since Archbishop Rotherham presented the new Schools. The King had come that way. They had not heard much of him since he began to rule last year; knew that he had come to the throne in a strange manner and had taken several unexpected heads off. He was said to be a pale little man with uneven shoulders and narrow eyes: a great change from the Rose of Rouen certainly. Then one morning he had come riding in, nobles and men-at-arms in front of him, a surprising number of clergy in his attendance; and the University had turned out to do him honour: the Vice-Chancellor, the Provost of King's and President of Queens' the Masters of St. Peter's, and St. Bene't's, Clare and Pembroke, Trinity Hall and Gonville Hall, Michaelhouse, King's Hall, and Provost Wodelarke's own foundation of St. Catherine's, the Proctors and Esquires Bedell, the Doctors, Masters and Bachelors of all the faculties and sciences. They had not had much time for preparation. House-fronts in Trumpington Street were hung with what arras could be found, the stinking quagmire of a lane between Trinity Hall and Gonville Hall was sweetened after a fashion, Latin orations were scrambled together and lads in statu pupillari forbidden, on pain of stocks and birching, to make themselves conspicuous. Everything was fluttering and uncertain : and into the turmoil there rode a tiny little white-faced man who smiled at everybody and looked as though he were ready to tumble out of his saddle with weariness : a ghost of a man. They conducted him to the new great Church of St. Mary on Market Hill, where Mass was sung and long speeches made and some degrees conferred. They took him to the hall of King Henry's College to sup and hear Latin disputations. They sang another Mass for him in the vast, unfinished Chapel of the College; and they left him for the night. He was not so formidable, after all. To-morrow he would ride off and forget them again. He did not. They had misread him there. He spent tomorrow talking to people and asking questions. When he left the day after, they realised very completely that they had a new make of King in England.

Provost Wodelarke leaned forward and touched his friend's knee.

"You've understood me too well. I confess I would dearly like to see a fit record of what has been done for us here written by one of us. We have the future to consider, Domine. Those who come to find learning here after we're gone ought not to suppose we were ungrateful."

Dr. Warkworth allowed himself a thin laugh.

"I used to think, Provost, that you were Lancastrian."

"I was," said Provost Wodelarke innocently, "until I met the King."

"Your founder would not thank you to hear that."

"My founder would thank him. You and I know, my friend, that Henry of Windsor was a man of God if ever one trod this villainous earth. Look out there."

He pointed to the towering greyness of the College

Chapel, just visible through the window like a solidification of the general mist.

"That lovely house of God was his best work. It was to be his monument: a place such as no University in France or Italy possessed, a Chapel like a Cathedral that would remind all us learned men what the beginning of wisdom is."

"You're an orator, Domine."

"Do you deny the postulate?"

"No, no."

"No learned place in Christendom would praise God with more seemly magnificence than Holy King Henry's College if that Chapel were finished. But he died before it was finished, unkinged and a martyr."

"Between four walls, Domine, there are plenty would say the King we have now martyred him."

"Do you believe it yourself?"

"I am not sure: and if I were sure I should not tell my hood, leave alone my friends."

"I do not. I am ignorant of politics beside you, but I disbelieve that tale. Thanks to King Richard, the work begins on King Henry's Chapel again to-morrow. He has promised me the money on his own word. We may live to see it finished."

"That is certainly something."

"Something? Then what do you say to his other charity to the memory of Lancaster: five hundred marks to Queen Marguerite's College?"

"I say it is a great sum of money."

The Provost was warming. He kicked the skirts of his gown impatiently and stood up.

"If you had heard him talk to me," he said, "as simply as I talk to you, about his other charities and foundations: a college of a hundred priests—no less than that—at York, the College of All Hallows in London, his works in Westminster. He is finishing the great Chapel of St. George King Edward began there. He talked to me so openly about all these things, and about Prince Edward, his son, and how he will educate him. It was in this room. He sent for me. There were a dozen great men with him: my Lord Treasurer Audley, the Viscount Lovel, the Earl of Lincoln, Sir William Catesby; and he treated me as though I were one of them. Mr. Kendal the Secretary came in whilst we were talking with a letter to King Charles of France for him to sign, and he asked my pardon to break off and attend to it."

"The house of York were always affable," observed Dr. Warkworth.

"Maybe. But I tell you I no longer believe the tales about him. He is a kind christian Prince: and he is not crouch-backed either. I say now that if he headed Lord Hastings it was because he deserved it; and the Duke of Buckingham was a foul common traitor to rise against him last year, Lancaster or no Lancaster."

"Yes, you're a proper Yorkist now, my friend. That is as great a prodigy as any I have recorded in my chronicle."

"Habeo! The charge lies. I confess to it. He has made a Yorkist of me. My old friend, I wish you would open that chronicle of yours again. I know why you closed it: because you would not record all the sorrows of this unfortunate realm after Edward came back again."

"And that's true. I would not risk my neck with telling the truth or cumber my soul with writing lies."

"But now there's a new kind of truth to tell. Consider this year's Parliament. They say on all hands it's the best and most just that's sat since Edward the Great's day. I believe as much as you do that our hold King Henry and his son after him were the only heirs of the crown of England. As to this Welchman, the Lady Margaret's son, I do not know what to say. But I will say this. I think that King Richard is a wise King and a kind King who has shown a most blessed disposition in all things. He has comforted the poor; worked to undo his brother's tyrannies; showed more mercy to his opponents than could be imagined. I have heard stories of the care he took last year, after the Duke revolted, to see that no innocents should suffer. I wish these things could be recorded; and I think you are the man to record them."

"Not I."

"You saw him too. You spoke to him. Did you see a tyrant?"

"I will say this, Domine. All I saw in the King's face was kindness: that, and more care and weariness than I supposed there was in the world."

"Then set down what he has done. A University being a place of learning, it is fitting and reasonable that useful truth should be stored up in it for the future. You should be our Livy, and set down these things you have witnessed. It is laudable, and you once took pleasure in it."

It was Dr. Warkworth's turn to get up now. He took his friend by the arm and spoke quietly.

"I should be glad to do it, if it were not for one thing. I have told you I will not endanger myself by writing dangerous truths, and I will not flatter. I would rather choose honesty and silence. Tell me where are the two sons of Edward IV?"

Dr. Wodelarke turned very white; looked at the door. His voice jerked.

"You should not ask such things; even here. It is dangerous. No one knows . . ."

Dr. Warkworth smiled at him with one side of his mouth.

"You see now. It is, as you say, dangerous. Even to talk : leave writing aside. All last autumn, until after the Duke's rebellion, they were seen playing and shooting at times in the royal gardens at the Tower. Now they are not seen any more. The story is that they tried to escape and fell from the bridge into the moat and were drowned. The Thames carried their innocent little bodies away so that there was not even anything to bury. Ascertain me for certain, Domine, that that is the true story, and I will take my pen again and write you the history of King Richard."

King Edward IV had built largely in his time at the Castle of Nottingham, the great central fort of England which faced all ways, dominating the roads from Scotland to London and from the Eastern fens to Wales. His brother, who loved stone and mortar, was continuing the work. The high, three-storied tower where, his face turned North again after the spring progress, he bent patiently and unrestingly over his morning's business was not finished even now. Clink of trowels and rough talking came down occasionally through the wide window and into the room. It was a fine room hung with a peculiarly beautiful arras whose scenes showed the hunting of the unicorn. Here, the noble solitary beast with its one horn ventured out of a wood of formal trees, lured by a virgin, ready to lay its wild head on her lap.

423

Now the hounds were slipped. They bounded forward in heraldic postures like lions salient on a shield. One of them seized it by the fetlock. The monster had turned, in the next scene, and scattered them; was galloping away over a meadow full of butterflies and coloured flowers. The hunt was after it: men with swords and boar-spears, servants with crossbows; small-waisted ladies in red gowns watched from a pavilion as it came to bay, levelling its horn at its pursuers. In the last picture it was ringed round with men and stabbed between the shoulders with a long sword. Beneath this part of the arras was the King's table, heaped regularly and orderly with papers. King Richard, wearing a magnificent gown of mulberry-coloured silk reversed with otter, sat at the middle of the board with Mr. Secretary Kendal on his left and the Lord Privy Seal, Dean Gunthorpe of Wells, on his right. The Comptroller and Treasurer of the Household, Sir Robert Percy and Mr. Walter Hopton, were together at one end, busy with their own affairs, pricking items on a long parchment list with a dagger and checking them from a raffle of small papers. Mr. Robert Bolman, clerk to the Privy Seal, was writing at the other. They had been at work since seven o'clock that morning and it was now almost noon.

Mr. Kendal looked sideways at the King: line of a wax-white cheek curving inward to the furrow round the mouth, and with the bone showing under it, the lips as tight as they had always been, but with less blood in them. God have mercy, he thought, how bad he looks! Less than a year of being a King has done it. He is, now how old, not thirty-two yet; looks forty-five. Well, and we aren't through the morning's work yet. The King looked up from the paper he had been reading: a sworn statement by the Mayor, bailiffs and burgesses of Cambridge concerning the impoverished condition of their town. It had been forwarded to him after he visited the University a month ago.

"We shall have to do something for these folk," he said. "What is the old fee-farm they pay?"

Mr. Kendal routed among his papers. "Seventy pounds to the Exchequer, your Grace, nine pounds to the Prior of Chaldwell and a pound to the Prior of Killingworth."

"Make a memorial, please, to consult Sir William Catesby about how much we can spare them."

"Yes, your Grace."

What an ugly face Sir William will pull, he thought. It's almost the only diversion we have now, to see the King cheating his own Chancellor of the Exchequer out of half-pence for charity. The same thought must have been also in King Richard's mind. His narrowed eyelids allowed the smallest twinkle of amusement to flick through them.

"And if he grumbles," he said, "tell him to be a little sharper in collecting the Crown debts and then we shall not need to squint quite so long at each groat we spend. What was it you wished, Sir Robert?"

Sir Robert Percy leaned over with two carefully engrossed documents.

"Appointments of two yeomen-poulterers of the household, your Grace."

The King waved them away.

"At your own discretion, Sir Robert, so long as you appoint no foxes. Mr. Secretary, please give me the inquisitions of the property of John Fogg."

His voice chilled on the name a little. Mr. Kendal, routing out the papers, thought : I wish we could have caught the bastard. Too many people had slipped overseas last year when the storm drowned Henry of Buckingham's rebellion : the smooth Morton of Ely, the Marquis Dorset and several more. They were in France and Brittany now, though one of them, the Marquis, might soon be home again, considering the strange course King Richard had just taken.

Before the King left London he had, with no warning, summoned the Lord Mayor and Aldermen and the Lords spiritual and temporal, as many as could be found, and before them all, coldly and unaccountably, as he did most things, promised and swore, verbo regio, that if the daughters of Elizabeth Grey, late calling herself Queen of England, would come to him out of the Sanctuary of Westminster and be guided and ruled by him, then he would see them in surety of their lives; would not suffer any manner of hurt to be done to their persons by way of ravishing or defiling contrary to their wills, nor imprison them in the Tower of London or elsewhere; but would treat them and find for them honestly and courteously as his kinswomen and marry them to gentlemen born, giving to each of them a dowry of the yearly value of two hundred marks, in land. To Dame Elizabeth Grey herself he would assure a pension of seven hundred marks a year; and he further promised that if any evil report were made of them to him he would not punish them before they had opportunity for defence.

What it cost him to swear this, John Kendal reflected, it would be wiser for a man without Plantagenet blood in him not to speculate: but it was clever. Queen Elizabeth and her five daughters must be growing mightily weary of Broad Sanctuary. Since Henry Stafford's head had bounced on the scaffolding before the Poultry Cross six months ago, there had been little hope that the eldest of them, the plump Lady Bessy, would ever see her Welch bridegroom come riding into London to crown her Queen by the right of Lancaster. Half a loaf, even to a hate-crazed polecat like King Edward's widow, would look vastly better than no bread. They would come out for certain, and then—Mr. Kendal grinned faintly over his papers—some gentleman born to whom the King owed a grudge could be found to make a husband for Lady Bessy. Bishop Morton's outrageous vision of a marriage-alliance between Wydvylle and Lancaster would blow out for ever. Yes, it was cunning: King Richard's device to the last letter: the removal of a great menace to the peace of England by just a few words and a little money, with no bloodshed.

The King looked up again. His eyes were very narrow.

"How this tick bloated himself on England," he said quietly. "Mr. Dean, did you dispatch that grant to Sir Robert Fenys?"

"Yes, your Grace."

"Kendal, you said something of some Scots papers."

"Only spies' news, your Grace: they say they can learn nothing of whether King James means to send the commissioners that he promised or not."

"These Scots: once let me have England settled as I'd wish to see it and I'll give 'em a sit up. In the meantime we need a truce till Christmas or at any rate All Hallows. We'd better send a herald to Berwick in case the commissions do come. I should suggest Northumberland Herald. What do you say, Sir Robert?"

"Good enough, your Grace: but if I may speak my mind..."

"Always."

"We'll never get a truce from the whorsons whilst we hold Dunbar. Albany gave us the wolf by the ears when he surrendered the pestilent place to us."

"We'll hold the wolf; but you may be right. I must do something with Scotland more than a truce : peace or war. You're a North-countryman, Robert. Why must I do something with Scotland?"

He gave them his first real smile and their first real rest of the morning, leaning back in his chair and twisting his ring. Sir Robert Percy grinned like a bright schoolboy.

"Imprimis, because they've earned it : item, because your Grace is also a North-countryman : item, because Louis of France has gone to the place where he belongs."

"Your arrow's in the gold. But it's deeper than that. I have assured the child who now rules France that I mean nothing against him : and I haven't named it for a lie in the confessional. I do mean nothing against him while the Welch milksop's at liberty. If he, or rather his governors, once so much as glimpsed my real drift—which is to leave my son the crown of France along with the crown of England—they'd have that little upstart out of François of Brittany's hands, lend him an army and send him here as though all the devils in hell were after him : and I will not suffer another war in England. We must clip Henry Tydder's sting for a beginning. Next we quiet Scotland. I've no great wish—pardon me, Robert—for conquests there. We'll keep Dunbar, and for the rest peace will serve us as well as war. There are more ways of killing a cat than putting it to death with cherry-stones. When that's concluded, why, when that's concluded we can pray God for a fair wind to France."

"Amen."

Not quite for the first time, Mr. Kendal felt his sceptical, phlegmatic mind stirred, listening to his master; saw the world he aimed to leave his son, the English Empire stretching from Ireland to Champagne and from the Tweed to the Garonne; its great cities equal in prosperity so that York was as Rouen and Nottingham as Tours; Spain, Brittany and the Low Countries its allies; Scotland spanieling at its heels with no Valois on the other side of St George's Channel to make trouble between them; subjects of one crown and one King meeting in innumerable open markets to exchange the wool of Yorkshire and the wine of France; the conquered French, even, in time, learning to bless God for the mild rule of Plantagenet after the iron rule of Valois. It could be done. Harry of Monmouth had almost done it, that man of stone whose nostrils loved the smell of a burnt heretic; and this man was not stone; was steel. He sat there, small as a frog, worn thin, just as a steel blade would be, on the incessant grindstone of his occupations, tired as a tree is tired of the wind; but sure. He was utterly sure : a carved image in a cathedral, sitting and abiding the flux and outcry round his seat, content in the purpose of God. He would reach his aims, because, John Kendal thought, staring through the paper in front of him at the future, he aimed at nothing for himself. England, my son : those were the two words with which he ordered everything. They were a talisman against failure. A man who did not regard himself could hardly fail.

He jerked his head. I'm growing fanciful; shall become a second Anthony Wydvylle at this rate. It's all fine and fair to talk of what we shall do when we've caught Henry Tydder, but we've to catch him yet. In the disconcerting manner he sometimes used, the King spoke his thoughts for him.

"Pierre Landois, Treasurer to Duke François of Brittany, is an upstart, avaricious like all upstarts. We can bribe him, and shall."

"To kill Henry Tydder, your Grace?"

"To cage him : that is sufficient."

Sir Robert Perccy rattled his parchment at the end of the table.

"Stone-dead has no fellow."

The liveliness went out of the King's face suddenly, as a candle-flame would go out in an unlooked-for draught, and left him staring straight ahead of him almost like a man at a loss. Then he reached for his papers.

"We have still work to do."

Mr. Kendal returned to the list he was engrossing of certain properties : the manors of Eydon and Thorphill in Northamptonshire of the yearly value of seventy-four pounds, the manor or lordship of Great Billing in the same of the yearly value of twenty-three pounds fourteen shillings and fivepence, late the property of Margaret, wife of Lord Thomas Stanley, now held for life, with their knights' fees, advowsons, stews, waters, stanks, woods, underwoods, markets, heriditaments and commodities, by the said Lord Stanley, with reversion to the crown. He clicked his tongue over them. The sullen-faced Beaufort woman, Henry Tydder's mother, had been as deep as the pit of hell in Buckingham's conspiracy. What mother, even were she not a lifelong enemy of the house of York, would not have taken art and part in a plot to make her son King of England? You could as soon wash an Ethiopian white as clear her of it. When Buckingham's head fell, John Kendal had looked to see her clapped up for life in the Tower or exiled to the Isle of Man, attainted, even put to the axe. Lord save your soul, no. He nibbled his quill irritably. She had not even been chased into a nunnery; had merely been re-manded into the custody of her husband, who was to enjoy her estates during his lifetime, with order that she was to be allowed no communication with her son. Certainly, it did seem as though the fat Baron himself were a safe man. He and his family had provided the bulk of the royal army for the bloodless West-country campaign last year, and he had been given the office of Constable in reward for it. Never-theless, thought Mr. Kendal, had it been he who wore the crown, the Lady Margaret would have been put where she could make no mischief. She was a schemer and intriguer to her fingertips, and whatever they had done against Buck-ingham, the family she was married into had the reputation of going where the cat jumped. Yes, the act of a thoroughly cautious man would have been to end her : but King Richard's clemency was a byword.

Clemency and generosity : certainly they were no ill weapons, and the bloodless, frigid little gentleman on Mr. Kendal's right knew how to use them. King Richard had forgotten the enemies but never the friends of Duke Richard of Gloucester. Mr. Kendal himself, as well as the offices of Secretary of State and Controller of the Mint, had just re-ceived a pleasant Easter gift of eighty pounds a year. His old friend Thomas Wrangwysh had an annuity too. Lord Lovel was Chief Butler of England and making a better showing in that office than Lord Rivers ever did. These things were for old friendship's sake; but only pure christian

429

charity could explain the King's dealings with the Countess of Oxford. Since her husband had been captured at St. Michael's Mount twelve years ago and shipped across to Calais to look out over the marshes from a barred window in Hammes Castle, the unfortunate creature, who had never mixed herself with politics, had been in a most miserable case. King Edward, after stripping her of every rag she possessed, had been pleased to pardon her misdeeds and leave her to God. For ten years she supported herself with her needle as a common seamstress. Her friends made interest for her to the King, who clicked his tongue sympathetically, wrote out a grant for a pension and forgot to implement it. She would have been sewing yet had not King Richard had the crown. She received a hundred pounds a year now.

Lord, the web of it, thought John Kendal, through whose fingers many strands of the web ran : the criss-cross out of sight of small decrees and grants and readjustments, the gift of a living, the reduction of a subsidy, the remission of a fine, seal upon seal, patent upon patent, day upon day, all for the one end : that King Richard might leave England a little easier than he found it. It had hacked the lines into his forehead and round his mouth as deeply as a knife would; had turned his skin as translucent as the rim of a candle. His scruples were ageing him as quickly as his pleasures aged King Edward. Well, he was not a man whose ways one questioned.

The King spoke again.

"I see Sir John Fogg had the guardianship and marriage-bargain of a boy, one Robert Arundel of Treriss, poor child. Sir James Tyrell spoke of it to me. Did I ask you, Mr. Dean, to make out a grant of them to him and some other person? I forget now."

Dean Gunthorpe snapped his fingers to Mr. Bolman, who passed a writing to him after a little search. The Dean cocked his silver spectacles at it and said :

"Yes, your Grace, the new guardians are Sir James himself and one Richard Gowld of London, mercer."

"I remember. Seal it, please."

"Yes, your Grace."

Wax spat in the little chafing-dish. It was as Dean Gunthorpe actually pressed down the seal that the door was knocked. Robert Bolman went to it.

"It's Sir James Tyrell here, your good Grace."

"He's come in pudding-time. Admit him."

Sir James was a tall, cold-lipped man. His usual face was as expressionless as his master's: but now the look on it seemed to pierce Mr. Kendal like a sword in the belly. His hands moved senselessly.

"Your Grace, your Grace . . ."

"What's amiss?"

The King was out of his chair. Sir James moved toward him draggingly, like a man exhausted with running; leaned one hand on the table as though he did not trust his knees.

"Speak out, man."

"A message from Middleham, your Grace: late last night, the Prince—it was a sudden sickness, your Grace; last night. God took him."

"Dickon, oh Dickon, you must sleep now."

"I can't."

"Oh, my love, it is two nights now. You must. You must, indeed. Oh, Dickon, aren't I suffering too? Come to me. Come here and lie down by me. Lie down and shut your eyes. Look, love, we'll hold hands, so, both with our eyes shut; shut out everything. We'll think of nothing at all; make our hearts quite dark and quiet as though we had drawn curtains round them. We shall sleep then. We are together. We're still together, Dickon, still. Only shut your eyes now."

There was no sound in the room. The bed was scented with musk and violets. The thick hangings were walls round them, darkening darkness. For a long while he might have been asleep. Then a noise began that she could not recognise; had never heard before. It terrified her almost out of the memory of her own grief when she understood that her husband in the dark beside her was weeping as though his lungs were torn to pieces.

"Dickon, oh, Dickon, Dickon, for pity's sake."

She got her arms round his cold, smooth body, dragging it to her. He lay on his back with his hands shut at his sides, and she threw herself over him. But the terrible rending noise of his sobs went on. His whole chest shook with them.

"Dickon, Dickon, Dickon!"

"Oh, God, my punishment is harder than I can bear."

"Our punishment?"

"Anne, forgive me. Oh, forgive me, forgive me."

"Dear heart, listen. You are out of yourself. Think clearly a moment. There is no punishment. I have nothing to forgive. God took him. He was quite innocent. His little soul is with God now. He is happier than he could have been with us. We shall see him in the end. Oh, Dickon, you know that."

"Forgive me, Anne."

"Love, there is nothing on the footstool of God I would not forgive you : but why now? You have done nothing. Didn't you give him to me, Dickon? You made me happy with him for seven years."

"Hush, for God's sake. You can't understand. I killed him."

"No, no no."

"I killed him, woman. The punishment for my sin : God took him from us."

"Dickon, you mustn't talk so. I won't hear you."

"God's justice : I wanted a quiet England."

"Hush, your wits are all shaken. You've not slept for two nights. You'll have forgotten all this after you've slept. You must shut your eyes now. There, I'll kiss them shut. You must sleep."

"Oh Christ in heaven, oh Jesus, you won't understand. We are punished for Edward's sons. I killed them after Buckingham had revolted."

CHAPTER SEVEN

THE ROASTED COCK

(England—August 1485)

'If this be truth,' King Herod said,
'that thou hast told to me,
the roasted cock that lies in the dish
shall crow full senses three.'

Oh the cock soon thrustened and feathered well
by the work of God's own hand—
and he did crow full senses three
in the dish where he did stand.

English Carol : N.D.

THE green of August leaves they rode under was livid;
suggested the corruption of metal. Heat, that clung deadly
round their armoured bodies, was stagnant. There was no
health in the sun. Leicestershire, ordered like a chessboard,
was spread out for them : one comfortable little swell of
land behind another, black-and-white houses, churches like
cats asleep. The land was sick and rotten; sick England a
widowed King rode through to fight civil war again.

Last year the trouble called the Sweating Death had
come; was a curse specially sent by God on England. Even
abroad, they said, it attacked only Englishmen. London
festered with it. It had packed Mayor Byllysdon and Sheriff
Chester into their graves. It had struck York, and Mayor
Wrangwysh and his Aldermen had fled out of the city. Men
working in the fields or treadling looms felt themselves
suddenly tremble, ripple upon ripple of shivering chasing
through them. Then they sweated, and presently felt the
cramp in their muscles, and began to die. It was rarely that
a man lived overnight with the Sweating Death on him.
The sexton, after a heavy day of making graves, was seized
with pains that were not rheumatism. The physician, with

a dried orange stuffed with helpful perfumes at his nose, felt the cold leap from the patient to himself. The priest, standing at the altar, began to tremble, and the hands he put about the chalice were sweaty.

It had been on England a year now. The land stank. Autumn woodsmoke, fog, smell of spring hawthorns, seemed to corrupt in the nostrils and become a stench of corpses. It did not help the towns that their dues were remitted and their gates not banged upon by rebels demanding shelter against one King or another. Infection bred in their narrow streets and the passing-bells lamented over their roofs all day and night. Poor people in cottages could have justice easily; but what oppressed them was outside the sheriff's jurisdiction and they could not appeal from death to Westminster. In monasteries and great houses, in cities, in the fat little villages snugged down between the wood and the hill, people died quickly, unreasonably, as though stabbed from behind. The saints did nothing. Prayers and incense, candles and vows, did not move them to one petty miracle. The land was as though under an Interdict.

As winter lengthened and the frozen sewer bred pestilence as freely as the running one, until death was the companion of the solitary, the third fellow when two sat together, the quickest mover in every crowd, Lollards and others who were not afraid of twisting Holy Writ whispered an atrocious thing. They whispered that when King David of Jewry had offended God by a great wickedness a plague was sent upon his people to punish them. King David's son had also been taken from him on account of his crimes.

They were called liars and struck across the mouth by honest men when they first whispered. Loyal people said that King Richard, who had punished the Wydvylles, who had abolished benevolences, who protected the poor, was not the King for whom God would afflict a nation. The bastards of Edward of Rouen had died as he said they died. But the carts still creaked down the streets with their piles of bodies, and the whispers still spread and multiplied like the very sickness; and in March of the new year the sun was darkened.

A shadow came over it in broad daytime. The light curdled unnaturally, thickening as if for evening, so that owls and bats in the countryside were deceived and flew abroad. Blackness appeared to eat inch by inch into the sun's very disk until, against a benighted sky, it was a disk of the dark with hell's flames burning round it. Wherever people had knotted at a street corner or in a market-place to watch the portent a low, formless sound broke out: a noise between a moan and a whimper, as though the courage of a sick land were audibly breaking; and the sound rose into a wild, bewildered clamour of desolation when the news ran about that a fresh scourge was laid upon the King: that at the very moment when the darkness was absolute, the Sweating Death had sent Queen Anne, Kingmaker's daughter, to join her son.

It was as though that lanced, but did not cure, a tumour; as though a gush of filthy matter broke out at a touch, the corruption of men's courage and wits. The whisperers were not silenced with blows now; could tell their tale at every market-cross and in every inn. England was under the anger of God. A sinner beyond all common measure stood between the people and mercy, darkening heaven to them as they had just seen it darkened to their bodily eyes. He had been marked out before all of them: the small, white-faced devilish creature with the face no one could read. Born unnaturally, bred up among calamities he had unnaturally survived, crowned after mysterious happenings whose truth no one would ever know, he was a man with a curse on him; had shed blood of his own blood.

The rumours maddened as the madness of fear increased. In London chiefly, the city King Richard hated and that hated him, impossible tales began to be told. Men who had never seen him learnt that their King was a hunchback with a crippled arm and eyes that whirled round continually in his head. He had stabbed Holy Harry of Windsor in cold blood, without King Edward's warrant; had murdered his unarmed and helpless son after the battle of Tewkesbury. Even in King Henry's lifetime he had aimed for the crown, and when the good Lord Hastings refused to help him he sent him to death without trial, swearing in a climax of rage that he would not dine until he saw his head off. For his nephews, kind King Edward's children, he had never proposed any better fate than murder. He had poisoned—they carried it that far in the South—his wife and son.

King Richard had laid hands on a few of the prattlers, Lancastrians all of them. A certain Mr. Colyngbourne of Lydyard in Wiltshire had been too clever; had nailed a rhyming couplet on the door of St. Paul's and been caught doing it.

> The Cat, the Rat and Lovel our Dog
> Ruleth all England under the Hog:

Catesby and Ratcliffe, and himself whose badge the dog was, rulers of grumbling England under the silver boar. Mr. Colyngbourne, who had served King Richard's brother and mother in his time, would make no more couplets. Tried at the Guildhall before the Duke of Suffolk, he had been proved a Lancastrian of old standing with a record as black as the devil's arse. He had had part in Henry Stafford's plot; was a friend of Lady Margaret who was Lord Stanley's wife but Henry Tydder's mother, and among the trusted tools of the fox, Morton of Ely, now gone to earth in Flanders. There was no doubt that he had had a hand in the worst setback to King Richard's policy. Last year, a little after Edward of Middleham died, the upstart Treasurer of Brittany, Pierre Landois, came to terms; would deliver up Henry Tydder so that there should be final peace in England. But someone had warned the little Welchman. Like a hero in a romance he changed clothes with his servant; got—though he was said to be no horseman—on the swiftest mount he could borrow; spurred for his skin over the border into France. The governors of the boy-king, Charles VIII, received him kindly.

Mr. Colyngbourne had had his part in that; no doubt of it. Well, they had paid him. A good new gallows was built on Tower Hill for his special use. The rope failed to kill him, for when the hangmen dragged his clothes off and had their knives at him he shrieked out hideously: 'Lord Jesus—yet more trouble?' and lived whilst the whole business of gelding, gutting and burning was carried out. If the job could only have been done two years ago, in the days when the world seemed real and King Richard human, they would not now be riding West from Leicester in harness.

This time the end had come. St. Albans, where the nobility of England had learned to kill each other, Bloor Heath and Northampton, Wakefield and the Duke of York's dead head with a paper crown on it, Noman's Heath and Mortimer's Cross, where Owain Tydder's head paid for the Duke's, Towton of the twenty-seven thousand dead, Hedgeley Moor, Hexham and Edgecote, Barnet and the fall of Kingmaker, the Bloody Meadow and the Bastard's siege of London : all the madness that for thirty years now had made England rip out its own bowels like a wounded wolf was coming to its end and resolution. This would be the ultimate bloodletting. The Cat, the Rat and the Dog were riding with all the strength of England behind the silver boar for that. Three Plantagenets, four Nevilles, four Beauforts, three Bourchiers, three Staffords, two Courtneys, five Wydvylles, had died in the garboyles that led up to this. To-morrow or next day some more would die, and they would have quiet for good; breathing-space to take order with England.

Henry Tydder the Welchman, the last bastard offshoot of the House of Lancaster—a little rat-faced man, those who had seen him said, with yellowish hair going thin already and small peeping eyes—had landed at Milford Haven in Pembrokeshire on the Feast of the Transfiguration, just fourteen days ago. He had with him two thousand Norman and Breton fighting men, under the command of Philibert de Shaundé; and in his company, as though ghosts walked out of their graves to trouble men, came his uncle, Jaspar of Pembroke, and John Vere of Oxford, whose wife King Richard had made his pensioner and who had repaid him by escaping from his prison at Hammes. Lord Lovel did not know for certain what could have moved the Welchman to this last risk, to fling himself under the very tusks of the boar with only two thousand soldiers of fortune, a superannuated captain shaking with gaol fever, and the good wishes of the rulers of France to guard his skin. Some said the Lady Bessy, Queen Elizabeth's daughter, had a hand in the business. That young lady, now kept in seclusion in the Castle of Sheriffhutton, had shown herself recently to be a proper Wydvylle; had suggested, a small matter of weeks after Queen Anne found rest, that her uncle the King might get a Papal dispensation to marry her, which would, she said, end all the grudging between her family and him. It seemed even that thin-jawed Medusa of Westminster Sanctuary, her mother, thought this incest a hopeful plan. King Richard, without change of face, had announced publicly in London that the proposal had been made to him and that he had refused it; that there would be punishment for those who even spoke of such an infamy. It did not touch him. But perhaps the pleasant news that Lady Bessy, if she could wear a crown, would not be particular who put it on her had helped to call Henry Tydder out of France. Women—Lord Lovel damned them wholemeal—had too many hands in politics. There was the Lady Margaret. King Richard should have killed her after Buckingham's Water. Now she had done her share for the corruption of England. They had found out a week ago at Nottingham.

The news had come to them there that Henry Tydder had reached Shrewsbury. In his own country of Wales no one opposed him. His little regiment of gaolbirds—the French had not gone so far as to provide him with men that could be trusted—had slouched from valley to valley behind the banner of a dragon passant, gules, on a field vert and argent, the standard of Cadwallader. That had been clever of the little Welchman. He claimed descent from Cadwallader as well as from John of Ghent and Brutus and King Lear; and there was a prophecy that a man of that blood would one day recover the ancient empire of the Britons. Welchmen in ones and twos began to join him : savage men with pedigrees as long as their pikes and bellies as empty as their purses : Gryffudds, ap Thomases, Morgans, Vaughans and Gams. Shrewsbury would have shut its gates to him but for his numbers. He got in, and the rumour ran about that there was one Englishman at least who was ready to fight shoulder-by-shoulder with the Welch and French against his King. Sir Gilbert Talbot had raised five hundred men and declared for Lancaster.

That was the news they debated in the tower-room at Nottingham.

"The rot is spreading," said John Howard of Norfolk. "We may hear worse things before we're done. This gives the Welchman four thousand at least : twice what he started with."

King Richard clicked his dagger and looked down. His face was a dead face washed clean by too much unhappiness. But he said quietly :

"I wish the Great Turk, with Prester John and the Sultan of Syria, were against me with all their power. For all their manhood I would be King of England."

A little stir went round them, like wind going through tired leaves in the autumn. It was not the King of silences that they had grown used to in the months since Lady Anne died, but their old Richard, who said that. But whilst they were still looking at one another with the sadness of men whom a relic had put in mind of a dead friend, Sir Richard Ratcliffe was in the room with them.

"Your Grace, I found my Lord le Strange with his horse saddled. He was making ready to leave Nottingham and your person on his own concerns."

Lord Scrope swore and grabbed for his dagger, and the Earl of Northumberland went white, when they heard that. Lord le Strange, who had raised ten thousand against Buckingham, was the son of Lord Stanley; and Lord Stanley was the stepfather of Henry Tydder.

He was brought in. They had taken his sword from him and there was blood on his mouth as though he had made trouble and been given a blow. The King's voice was as gentle as the croon of a pigeon and his face was blank.

"Lord le Strange, why were you leaving Court without my word?"

Suddenly, with the quickness of a frightening accident, Lord le Strange dropped on his knees. He was a young man, big and fattish, and his face was as flabby as a dead fish with terror.

"Mercy, your Grace, for Christ's sake mercy : I'll tell you everything."

"Lord God," whispered John Howard of Norfolk to Francis Lovel, "what's this to mean? Are the whole Stanley pack in it?"

"You will tell me everything," said King Richard, looking down at his hands, agreeing with him.

The story came, Lord Lovel thought, almost too freely. He had listened to his stepmother, the Lady Margaret.

She had begged him to help her Welch son to the crown of England; had talked of rewards. She had said King Richard could never prosper now the world knew he had killed his nephews. Like a disloyal fool, he had come to terms with her. So had his cousin, Sir John Savage. Let the King have mercy. His uncle, Sir William Stanley, was not clean of the matter either. He would tell the whole truth. His uncle had sworn to give King Richard such a breakfast as no knight had ever prepared for a King.

"And your father?"

"Your Grace, do what you please with me. Kill me. But if I were at the edge of the block I would tell you the same. My father never conspired against you. He would not listen to her. He knows nothing of all this. I swear it on the sacrament."

"You will write a letter to your father. Tell him that if he does not join me with five thousand men to break this Welchman, you will pay me your debt. Your uncle and your cousin I shall proclaim traitors. They will answer to me. in my own time. If your uncle keeps his promise to this woman, if he sends one man to the aid of Henry Tydder, you pay."

Sir Richard Ratcliffe cut in then.

"Your Grace, for the love of God you'll never trust a Stanley now? Trust none of them. We've plenty of men. Send ten thousand into Cheshire to pull down the gryffon's claw wherever it flies. Christ's body, you can't trust them now."

"I trust this coward's love of his life."

"No, no, your Grace, for all hallows' sake remember Henry of Buckingham's last words to you. Everything is for sale in England."

"And I have bought Lord Stanley with his son's head. Will he fight against me with his son in my hands? and if he fights for me, will his brother fight for Henry Tydder? Write your letter, George Stanley, and save your neck from the axe and your father from the sin of treason."

"Ah, let me cut his throat now and his father's to-morrow. We've time yet before we deal with the Welch-man."

"No."

No one argued with King Richard now. Some ranks ahead of him, in the middle of a thick clump of spears,

Francis Lovel could see Lord le Strange riding with his feet lashed to his stirrup-leathers. Lord Stanley had heard what the conditions were on which he would see his son alive again. He lay ahead of them, camped in the Deer Park before Market Bosworth, with his five thousand. If his honour was for sale, it seemed the King had got the price for it.

They had power enough without him. John Howard of Norfolk and his son the Earl of Surrey, Henry Percy of Northumberland, young John de la Pole of Lincoln, Neville of Westmorland and Gray of Kent, Lord Dacres, Lord Ferrers, Lord Zouche, Lord Ogle, Lord Beauchamp, Lord Greystoke, Lord Scrope of Upsall and Lord Scrope of Masham, and fifty-nine knights, each with his following, were somewhere in the long fourfold column, flanked on each hand by a single line of outriders, that churned the August dust up. The metallic, comfortable noises and sweaty smell of a great army on the march came to Lord Lovel as he rode. He felt a sudden keenness of liking for the archers slouching beside his horse : sun-bitten, red necks and unthinking faces. Sweating Death or none, treason or none, these—some twenty thousand of them— had turned out to have a hand in the finish of it; put an end to the madness of the two roses.

Someone had pulled his horse out of the line ahead of them; was standing and letting the column pass him, shouting to each captain as he came up :

"Stapleton Village ahead : we harbour this side of it where the bridge is."

He swung in his saddle, acknowledging the order with a lift of the hand; shouted to his men :

"Harbour in a moment, lads."

A kind of muttering cheer wandered from mouth to mouth. The sun had flogged the spirit out of them. The whole column moved a little sullenly, heads down, eyebrows drawn, hating the dust and the hedgerows that looked cool but were not. Sooner we get them off the road for the night the better, he thought, and shouted to his harbingers to get ahead and pitch camp.

Only the church-tower showed above the trees from Stapleton village. The Camp-Marshal's pickets were out on the road to turn back those who dreamed of the alehouse.

Like King Edward in his great days, King Richard kep[t] his men sober on campaign. In a hollow meadow by th[e] roadside, with a stream through it, horses were bein[g] picketed and tents put up. The harbingers quarrelled and advised each other. He let a groom take his horse, and stood at the roadside watching one company of me[n] slouch past him behind another. Presently someone sai[d] behind him:

"Well, my Lord Viscount?"

The face of John Kendal, Secretary of State, looke[d] strange with the steel frame of basnet and gorget roun[d] it, like the face of a friend seen suddenly in the dark by [a] tinder-flash.

"Well, Mr. Secretary?"

"The King is to sup alone: but you and Sir Richar[d] Ratcliffe sleep in his tent."

"Very good: is there any news of Lord Stanley?"

"The King has sent an outrider."

"Then we shall have news soon."

"Yes."

There did not seem any more to say. Almost horizonta[l] beams of sunshine, as red as blood, stretched over the half pitched camp. The voices of men unloading carts and setting up tents sounded flat and low. It's queer, though[t] Francis Lovel, the little crew of us who stand round ou[r] King like mourners keeping the month's-mind round th[e] grave of a friend, and queer how we come together i[n] corners when we think no one's looking, and then fin[d] that we have nothing to say. Ah, Lady Anne, wasn't i[t] hard enough for us to lose you: need you have take[n] Richard away as well? John Kendal lifted his hand in [a] kind of salute and slouched off, clumsy in his unfamilia[r] harness, and Lord Lovel went to see if his supper wer[e] ready.

It was nearly dark when he was called to the royal tent[.] The great cloth-of-gold pavilion, as big as a barn, wit[h] the leopards and lilies hanging lax over it in the unmovin[g] air, was the one King Edward had used in France te[n] years ago. The gold thread was a little tarnished now[.] The captains were all there: Norfolk, dark-eyed an[d] thoughtful as he always was; his livelier son, the Earl o[f] Surrey; handsome young John of Lincoln; Henry Perc[y]

442

of Northumberland, thin-faced, unsure in his movements, not looking much like a man who had the blood of Hotspur in him. Sir William Catesby was there too, the Cat; and the Rat with him. Colyngbourne deserved to be hanged only for calling that honest mastiff of a man a rat, Lord Lovel thought. John Kendal and Sir Robert Percy were in attendance.

The King sat in a small, low-backed chair. He had his harness off and wore black velvet. The men stood around him, some talking, but he did not appear to see them. His hands with their many rings lay on the chair-arms and he was looking down. His face was deathly, the bones standing out as though to cut the skin and the muscles round the mouth like wires. After a little, he held one hand out and John Kendal put a paper in it. He read it through, drawing his colourless under-lip backward and forward over his teeth; then talked. His voice was as dead as his complexion.

"Gentlemen, this is an assurance from Lord Thomas Stanley that he is and has been loyal. He will fight tomorrow. He has implored his brother, Sir William Stanley, either to seek my mercy or at least not to draw his sword on me, and he has a certain confidence that his appeal will be heard. None of the name of Stanley will be on the Welchman's side to-morrow. He gives me news of the rebels. Their force, he says, is not above five thousand, and their French and Breton mercenaries are of the poorest. John Vere and Jaspar Tydder are old men. As to Henry Tydder, he would seem to be altogether what we supposed he was : a milksop who never saw an army. It seems he is regretting his hardiness already and wishing himself back in Britanny; Lord Stanley tells me for the truth that on his road here from Lichfield he tried to desert his own army and hide alone. His uncle Jaspar prevented him. That is the man we are to fight.

"Now, gentlemen, here is the disposition of the matter. The Welchman and his five thousand are at a place called the White Moors, three miles away on our left hand. Two streams lie between us and them and there is no good road. Sir William Stanley, in whom the rebels put all trust, lies almost two miles north of them near a village that is called Market Bosworth, and a mile from him and on the other side of Bosworth Park is his brother, Lord Thomas. We have assurance that these two will not join the Welchman. Then he must join them. To do this, he must cross the River Sence at a certain bridge and take a road about a marsh there. A hill overlooks this road. Its name is Ambion Hill upon the edge of Radmore Plain. We shall station ourselves there to-morrow. From it, we can see the Welchman and both the Stanleys, and we can force a field when we desire. If we engage the Welchman when he is round the marsh, Lord Stanley can take him in the rear. I have commanded him to do this. As for our marshalling: Norfolk, you take the vanward and form it on my left when we pitch field. My Lord of Northumberland, you take the rearward. I shall command the middleward. Sir William Catesby and Sir George Buck will remain here to oversee the camp.

"I have only this to say to you. With Sir William Stanley and Lord le Strange, since their treason has stopped short of battle, I shall deal with a certain mercy when this is over. For the rest, I require no prisoners. The Welchman and his five thousand are to be destroyed. We outnumber them by more than four to one. See you to it. These shameless foreigners and the unnatural Englishmen who are with them have brought civil war into my country again. For that, every mother's son of them is to die. Kill without quarter. Every one of Henry Tydder's part-takers whom I find alive after the field will be hanged and drawn. I shall give a reward for the head or body of Henry Tydder, or for Jaspar Tydder or John Vere or Gilbert Talbot. For the Frenchman, de Shaundé, I offer nothing. If he leaves the field, he cannot leave England. Repeat all these orders to your men. Has any of you anything to urge?"

"Aye." Sir Richard Ratcliffe took a pace forward, his bull's head of reddish-yellow curls down and his jaw fixed.

"I am listening."

"You trust the Stanleys too far, your Grace."

"I do not think so. Even in England a man thinks twice of a treachery that will cost him his son's head; and no word was ever said against Lord Thomas. I have made him Constable of England and spared him his wife's estates. Also he knows that if he does fail me I shall root his house out to the ninth generation and divide his lands from Lancaster to Shrewsbury."

"And if your Grace miscarried by his treachery, d'you not think he'd count it worth his while to lose a son if he could have a stepson a King? By Christ, I do. Remember Henry Stafford, your Grace."

"Henry Stafford was mad."

"Your Grace, we *know* Sir William Stanley meant to turn on us. How can we trust any one of them?"

It was the Earl of Northumberland who spoke now. His meagre face was more anxious even than before and he gesticulated like a Jew, hunching his shoulders.

"We have a hostage. We have Lord Thomas' assurance."

"Then by St. Cuthbert, why isn't Lord Thomas with us now instead of camping hip-to-haunch with his brother who's a proved traitor?"

"He is of more use to us where he is."

"Your Grace, as the blessed Trinity looks on me, I don't like it. I don't like these four camps scattered over half the county. Wherever we turn there will be someone who might fall on us. It's poxily unsafe. I'm for retreat until Stanley's proved his word and joined forces with us."

"You are for what?" asked the King tonelessly.

"I'm for withdrawing from this trap until we know who are our friends."

"My Lord of Northumberland," said the King without any change of voice, "if you are afraid you may leave us. When you are back in the North, tell the common people there that you deserted King Richard. They will rise in a mob and hang you. I know who are my friends."

"I'm not afraid, your Grace, indeed not: no, by God."

The man's face was white, Lord Lovel noticed. I would not give him a ward to command, he thought, if I had my way.

"I am glad to hear it. It would be a new thing in the history of the Percys. We do not withdraw. Listen. Stanleys or no Stanleys, the Welchman cannot hold the field against us for half-an-hour. This is our opportunity to do England the greatest service that King or nobles ever did her : clean her for ever of civil war. All the disturbers of our peace— the old Lancastrians, the Welch partisans of the house of Tydder, the lice who clung to the hem of the Wydvylles' gown—are gathered together in one heap at White Moors to-night. To-morrow, we and every one of them, fall back, fall edge. A new England will begin to-morrow."

England, thought Lord Lovel, you plague-stricken old bitch who'll bite your master's hand, when were you worthy to have that said of you? Why should we risk a single honest life for you? We do, for all that. He says it, and we obey.

"Does anyone else wish to speak? Then good-night to you, gentlemen: get your rest. We shall be busy to-morrow."

He stood up, a black little figure like a page in mourning or a scholar who has puzzled over his books too long, and they left him.

There were two straw pallets in the outer compartment of the royal tent. Someone had put a jug of wine and two cups beside a lantern on the table. Alone together, Lord Lovel and Sir Richard Ratcliffe looked at them and at each other; nodded; filled; drank without saying anything. The wine was Beaune, and very good. The moon was up outside and they could hear stamping and, once or twice, a long, shaking whinny from the horse-lines. It was a feverish night: the air warm and thick like a cat's fur. At Market Bosworth, over there in the dark now, Sir William Stanley would be breathing this same air and praying that, since he was to hold his hand to-morrow, the pale-faced King would hold his afterward and not visit his treachery too heavily on him. Beyond, in the Deer-Park, Lord Thomas Stanley must be cursing the wickedness of his wife and brother that had endangered his own honour and his son's head: and westward from them, not dreaming the prop in which they trusted had been struck from under them, the yellow-haired Welch-man and his tagrag of renegades were lying close, waiting uncertainly for a dangerous morning: treachery and counter-treachery scattered in arms over the miles of English innocent countryside, and above it all the insensible thick miasma of pestilence.

Sir Richard Ratcliffe stretched himself. Lord Lovel could hear the muscles in his big arms crack. Then he whispered:

"Be hot to-morrow."

"To-morrow, yes, to-morrow should be a strange day on all counts."

"I could wish for rain. Foul weather's York weather: snow at Towton, fog at Barnet, storms before Tewkesbury, Buckingham's Water."

"We shall do the work whatever the weather is."

"I wish I were a little surer of the Stanleys."

"Ah God, man, d'you think anyone would send his own son to the block for the sake of making a fresh King?"

"In England, yes I do think it. See what's happened in England before. Edward of Rouen killed his own brother. Someone else killed Edward of Rouen's two . . ."

"It's better not to say it, Ratcliffe."

"Happen it is: but the sister of those two was ready to commit incest with the one who killed them, if only he'd put a crown on her head. That's what can happen in England when it's a matter of Kings and Queens."

"Aye."

"All because they want something for themselves: an office, a castle, money, a grant of land, just a name sometimes: that's what they want power for."

"And the man who has the power wants nothing whatever for himself. That is why he will keep it."

"You're in the right of it, my Lord Viscount. Aye, Christ yes, you're in the right of it there: Stanleys or no Stanleys. I wish I may get a cut at Henry Tydder to-morrow. His head would be worth money."

"It's only three miles to his camp. Don't wait for to-morrow. Go out and take his head now."

"Only three miles: blessed St. Peter, think of him saying his prayers over there in the dark, wishing to God he'd stopped in Brittany and damning his mother for having fetched him here. He'll be sweating as if he'd the plague."

"He couldn't die much sooner if he had. There'll be some hangings in Wales too when this is done."

"I'd string up every whorson jenkin from Flint to Cardiff if I'd my own way. Our master won't."

"I think this time he will."

"Maybe, but look at the plague of mercy we had after Henry Stafford's garboyle two years ago."

"He is different now."

"God have pity on us all. He's different. You know, I've

been thinking a crowd of odd things these last months."

"I suppose we all have."

"And I've been thinking about the chronicles will come to be written after we've gone, a hundred years from now and more. We'll be in them: what we did for King Richard, how we helped break the Wydvylles and the Tydders. They'll say I was a rough make of a fellow who did the King's butchery for him. Good luck to them: it's what they'll say about him puzzles me. They'll say he was a man with no blood in him, nothing of what you'd call humanity, a cold man that went his own road."

"They'll say that."

"Aye, but the devil fly off with it, they'll be wrong. They'll not know what he was like before the little Prince and our dear Lady—God rest them both, amen—were taken away. They'll not know the truth about him. They'll be talking common lies."

"They will."

"Do you suppose all the chroniclers are liars, then? D'you think the tales we hear tell of Harry of Monmouth and Edward of Windsor are lies too?"

"I see no cause why they shouldn't be. Look you, Ratcliffe, we've a piece of work on hand to-morrow for them to tell lies about when the time comes. Let's get our rest for it."

"We'll be best to."

It was barely cocklight when Lord Lovel woke again. He did so sharply, with the awareness that something had been moving in the tent. The beginning of morning showed Richard Ratcliffe asleep face-downward, his head in the curve of his arm like a child's. He had not shifted. It was someone else. The gold hangings spangled with silver fleurs-de-lys looked grey now; were not stirring. Have we had ghosts with us to-night, Lord Lovel wondered. Have all the multitude of dead come to watch the end of the troubles; Kingmaker and Somerset and Holy Harry come to see the last battle and the stopping of the wheels that went over them all? Something has been through here. He got up; went to the tent opening in his shirt and hose; looked out. The sentry was there, the early light sliding coldly over his steel jack and sallet, his pike held stiffly.

"Has anyone passed?"

The man twitched a frightened country face with a rough fuzz of beard round to him; pointed; did not say anything. The camp was as quiet as a cemetery; big round tents asleep like tombstones, guards standing as dull as monuments. There was no smell of smoke yet. The morning was clean, not hot and brooding as the day would be, but full of a kind of joyful and silent life. Among the pale lumps of the tents, as a child might walk among bushes in an orchard, a small black figure was twining, stopping now and then as though to take a breath of the coolness, sometimes peering at a tent or a stack of arms. Except that it left a black spoor of footprints in the grey of the dew, it might have been a homing goblin.

"Holy Jesus," said Lord Francis, "it's not right he should be wandering by himself." He took his sword from beside his pallet and strapped it on. "Tell Sir Richard Ratcliffe when he wakes," he told the sentry, and began to walk over the dew.

He did not at first try to overtake the King; allowed him fifty yards' law and kept his eyes on him. He moved slowly, for all the world like a country gentleman taking a morning stroll in his orchard, looking up now and again at the sky, which was turning from white to blue. They walked through the whole camp; halted at the brown welt the road made over the grass. The King had his hand at his side, and Lord Lovel knew he was playing his familiar trick with his dagger. Thinking of what : of the new day this was going to be for England, of the Stanleys, of his dead? No one, thought Francis Lovel, has ever known what King Richard thinks. But whatever he is studying over now will come to pass as he wants it. I have known just one man in my life from whom fate took orders. You Welch fool over there at White Moors, wishing to God you were a hundred miles away, what madness brought you out of your hole to try conclusions with a man nothing can hurt? If I were a Lancastrian I could believe the old fairy-tale that the devil fights for York. Buckingham lifts himself against King Richard and the very rivers turn on him. Lady Margaret plots, and her husband's son tumbles into our hands for a hostage. Doubtless

449

a thunderbolt will drop out of a clear sky and split Henry Tydder's head for him. At this moment, the King turned round and they were looking at one another.

Lord Lovel spoke first.

"God give your Grace good morning."

"Good morning, Frank."

It was almost the old voice, soft and encouraging like the voice of a man speaking to an animal. The King's face was as it had been the day before, but there was a kind of calmness about him as though he had been soothed, purged of something. His next words were a surprise.

"I could not sleep. I was dreaming of devils."

"Devils?"

King Richard nodded, beckoning Lord Francis nearer to him. They stood together looking into the rutted brown of the road as though into a stream.

"Devils, Frank, all the devils pulling and haling me from side to side so that I couldn't rest. They had the faces of people I knew. One of them was the Wydvylle woman and another was her daughter, my niece, who wished to seduce me into incest with her; and one of them was Henry Stafford."

Lord Francis crossed himself.

"No, Frank, I do not think it was an omen."

"God forbid."

"I think it was a parable."

"A parable?"

"Why, yes, of all my life: devils have been pulling me from side to side ever since I can remember. I have not had much rest."

God knows you have not, thought Lord Francis. Ah, Dickon, what has come back to you this important morning? You have been a shell or a corpse these months back, like a ghost watching us and giving us orders. You have not called me Frank for a long while: but talking to you now is like being at Middleham in the good days.

"No, you have had little of that, your Grace."

"It was Edward's fault, God pardon him," said King Richard simply: "Edward, who cared more for men's ordinary pleasures than for his kingdom. He should not have done that. It is not allowed a King. I was only

450

eighteen when Kingmaker quarrelled with him over the Wydvylle woman, and I have been doing penance for his sins ever after that. I'm thirty-three now. It's a long while. Thank God it's over."

"Over, Dickon—your Grace?"

"Call me Dickon if you wish. I almost am Dickon of Gloucester again. Perhaps after to-day I shall be."

"God knows, my dearest friend as well as my King, you have been to me always."

"I have not been to myself lately, Francis. I loved her, you see; and our son. He would have been such a fine lad, and I killed him. That killed her. It was a large price to pay."

"What are you saying? You mustn't say such things."

"It is true. I can talk to you this morning because it all belongs to another age now; is not part of us. God has been very merciful. Listen, Frank. You heard that good faithful Ratcliffe of ours preach and preach Henry Stafford's sermon to me, how there is no honesty in England. He thinks I do not know. I knew it as soon as Henry Stafford did. That was the England Edward left me: all perjured, all rotten, as unstable as sand. What else would it be when its King sold it to that abominable woman who sold it over again to the French? Edward made England what it is, and as soon as Bishop Stillington told me the truth, I knew my duty: to make it honest again. My God, it haas been like walking in a swamp. Hastings betrayed me. I would have trusted him with my soul twice over. Henry Stafford betrayed me. He had most cause to be true. When I found that devil Morton has corrupted him I knew what sort of an England it really was. Then I was tempted. I saw the only hope for it was to take every occasion of falsehood away, as one puts knives and razors out of a child's reach. There would have been another rising in favour of those Wydvylle bastards in the Tower. I knew that; and I remembered something that had been told me that Edward said before he died. His conscience troubled him because he had corrupted everything he touched. He said in the end that it would be the less loss if they died than if there were a fresh war on their account. I am assured of those words. So I killed them.

451

"Don't look so startled, Frank. You know it. All England knows it. I was wrong. It is folly to be unjust for the sake of justice. Now men will always use my name as an example of cruelty, as they use Edward's as an example of lying.

"God has been very good to me, Frank. He has punished me terribly: my son first, and then my dear, dear Anne. I bore it, but I was so afraid. If I've seemed strange these months past, it's not been only grief. I was terrified beyond all words of what the rest of my punishment was to be. I was afraid God would punish me by the ruin of England. The plague made me think that. Perhaps he meant to take everything away from me: my work too. People hate me. They have a murderer to rule over them. I thought I had forgone my right to build England up again.

"How can we ever find words for the mercy of God? He has punished me in all my affections so that my soul bleeds day and night. I think of her so often at night. He has broken my heart so that I may continue King and do my work. You see there is no more punishment now. England is not to be taken from me. Henry Tydder is the last of all those devils I dreamed about last night, and he is helplessly in our hands. We break him, and then I can go on. Do you remember those verses Anthony Wydvylle made before I headed him?

My life was lent
Me to one intent . . .

I know my life and intent are spared. Nothing else matters."

Behind them, suddenly, like a cock crowing, the morning trumpets began to blow.

The marshalling of the troops was a quick business that morning. The smell of frying and boiling had not cleared from round the tents before they began it. Lord Lovel walked down the line of his division, looking at jacks and bows, scolding a man with a rusty sallet, joking with an archer whose leaden mall looked almost too heavy to lift. The man was a smith by trade and grinned when his Lord felt his arm-muscles and said: "I renounce

Mahomet, but I believe it's not too much for you after all. If you meet one of the rebel captains, be sure you do not beat his head so flat that it won't be known or you'll lose your guerdon."

Then the trumpets blew again. King Richard was out of his tent. He wore the beautiful white harness, damascened with rayed suns and silver boars, that he had carried at Tewkesbury, and rounded his basnet, like a halo, was the gold circle, crosses alternating with fleurs-de-lys, that stood for a King. White Surrey, the big, pink-nosed charger that he only used on state occasions and at war, was held for him. A groom swung him up, and he lifted his battle-axe so that it caught the sun and split it into needles of light, signing them to ride on. Now for it, thought Francis Lovel, now for changing England.

Their way led up first: over a brow, down and across a brook, then up a slope which had a village on top of it. They swung left and saw a lump of wood, rich green in the morning, and a high ridge, hollow fields between them. They had come to Radmore Plain. Like a hairy caterpillar made of metal, a long undulant thing bristling with points, their line wormed up toward the ridge. John Howard's banner was ahead, and just in front of Lord Lovel rode the King's standard-bearer, Sir Percival Thriball, sitting very stiff in his saddle and holding up the gilt pole with the leopards and lilies. Then the view opened to them. From the ridge the ground ran very sharply down and there was a flat space, green and unpopulous, with a bright little river through it. Beyond that again, they could see trees and tents. With difficulty, in his armour, Lord Lovel swung himself up in his stirrups to look. Yes, perhaps a mile away and a mile apart, there were two camps separated by a wood and a church-tower peeping over it: the Stanleys. Nearer and on his left he saw the marsh that Henry Tydder must come round. A very distant sound of bugles disturbed the air.

They halted: three blocks of metal and colours sat like three stones of a battlement along the ridge of Ambion Hill. A call sounded, and the captains of the two wings touched their spurs to their mounts and rode in toward the centre. The King sat his horse under the limp standard, his axe in his right hand and his left bunched on his hip. He had turned to face his own men. There was a lark singing.

Lord Lovel watched the officers. The Duke of Norfolk, in black armour with the silver lion on his basnet, looked as he always did. His son, the Earl, was smiling happily as though he expected a good morning. Henry Percy looked old. Confound the fellow, Lord Francis thought, I know it's the truth that no Percy for four generations has died in his bed, but need he look as though we were at a funeral? After all, this need not be his last day on earth. He might die in some other battle.

"My friends . . ."

The King's voice was as gentle as ever; would not reach far enough, Lord Lovel thought.

"My friends, I shall not make you a long oration. You know that the devil has entered into the heart of an unknown Welchman whom none of us ever saw, exciting him to try for a crown, and at that the crown of England. You know that he is a man of small courage and less experience. You know that most of his force consists of Frenchmen, men whom our ancestors overthrew oftener in a month than they would have supposed possible in a year. You are not afraid. You are Englishmen and know how to deal with Frenchmen and traitors. Your work's easy. If this Henry Tydder, this bastard begotten in double adultery, were to be King of England it could be only by the utter disinheriting and destruction of all the noble blood of this realm. If a Welchman and a bastard sat on the English throne of the Plantagenets, can you imagine anything so monstrous or unnatural that it might not follow from it? Old England itself would crumble. There would be nothing left secure, nothing of our familiar life safe. Murder, incest, adultery, the subversion of Holy Church, the sale of England not simply to the French— for this fellow has already pledged himself to surrender our true and just title to the crown of France—but to the Scots or the Easterlings, for what I know : all this would follow the victory of Henry Tydder. Let us thank God such a victory is not possible. What is a handful to a whole realm? Every one of you give but one sure stroke and the day's ours. Do this to save our old England that we know and live in. God and St. George!"

454

The blare and rumble of voices went up round them:
"St. George! À Richard! À King! God and St. George!"
The noise had not died down when he shouted in a new
voice, high and carrying:

"Look! Look!"

Lord Francis trotted his horse to the edge of the slope
to look. They were there. The marsh was a big smudge
of green spotted with clumps of purple flags like ulcers
and wrinkling up here and there into a little mound
where a bush grew. It looked like a disease of the land-
scape, a place of leeches. Round its far side a curved
glimmer, recalling water in moonlight, was slowly crawling. He could make out individual heads under steel
coverings, a few horses. The rebel army was deploying,
moving from left to right in front of them. There were
two divisions. The first, like the head and neck of a
snake thrusting out of its hole, was past the marsh already.
Lord Lovel, working his two-handed sword out of its
sheath, could see the banners. A silver mullet dropped in
front: John Vere's blazon, the old star of Lancaster and
defeat. The man whose wife King Richard had pen-
sioned was ordering battle against him. A spotted dog
showed up next. Lord Lovel, thinking of his own blazon,
grinned. There are curs as well as hounds. Sir Gilbert
Talbot had been a trusted subject once. A queer blazon
next: he narrowed his eyes at it: a white hood. That was
Sir John Savage. A white shroud to you, Sir John, you
whorson: you're the blackest traitor of the whole pack of
them. But no matter: you are the only Stanley who will
draw sword against his King to-day. That was the first
division: not more than two thousand. Jesus, thought
Francis Lovel, this will be a massacre. Here was another
device, heading the second ward: three ravens and a
chevron. That looked Welch: aye, Sir Rhys ap Thomas
of course. Wales was doing its best for the Welchman,
but a raven was the right sign. The ravens would be
dining presently. That was what was oozing out from
behind the marsh and spreading itself on the plain: a
raven's dinner, carrion that did not know it was dead yet.

The last standards, a clump together, were in sight
now, not forming beside the others but halting behind
them: a red dragon on white and green, a portcullis, a

red rose. Lord God and all angels, thought Lord Francis, the little man's not even going to fight. He'll wait in the rear and let the others die first.

A trumpet seesawed a long chain of notes.

"Lord Lovel, Lord Ferrers, Sir Richard Ratcliffe, Sir Gervaise Clifton, Sir Robert Percy, Sir Percival Thriball, remain horsed and keep by me. My Lord of Lincoln, take the rest of the middleward and advance. Strike hard. God be with you."

It was the King's voice. Lord Lovel saw the others who had been named closing in round him: Lord Ferrers, short and fresh-faced, Sir Gervaise Clifton with his red cheeks and gentle black eyes looking almost girlish under his basnet, Sir Percival Thriball with the standard. Drums and trumpets were making a great racket now as the Duke of Norfolk's and the King's ward began to move together down the hill. The Earl of Northumberland and his division did not stir; were a reserve for the moment.

There was a thump of hooves behind them. Sir Robert Brackenbury, a big, slow-spoken man, had ridden up. King Richard turned in his saddle to look at him. His face was ten years younger than it had been overnight.

"You gave my message to Lord Stanley?"

Sir Robert Brackenbury was out of breath.

"Gave it, your Grace. I said: My lord, the King salutes you and commands your assistance, or by God, your son shall instantly die."

"He said?"

"He'll come. Sir William Stanley will do nothing either way; won't join the rebels. His brother swears that of him."

"Good."

"If he's coming," said Sir Richard Ratcliffe, "he should be here by now. I can see his camp as plain as my hand. He's not stirring."

Things had begun to happen on the plain in front of them. The thick line of the King's people had gone swinging down the slope of Ambion Hill at a fast walk. Sun took their basnets and sallets and the heads of their long pikes. John Howard of Norfolk led his ward on foot. They could see him wave his long-hilted five-foot battle-sword. Some of the men were still cheering. The rest had taken up songs, or whistled and called insults to the French and Welchmen. At the same time, the two little clumps of men beside the marsh had joined together, as if huddling themselves small before the attack. Now they reformed themselves in an odd way: a straight line broken at regular intervals by wedges of men standing out from it like prows of ships.

"Array triangle," said Sir Richard Ratcliffe, and whistled.

It was the terrible old device on which, in Harry of Monmouth's day, the French had broken themselves again and again: wedges of archers joined by lines of knights and pikemen, a toothed thing like a wolf-trap. A frontal charge against it was almost suicide.

The King's divisions had halted. Those who watched them from the crest of the ridge heard the short sudden "Ha!" of the archers, and saw men pitch forward suddenly out of the jag-toothed rebel line, falling down with the clothyard shafts in them. It would be an archery-duel for now.

"The devil take that double-tongued Stanley," shouted Sir Robert Percy. "What's he about? Now's the moment to take the bastards from behind. Why doesn't he charge?"

No men were issuing from Lord Stanley's Camp that made a distant splodge of white and colours against the green of Bosworth Park. But in the camp of his brother, Sir William, there appeared to be a certain stirring. The conspicuous blood-red surcoats of his men could be seen massing and clothing, forming into some sort of order. They looked remote and meaningless, like red ants on a turf.

"Didn't you say," said Percy to Sir Robert Brackenbury, "that Sir William would not fight?"

"All Stanley said was he would not fight against the King. He must have changed his mind and mean to join his brother. They'll both come in together on the Welchman's rear."

"I hope . . ." said Percy. "Great Jesus, look!"

A loud noise of voices, a pandemonium, came up the hillside. The divisions of Norfolk and Lincoln were charging with their pikes levelled.

"The fools," shouted Richard Ratcliffe.

King Richard's face had changed suddenly. He lifted his hand, opening and shutting a steel fist on the air.

"Norfolk, Jockey," he said in a small, suffering voice, "never charge that man. Stand and use the bows."

The smash of the lines meeting was like the smash of a shipwreck. John Howard of Norfolk had been at the foremost of his division. Now, as the two sides swayed a little apart again after the first shock, they could no longer see him.

"Jockey," called the King again, and beat his steel fist down on the pommel of White Surrey's saddle. Lord Lovel heard himself groan.

The lines had joined again; were a long, writhing snake of men that twisted about on the flat ground. Whoever had fallen at the first impact would be trampled to mud now. Behind the mêlée, clear to be seen, the standards of the red dragon and the portcullis, cognisances of Tydder and Beaufort, stood quite still. The little Welchman who never saw an army until today was letting his friends fight as they best could without him.

"I am thirsty," said King Richard in a small voice.

"There's a well behind us," Lord Ferrers said.

The King wheeled White Surrey suddenly.

"Come with me. I'll have no more of this. I'll put an end to the business. We'll not wait for Stanley."

They swung back toward the low trough of plain between the hillocks. A foolish exultation beat up and up, like the voice of the lark still charming the air above them, in Lord Lovel's chest. This was the way to end a battle: King against would-be King, a charge and the swift killing of the right people. This was a tale that would please Ratcliffe's chroniclers. He wanted to throw his sword in the air and cheer. The well was only a little spring in the low ground. King Richard's basnet, with the gold circle in which the Black Prince's Ruby glowered like a drop of blood, shimmered as he slid quickly over his horse's side; knelt and pushed his face down like a dog and sucked water. Then, without help, he was on his feet again. His eyes were as open as a hawk's, glaring. He smiled through the water that ran down his face. Sir Richard Ratcliffe leaned out of his saddle to help him up. He put his hand to his vizor to snap it down over the white joyful smile on his face.

"Now!" he shouted.

The earth complained of their horse-hooves. Their harness clattered. Moved by the wind of their speed, the English banner unfurled itself with a thick crackle like eagles' wings. Lord Lovel, peering through the bars of his own vizor, swinging his sword as he rode, saw trees and greenery curve past him. They were round the hill and heading for the marsh, calling to one another like peewhits.

"St. George!" yelled Robert Brackenbury. "King Richard!"

"God and the King!"

"St. George!"

Their horses snorted, thrusting their necks out. They had passed the edge of the marsh now. The battle was to the right of them; was a hubbub, a dense contention of colours glimpsed with the tail of the eye. But straight before them was what they had come for: the little clump of men staring with white faces at their charge, the banner of the red dragon amongst them on its gilt pole. Henry Tydder was there, the bastard-descended Welchman who had dared to rouse the old devils of England against King Richard.

Lord Lovel, gripping his horse between his thighs, saw the King pass him; gold of the crown, steel of the axe, on fire in the sun. Someone—he looked a giant on his tall horse—had hurled himself forward from among the Welchman's guards. Like an oak over a shrub, he impended above the King, whirling a sword. There was a crash, and King Richard was charging forward, heading straight for the standard. The giant lay on his back on the tramped marshy turf; lay still.

The pattern of men had changed. There were dead bodies around Lord Lovel in the track the King had driven. He fancied that he himself had killed one of them. Ahead, he saw the red dragon standard waving like the standard of a ship in storm. A gold-ringed basnet and a whirling axe were coming down on it.

"St. George!" shouted Lord Lovel. "St. George and King Richard!"

459

He saw the standard go down in the mud under White Surrey's forefeet, the standard-bearer dropping with his head smashed; saw the leopards and lilies of England streaming on behind the King, and a little figure in new armour that could be, must be, only Henry Tydder, wrenching frantically at its horse's head, trying to turn out of the mêlée. He saw more than this now. Fresh men were coming up behind the shattered and shrinking knot of Welchmen. There could be no mistaking the blood-red coats of Sir William Stanley's following. He has thought better of it, he told himself, urging his horse on. He has thought better of treason and skulking like a dog whistled by two masters; has joined us. He cheered: now England, a clean England again and the troubles done with.

"King Richard! St. George!"

Something new was happening. Henry Tydder had got his horse round; rode like a possessed man, hunted by devils, toward the red jackets. No blow was aimed at him. The pikes stabbing upward and the swung blades that Lord Lovel looked to see mangling him dropped or swung sideways. The line opened, and he was through; then closed again, making a barrier between him and the King. At the same moment, the or and azure of the English banner swayed sideways. A man in the Stanley colours had struck with his pole-axe at the standard-bearer.

Above the noise of it all, clear and desolate as the cry of a seagull, Lord Lovel heard the King's voice. It shouted one word; repeated it:

"Treason! Treason!"

His axe whirled up and down again. A crowd of the red coats were between him and Lord Lovel. Lord Lovel, cursing, slashed right and left at them; felt his sword bite. Over their heads he saw Richard Ratcliffe, at the King's side, drop from his saddle. He saw the King's axe lift again. Men in red jackets were all round him, thrusting up at him with pikes, chopping with maces. White Surrey seemed to disappear and go down in a swarm of red that closed over the crowned basnet of his rider.

"No!" shouted Francis Lovel. "No, no . . . ."

A Selection of Popular Fiction from Sphere

A Selection of Science Fiction from Sphere

A Selection of Historical Fiction from Sphere

THE GAME OF KINGS	Dorothy Dunnett	40p
QUEENS' PLAY	Dorothy Dunnett	40p
THE DISORDERLY KNIGHTS	Dorothy Dunnett	60p
THE BLACK PLANTAGENET	Pamela Bennetts	30p
BORGIA PRINCE	Pamela Bennetts	35p
THE BORGIA BULL	Pamela Bennetts	35p
KATHERINE OF ARAGON	Julia Hamilton	30p
ANNE OF CLEVES	Julia Hamilton	30p
ANNE BOLEYN	Margaret Heys	30p
JANE SEYMOUR	Frances Clark	30p
KATHERINE HOWARD	Jessica Smith	30p
KATHERINE PARR	Jean Evans	30p

The above six titles are also available in an attractive slipcase at £1.80